Three-times Golden Heart® finalist **Tina Beckett** learned to pack her suitcases almost before she learned to read. Born to a military family, she has lived in the United States, Puerto Rico, Portugal and Brazil. In addition to travelling, Tina loves to cuddle with her pug, Alex, spend time with her family, and hit the trails on her horse. Learn more about Tina from her website, or 'friend' her on Facebook.

Louisa Heaton lives on Hayling Island, Hampshire, with her husband, four children and a small zoo. She has worked in various roles in the health industry— most recently four years as a Community First Responder, answering 999 calls. When not writing Louisa enjoys other creative pursuits, including reading, quilting and patchwork—usually instead of the things she *ought* to be doing!

THE VET, THE PUP
AND THE PARAMEDIC

TINA BECKETT

MIRACLE TWINS
FOR THE MIDWIFE

LOUISA HEATON

MILLS & BOON

First published in Great Britain 2022
by Mills & Boon, an imprint of HarperCollins*Publishers* Ltd,
1 London Bridge Street, London, SE1 9GF

www.harpercollins.co.uk

HarperCollins*Publishers*
1st Floor, Watermarque Building,
Ringsend Road, Dublin 4, Ireland

The Vet, the Pup and the Paramedic © 2022 Tina Beckett

Miracle Twins for the Midwife © 2022 Louisa Heaton

ISBN: 978-0-263-30146-5

12/22

MIX
Paper | Supporting
responsible forestry
FSC™ C007454

This book is produced from independently certified FSC™ paper
to ensure responsible forest management.
For more information visit: www.harpercollins.co.uk/green.

Printed and Bound in Spain using 100% Renewable Electricity
at CPI Black Print, Barcelona

THE VET, THE PUP
AND THE PARAMEDIC

TINA BECKETT

MILLS & BOON

To my family, as always.

CHAPTER ONE

CABE MCBRIDE ONLY shifted his attention for a minute. Just enough time to peer into some of the scrub brush that lined this particular path on the mountain. The narrow, winding way had been treacherous, even though they were still well below the line of snow that clung almost year-round in this part of the Sierra Nevada range. He and Soldier always worked as a team on these rescue missions, his bloodhound's nose an invaluable tool in finding missing persons. And this time was no different. Soldier had alerted him to a scent near this area, which was where Sandra said her husband had last been spotted. And possibly suicidal after losing his job last week.

He turned to see if Soldier was scouring another area, but his dog was nowhere to be seen.

He gave the quick double whistle he used to call his companion back to him. But there was no response. No deep howl to indicate he'd found the missing man. No nothing. There were two other volunteer members of the Sierra Nevada Search and Rescue team also out here, on different ridges. The three college friends were part of the same paramedic squad. There were also two officers out there searching.

He tapped his earbud and spoke into the headset. "Any sign?"

Bradley Sentenna was the first to respond. "Nothing here. Doug, you have anything?"

"Nada." Doug Trapper, who looked like a Grizzly Adams type with his thick beard and longish hair, was a man of few words, but had a huge heart.

"Soldier alerted to something, but I'm having trouble finding him, which isn't like him. Stand by."

"Gotcha."

He switched off his mic and this time called to his dog. "Soldier! Come!"

A faint sound came from the scrub about ten yards to his left. Alarm bells rang in his head. Never had his dog ever failed to respond to him. After rescuing him from a local shelter several years ago, Cabe found his pup had had a natural aptitude for finding things. Including people. So much so that he'd sailed through a rigorous training course with ease. And so began their partnership with the search and rescue team here.

He moved sideways and although the sun was still high in the sky, the shadows cast by the low-lying bushes made it hard to see. Suddenly he spied a shadow crouched in the midst of them. And a pair of shoes. They were as still as...

Hell! He tapped his mic. "Found something. Head this way."

His friends both acknowledged without asking any questions. He pulled in a deep breath and then parted the first set of branches, hoping he was wrong.

"Stay right where you are. I have a gun." The growled words hit him in the midsection. Had he hurt Soldier?

He forced himself to respond calmly, even as his heart pounded in his chest. "Are you injured?"

"No. Not yet. Just don't come any closer. Please."

Not yet?

There was an edge of desperation to the words that made Cabe take another step. He needed to notify law enforcement about the gun, but to do so right now, in front of the man, might bring consequences neither of them wanted. Especially if his wife was right. The psych training he'd had in both the military and as part of his SAR training was telling him she was. So he decided to stall as he assessed the situation. "I'm looking for my dog. Have you seen him?"

There was a pause before the voice came back. "I—I think he went over."

"Over?" Just then he realized what the man meant. There was a steep drop-off just past where the man had hidden himself. Had he heard them coming before he could jump to his death?

The thought of Soldier lying at the bottom of that crevasse broken and bleeding filled his throat with bile.

Stick to the matter at hand, Cabe.

"I think he fell." The man stood. Dressed in a suit and tie, there was no sign of the gun he'd claimed to have. That was a relief. But dirt and sweat were streaked across his face, and his hair looked like a million fingers had tunneled through it. Trying to get up the courage to end it all?

It would be at least twenty or thirty minutes before Doug and Brad made it here. And the officers were also somewhere out there. Probably down at the bottom of the mountain. His medic bag was just to the left of him. Could he make a grab for the man if he turned and tried to leap off the cliff?

Doubtful.

He needed more time. Maybe he could get the guy's mind fixed on something besides his own troubles. Gain some kind of rapport with him.

"Where?"

"Over there. He was coming toward me, and then all of a sudden he seemed to scrabble for his footing and disappeared." The man's eyes met his. "I—I didn't push him. I swear. I would never hurt an animal."

No. Just himself.

Damn, if Soldier really had fallen, he needed to act. But first he needed to make sure of the man's intentions. "Where's the gun."

The other man shook his head, eyes shifting away. "I don't have one. I just wanted to be left alone."

Cabe decided to take him at his word. "I don't know why you came up here, but right now, I need help with my dog. Can you see clear to give me a hand?"

"I guess so."

This was obviously not how the man had expected his day to go. Or to end. And maybe that was a good thing.

"I have some rope and climbing gear behind me. If he's down there, I'll need you to feed the rope through a pulley. Can you do that?"

The man nodded.

Cabe looked at him a little closer. "I take it you're Randolf Meridian?"

Another nod. A little sharper this time. "How do you know who I am?"

"Your wife is really worried about you. She called search and rescue."

"I wish she hadn't. She'd be better off if..."

"Why do you think that?"

He gave a half shrug. "She's smart and successful and her daddy once told me she could do a hell of a lot better than a stockbroker. I'm beginning to think he was right."

Cabe bit off a swear word. "He's not. Your wife loves you."

Hell. He paused, trying to decide whether to impart the next bit of information or not. But the guy needed to know it was not just his wife who would suffer if he did what Cabe thought he was planning to do. "There's more. She was going to tell you today. She's expecting a little one. She baked a cake and everything."

Randolf's eyes closed, and he pressed his fingers to his temples for several long seconds. "God! A— a baby? There's no way I can be a father."

"Yes, you can. That little one deserves to know who you are."

The man shook his head. "Like I said, they'd both be better off without me."

Had he really just said that? A sliver of anger went through him. He had heard those words over and over throughout his childhood. A litany that repeated endlessly. Until one day it really had ended. Forever. "Do you really believe that? Do you really want your child to know that his or her father threw his life away... that they didn't mean enough for him to at least try?"

Realizing his voice had risen slightly, he sucked down a breath. "I think both your wife and baby deserve more than that." He gave him a pointed look. "Don't you?"

Soldier was still down there somewhere. But unless Cabe sorted this out right now, it was doubtful he would get much help out of the man. He might even take off once Cabe had climbed down the steep slope. But if he could turn him into an ally, maybe he could turn this around. And right now he sensed if he tried to radio law enforcement, his chance to do that would probably be nil.

"I guess so. I don't know. I can't think." His palm scrubbed at the back of his neck.

"I know it's all confusing right now. But don't make a decision that you can't take back. That you'll never be able to take back, without at least talking to your wife. I wouldn't be out here on this mountain, if she didn't care. *Really* care. Will you at least think about calling her?"

Randolf gave a defeated nod. "Yes."

Cabe studied him for a moment, before deciding the man was telling the truth. A trickle of relief chased the perspiration down his back. Now to seal the deal.

"Good. There's time to sort all of that out later. But right now, I need your help with my dog. He came up here to help me help you. Can't you do the same for him?"

Randolf's chest heaved, and he nodded. "Yes. I'm pretty sure I know where he landed. I heard a thud to our right."

"That helps. Stay close, okay?" Cabe's gut clenched. How big of a thud?

He peered over the edge but couldn't really see much. "You're sure he went down here."

"Yes. What do you need me to do?"

Grabbing the basic equipment he'd brought, he attached one of his pulleys to a nearby tree, attached the rope through it and then fastened the other end to the D-ring on his climbing vest. "I'm going to climb down and take a look. Just keep tension on the rope and feed it through the pulley. Can you do that?" He wouldn't be able to use his manual ascender for the trip back up, because he'd have his hands full with Soldier.

"Yes."

"I'm counting on you." He kept one eye on Randolf and the other on his gear.

"I know."

Cabe blew out a breath and then backed up to the edge of the slope, sending a couple of loose rocks skittering down the embankment. A soft whine sounded from below. At least Soldier was alive. For now, anyway.

I'm coming, boy.

He looked at Randolf. "I have a couple of friends who are on their way to help, so just follow my instructions until they get here, okay?"

"Cops?"

"No. But there are a couple of officers at the base of the mountain awaiting word. They're concerned for your safety. Nothing more."

"She really called out the cavalry, didn't she?"

"That should tell you something."

"It does." He looked Cabe in the eye. "She's really having a baby?" Those words seemed firmer, as if he'd come to some kind of decision. Cabe only hoped it was the right one.

"She really is. Feed the rope for me, okay?"

Randolf gave a nod.

With the immediate threat pushed to the side for the moment, Cabe took a deep breath and hoped beyond hope, Soldier wasn't mortally wounded. He slowly put one foot behind the other as he let the rope take some of his weight. Everything held. At least so far. And Randolf was doing just as he instructed, giving him support as he inched his way down the slope.

It seemed to take forever, although it was probably only a period of five minutes before he could see the lower part of the mountain. Then his feet hit a flat area. Rocks went over the side, making an ominous skittering sound as they bounced off whatever was beyond it. Hell. This was little more than a ledge followed by another sharp drop. He doubted there was enough rope to get him all the way down it. If Soldier wasn't here… If he'd struggled…

"Soldier! Where are you boy?"

Another whimper came from just past a patch of scrub. He called up to Randolf. "I'm going to move to your right. Just keep feeding the rope as I move."

"Got it!"

His voice was still firm. Solid. That was a good sign.

Crab-walking sideways, he moved in the direction of the sound. "I'm coming, boy."

Another whimper. At least he was alive. He'd adopted Soldier almost five years ago, just as he was leaving army life behind. As a tribute to all the men he had treated on the field as a medic, he named the dog after them. Brave and loyal, his pup reminded him of the men he had served during his ten years of service.

"Almost there, Soldier." He stepped over another low bush and saw a patch of red fur. Another large step and his dog came into view. The second Soldier saw him, his thick tail thumped on the ground, making Cabe's heart cramp. "I'm here, boy." He crouched beside the dog and immediately saw the problem. He'd fallen on a sharp branch that had impaled the fleshy part of the dog's thigh. He tried to move toward Cabe then fell back with a sharp cry.

"Stay!" He forced his voice to give a sharp warning, not because he was angry, but he didn't want the dog to do more damage to his leg. So he called up. "I found him. Can you give me just a little slack?"

The rope went loose. For a second his heart leaped into his throat, then from above him, Doug's voice came. "I'm here, Cabe! Let us know what you want."

Thank God.

"Soldier's impaled himself on a pretty big stick. I need to cut it close to the wound and..." He couldn't bring himself to say the rest. Hell. He was as cool as a cucumber with almost every emergency situation he found himself in, but the thought of causing his dog any more pain...

"Got it," Doug called. "Let us know when you're ready."

"Will do. Randolf, I'll need you to give Doug a hand, okay?" He was thankful at least one of his friends had arrived. Both for his and Soldier's sake, but also for Randolf, who had a lot of things on his mind right now.

"I will."

He looked at the area around Soldier. There was some blood, but not enough to indicate that his boy had severed a major vessel. But canine anatomy was not the same as human. He had no choice but to try to free him. The leg that was trapped was the hind one closest to the ground. Taking a pair of sharp cutting pliers from one of the pockets in his vest, he patted Soldier's head. "Easy, boy. We're going to get you out, but it's going to hurt like hell."

Soldier's tail patted the ground as if he understood.

He eased the cutters as close to the dog's wound as he dared. "Stay."

Soldier had been trained to freeze like a statue at that command. But the dog had never sustained an injury like this one either. And he had nothing to cover his eyes or face with. Hell, if he bit him, so be it. But there was no way he was leaving him for one second longer than necessary. The powerful nippers easily cut through the branch, but not without bringing a sharp cry of pain from his dog. Now he somehow had to ease Soldier off the remaining part of the branch. He didn't dare try to reach under him to cut the bottom part.

"This is going to hurt, boy. I'm sorry." He made his hands as flat as possible and slid them under the dog's thigh on either side of the branch. "One, two, three!" Whether he was counting for Soldier's sake or his own, he had no idea, but he lifted the dog's leg up and off the spike of wood, bringing a gut-wrenching howl from his friend.

But he couldn't stop now. He pivoted the dog's body so that he could set the leg back down on top of his own, to avoid contaminating it any more than necessary. Warmth that could only be from blood seeped through his pants, but although he held his breath and waited, the flow didn't pulse in thick streams that would signify an arterial bleed. He exhaled in relief as he did a quick check of the rest of the dog's body, palpating ribs and limbs as best as he could. Nothing broken that he could tell.

He called up to the top. "I have him free. But you guys are going to have to drag us both up, since I don't have a free hand. Can you do it?"

"We're all here now, so between the three of us we have you. Tell us when."

Okay, so Brad was there as well. The only way he figured he could do this was to cradle Soldier on his lap and wrap his own body around the hundred-and-fifteen-pound dog. His rope was geared for two good-sized adults, so it should hold.

Soldier thumped his tail again, lifting his head to look at Cabe. The threat of moisture made his vision blur for a second before he blinked it away. "Good boy. You're doing great. Another big ouchie coming."

Sliding his left arm under the dog's shoulder, he dragged him the rest of the way onto his lap. This time there was no cry, not even a whimper. Pulling him closer, Cabe drew his knees up and curled his torso over the dog to lock him in place, using his arms to hold him there. Hopefully it would cushion his ride at least a little. He yelled up, "Okay, start pulling."

Since he'd moved sideways to get to Soldier, the first pull of the rope dragged him diagonally across the ground. With each upward heave, his back glanced off rocks and branches tore at his protective clothes. But he didn't ease his grip. It was the least painful way to move his dog, and Cabe would rather take the brunt of whatever they were going over.

Damn! His right shoulder hit something with enough force to make him see stars, but somehow he managed to hold on to Soldier. After ten minutes of effort, hands reached down and hauled them over the side of the embankment.

Brad took one look at him and winced. "Man, you look like hell."

That got a smile out of him. Cabe could have guessed that. His cheek stung from one of the branches that had grabbed at his skin. "That doesn't matter right now."

His eyes searched out Randolf and found him standing beside his two friends, the rope still in his hands.

"How is he?" The man's voice was a bit shaky as he looked back at him.

"He's alive, but I need to get him to a vet. Thanks for helping."

Cabe hadn't moved. In reality, Doug was right. He was beat up. Every muscle in his body ached, and he wasn't sure he could straighten up. At least not easily. He glanced down at Soldier to see liquid brown eyes meet his with a lot more calmness than his own tripping heart.

Brad nodded. "Randolf's going to help us get Soldier down the mountain."

His friend's voice told him, he'd assessed the situation without Cabe needing to fill him in in front of the man. That was good. And Doug was standing off to the side, his cell phone to his ear. Probably talking to the officers. Or maybe calling Randolf's wife.

Pulling out a square foil pack that Cabe recognized as a reflective survival blanket, Brad shook it out and laid it on the ground just as Doug rejoined them. "I think this will hold under Soldier's weight. We'll put him on it and carry him down the hill like a gurney."

"Yes, that should work."

Uncurling his stiff body, he watched as his two friends and Randolf carefully took Soldier from him and laid him on the blanket. The dog whimpered once and then lay still.

Now came the test when Doug came over and held his hand up. "Can you stand?"

"Yep." He allowed his friend to help him to his feet, his muscles screaming with each movement. It was a small price to pay.

He glanced at Randolf. "Hey, buddy, there are some officers you'll need to talk to. Doug or Brad will help you find them. You have to promise me you'll be honest about your struggles, and that you'll go and talk to your wife."

"Will they arrest me?"

"Like I said, they're more interested in your well-being. They can help you find someone to talk to. Do it. Not for me. Not for Soldier. Do it for your wife and your new baby. And most of all, for yourself."

"I will. I promise."

Cabe pulled a card out of his pocket. "This is my number. I want you to call me in a couple of days and let me know how it's going. If you don't, I'm going to pay you a visit."

Randolf held up his hands. "I know it was stupid. The shock of losing my job, just as we were in the process of buying a house came up and overwhelmed me."

He understood. All too well. When his father had been at his worst, he'd been overcome by emotions that never should have seen the light of day. At least Randolf didn't seem to have lost himself in a bottle. Which meant he could still think, could still take control of his life. And it sounded like he'd have help doing that, from how scared his wife had sounded. He hoped they would both seek help to get past this.

"I get it. Just don't do anything like that again."

Randolf nodded. "I'd like to help you get him down the hill, if that's okay. And then I'll talk to the officers. As soon as I call my wife."

"I think that is the best idea I've heard all day."

Jessie leaped up from her little garden, brushing the dirt from her hands as soon as she set down the phone. Her first emergency case as the new vet in the area. And it had to be on a Saturday when her only employee was out of town on a fishing trip. She reached in her pocket for the key to the medical cabinet in her office and squeezed it tight. A habit from her last several weeks in San Francisco. She forced her fingers to uncurl.

Well, she wasn't in San Francisco any longer, and from what old Doc Humphrey had told her last week as he was retiring, the Santa Medina Veterinary Clinic sometimes saw pets who were injured while exploring the wild surrounds of the area. Only this time it wasn't a tourist's pet, it was a search and rescue dog who'd evidently fallen down a steep embankment and been injured during a rescue.

Fortunately Doc Humphrey had bequeathed her the small cottage that was on the clinic's property, where he'd lived. He was moving to Idaho where his daughter was, wanting to make the most of his time after getting a diagnosis for the slight palsy he'd developed. Parkinson's. It was still in its early stages, but her heart hurt at the pain in his eyes when he realized he'd have to give up his practice here. He'd been in a hurry to find a replacement, and she'd been in a hurry to relocate out of the city.

Not bothering to change her clothes, knowing they were on their way in now, she washed her hands and grabbed her lab coat off its hook by the door and walked over to the clinic to get things laid out in case she needed to do emergency surgery on the dog. God, she hoped the rescue guy wasn't going to go all squeamish on her if she needed an extra set of hands. Her ex certainly had the time or two she'd encountered an injured animal during her travels. Then she rolled her eyes. Of course he wouldn't. He was search and rescue. Not a baseball player who was worried more about his pitching arm than anything else. Including the damage he could have done to her reputation if he'd succeeded in using her key.

Fifteen minutes later, she heard a car drive up, horn giving two sharp beeps as it parked in her small gravel lot.

She met them at the door, her breath catching at the man who carried what looked to be a very large bloodhound. The man's black hair was sticking up in every direction, and he had blood caked on the right side of his face, and there was still more flowing from a deep gash on his cheek.

Needed stitches. Her brain was already processing what she saw. "What happened?"

"He fell quite a distance. Landed on a thick branch which went all the way through his right hind leg." The man was out of breath, probably injured himself. Had he fallen as well?

There was another man behind him. "Let me take him, Cabe, dammit. You can barely walk."

"I'm fine. I've got him." His tone brooked no argument.

Running to open the door for the pair, she motioned them into an exam room. "Set him here."

Gingerly setting the injured dog on the table, the man waited as Jessie unwound her stethoscope from her neck, murmuring little words of reassurance to the hound. She'd long learned that the words themselves didn't matter, it was the tone that either soothed or caused fear. When the dog lifted his head to look at her, she held out her hand, fingers curled in so he could sniff it. "That's a good boy. Let's see where you hurt."

His head flopped back onto the table, long ears akimbo, as if exhausted. He probably was. As was his owner if that's who he was. "Whose dog is he?"

"Mine. His name is Soldier."

She blinked. Okay, that was an unusual name. But then his owner seemed a little unusual himself. She looked at him. "Are *you* okay?"

"I'm fine. Just see to him. Please."

The last word had been added in a tone that sounded slightly strangled, belying his gruff manner. He was worried. As any owner would be.

He turned to his companion. "Thanks, Doug. I can take it from here. Go home to your family."

"I'll help you get him home. He weighs a ton."

"I don't think so." She looked up after listening to the dog's heart. "I'd rather he spent the night here." For some reason the words sounded funny to her ears, so she added, "Soldier, I mean. I don't want him moving around, and it's already six o'clock. Unless you need your friend to stay to help me with my exam. It's just me tonight, I'm afraid. And you look…"

"He looks like hell. I've told him that several times

already, but you'll find Cabe is as bullheaded as they come." Doug's face softened. "And that dog means everything to him."

She watched as Cabe fixed him with a look that would melt lead. "I'm fine. Go home, Doug."

Doug held up his hands. "I'm going, I'm going. But call me and let me know how he's doing."

"I will."

With that, Doug waved goodbye to her and headed out the door.

Then those steely blue eyes fixed themselves on her face. "Now tell me. What do I need to do?"

Fifteen minutes later, they were in the small surgical area in the back of the clinic. Soldier had gotten a dose of a short-acting anesthesia so she could irrigate his leg and then X-ray him to check for fractures.

Cabe surprised her, by handling everything like a pro, not balking at anything she asked him to do, including helping cut sutures as she tied them off. "You're a paramedic?"

"That's right. Before that, I was a medic in the army. I went to one of the local shelters soon after I got out... and well, the rest is history." He smiled, glancing at his dog.

"Ahh..." The dog's name suddenly made more sense. So did Cabe's skill in the operating room. "That's why you're not put off by the messier parts of medicine."

"I've seen my share of trauma. But this is the first time with Soldier."

"From what I can see, he's going to be fine. One cracked rib that should heal without a problem with some downtime. And no major vessels lacerated, which is a small miracle considering where that branch went through. We normally recommend leaving the object in just in case—"

"The branch was still attached to the bush, and he was lying on top of it. No way for me to get underneath him to cut it. And we had to drag him up the hill."

She swallowed. Cabe's own injuries suddenly made more sense. "You held him, and they dragged you up."

He gave a short jerk of his head. "They pulled us both up."

Their eyes caught and held for a few seconds, before Jessie hauled hers away and fastened them back on the dog. Where they should be. She bandaged both sides of the wound, affixing the tape to the area she'd clipped before surgery. "Let's put him in a kennel and let him wake up. I've given him an injection for pain, so that should help him be more comfortable."

She hurried to put a fleece blanket in the largest kennel they had before realizing there was no way he was going to fit in there without it hurting him to move in and out of the door. "On second thought, let's just put him in the exam room we were in before this. He should be more comfortable in there."

Before she had to ask, Cabe scooped the dog into his arms as if he weighed nothing. It sent a shiver through her, and she wasn't sure why. The paramedic looked like he was impervious to anything. Even emotions.

Except for that tiny quaver when he'd murmured to the dog before the anesthesia had taken effect.

They got him into the room, and Cabe set him on the fluffy blanket that she'd wound into a circle on the ground. Then she set water down for him. "I don't want to give him food until I'm sure we're not going to need to put him back under."

He frowned again. "How long will that be?"

"Just an hour or two."

"I'll wait with him, if it's all the same to you. You don't need to stay. I can lock up for you, if you'd like."

She tensed, before forcing herself to relax. "I was already planning on waiting with him. But first, I'm going to need you to hop up onto that exam table so I can get a better look at your cheek. Let me just lower the mechanism a bit first, though."

"The cheek's fine. But if you have something for this headache, I'd accept it."

"I have Advil. And that's it." Was she going to tense up every time someone asked for a simple painkiller? Maybe. "And your cheek is not fine, and it wasn't a request. If you want to stay here with him…" She left the sentence hanging. He'd get the meaning.

He glanced at the table as she pushed a foot pedal to bring it down a little. "Is that thing going to hold me?"

"Yes." Even saying the word made her smile, though. The man had to be six-three or six-four, if he was an inch. But he wasn't tall and scrawny looking. Instead, he was filled out in all the right places. The fact that she was just now noticing that made her kind of proud. At least she hadn't ogled him the second he'd walked through the door.

Well, she wasn't going to ruin that record by staring at him now. Gathering some supplies while he got onto the table, wincing as he did, she tilted her head. "Are you sure you don't need to visit the ER and get a few X-rays of your own?"

"I'm sure. Just got a few bumps and bruises." He

glanced at his dog, who was still sleeping off his adventures, thanks to the pain meds. "Are you sure Soldier needs to stay here? We haven't been separated since... well in a long time."

"I'm sorry, but I'd feel better if he were here where I can keep an eye on him."

He frowned. "Are you going to spend the night at the clinic?"

"That's the plan. I have a little sleeping area set up in back." She soaked a piece of gauze with antiseptic. "This is going to sting a little."

She gently cleaned the area on his cheek. She was right. It was fairly deep. "This looks like it needs stitches."

"Okay."

The gauze went still. "So you'll go have it seen?"

"Can't you do it?"

"I'm a vet. Not a human doctor."

His mouth twisted. "Okay... Doc. If I trusted you with Soldier, I sure as hell trust you to knot a few sutures on me. But if you won't, and you have a couple of butterflies or some superglue I can use, I'll just close it myself."

Was he kidding her? Then again, he'd been a medic in the army, he'd probably had to make do with what he had more than once.

"I'll close it with a butterfly bandage. But you're probably going to have a scar if you don't get it done right."

He actually cracked a smile. "It won't be my first one."

The man was ridiculous. Not only because of what

he'd said, but because now she was wondering where those other scars might be hidden.

She switched to a fresh gauze and cleaned up some more superficial cuts on his temple. "Let me check your head."

Her fingers tunneled deep into his dark hair and sifted through the crisp strands as she felt for other injuries or telltale signs of a head injury. No bumps that she could find. He pulled back with a weird sound. "I think I'm fine. If you could just patch up the spot on my cheek, I'll be good to go." He seemed to think for a minute. "Are you sure I can't sleep in your spare room at the clinic so that you can go home to be with…whoever needs you."

Not a chance in hell.

"That would be my bird, Dumble. And I live right next door, so I'll run home to feed him. I'll be gone all of five minutes."

She'd lost her dog, Chloe, to cancer, before leaving San Francisco. It was part of what had prompted her to move to Santa Medina. She'd had Chloe ever since she was a junior in high school and losing her had been harder than breaking it off with her long-term boyfriend, Jason. Of course finding him with the keys to her drug cabinet and suddenly realizing why Chloe's pain meds had run out much sooner than she'd expected had left her reeling. Jason had been stealing them. At first he denied it. Then claimed he hadn't wanted to go to the doctor for a shoulder injury, he'd told her. None of which she now believed. Nor had she believed his story of finding her keys beside her car and picking them up to return to her. If he'd actually made it to the vet clinic where she worked and stolen drugs… She would have been finished. Anger washed over her all over again.

No. She wasn't trusting anyone the way she'd trusted him, ever again. That included letting someone sleep in her clinic.

"Dumble, huh? No cats or dogs?"

His words jerked her back to the present. "Not anymore."

He frowned and looked at her for a long moment before murmuring, "I'm sorry."

An unexpected wave of emotion overcame her, and a half shrug was all she could get out for several minutes. She hadn't even been able to grieve Chloe's loss properly because of the drama with Jason soon afterward.

She covered by cleaning up the discarded gauze and putting away the disinfectant. Then she pulled out a small, covered tote that held various Band-Aids and found a couple of butterflies. She also retrieved a couple of ibuprofen.

Affixing one side of the dressing and then pulling the edge of the skin to meet with the skin on the other side of the cut, she finished up and stood back to look. "Make sure you have it checked if there's any sign of infection. And you should probably get a tetanus shot if you haven't had one in a while."

She went to the small fridge around the corner and got a bottle of water, then handed it to him along with the ibuprofen.

He twisted the cap and put the bottle to his mouth, downed the pills with a powerful movement of his throat. "Thanks." He slid off the table. "Is that it?"

"Yep, I think we're all done. Go home. Please. He'll

probably sleep most of the night, and you look about done in. I'll call you if there's any change."

"Are you sure?"

"Absolutely." A frisson of relief went through her that he was about to be out of her clinic. Something about him made her uneasy. Not in a creepy way, but in a way that said she wasn't sure of her own reactions. And it was strange. Jason had been stunningly attractive with a runner's body and a great sense of humor. And not a scar in sight. But Cabe...there was something darker about this man. More closed off. As if he had a million secrets tucked away behind those blue eyes of his.

He was a combat medic. Who wouldn't have a darker side after that kind of career? Or secrets.

Then again, so had Jason. And none of them had been the good kind.

He patted his vest pockets before shaking his head. "My wallet's in the car...let me get it."

"We can settle up tomorrow when you come get him."

"Are you sure?" As he turned toward her, his hand knocked the leash she'd used onto the floor.

"I'm sure."

He bent over to pick up the neon-green length of nylon, and Jessie's eyes widened, a shocked squeak coming out before she could stop it.

Because a section of jeans that should have been covering his ass was now a useless flap of fabric that hung to one side, and there, in all its glory, was half of the man's butt, bared for her viewing pleasure. And the knotted muscles there...

Oh, God! Stop looking, stop looking, stop...
She swallowed hard and stared at the wall over his
head, waiting for him to turn around.

CHAPTER TWO

THE SOUND THAT came from behind him made him straighten slowly and glance toward Soldier, thinking the dog had done something that had alarmed the vet. But the canine was still resting on his side, snoring slightly.

He turned around. "Are you okay?"

"Your, um…" Her hand did this funny swirly thing in the air and then she patted her backside.

What the hell?

He frowned, having no idea what she was talking about. He reached around to that area on his own anatomy and felt his vest. His head tilted sideways, the movement stretching the skin under the butterfly and making it burn.

"No. Not there. Underneath that coat thing." She pulled off her lab coat and held it by her side, revealing a snug brown T-shirt with just a hint of cleavage visible above the V-shaped neckline. She had a smudge of dirt on her right upper arm. "I have a feeling you might want this."

He was pretty sure his eyes might have burst free of their sockets, before he realized she wasn't referring to her body, but to the white coat which she was now holding out.

"I don't understand."

Her brows went up and a trace of a smile curved the edges of pink lips. "Just. Feel. Your. Ass."

Feel his…?

What the hell? He felt the area again, this time reaching under his vest. His hand met bare skin. The skin of his…ass.

Well, damn.

That's what that cute squeaking noise had been about. His worn jeans must have ripped apart as he was being dragged up the hill holding onto Soldier. Seeing as his buddies hadn't ragged on him about it, it must not have been visible because of his hiking vest… until he bent over. Right in front of the brand-new vet.

Fire marched up his neck and his head pounded until he thought it might explode. Grinding his teeth, he forced the tide back. He was being ridiculous. It wasn't as if no one had ever seen his backside before, but it also wasn't something he wanted to foist onto someone without them being aware of it…and wanting it.

"Sorry. I didn't realize." He looked at the lab coat she held out. "But I doubt that is going to fit me. Do you have a surgical drape I can use by any chance?"

"Yes…er…just a minute." She discarded her coat on the front desk and went into the back before coming back with a square blue piece of paper. And *her* backside was completely covered by black denim jeans, which hugged every curve.

Damn. He'd come into the clinic assuming that the Jessie Swinton DVM who would emerge was going to be an older man, kind of like Doc Humphrey had been.

She was about as far from that image as one could get. She looked like she was nineteen, only there was no way she could be that young. Besides, Doc had been his vet ever since he got back from the army. He'd watched Cabe go through his divorce and the aftermath. That break hadn't been quick or easy. But he'd seen it coming down the road long before she finally uttered the word *divorce.*

He wasn't sure how he felt about another vet taking his place, even though the man's hands had developed a slight tremor that probably marked the end of his career.

There were other vets, but to change just because Dr. Swinton was different from his last one would be... stupid. How about changing due to embarrassment?

Also stupid.

Besides, it was worth a little bit of a red face as long as it meant Soldier was going to be okay. He realized she was still holding the paper drape. Taking it from her, he tucked it into the back of his jeans, letting it hang behind him like some kind of ridiculous kilt. "Thanks again for coming in and taking care of him after hours."

"Of course. Thanks for assisting, since my only lab tech just went out of town for the weekend."

"Fishing?" When she nodded, he smiled. "Margo does like to fish."

"You know her?"

He nodded. "I grew up around these parts and besides, Margo was also Doc's assistant."

"Does everyone just call him Doc?"

"As far as I know." Belatedly, he realized it might bother her that the town treated the previous veterinarian with such affection. "He grew up in Santa Medina too."

She smiled, the warmth of it washing away some of the sting of being caught with his pants down—or at least a piece of them. "Is there anyone here who *wasn't* raised in this town?"

It was on the tip of his tongue to say "you," but he had a feeling it might make her feel like an outsider, and that's not what he would mean, so he simply said, "People come through all the time. Some stay. Some don't."

And that didn't sound much better, but he suddenly didn't seem to be thinking straight, so names of specific people had eluded him.

He reached in his vest and pulled out yet another business card. "Here's my number. It's my cell. Just call if you need anything or if Soldier does."

"Thanks." She took it from him. "Sorry about not looking you up on the computer, but Margo hadn't shown me how to work all of that yet."

"Not a problem." He crouched down next to his dog, glad of the drape, since he didn't want to make the same mistake a second time. Stroking the hound's soft ears, he drew a deep breath, realizing how badly today could have gone. Randolf could have really had a gun and could have hurt himself or someone else. And Soldier could have died in that fall. But none of that had happened, and hopefully the man would get the help he needed. "Well, boy, I'll be back tomorrow to get you. Don't give Dr. Swinton any problems, okay?"

His pup's eyes rolled around in their sockets for a second, but they didn't really open. Cabe frowned for a second. "I don't know if he hit his head on the way down or not."

"I'll keep an eye on him. I promise." As he stood to his feet, she continued. "He was very lucky. You both were."

"Yes, we were." He looked at her again. "Thank you for letting us come in on your day off."

"It wasn't a problem. I was just out working in the garden."

He smiled. "I thought maybe you were doing something like that." He touched his arm, mimicking what she'd done earlier. "You have something right there."

She glanced down and then laughed, the sound ringing with amusement. "It figures. You're lucky it isn't worse."

"I know. You could be missing part of your clothes."

She blinked for a second and then laughed "Yes. And I can see how that would be much, much worse."

No. Not worse. But much more dangerous. And something he didn't need to be thinking about. Now. Or ever. So he said goodbye and reached down to give Soldier one more pat, promising he'd be here whenever she was ready to send him home and thanking her again for everything.

"Even this." He fingered his cheek, where the butterfly dressings made their presence known every time he smiled.

"I hope you found who you were looking for."

He hesitated. "Yes, I did. See you tomorrow."

As he left the clinic her words came back to him. "I hope you found who you were looking for."

He knew she'd been talking about the rescue, but for a split second he thought she'd been talking about relationships. He'd thought he'd found who he was looking for in Jackie, his ex. But in the end, the couple who'd been voted most likely to marry in high school had indeed married. Only it hadn't lasted. He'd married her right before shipping out with the army. But once he came home from his...

Well, things had changed.

He climbed in his car and started the engine, glancing at the vet clinic with its Closed sign in full view. As he pulled away, he could have sworn he saw the curtains in the front window twitch. But when he looked again, they were in the same spot they had been. Must have been his imagination. But man, that had been nothing like his interactions with Doc had been.

And he wasn't sure how he felt about that.

Cabe felt like he'd been hit by a Mack truck. Every bone in his body hurt, and he had bruises everywhere. And his shoulder was killing him.

He figured he'd be a little sore today from how hard it had been to get his clothes off last night. His ripped jeans had gone straight in the trash. But the word *sore* didn't describe what he felt like today. He'd tried to call the vet clinic before going into work, but there'd been no answer. It was supposed to have been his day off, but one of his fellow paramedics had called in sick. Cabe probably should have said he couldn't do it. But his nature was to gut it out no matter how hard things got.

Except with Jackie, evidently, although the decision hadn't been his by that time. And he couldn't really blame her. He knew who he was, and despite her best efforts, he hadn't been able to shake his past.

He didn't want Dr. Swinton to be stuck babysitting Soldier today, so he'd hoped to catch her early and pick his boy up before work. He hoped things were okay.

She would have called him if there was a problem, right? She'd promised.

Maybe another emergency case had come in.

He hoped not, although first responders never quite knew when those calls would come in either. Like today.

He got to the station, parking around back. But when he went through the doors, he saw the man from yesterday standing in the kitchen area talking to a couple of the other guys. Next to him stood a young woman.

"Randolf?" He stepped around so the man could see him. "Everything okay?"

"Yes, it's okay. I just wanted to come by and say thank you again. If you hadn't found me yesterday..." Randolf paused. "Wow. Are *you* okay?"

Evidently he looked as awful as he felt. "I'm fine."

His wife gripped the man's arm as if afraid he'd disappear if she let go of him. "Yes, thank you." She frowned. "I heard your dog was injured, I'm so sorry. Will he be okay?"

Her voice was so soft he almost didn't hear her. "Yes. Doc... I mean the new vet, got him all patched up. He's still there for observation, and she's taking good care of him."

At least that was his hope.

"Can we do anything? Pay for his care?"

"Search and rescue provides emergency insurance for him. It should cover it. I'm just glad everything turned out the way it did." And that Randolf's resolve to do himself harm had faltered as he realized just what he stood to miss out on.

She smiled. "We're actually on our way to see a counselor. But Randolf insisted on stopping by to see if he could thank you in person. Are the other two men here?"

"No, Doug and Brad are off today, but I'll pass your message along."

Randolf reached out and shook Cabe's hand. "Give my best to Soldier. I'd like to send him over a box of treats, if that's okay."

That made him smile. The man sure sounded better than he had yesterday. "I'm sure he would love that. Come by and let us know how you're doing when you get a chance."

"Thanks. I will." He glanced at his wife. "We'd better get going."

"Yes." She smiled at Cabe. "I can't express how—"

"You don't have to. It was my pleasure. Just take care of each other."

He hadn't been able to rescue his dad from his own demons, but this kind of rescue he could do. Not emotional rescue, but physical rescue. Where you could save a person's life. The rest was up to them. Maybe there was a little part of him that saw it as doing what he hadn't been able to when he was a kid.

Randolf's wife nodded. "We will."

They left just as Sam Murray handed him a wide-rimmed bowl that held some chili and corn bread. "Thanks. How old is this stuff?"

Sam grinned. "Ha! No, my wife took pity on us after that last canned stew incident and made a big pot of chili. From scratch."

The stew had sat on a shelf in the squad's pantry long past its expiration date. After it was heated up on the stove, there'd been no takers when it came to eating it. Not even Sam, who'd been the one to dump it into the pot. But you never knew when a call was going to come in, so there wasn't always time to do a lot of real cooking.

He had to admit, despite his achy joints, the food smelled wonderful. "Well, tell her thank you for me."

"You've got it."

Clay, another of the firefighters, was already at the table digging in. "Are you sure she doesn't want to join the squad?"

"I'm lucky she lets me come in as often as I do." Sam was nearing retirement age, but you'd never know it from his youthful appearance.

Just as Cabe took his first bite, his phone went off. He glanced at the readout and frowned, then held up a finger to the two men. "I'll be back in a sec. Nobody touch that bowl."

Walking a short distance away, he answered. "Is he okay?"

"He's fine. I told you I'd call if he wasn't."

Her voice was soft and lilting with no hint of irritation over the fact that he'd tried to reach her twice. "Sorry for the calls. I wanted to let you know I got called in to work unexpectedly but will try to work out a time to come get him sometime this morning. Is he okay hanging out at the clinic for a little while longer?"

"No hurry. I didn't want to leave him locked in the exam room, so he's actually following me around the yard. Glad I don't have any bodies buried out here. He's been nose-to-the-ground the whole time."

That made him chuckle. "He loves his job. How about his leg?"

"He's limping but getting around okay. I don't think there will be any permanent damage to the muscle or nerves. He was very lucky."

Lucky. That word seemed to be thrown around a lot.

Before he could say anything, she said, "Well, I just called with an update. No hurry coming by. But I would like to know what he normally eats for breakfast and how much."

"Oh, of course." He named the brand of food that he normally gave Soldier and the amount. "But if you don't have it, I'm sure he'll be fine with whatever you've got on hand. But don't let him sweet-talk you into giving him more than his portion. He'll make you think he hasn't eaten in forever."

She laughed. "Oh, I can see he's well fed. In a good way. His weight is perfect. How's the offending cheek?"

"Pardon me?"

"Your cheek… Oh! I mean the one on your face."

Dammit. Of course she had. What was wrong with him?

"It's fine. The butterflies are holding. Thanks for agreeing to do them…and for the ibuprofen. I was beat yesterday."

And why had he said that? She didn't care if he was tired or not.

He was going to need to tread carefully around Dr. Swinton. His ex had laid things out about as clearly as she could. He was not good husband material—although she'd seemed to like him well enough in high school. Except the "I love my bad boy" endearments she used to whisper during lovemaking had shifted to shrill accusations that he was emotionally stunted and unavailable. And he had to agree with her. He'd probably no business getting married to her...or to anyone. But he'd convinced himself that he'd be able to do it: that despite the scars from his dad, he'd still be able to connect with someone on an emotional level and sustain a relationship. How wrong he'd been.

He wasn't going to put anyone else through what he'd put her through.

"I'm sure you were. Hope you're feeling better today."

Not really. Although he was glad Randolf and his wife appeared to be headed down the right path. At least counseling would work for someone. He'd suggested counseling to Jackie, thinking it was the expected thing to do, even though his heart wasn't in it. But she hadn't even wanted to try. To say he'd been relieved was an understatement. And once she walked out, he'd canceled the appointment. Maybe that made him a hypocrite for making Randolf promise to go see someone. But then again, Randolf wasn't him.

"I'm fine. I'm glad to hear Soldier is up and moving around though. Sorry for not being able to come get him right now."

"He's good company, actually. So no hurry. Just let me know when you're on your way, so I can meet you at the clinic."

"I will. And thanks again."

"See you in a while."

He sighed, not sure seeing her again was something that was smart, but it was necessary.

"Hopefully it won't be too long. I'll call you."

"Yes. Do that." And with that, his phone showed that she'd already hung up.

What was she doing at home that had Soldier following her around? More gardening?

Somehow picturing her digging in the garden with a spade, another smear of dirt on her arm, and maybe one across her forehead made his gut tighten in a way that he didn't like. Well, he'd better get himself together and start concentrating on work and figure out when he could go get Soldier and take him home.

Because the sooner he went to pick his dog up, the better. Before there was any more mention of his cheek. The one on his face or any other one.

Jessie was nervous. Not because of Soldier—who was doing fine—but because she'd just had the idea of the century. Or at least the idea of the last fifteen minutes. And she had Cabe to thank for it, since it turned out that Soldier was a shelter dog. But she wasn't sure he would go for it. Or if she should even ask. But one of the things she'd hoped to carry over from her last job was the series of community education seminars about how having a pet can benefit not just the person who owns them, but also the community at large. The seminars had always been a big hit in San Francisco.

She'd already called one of the animal shelters and they were on board with doing a seminar on pet adoption, and they were planning on bringing some of their charges with them. But how great would it be to have someone in the search and rescue field—who'd adopted his dog from a shelter—talk about what it entails and the type of training their dog undergoes.

Cabe was due at the clinic any minute. And she was perched precariously on a stepladder trying to get the stupid battery-powered screwdriver to cooperate.

Soldier gave a low woof as if commiserating with her.

"I know. The stupid angle isn't helping any, boy." The driver slipped yet again, and this time hit her thumb, and the screw fell to the floor. "Dammit!"

"Something I can do to help?"

Her head whipped around so fast that she teetered on the ladder and would have fallen, if warm hands hadn't landed on her hips.

Oh, God. Of all the stupid…

"Sorry." The man was basically holding her in place, and there was nothing to grab onto to pull herself back upright.

Before she could try to figure it out, he lifted her feet free of the ladder and set her down on the ground. She swallowed, the picture of him cradling his dog sliding back through her head. Those muscles weren't just for show. Although it made sense if he had to go on rescue missions.

Turning toward him so she wasn't tempted to lean into his touch, she bit her lip. "Talk about clumsy."

"I startled you. I should be the one apologizing."

Looking at him though, he didn't look the least bit sorry. In fact there was a ghost of a smile on the man's face. The darkness she'd sensed in him yesterday was nowhere to be seen right now. And she found she liked that. It made her more optimistic about what she wanted to ask him.

Soldier wound around them, tongue hanging out with excitement. "He's barely limping at all now. I think he's happy to see you."

"I'm pretty happy myself. There was a time yesterday when I thought…" His voice faded. She could imagine where his thoughts had gone.

"He's fine, as you can see. I gave him a pain pill this morning, but it should be wearing off by now."

"Do I need to give him something when I get him home?" His hands went onto his lean hips, perching there in a totally sexy way that made her mouth go dry.

Her so-called brilliant idea suddenly didn't seem quite as wise as it had a little while ago.

"I want him to continue the antibiotics. One pill a day, but unless he seems uncomfortable, let's hold off on the pain pills. I'll send two home with you. They can affect his motility. I mean—"

"I know what you mean."

She wasn't sure how to say this, but really felt it needed to be made clear. "If you don't have to give him the pills, I'd appreciate it if you returned them to me so I can dispose of them."

His head tilted as he looked at her. "The antibiotics?"

"No. The carprofen."

"Not a problem. I know they shouldn't be flushed."

Her muscles went slack all at once. Why had she said that? Was she seriously going to ask every client to return unused pain meds? No. But something inside her had blurted the words before she could stop herself.

Before she could try to come up with a logical explanation, he motioned at the bulletin board on the wall that was sitting askew, since it only had one screw in it. "What's this?"

Well, if she was going to do it, she needed to do it now.

"At my last clinic, we had a series of educational seminars on pets in the community. So far I have one of the local shelters scheduled to speak on their community ambassador program." She cleared her throat. "You wouldn't be interested in bringing Soldier in and talking about your and his work in search and rescue, would you?"

His hand reached down to his dog and fingered his ear as if needing time to figure out how to politely decline her offer.

She hurried to say, "I mean, I'll understand if you don't have time between your job and everything, so please don't feel pressured to say yes. It's just that it would be great for people to see that shelter dogs can bring so much benefit to society at large."

"I think it's a great idea. I don't think Doc had anything like this when he was here. How often are you thinking?"

"Once a week was what we did in San Fran. Search and rescue, though, I think would be a big draw. If you had the time, you could take two or even three sessions. And if you know of someone who trains dogs to do what Soldier does, that would be a great way to close out the subject, in case anyone might want to pursue that line of work or get involved."

"It's harder to get people involved in SAR when it's not a paid position."

She frowned. "You volunteer?"

"Yes. I should clarify that I get paid for being a

paramedic, but not for my work with SAR. I help when I'm available."

That surprised her. "You must really love it, then."

"Soldier definitely does." He paused. "Which makes me ask. Will he continue to have problems with his leg even after it's healed? Do I need to think about retiring him?"

"I don't see why he wouldn't be able to go back to work. He's limping now, just because the muscle is sore. Unless there are unforeseen complications, he should be as right as rain in a few weeks." She smiled. "From what I saw of him, retirement wouldn't suit him."

Or you. The words hung on the tip of her tongue, but she didn't say them. After all, she really didn't know him. At all.

And that wasn't likely to change, even if he agreed to participate in the seminar program.

Cabe took the screwdriver from her and picked up the screw that had fallen to the floor. Without asking, he stepped onto the lowest rung of the ladder and finished securing the bulletin board to the wall. The man was definitely tall. She'd almost been on the top of the ladder and had still had to stretch up to reach it. She hadn't wanted it to hang so low that little kids or large dogs might be able to reach the tacks. "How's that?"

"It's great, thanks."

He stepped off the ladder and handed her the screwdriver. "What day of the week are the seminars on?"

She'd half expected him to come up with an excuse of why he couldn't participate, but so far, he hadn't.

"Right now, I have them planned for Saturdays. But I can be flexible."

"Let me see if I can get two Saturdays in a row off, although I don't think it will be a problem. Which weeks do you want me to take?"

She blinked. "You mean you'll do it?"

"It certainly sounds that way."

She smiled. "Great! Since I only have the shelter signed up so far, and they're coming this week, do you think you can do the following Saturday and the one after that?"

"Let me double-check with the station, but I'm pretty sure I can trade with someone, if I'm scheduled. After all it's the least I can do to repay you."

That threw her. "Repay me?"

"For not letting me walk out that door yesterday knowing what you did. I'd planned on going to the pharmacy for some painkillers, and I wouldn't have wanted to be on...display. So you saved me both the trip and the embarrassment."

Oh! She got it. Motioning to the ladder, "I think you just repaid me by not letting me crash to the ground."

He grinned. "So we're even?" He pulled his wallet from his pocket. "Except for the emergency vet service that is. I have Soldier's insurance card."

She waved him away. "I'll donate that in exchange for your expertise in doing the seminar." In case he was thinking of arguing with her, she added, "I'm donating services to the shelter as well, in exchange for them coming to speak."

This time it was Cabe who frowned. "You'll go out of business pretty quickly if you keep giving away services. Seriously, though, I don't know what I would have done if you couldn't see Soldier. The next clinic is thirty miles away, and I didn't want him to have to wait that long."

"Of course! I'm happy I was home."

They both stood there for a minute or two in silence. Then Soldier nudged at Cabe's hand, and he drew in a quick breath, his demeanor seeming to change instantly. "I think he's hinting that he's ready to go home. I'll confirm my participation in the seminar."

It wasn't her imagination that he suddenly didn't sound as enthused as he had moments earlier about doing it. But that was on him. If he didn't want to, he could speak up and say so.

"Thanks for considering it." Her fingers reached up to touch his injured cheek before she had time to think. When his brows went up, she hurried to say, "This looks better. It's not as puffy today."

"It feels pretty good, all things considered. Thanks again for putting me back together."

Except she had a feeling she hadn't. And whether or not what she'd sensed was part of her imagination or something very real, she'd treated enough sick and injured animals to know that some living creatures couldn't be put back together. Not by her. Not by anyone. Just like Jason.

Knowing where that line was was an important part of her job in alleviating suffering. But not with humans. That wasn't her job. And certainly not with this man. The sooner she remembered that, the better off she would be.

CHAPTER THREE

TWO DAYS LATER, Cabe walked out of the small office in the fire department that housed the Santa Medina Search and Rescue Center and rolled his eyes. Not only did his boss think that taking part in Jessie's seminar series was a good idea, he wanted to go all out and put on a demonstration of all it entailed. And that meant that Cabe had to set up a mock rescue of another team member, have Soldier find him, and then climb down to "save" him. His banged-up shoulder still hurt like anything, so the prospect of climbing didn't thrill him all that much.

Was that the only reason?

No.

Startling Jessie and having to almost catch her had done a number on his nerves. He'd found himself reliving that scene in microseconds over the last couple of days. He'd almost…almost…turned her toward him and…

And what? Kissed her?

Oh, he was sure *that* would have been well received. Not. His mouth twitched sideways. He'd also imagined the possibilities of the aftermath of that kiss in stunning detail. And some of those possibilities had been…

But "the kiss that wasn't" wasn't the only thing that bothered him about that day. Cabe had stood there chatting with her as if she were an old friend. It had felt warm and comfortable. Something he hadn't felt in a long time.

But Jessie was not a friend. And he wasn't even sure why he'd gotten so worked up over lifting her off that ladder. He hadn't kissed her, although the urge had certainly been there.

He could only chalk it up to gratefulness over the way she'd taken care of Soldier, taking his dog home with her and letting him follow her around.

And now he had to call her and tell her what Terry had said about the seminar. Maybe she wouldn't want anything that in-depth and would say "thanks but no thanks" to anything but the informational talks, although she'd seemed keen to let him do as much or as little as he felt comfortable with. Well, his comfort level was pretty much nil at the moment.

Maybe he could pass the job off to Brad or Doug. He rolled his eyes, remembering that she wanted to show how *companion animals* as in shelter animals helped the community. It wasn't just about SAR. And Soldier was the only search and rescue dog in this area, although there were others they could call on if there was a massive search effort underway, just like he and Soldier could go and help another team if they were ever needed.

He opened the back door to his car to let Soldier jump in, noting the dog's leg and ribs weren't giving him any trouble, before going around and climbing into his own seat. Only then did he dial the number to the clinic. In the back seat, Soldier gave an enthusiastic bark, anxious to be on their way.

She answered it on the first ring. "Santa Medina Veterinary Clinic, may I help you?"

"Jessie? It's Cabe." Surprised that he'd recognized her voice instantly, he'd forgotten to use her title. If she noticed she didn't let on. "Did Margo not make it back yet?"

"She did. She's just on her lunch break. How's Soldier doing?"

"He's great. Barely even a limp." It had been two days since the injury, and it was looking better each day. Like his cheek.

"That's great news. So if you're not calling about Soldier…"

"Do you have a patient right now?"

"Nope. Do you want to come over?"

Maybe this would be better done in person. Then he could gauge the reaction on her face. If there was any hesitation, he would gladly scale his participation down to a simple speech, with Soldier standing next to him. "Sure. It won't take long, I promise."

"You're not going to speak, are you."

It took him a second before he realized she was talking about the seminar itself and not about her wanting him to remain silent when he arrived at the clinic.

"No, I am. It's just…" He thought fast. "Do you have time for a coffee?"

There was a pause. "How about if I put a pot on at the house. Then you can tell me whatever it is that's on your mind."

That was probably a better solution. "Are you done for the day?"

"Pretty much. Barring any unforeseen emergencies."

He and Soldier had been one of those. "I have Soldier with me, is that a problem?"

"I already know he doesn't gobble up birds so no, it's not a problem."

That made him smile. "Okay, we'll be there in about twenty minutes, if that's not too soon."

"I should be just about ready for you by then."

The words sent a shard of something through him. According to his ex no one was ready to deal with him. And she was probably right. He'd never seemed to be good at relationships...whether they were familial or romantic.

Which basically ruled out relationships in general, except with his mom. And even their relationship wasn't the best in the world, although it was certainly better than it used to be. Mainly because she'd finally realized that she had an issue with codependency, getting involved with men she thought she could heal. Only it never worked out. Not with his dad. Not with the three other relationships she'd had since then.

But thank God she'd booted the last guy out. Now if she could just keep it that way.

His ex had basically booted his butt to the curb for the same reason. He wasn't a drunk. But growing up with one had made him guarded with his feelings. Not the ideal kind of person to be with if you wanted emotional intimacy. Which Cabe didn't. Not anymore.

Starting up the car, he pulled out of the space and headed toward the clinic.

Jessie's house still looked like Doc's. Probably because she'd just moved in not that long ago. Except there was a huge birdcage in the middle of the living room. What was—unfortunately—*not* in the cage, was a huge white cockatoo.

This was her bird? He'd pictured something…well, smaller. Less threatening.

As it was, the feathered creature was sitting on a large perch that was just about at face level.

The better to peck your eyes out.

Cabe had never been around birds, not even chickens, so he stared at it warily.

The bird's head twisted sideways and tilted as if studying them. When he saw Soldier, his comb went up and he stepped with funny jerky movements along his perch, moving closer to the intruders. "Nice doggy." The singsong words were followed by a whistle that was definitely not politically correct.

Cabe thought his brows were going to shoot straight off his forehead.

"Dumble! That's not nice."

The bird repeated the whistle, then said, "Not nice. Dumble not nice."

The cockatoo didn't sound in the least sorry for what he'd done.

"Oh, jeez." Jessie's face colored. "I'm sorry. I can't seem to break him of that."

"I take it you didn't teach him that."

"Nope. That definitely wasn't me. I sort of inherited him. I did a stint in vet school studying exotic birds, and one of my professors died midyear. It was terrible. Dumble was his. He had nowhere to go, and so I…"

"Inherited him. Did you inherit his name too?"

Jessie certainly seemed to be a softy when it came to animals. Which made sense.

"Yep. My professor said his kids had grown up with a children's book series and they'd named him. Dumble's close to twenty-five years old now." She smiled. "Anyway, come in and sit down. I have the coffee made. How do you take it?"

He moved further into the room and sat on a sofa that had to be the same age as the bird. The upholstery was dark beige with kind of a velvety texture. It did not fit Jessie—or her bird—at all.

As if reading his thoughts, she smiled. "I haven't had a chance to redecorate yet. And I'm more of an outdoor girl than an indoor one. Working in the garden seemed preferable to replacing all of the furnishings in the house."

Dumble had swiveled on the perch, continuing to eye Soldier and Cabe in a way that made him slightly uneasy. "He won't come down and visit us, will he?"

She gave him a funny look. "You don't like birds?"

He shrugged. "I've never really been around them."

"Don't worry about him. He's harmless. And he's not a spring chicken anymore. I can put him in his cage, if you want, though."

"No. It's okay." Soldier had flopped down onto the floor, his injured leg facing up, and seemed totally unconcerned about a possible visit from Dumble. If his dog wasn't worried, then he wouldn't be either. "Can I help with the coffee?"

"Nope. I'll get it." She paused. "I don't think you ever told me how you take it?"

"Just black."

"Of course you do," she muttered, then as if she hadn't meant to say the words out loud, she added. "You're kind of a no-frills guy."

The words made him tense. If she only knew how right she was.

He didn't do soft and mushy, or romantic and sweet. Not easily anyway. Oh, he knew what was expected out of a partner, and could occasionally get with the program and do the prescribed flowers and chocolate. But it always felt like an act. Like he was playing a part without really feeling any genuine emotions. And that worried him. His ex had deserved more, and she knew it. But he felt like he didn't have more to give.

Which was why he had sworn off relationships. He felt like he had more of his dad in him than he might like to think. And now that he was divorced, he could make a conscious decision to not be put in that position ever again.

Realizing she was waiting for a response, he said. "You're exactly right. No frills here."

She gave a weird kind of smile and then said, "I'll be right back with the coffee. Dumble…be good." And then she left the room.

"Dumble not good. Dumble not good."

Cabe shot the bird a look. "You're not the only one, pal."

"Not the only one. Not the only one."

Hell, the last thing he needed was to have the bird start repeating what he said. But if there was an off button, he had no idea where it was.

Jessie came back a couple of minutes later with a tray and two heavy white coffee mugs. He wasn't the only one who did no frills, evidently. No delicate porcelain cups in sight. She set the coffee on the table in front of the sofa and handed him a mug.

Dumble squawked and then parroted. "Not the only one." He repeated the phrase a few more times.

The veterinarian frowned at her bird. "Sometimes I have no idea where he comes up with these things."

Cabe busied himself taking a drink of coffee, to avoid commenting, while she sat in the chair across from him. Soldier's tail thumped a time or two, although the dog didn't open his eyes. He was asleep on the rug.

Her lab coat was long gone. Instead, she had on jeans and a black tank top, its narrow straps showing off her shoulders to perfection. Something he shouldn't be noticing. And her wavy blond tresses were pulled back in a high ponytail, making her neck look incredibly long. Incredibly kissable.

Coming here had been a bad idea.

Oblivious to his thoughts, she glanced at the dog and then at him. "He looks like he's doing pretty well." She nodded at him and then added, "And your injury seems to be healing."

"It's much better, thanks. I figure seven days, and I can take the butterflies off?"

"About that. Depends on how often you smile."

That made him look at her.

"Sometimes if sutures are in an area of high movement, we leave them in an extra day or two to make sure things are going to hold."

Ah, that made sense. "Well, in my case, seven days should just about do it." Although he could feel the muscles in his cheek twitch as if trying to pull his lips up. Great. It was as if she'd just said "don't think about the word gorilla" and of course that was impossible to do once the suggestion was made.

"Are you saying you don't smile much?" Before he could answer, she took a drink of her own coffee, staring at him over the rim of her cup. "So, you wanted to talk about the seminar? Were you able to get the time off?"

"Yes, but there's a catch. Kind of a big one."

As expected, he watched her frown before he added, "If you decide it's not what you're looking for, feel free to say so. But just so you know, it wasn't my idea."

"Okay..." She drew the word out slowly. "What's the catch?"

"My boss, actually. To promote our work, he would like to do a mock rescue on-site at the Stately Pleasure Dome."

She gave him a look. "Pleasure Dome? Okay. I'm not even sure what that is, and I'm a little afraid to ask."

The name was so ubiquitous to the area, that he never even gave it a second thought. But he could see how it sounded to someone who wasn't from the area. Maybe he needed to backtrack a bit. His lips twitched and then he smiled.

"It's kind of an unofficial name for one of the rock formations in the Tuolumne Meadows area."

"I see. It's kind of a weird name."

"The rumor is it was named after a poem. Anyway, it's a popular climbing area, since it's easily accessible."

"And where are the meadows? Too-All-Oh-Me, did you say?"

Another smile at the way she drew out the name. "We're not that far from there, actually. You've never been to Tuolumne Meadows?"

"I'm from San Francisco, remember? I mean, I've

researched some of the nearby areas, but since I've only been here a couple of weeks, I haven't had a chance to visit anything."

Of course she hadn't. He'd been stupid to assume otherwise. "Sorry, I should have realized that."

"It's okay." She took another sip of her drink then set the mug on the table. "So what would this mock rescue entail?"

"Soldier would show how he tracks a scent and then once the 'injured hiker' is found, me and three other team members would stage a rescue."

"Would this be one of the two weeks you agreed to present?"

"No, it would probably need to be the week after the presentation. Maybe have anyone interested meet us at the site. Terry—my boss—would like to hand out brochures afterward telling people how to get involved with our team and what's required."

She sat there for a minute before saying, "Wow."

Okay, so he had no idea if she meant that "wow" as in did he really expect her to agree to that? Or a "wow" as in the request was so much more than she'd hoped for.

"So what do you think?"

"I think it's perfect. I feel lucky to be able to see how a rescue takes place."

"Really?"

"Really. I would like to go and visit the site for myself, though, if possible. The accessibility and so forth might be an issue if we have a lot of interest."

He'd really expected she would balk at the idea. Had halfway hoped she would. But instead, there was a gleam of excitement in her eyes.

"Can you tell me how to get there? Or is there an address I could look up?" she asked.

"Maybe it would be better if I just take you there."

And where the hell had that just come from?

"I would love that. When?"

If they were going to do this, it needed to be soon, so his team could plan and figure out what they were going to do. He had no idea why, but part of her enthusiasm was rubbing off on him. They did training sessions all the time, but normally there wasn't an audience. And lately because of the challenges involved in organizations like theirs, there had been talks of financial cutbacks. Most of the team were volunteers, so the savings couldn't be taken out in salaries. Instead, it meant equipment that couldn't be replaced or repaired, and they would have to make do. That meant possibly putting team members in danger.

"Do you have time this week? You said the shelter is taking this coming Saturday, right?"

"Yep." She stood and retrieved her phone from the back pocket of her jeans. "Let me check what I have scheduled for the rest of the week."

She sat back down and ran her finger over the phone screen. "Wednesday is pretty booked. And Thursday. How about Friday? Are you working?"

"I work 1:00 a.m. until nine. Could we meet at the clinic around ten?"

"Are you sure you want to do a field trip after working those kinds of hours?"

He smiled. Cabe actually thrived on the long hours. It gave him less time to think. Or to think too far into the future. A place he didn't really like to visit. "I'm sure. It'll take about thirty minutes to arrive at the

Dome. But it's a nice view and there's a road that runs right beside it."

"Parking?"

"There's some on the road along that area. Even if there's a large group, there'd be less than a quarter-mile walk to get there."

"Sounds perfect." Her smile widened. "Thank you for being willing to participate. I imagine this will pull in quite a few people."

"That's what Terry is hoping. And if we can get some experienced climbers involved that would be ideal. If you have time maybe stop in at the office and meet him before we go. And I'll let him know that you're in agreement with it."

He hadn't been to Tuolumne Meadows as a tourist in years. Strangely, he was looking forward to seeing it through Jessie's eyes. And maybe even looking forward to a little more of her company? That was something he was not going to say anywhere near her bird. The cockatoo appeared to have lost interest in them and looked to be dozing on his perch at the moment. A very good thing.

He stood, finishing the last of his coffee. "Well, we've taken enough of your time. Thanks for the coffee." He looked down at where his dog was looking up at him with expectancy. "You ready to go, boy?"

Soldier leaped up and stood right beside him, waking up Dumble, who turned on his perch to stare at them again.

Cabe reached down and rubbed the dog's head. He took back what he'd thought about emotions. He loved his dog. But then Soldier's expectations of him were fairly low, and there was no prevaricating or hinting or getting upset if Cabe didn't say exactly the right thing. That was the kind of relationship he excelled at. Where things were pretty much mapped out and rarely strayed from the prescribed path. He glanced up at Jessie and something in his chest thumped.

Not so with the woman in front of him. Or any woman, for that matter. In that, he felt totally lost and out of his element when he was around them.

"Not the only one," Dumble mocked.

For some reason, the words made Cabe laugh. "Remind me not to confess to any crimes around him."

"Yes, that would not be good, although I'm not sure how admissible it would be in a court of law. Especially if he started in with his infamous whistle."

She handed the bird a peanut, which he deftly cracked open and ate, dropping the shell onto the papered shelf beneath him. Then she gave him a scratch beneath his beak with the tip of her fingers, which the bird leaned into.

Cabe couldn't blame him. Her ponytail swished as she leaned forward to give the bird a quick kiss.

Something tightened in his gut. A thin thread of longing that he didn't recognize. Didn't want to recognize. And on that note...

"Well, I'll get out of your way. Until Friday?"

She straightened to look at him, tucking a stray lock behind her ear. An image went through Cabe of him being the one tucking that strand back in place. Of leaning forward to...

"Until Friday."

Friday at the Pleasure Dome. Oh, hell, he should have chosen another place. Any other place. For not the first time, he was thinking how stupid it had been to suggest taking her up to Tuolumne.

To survive this, he was going to have to make sure he kept his mind on work and off...

Well, anything else.

CHAPTER FOUR

THE PLACE HE indicated had no cars in front of it, which surprised her. But then again it was before noon and most locals worked on Fridays, Cabe had said.

He'd picked her up from her clinic a half hour ago, and she'd carried most of the conversation on the short trip. Maybe it was nerves, but she had the feeling that's just the way Cabe was. The strong silent type? It appeared that way. But he didn't seem irritated by her chatter, which was a huge relief.

He found a spot right in front of a rock formation and pulled alongside the road. "Well, this is it. The Stately Pleasure Dome."

"Wow. You weren't kidding when you said the road ran directly in front of it." She glanced in the distance and saw several other mounded rock formations scattered throughout a huge flat area. "So is this the meadow you were talking about?"

"Yes, and this is probably the best spot to do the demo. It'll provide a great view of what's going on." He paused. "Since we're only about three weeks out, Soldier should be healed enough to make it up that slope?"

"I think so. Is he limping today?"

"No, and he got into the car fine. I'm not seeing any discomfort in the leg or his ribs."

"Animals heal remarkably fast. Probably because their ancestors had to in order to survive." She peered toward the east side of the formation. "Will the display be on the front side of the rock or in back."

He smiled. "Unless you or your group can walk on water, it'll have to be on this side. I'll take you around and show you why. There's a road around part of it, but there's water on just the other side of it."

Exiting the car, he let Soldier out. The dog immediately started tracking scents. The scent hounds had always fascinated her.

"Does he ever find something you haven't asked him to find?" Jessie followed his lead out and stood on the embankment watching the bloodhound's intent search.

"All kinds of things. He's almost always nose to the ground. I imagine scents are like tastes to us. So many different smells out there to sort through."

Cabe turned to the side, and Jessie couldn't resist letting her glance alight on his butt, where his black jeans covered taut well-muscled flanks. He turned before she was ready for him to, and he caught her. When her face heated, his mouth canted to the side for a second or two. But thank God, he didn't say anything. Maybe because he couldn't be positive about what she'd been looking at.

Hurrying to find another topic, she said, "So how will this work? Is the person who's pretending to be injured going to be on one of those flat areas and you'll climb up to him?"

He put a hand up to shade his eyes and looked at the rock. "Yes, although we haven't decided if I'll be climbing down to him or going up. It depends on what's needed. If someone falls while hiking or mountain climbing, for instance, we might have to climb up one of the main tracts and then descend to their level. Fortunately these domes are popular climbing spots, so there are already bolts left by other climbers that we can anchor to. People have even mapped out the best travel paths."

"I'm not sure what any of that means, since I've never climbed before."

"It means we can get to someone faster than we would if we had to set our own spots to anchor ourselves to."

A shiver went through her as she imagined how it might be to fall from a height and have to wait for someone to come help her. "Got it."

Just then he gave a shrill set of whistles that made Soldier's head come up. He immediately headed their way with a big lumbering trot that made her smile. His long ears were flipping and flopping with every footfall. "Those ears. I just can't get over them."

"He's a pretty special guy."

"I can't imagine how awful it was when he fell."

He blew out a breath. "It was pretty terrible. I expected to climb down and find him either dead or at death's door. But he's a tough one, aren't you, boy." He rubbed the dog's ears when Soldier pulled up next to him.

"How often do you get called out on rescues? Are most of them climbing related?" She'd never actually met anyone involved in SAR. She found she was looking forward to the demonstration at least as much as anyone who might come to watch.

Cabe was so totally different than Jason had been. At least on the surface. As far as what was underneath, who knew. It was hard for her to trust her judgment in that area right now.

Her ex had been a true urbanite at heart, self-assured, soaking up the attention after a successful ball game. He also had no problems expressing himself. She had no doubt he would hate Santa Medina. His passion was baseball and his earnings had been a lot more than hers. She and Chloe and Dumble had lived in one of his posh residences with him for over a year. But Jason had not been a fan of Dumble's incessant talking, and Jessie had chafed at the lack of green space around the building, although the views from his apartment had been breathtaking. Then Chloe had gotten cancer, and Jason had made some unforgiveable choices during that time. Even so, her decision to leave him had been hard. Even now, she could remember the sick churning of emotions as he asked her to give him another chance.

She couldn't afford to. Not with that kind of betrayal.

And she would never put herself in that position ever again. From now on, she was going to guard her heart with as much diligence as she guarded the keys to her medicine cabinet.

And Cabe? He didn't do a whole lot of talking. Nor was he open with his emotions, from what she'd seen of him. But what she had seen were snatches of the deep love and admiration he had for his dog.

But, like Jason, he also didn't seem to be Dumble's biggest fan, although it didn't matter, because she didn't have to live with the man. Nor would she. It had been such a relief to be on her own again after Jason's unconscionable acts, that she couldn't see wanting to change that anytime soon. And if she did, it would be with someone who wanted the same things out of life as she did. Someone she came to trust. And that would only come after years of knowing that person. After years of digging for any secrets that could bring heartache. And honestly, she wasn't sure if she would ever take that leap again.

She blinked the thoughts away, when she realized Cabe had said something to her. "Sorry?"

"I was saying that we can go up onto the lower part of the Dome if you want. We wouldn't need any equipment for that, since the pitches are fairly low key."

"Really? I would love that!"

Although there were mountains accessible in the distance in California, it wasn't something she'd done a whole lot of as a kid, since her parents, like Jason, were pretty much indoor people.

Another car had pulled up and a couple exited with what looked like rugged outdoor gear. Both of them had a variety of bungee cord type thingies clipped onto their belts. Although she wasn't the biggest fan of heights, she could see how rock climbing could be fun. Maybe she'd take a class or two on some of the tamer slopes.

The couple waved to them as they passed by.

"Which slope are you doing?" Cabe asked.

"We're thinking we might head up to the Boltway."

He nodded. "Have a good climb."

"Thanks, we will." The pair went on their way, scrambling up the lower surface of the rock formation before things got steeper. At that point, they began using their hands and the girl pulled something off her belt. One of the bungee-looking things.

"What are those straps?"

"They're climbing slings. They're used to help you anchor to different points during the climb." He peered up at the couple. "Let's go ahead and go up one of the outcroppings where we can sit. I'll explain what our plans are for the demo, and you can see if it'll fit in with what you want."

She smiled. "Oh, I'm sure it will be. You guys are giving me a lot more than I even dared to hope for."

Following Cabe up the slope, she was glad she'd worn tennis shoes rather than sandals. She'd needed the grip of the rubber several times as the terrain's slope increased. When she hesitated for a second, Cabe reached his hand down for her.

Grabbing it, she let him haul her up to the ledge he was standing on. "I can see why people carry all that gear now. This isn't as easy as it looks." And she considered herself to be fairly athletic.

"No, it's not."

Soldier had had a much easier time scrambling up the hill than she had. "He doesn't seem traumatized by his fall."

"No, and I'm very glad he's not hesitating."

Quite the opposite, actually. The dog plopped down on a horizontal stretch of rock that was shaded by an overhang. Cabe took the backpack he'd slung over one of his shoulders and produced two water bottles, handing her one of them.

"Thanks." She definitely hadn't come prepared. She hadn't even thought to bring water. But then again, she hadn't thought she'd be actually scrambling up a slope.

She lowered herself onto the rock, which felt surprisingly cool compared to the warm temperatures of the air around them.

Cabe poured a little of his own bottle out into a depression in the rock near the dog, and Soldier lapped it up, without even getting to his feet.

Then he sat down beside her. Another car had parked, and hikers were getting out of it as well. "I bet this place gets congested with climbers on weekends."

"Definitely. And not just on weekends. It's one of the most popular climbs in the area because of how easy the access is."

She looked out over the road and beyond. It was surprisingly quiet. "It's beautiful."

"Yes, it is. The lakeside is even more so."

Soldier stretched out on his side with a sigh of contentment. Chloe would have loved this spot too, although with her little legs, she'd have probably needed to be carried up. The thought that Jason had used some of her pain meds for himself instead of giving them to her still made her heart cramp. It was an ache she'd probably never be rid of.

"I bet the views from the top are spectacular."

"Yes, they are." He glanced at her. "You should take some classes in climbing. You might find you like it."

"I was just thinking that, although I'm kind of terrified of heights."

"You might surprise yourself. I'd stick to the easy slopes at first, though. They have some pretty impressive views as well." His smile reached his butterfly bandage and made lines radiate out beside his eyes. The expression was warm and so genuine that it made her stomach twist.

She found herself smiling back, her gaze moving to take in the snoozing dog. What a perfect day. If she had thought ahead, she could have packed a picnic lunch, although Cabe might have thought she was being presumptuous, if she had, since he'd made no mention of sharing a meal on this trip. "I'll have to make it a point to take in more of the sights. Yosemite is gorgeous, if this is any indication."

"Yes. It's beautiful."

She hesitated, before asking, "Can I look at your butterflies to make sure they're holding up okay?" Although she wasn't sure what she was going to do if they weren't.

His eyes fastened on hers for several seconds. "Go ahead."

Jessie got up on her knees and leaned in to look at the bandages, which weren't quite as white as they'd been when she'd put them on. Her fingers touched his warm cheek and slid to the edge of the first butterfly, her gaze taking in the sealed skin around it. It looked like it was healing well. She tested the edges of the skin. It remained sealed. "It looks just about perfect, I think."

"Yes. It does." His murmur rumbled through her, the tones warm and hypnotic.

And when she looked closer, her mouth went dry as she realized their faces were now mere inches apart. She hadn't realized she'd gotten quite that close. But she found she didn't want to move away. Not just yet.

Cabe's hand came up and covered hers, pressing her palm against his cheek. His skin was warm and slightly rough with a hint of stubble. Jason had always shaved twice daily, as he couldn't stand having a five-o'clock shadow. It didn't seem to bother Cabe, though. And she found his rough exterior…sexy. Her fingers itched to wander across those whiskers and explore more, but he was still looking at her in a way that made her go totally still.

Then his other hand came up and cupped her cheek, and she couldn't stop herself from leaning into his touch. The world around them seemed to shrink until it encompassed only her…and Cabe.

Her gaze went to his mouth, and she started to lean forward…

A sudden scream split the warm sensuality of the moment in two, and it took him a second to realize that Jessie was not only *not* kissing him, but that the scream hadn't come from her either.

She wheeled away from him in an instant, and Cabe's eyes scoured the area above them for the source of the cry. It came again, but this time ended in a shrill laugh.

Ah hell. It wasn't a distress cry. It was that first couple playing around as they ascended the rock.

When he glanced at Jessie, her eyes were also on the upper area of the dome, and when they came back down to meet his, she put the back of her hand over her mouth, a horror in her eyes that was worse than it should have been under the circumstances. Hell, it hadn't even been an actual kiss, so no harm no foul.

And if it had been?

And then, when she finally lowered her hand…she giggled.

What the…?

"Sorry," she said between gulped chortles. "I had no idea what that was. I thought someone was plummeting to their doom for a minute. And there we were in the middle of...well, who knows what that was."

He couldn't stop the smile that crept across his face. "I thought the same. I always have my climbing gear in the back of the car, just in case." Not that he could climb away from what had almost happened, as much as he might want to.

"Thank God it was a false alarm."

"Yes." What hadn't been a false alarm was how intent he'd been on her as she'd come closer, as she'd examined his wound. As her scent and warmth had surrounded him. So much so that he'd lost track of the world around him. Not good. This was a very public place. The last thing he needed was to see someone he knew and to have to explain why he'd been up here almost making out with the new vet. Only he hadn't been. And maybe she wouldn't have kissed him at all. Could be it was all in his damned imagination. He glanced over at Soldier to see he was still fast asleep. Yep. Not even that scream had woken him up. Maybe because in his subconscious he'd been able to tell the difference between what was real and what was not.

Kind of like Cabe was trying to do right now.

Well, what was very real was the fact that he didn't want to get carried away and end up in another relationship that had no business getting started. No matter how attractive he might find her.

He decided to prevaricate.

"Sometimes the beauty of the setting can kind of get the best of people. In a whole lot of ways."

"Evidently. I have no idea why I got so..." She shook her head. "This isn't, um, going to affect your participation in the community series, is it?"

He shook his head. "Why would it? If you think I'd pull out over a whole lot of nothing, I would say you don't know me very well, but in this case it's true. You don't know me."

If he'd been looking to drive home the fact that they were strangers, it seemed to have worked, because she scooted over to put some distance between them. "You're right. I don't. And I didn't come here to make friends, or anything else. I came here to do a job. And that's what I need to focus on right now. My work."

Why did he feel like he'd just made a mess out of something that he'd just called "a whole lot of nothing"? Maybe because that's what he did when it came to the opposite sex: made messes that were hard to clean up. But if he tried to backpedal, he might give her the wrong idea or make her think he was interested in anything she might have to offer. Well, she hadn't offered. And he wasn't interested. And it needed to stay that way. He knew what he could give someone. And he knew what he couldn't.

"I think that's something that we can both agree on. That our jobs are what are important to us—what we both need to focus on." He forced a smile. "So now that that's settled…"

Another screeched laugh came from somewhere above him and all of a sudden, he didn't want to sit here and listen to another couple's happiness. "Can I take you around to the lake side so you can see it?"

"Yes. Let's go."

He hadn't been kidding about needing to walk on water to see a display on this side. The road beside the Dome was narrow and there was nowhere to back up to in order to see a demonstration, until you were swimming offshore, and she didn't imagine anyone was going to want to come in their bathing suits.

Damn. What had almost happened? And there was no mistaking what she'd been about to do. It was as if she'd been mesmerized by him. After all the lectures about not leaping in and trusting another person…about it taking years before she felt safe enough to let her guard down. And here she was. Letting her guard down.

Well, up you go, Mr. Wall. Back in place.

She hadn't moved all the way to Santa Medina just to make the very same mistakes again. Yes, Cabe and Jason seemed very different. But that didn't mean that Cabe was any better for her than Jason had been.

So why had she almost done the unthinkable?

Like he'd said, maybe she'd been caught up in the scenery. Or seeing that first couple walking along in such unity. A unity she'd once dreamed of finding with her ex, only to have that dream turn into a nightmare. And something inside her now wondered if she was cut out for long-term relationships. If trust could ever truly be rebuilt.

"Which lake is this again?"

"Lake Tenaya."

She stared out at it, thankful for the stiff breeze that was not only whipping her ponytail around her face but also helping to blow away her troubling thoughts.

Jason was out of her life forever. And she needed to try to put the ugly things that had happened behind her.

Soldier sidled up next to her, and she reached down to pet his silky head, liking the way he leaned his weight against her hip. She wasn't quite ready to get another dog, but maybe that day was coming. He or she could never replace Chloe in her heart, but she knew the human heart was an amazing thing, able to carve out a new space and a different kind of love.

She glanced at Cabe.

Which was also why she needed to be on guard. While it might be okay for it to carve out a new spot for a companion animal, she didn't want it to think she was in the market for a new *human* companion.

"It's amazing." And it was. The sun glinted off the crystal-blue waters, mirroring the sky above. Both the lake and the sky were a beautiful contrast to the evergreens and rock formations that surrounded the area. A long sandy strip lay a short distance away, and there were several people sitting on the beach. "Do people swim here?"

"They do, but it's pretty chilly, even in late summer. Any other time, it's frigid."

"You're not a fan of polar plunge challenges?"

He smiled, his bandage crinkling slightly, which was what had gotten her into trouble before. She averted her eyes. "Let's just say, I'd choose my rock climbing over icy water any day."

"I would have to agree with you there. Even though I'm not crazy about heights, I think I might take your suggestion and find someplace to take lessons."

"I know a couple of good places. Or I could show you the basics."

He was willing to do that? Even after she'd almost kissed him? It could be she was making a bigger deal about it than she needed to. He'd almost said as much.

But wouldn't being with him any more than necessary be playing with fire? Probably, but she was going to have to be with him for the seminar series. She could incorporate planning time into it and get a tiny glimpse into what search and rescue was all about.

"Are you sure? That would be great. It would be nice if I didn't go into your sessions having no clue as to what your team does. So can you talk me through a rescue as you show me those 'basics'?"

His gaze was on the lake, so she couldn't read his expression, but he seemed to have just tensed. Was he having second thoughts about his offer? Or just not thrilled about having to explain everything to her?

"We could just do one of the easy passes here on the Dome. I could show you how to use anchors and how to belay."

"Belay?" She gave an internal eye roll the second the question left her mouth. Case in point. Every time he mentioned something about climbing she sort of went *Huh?* But she wanted to learn. Wanted to know how the Santa Medina Search and Rescue team did what it did.

"Belay is a safety measure so you don't fall. It's why climbing in pairs is so important."

Her eyes widened. "Not falling would definitely be preferable to the alternative." She thought for a minute. "If you could show me some basics, I could decide if it's something I want to pursue further. With an actual instructor."

"They say some things are addictive. Rock climbing is definitely one of them."

She tensed. If anyone knew about addiction, it was her. And things about Jason made so much more sense now that she could look back on them. His single-minded pursuit of his sport. His seeming inability to get enough of her in bed while recovering from his shoulder injury. His secret drug use and subsequent denial that it was a problem. It seemed he could replace one addiction with another at will.

And Cabe's intensity about his work. Could it fall into that category? Somehow she didn't think so. But she had to admit, the man himself could be very, very addicting, if he put his mind to it.

She needed to be careful.

But what could it hurt to get a few pointers from the man? Maybe it would even help her understand more about the demonstration he and his team would put on in a few short weeks. If he even had time before then.

Soldier was following the edge of the lake, his nose to the ground like usual. She could see why Cabe loved him. The dog was very friendly and personable. Which was a testament to how well the paramedic treated him. And he was right about Soldier not limping anymore. If she hadn't treated him that day, she would have doubted anyone who told her the dog had been severely injured less than a week ago.

She re-found her train of thought. "Well, I don't know that I'll find rock climbing 'addictive,' but I'll certainly thank you for showing me a thing or two."

"Any other questions?"

A small part of her wished she had a million more questions. Because she had a feeling Cabe was bringing this trip to a close, and she found she wasn't quite ready for that. Wasn't quite ready to leave the magic of this place behind.

But she couldn't stay here forever. Because this wasn't the real world. Or at least not her real world. So the sooner she could get that through her thick head, the better off she would be.

CHAPTER FIVE

HE WASN'T SURE why he'd come here today.

This was the first of Jessie's community seminars, and his participation didn't start until next week.

He'd told himself it was because he wanted to see how the format was laid out, so he kind of knew what to expect.

He sat in one of the plastic chairs in the waiting room area of the vet clinic, surprised by the fact that there were very few vacant seats. Maybe everyone else was as curious as he was about what these seminars were all about.

The trip to Tenaya Lake and the Dome had surprised him. Jessie had an easy way about her, from her curiosity about rock climbing to the effortless way she could keep a conversation alive. And better yet, she hadn't expected him to dive into any and every subject she brought up. He'd found it...restful.

And so different from his ex who'd expected him to weigh in on almost everything she said. It had been both exhausting and exasperating. And he knew part of that was his fault. He wasn't geared toward what he could only call chattiness. But he could have at least tried. The fact that he hadn't, was very telling. The weird thing was that her expectations after marriage had seemed very different from when they were dating in high school. But then again, their hormones had done a lot of the talking for both of them back then.

And then when talk of babies and children had started, he'd talked even less. Because he hadn't felt ready. Had still been dealing with some of the scars from his childhood and his father's drinking. Starting a family of their own terrified him. And he hadn't been able to find the words to tell her any of that, so he resorted to passively avoiding the subject, leaving Jackie to cajole and ask and finally to press the issue. Until he finally said, "Not right now." She'd gotten angrier than he'd ever seen her and replied, "Forget it. Having kids with you would be the biggest mistake of my life."

She'd moved out the next day.

Cabe had let her go without a fight. Mainly because he couldn't have agreed with her more. Having kids with him would be the biggest mistake of both of their lives. And in saying that, she'd done the job his father hadn't finished. Convinced him that he wasn't fit for the role of husband or father.

And yet he'd been willing to kiss Jessie, if their lips had connected that day on the Dome. Had sat there in full view of anyone passing by as if they were an ordinary couple.

They weren't.

So he wasn't sure why he'd offered to show her the basics of rock climbing. Or why he'd felt it important to show up at her clinic today.

Was it really just the curiosity? Hell, he hoped so.

Jessie was walking around the room, introducing herself to the people who'd showed up. Either she hadn't seen him yet, or she was purposely ignoring him. Her eyes hadn't made contact with his. Not even once.

And then she was on his row. In front of him. Holding her hand out, she waited for him to take it, just like she'd done with all the other strangers, before giving it a quick squeeze and releasing it. "Thanks for coming. Although you didn't have to."

"I wanted to see what to expect." He nodded at the front, where there were several kennels lined up. "I see they came prepared."

"Yes, I think they're hoping for a few adoptions today. Lillian is great, as is everyone I've met so far. She's going to talk about adopting out pets to companies who would like a mascot. She said it would be kind of modeled after a furniture store in Santa Medina that has a greeter dog. I haven't visited there yet, but I've heard it's a staple of their business. We never had anything like that in San Francisco, that I know of. Maybe because the city is so huge."

"Santa Medina Furniture. Yes, that would be Bosco. He's been there for years and is much loved by the owners and, I would dare to guess, by the store's patrons as well."

"It doesn't cause any problems?"

"Problems? Like what?"

"I don't know, allergies? People who don't like animals?"

"I don't think so. Most people here know what to expect when they go into those particular shops in town. And there's a sign in the door with Bosco's picture on it that says *Warning: Puppy Kisses Happen Here.* So even out-of-towners know what they're getting into if they go inside. Although Bosco is very well-behaved."

"Well, I certainly think that after meeting Soldier, there are dogs in shelters that could be trained as therapy or emotional support animals. Or maybe could even be used in a hospital or hospice setting as a source of comfort."

"I think that's a great idea."

One of the waitstaff from the local diner came over, reaching out to give Jessie a hug and thanking her for helping the shelter here in town. "I've taken in three dogs, but my husband has said no more. So I'm thrilled to see them getting some much-needed exposure."

"Of course. Every pet deserves a good home. And they're just as committed to making sure every would-be adopter gets the dog or cat that is perfect for them. I was pretty impressed with their vetting system."

Despite how new she was in town, she was obviously good at getting to know people, her natural warmth making them want to move into her circle of acquaintances. Including him.

Not only that, but her passion about finding homes for shelter dogs was obvious and it was hard not to get caught up in her enthusiasm. Her cheeks were flushed, and her eyes sparkled as she talked. Her high ponytail bobbled and swung, caressing her neck with each tilt of her head. The look suited her. Long and impossibly silky looking, it was hard not to imagine winding its length around his hand and...

Ah hell. There he went again.

The person moved away, and Jessie glanced up at the front where Lillian Crane was setting papers on a podium. "I think she's getting ready to start, so I'd better go introduce her."

"Okay."

He watched her walk up to the front of the room, hips twitching in a sinuous dance that was totally natural—and had none of the artifice that he'd seen in some other women.

Enough comparing, Cabe!

He got it. She was different. But that didn't mean it was going to change anything. He didn't want *anyone*. Didn't need anyone. And she certainly didn't need someone like him.

Jessie got through the introductions and then sat in the front row while Lillian gave a short speech on how the Santa Medina Animal Shelter was starting a campaign of making pets an integral part of the community and helping show their usefulness in the private, professional and the health-care sectors. That included business owners. Of course only *people* could adopt animals, not business entities themselves, so that pets would be cared for no matter what happened with a person's professional life. And the dogs that would be involved in public settings were to receive specialized training to make sure they had the qualities required and that they would actually enjoy interacting with people they didn't know.

Lillian rattled off eight businesses in the surrounding towns where companies had done just that. Taken the "bring your pet to work" idea to a whole new level, while raising community awareness. It also gave hope to dogs and cats that might languish in the shelter for months or even years. And it was catching on. After all, cat cafés were all the rage in some of the more urban settings. People went in for a coffee and the experience of having cats lounging around the shop or winding around their ankles. And the snapshots of daily adoptions that were sent across social media said that ankles weren't the only things those felines managed to wind around. For some, it was those same humans' hearts. More and more shelters were turning to inventive ways like this one to forge connections between people and pets.

Soldier was the closest thing Santa Medina Fire and Rescue had to a mascot, but since he was Cabe's pet, it wasn't quite the same thing. Maybe he should talk to Terry and see if that was something the department might think about doing.

Once she finished, Lillian proceeded to introduce different dogs to the audience, walking them around and letting people interact with them.

"Any one of these guys would be a welcome addition to a home or business. They're social and friendly and we did some training to measure temperament around people and children. They all passed with flying colors. They'd make wonderful companions or therapists. They're also good with other animals."

Thirty minutes later, Lillian was back at the front of the room, while people gathered around the four dogs she'd brought. He stood in the back and watched as one by one, each of the animals, with the exception of one, found a home. With good people. He knew each of them and had no doubt that the dogs were going to be well cared for.

The one dog that was left was a small fluffy-looking

thing with wide-set eyes and a slightly crooked nose. When Lillian went to put her in her carrier, the dog looked around as if seeking someone…anyone.

Damn. He shouldn't go over there. He knew he shouldn't. He had no idea if Terry would even be open to the possibility of having a dog besides Soldier at the station house. But…

He went over and smiled. "Can I see him…her?… for a minute?"

"It's a her." She tilted her head. "I'm not sure Carrie is suited for search and rescue. She's kind of a couch potato."

Lillian put the dog into his arms and she immediately curled into them, tucking her nose into the crook of his elbow. "Not search and rescue, but maybe the squad would be willing to take on a mascot. I'm thinking her small size might be a good thing in this case. She's crate-trained?"

"Of course. And great with kids. She'd be good for all of those elementary school kids who come by on field trips."

"You don't have to sell me. You have to sell Terry."

"Terry's a cream puff. I'll call him myself."

He gave her a crooked grin. "Any chance you can keep my name out of that conversation?"

"Um…no. So maybe you'd better bring it up before I make that call."

He stroked Carrie's silky ear. "Okay, I will. But I can't promise you anything."

"Hey, if you guys aren't smart enough to take her, I'm sure we'll find a good home for her. Her quirky features are pretty endearing, you have to admit."

Yes, he did. Which is why he needed to hand her back. But not before promising he'd do his best for her.

Lillian slipped her back into her crate. "Let me know, okay? Soon."

"I will."

As the audience members filtered out, he went to find Jessie. To what? To congratulate her? The seminar hadn't directly benefited her, from what he could see, but it had done both the community and those dogs a lot of good. Maybe even Carrie, if he could talk Terry into it.

He found her by the side door thanking people for coming. He got in line behind everyone else. When it was finally his turn he shook her hand yet again, smiling at how silly that custom seemed right now. "I'm impressed."

"Impressed?"

"Lillian came with four dogs and she's leaving with one. And I have hopes that maybe the station house will take her on."

She smiled. "That was kind of the idea behind the series."

"Finding homes for dogs?"

"No. Making animals a normal part of close-knit communities like Santa Medina. Maybe with enough education, there will be fewer dogs and cats that wind up in shelters. And those that do will have an easier time finding homes."

He got it. "Well, if today is anything to go by, then you're certainly on your way to doing that. Did you get any other organizations besides me lined up to participate?"

"Yep. As a matter of fact, I did. I have a farmer

who's going to come in and talk about working dogs on farms, like Aussies and other breeds. And then I have a local school for developmental disabilities coming in to talk about service animals. The police department is trying to clear a date too."

"Well, it sounds like the seminars are going to be a success. And here you were worried about not having enough people to participate."

"I think I have you to thank, honestly."

"Me?" He had no idea how he could have anything to do with it.

"It got around that Santa Medina Search and Rescue was participating, and suddenly I started getting phone calls from other people wanting to know if I'd be interested in their organizations joining in."

"Well, I'm glad, although I had nothing personally to do with anyone finding out." If anything, he'd kind of kept it on the down low, but… "Maybe my boss had something to do with that."

"Whoever it was, I'm thankful."

Realizing there was someone behind him, he started to move out of the way before pausing. "About that rock climbing. Do you have time this next week? Before my seminar?"

"Let me look, and I'll give you a call."

Then she was greeting the woman behind him, and Cabe headed out the door, hoping that agreeing to give her a few pointers wasn't a huge mistake.

It would only be a mistake if he let it be one. If anything, this would give him the chance to work with Jessie and do a reset of their interactions. Putting that visit to the Dome firmly behind both of them. Where it needed to stay.

As long as he could remember that. No more fantasies about that ponytail or any other part of the veterinarian.

The climbing vest felt like a foreign entity. Jessie found herself dressed in a mess of curling cords and clanging metal. It reminded her of Medusa. And as Jessie glanced up at the Dome, it suddenly seemed a whole lot more formidable than it had the last time they'd been here. This time Soldier hadn't accompanied them, and it made her wonder just how high Cabe was planning to go that he couldn't bring the dog with them. Maybe she should double-check.

"You do remember I've never done this before, right?"

"Yep. Don't worry, I'll take it easy on you. Nothing you can't handle."

He had a lot more confidence in her abilities than she did, evidently. "You have no idea what I can handle," she muttered.

"I guess we'll find out."

Great. She hadn't meant him to hear that last phrase but leave it to her to have an instructor who had super sensitive bat hearing.

He stepped over to her and clipped what seemed like a hundred more carabiners onto the rings on her vest.

"Holy cow, am I going to need all of those?"

"No. But you always want more of them than you'll need. See?" He showed her his own harness.

"Heavens."

He pressed something into her hand. "This is a belay. We talked about this a little bit the other day. This is how it works."

He demonstrated how to feed the rope through the device hand over hand. "It's important to remember that your brake hand never ever leaves the brake side of the rope, which should always be on the bottom." He showed her one more time. "Now let me see you do it."

She felt like she had a thousand fingers—none of them very coordinated—as she practiced the counting and hand switching from the top to the bottom rope as she showed him. "Like this?"

"Yes. Try it again."

When she started to take her hand off the brake, he made a sound, and she stopped. "Right. Brake hand never let go. Got it."

They went through several other safety features, and he showed her how to build in redundancies. "In the climbing world, redundancies are a good thing. They provide extra security in case something fails."

"Ugh. The last thing I want to think about when I'm up there is something failing."

He smiled and repeated, "Redundancies. They're good."

He also showed her how to load her carabiner in the right way so that her slings and cordelettes were always on the strongest side of the metal clasp.

Lordy. To show her half this stuff, meant he had to get close to her. So close, she could smell the light aftershave he wore. Could feel him loading things onto her body. And she got a close-up view of those tiny stubbles that had tempted her fingertips. The man was sexy beyond belief.

And now she was going to climb the Dome. With him.

Well, at least an easier part of it.

"So we're going to head up to the first anchor bolt and I'm going to show you how to tie off and how to belay."

"You don't really expect me to stop you from falling, do you?"

"I do."

The matter-of-fact words made her shiver. "And you'll keep me from falling?"

"I will."

The solemness of his words made her wonder if they were talking about falling as in mountain climbing, or some other kind of falling.

And maybe they were. Because over the last couple of days, she could see how it might be possible to fall for this man. And she did not want to. Heavens, she so did not want to.

She'd just gotten out of a relationship that at one time she'd thought was wonderful. It turned out it wasn't. At all. She did not want to jump back into another one that would either end in the same way...or worse. She liked Cabe. She didn't want to ruin things by developing some kind of crush on the man. It was okay to find him attractive. And she did. Very much so. But what was not okay was to think of him in terms of a romantic partner.

Especially not when she was just establishing herself in this community. She'd seen how her community seminar program had grown once it became known that Cabe was participating. If they had some kind of falling-out, it could have the opposite effect. She needed to get established in Santa Medina on her own terms and because of her own skills rather than riding on someone else's coattails.

That wouldn't be fair to Cabe. And it wouldn't be good for her.

"Okay, ready? I'm going to go up to the first point, while you work the belay."

A quick thrill of fear went through her. "Are you sure, Cabe? What if I drop you?"

"You won't. And even if you get confused, it's a short climb, and I'll have a good grip. Okay. On belay?"

She checked everything and then repeated the response he'd taught her, signaling she was prepared. "Belay on."

As he headed up, she kept the slack at a minimum while he was actively climbing. And then when he stopped, he asked her to let him have more.

"Okay, I have the anchor and sling set up up here. Rope?"

"Okay."

He threw the length of rope down to her, while she fumbled around with it to get it where it needed to be. Oh, God, she couldn't believe she was about to do this, even though it looked pretty much like she could walk up it without needing the rope. But beneath the fear was a slight tingle of excitement. Very slight. But it was there nonetheless.

He gave her instructions each step of the way. And with each footfall that successfully landed on solid rock, that tingle of excitement grew, until she was within an arm's length of him. He held his hand out and the second hers connected with his, the warmth of his palm set off a series of tiny explosions as he pulled her the few remaining feet. She stood there staring at him, breath sawing in and out of her lungs until he finally turned away and showed her how to clip herself to the locking carabiner he'd set up. Then they were both tethered to the rock on hooks that looked like a tiny pop tab from a soda can. The fear came creeping back. "Are you sure that's going to hold both of us?"

"Positive. They're drilled deep into the rock. It can hold a couple thousand pounds each. Just lean back against your harness. It'll help you rest your muscles."

She gingerly did as he suggested and found that it actually didn't feel as scary now that she was up here as she'd expected it to. She glanced up at the clear blue of the sky above her. It seemed so much closer than it did from the ground, although she knew that was her imagination. But still. "Whew. My mom will never believe that I did this."

"Really? Why not?"

Jessie laughed, her gaze settling back on him. "Because neither of us like heights."

"We're not that high up. But the key when you're climbing is to keep looking up. Just take one anchor bolt at a time and always be looking for the next one."

"So what you're saying is never look down." Almost as soon as she said it, the urge was there to do exactly that.

As if he knew, he leaned closer. "Don't do it."

She pulled in a deep breath, seeing wisps of his dark hair as they blew across his forehead. She resisted the urge to brush them back.

He glanced at her. "So what do you want to do now? Ascend to the next bolt? Or head back down?"

She thought for several seconds, remembering how thrilling making it up this first section had been. "Is it exactly the same process?"

"Exactly. It's constant repetition. Until it all becomes muscle memory."

Constant repetition. Muscle memory. Was it really that easy? "Okay. One more."

In the end, they climbed to three anchor bolts before her leg muscles started screaming in protest. And she still hadn't looked down. That had to be something, didn't it? Part of conquering that fear?

She leaned against her harness to catch her breath. "This is hard work. Really hard work. But it feels good too." She could see where he got his muscles. Even now, the bulges in his biceps were obvious, and she'd bet his legs had the same corded muscle as his arms. She knew for a fact that his glutes were well defined. She'd seen the evidence firsthand. She smiled at the memory.

"What?"

"Nothing."

His head tilted, but he didn't try to press her for an answer. Instead, he said, "Okay, if you want to look out over the view, now is the time."

Her brain seized for a second at the thought. "You mean it's okay to look down?"

"Yep. Once you reach your goal, it's okay to look."

Taking a deep breath, she turned her head to look and a sense of wonder came over her. God, it was stunning. All of it. Including him. "I'm at a loss for words." She made herself pull phrases out of thin air. "It—it's staggeringly beautiful."

They were higher up than she thought they were going to be. And really, Cabe had done most of the work as the lead climber, but the exhilaration that came over her as she gazed across the scenery threatened to overwhelm her. "Now I get it, Cabe."

"Do you?" His blue eyes were focused on her face, and it caused the tingle from earlier to spread, sliding over in her midsection and beyond before pinging back and lodging in her heart.

"Yes. I do."

His fingers reached out and traced across her cheek. "I think you do."

Then his touch was gone, and he was no longer smiling. Instead a muscle worked in his cheek, and strange longing built in the pit of her stomach.

Not good.

Before she had time to dwell on it, he was reviewing the steps to get back down again. They would do what was called short roping, where they would be attached to each other with a short rope, and he would follow her down since the slope wasn't that steep. "I'm going to undo our anchors, and then we'll go."

Once he had everything stowed away on his harness, he told her to go in front and she walked down the way he had showed her earlier, praying she didn't trip over her own two feet. She didn't, and they made it back down to their starting point a lot more quickly than it had taken them to go up. Thank God. There was something cathartic about having conquered one of her fears. But she was also very glad she was back in control of her own movements. Something about having Caleb direct her steps had made her feel vulnerable in a way she hadn't felt in a long time. And she wasn't sure she liked it.

When they were on the ground, he detached the

rope. "And now you can say you've rock climbed the Stately Pleasure Dome."

"Well, at least a tiny part of it." She smiled. "Seriously, thank you so much, Cabe. I can honestly say that wasn't even on my bucket list of things to do, but it should have been. I actually think I might take classes. I'd like to try to do one of the easier climbs."

"I think you'll make it." He scribbled something down on a piece of paper he had in his vest. "Here. This is the name of someone I trust. He'll get you up there safely."

A tingle of disappointment went through her that he hadn't offered to teach her, but then again, he'd told her he was willing to show her the basics but had never promised anything more than that. Why not just be glad that he'd helped her see rock climbing through different eyes?

Yes. She would do exactly that. "Thank you again. Hopefully I'll never need SAR as I'm learning."

"I think you're going to do just fine."

"Hey!" A frantic voice called from above them. "We need help! Injured climber at the top of the Dome."

It was like the scream they'd heard the last time they visited the Dome. Only this time, no one was laughing.

CHAPTER SIX

THE MAN WAS climbing down the Dome.

"Go back up and wait. I'll be right there!"

Cabe turned to Jessie. "I need you to call Doug or Brad over at the SAR office and get them over here. They're both paramedics." He threw the number at her and waited until she'd punched it in.

He was going to need to self-belay to the top. As a beginner, there was no way that Jessie could follow him up. Besides, this was one of the more challenging climbs. He didn't have his medical gear with him, but Doug or Brad would be bringing that.

He did a quick check of his gear, making sure he was ready and then went into rescue mode, starting up the Dome.

"Good luck, Cabe!"

Unable to answer at the moment, all he could do was climb. And climb.

It seemed like forever until he reached the peak of the Dome, and his breathing was the deep gasps that came with heavy exertion. The man that had called down met him. "A little dog tried to follow us up the Dome and got in trouble. When my wife tried to help it, she fell. The rope caught her, but she's not answering when I call to her."

The man motioned to the side and sure enough a little white ball of fluff was crouched on the edge of the cliff, shivering. Damn. How on earth had it made it up this far?

Leaning against his harness, he called Jessie's cell phone. She answered on the first ring. "Are you okay?"

"Fine. There's a dog in trouble up here. If we can get him or her lowered down, can you take it?"

"Absolutely. Tell me where and when."

"I'm handing you off to another climber." He glanced at another man in the group. "Can you get him in your pack without getting injured? There's a vet on the ground."

"Yes. I'll meet her partway down."

"She's a novice."

"Got it."

Cabe handed over the phone and turned his attention back to the situation at hand. He peered over the side and saw a woman hanging from one of the outcroppings. The wind was stronger up here and kept blowing her back to the rock, periodically knocking her into it. She was unconscious. "Did she just lose her balance?"

It only made a difference in that it would let him know if there was equipment failure or she'd simply moved the wrong way and slipped.

"Her foot slipped on some loose rocks…" The man's voice caught, the anguish on his face evident. "We have a little girl at home. If something happens to her, I'll never forgive myself."

"We'll get her down." Just then his cell phone went

off and the other man handed it back to Cabe. "Mc-Bride here."

"Cabe, it's Doug. What have you got?"

He quickly relayed what he knew so far, before saying, "I'm going to head down. She's swinging from the southeast face. I don't have enough rope to lower her from there, but…" He turned to the woman's companion. "How much rope do you have?"

"I have enough."

"Good. Give it to me."

The man handed over a heavy coiled rope. Out of the corner of his eye, he saw the second man picking up the dog, who offered no resistance. He tucked the animal into his vest. Then he put his own phone to his ear giving some logistics. He must be talking to Jessie. Good.

"What's your wife's name?"

"Gloria. I'm Jerry, her husband. I—I didn't dare try to lower her myself."

Cabe was glad he hadn't. "You did the right thing. Wait here until I tell you it's safe to descend." The last thing he needed was someone to follow him down and get tangled up in his gear or go all emotional on him. This was where Cabe excelled. The lack of emotion in his marriage that had ultimately destroyed it, served him well in SAR. He could make decisions based on true objectivity rather than putting himself in someone else's shoes and imagining what they were going through.

"Doug, you still there?"

"Yep. I'm around on that side now. I see her."

"Good. I'm going to set up belay on the rope her

partner gave me, and you can use that to lower her once she's clipped in."

"Got it. I'll be ready. I saw Jessie. She said someone's bringing down a dog? From up there?"

"Yep."

He couldn't see Doug because of the outcropping, but that didn't matter. He would have to hope he could catch the bottom part of Gloria's rope and pull her in long enough to get the longer rope hooked to her harness. If he knew Doug, the squad was already en route.

Painstakingly making his way to the outcropping, he anchored himself in and then laid out flat along it to look at the conditions. She was about ten feet below him, still free-swinging, still no signs of consciousness. "Gloria? Can you hear me?"

His call got no response the first time. He tried again.

This time he heard a loud groan, but she didn't move. There was blood on her temple and on the shoulder of her climbing harness. He was right. She had some kind of head injury, which meant they needed to get her down as soon as possible. He looked up the way he'd come at her companion.

"Jerry, I'm going to finish making my way down to her. It looks like she hit her head. The plan is to lower her down with my partner on belay."

"Okay."

Cabe found a good bolt and anchored to it, then went over the side of the outcropping, feeling for toe and finger holds until he got to a more vertical section of rock, and thankfully found another bolt. The trick now would be to guide her close enough to clip her and hook her in above, while Doug guided her down, hopefully without her hitting the sheer wall any more than necessary.

The wind blew the loose end of her rope toward him, and he caught it on the first try. Rechecking his attachment point, he threaded her rope through one of the relays and using it as a pulley, guided her close enough for him to reach. Once he'd secured her to the master anchor, he checked her over as quickly as he dared. She was breathing and pupils were equal, thank God.

Satisfied she wouldn't swing back out again, he put Doug on speaker. "I've got her hooked into me. I'm going to throw you the excess rope."

"Go."

Taking a good swing that he hoped would clear all of the jutting rocks, he tossed the rope into space. He clipped his phone to his vest, leaving the line open.

"Got it, Cabe. Setting up belay."

Five minutes later, his partner's voice came back through. "Ready when you are. The squad is here."

"Good news."

With each of them working on opposite ends, Cabe fed his rope through his carabiner to slowly lower the injured woman, while Doug kept the line taut and stable and guided the path of the descent. For five nerve-racking minutes there was silence over the line, other than the grunts of exertion as Doug worked to keep the pressure exactly where it needed to be.

"She's down, I've got her!"

Cabe's rope went slack along with what seemed like every one of his muscles. He clung to the rock for several minutes, knowing he wouldn't be able to descend fast enough to help with her care. And he needed to rest, or his own descent wasn't going to be pretty. He called up. "Jerry, she's down. Do you have enough rope to get yourself down?"

"Yes. God! Thank you! We were so lucky you were here. I'm heading down. Lloyd just texted that he got the dog down to your wife, too."

Wife? Oh, hell, no. But then he hadn't recognized any of the trio, so there was no way they could have known that he and Jessie weren't related. But it still made his gut twist in a way that said the words had hit a nerve. And to try to explain it to Jerry? Not going to do it.

So all he said was, "Safe climbing."

With that he let himself lean his weight against his harness. Now that the crisis was over—at least his part of it—his adrenaline seeped away in a rush, along with any reserve energy he might have had left. But he couldn't hang here forever, and he needed to get back down in case the dog was in bad shape, and he needed to drive them back to the clinic. Or maybe she'd already gone. So he began the painstaking process of heading down the Dome on one of the more challenging tracts. But it was either that or climbing back over the summit and then going down the other side. In the spots he could, he bounced off the face of the Dome and could go quickly. Where it was too treacherous, he locked himself in and toed his way down. And then his feet hit solid ground and he stood there for a minute pulling down deep breaths.

Suddenly he felt a hand grip his, and when he looked, Jessie was there, her face pale. The white dog was tucked under her arm. Was it in worse shape than he thought?

"Is he all right?"

She opened her mouth several times to speak and finally she said. "Yes. *She's* fine. No injuries that I could find. But please, *please* tell me that's not what the demonstration is going to look like. I was paralyzed the whole time you were up there."

Hell, she *sounded* like a wife.

All of a sudden, Cabe laughed. Big bellowing laughs that were much larger than the situation warranted, but the relief of getting Gloria down hit him all at once, and he found himself turning and enveloping her in a big hug that went on and on and on.

From the region of his chest, her muffled voice came back to him. "They think she's got a mild concussion, but they're obviously taking her in to be sure there isn't anything more serious going on."

"And Jerry, her husband?"

"He made it down, and he's in the ambulance with her." She leaned back to look up at him. "He's very grateful. And so am I, for..." She nodded toward the tiny bundle tucked against her body. Suddenly her lower lip trembled, and a tear slid down her cheek.

He got it. He really did. He always imagined the rescues looked worse from the ground than they did from his perspective on the rock. Although this one was pretty hairy.

He caught the tear with his thumb. "Hey it's okay. We all made it. Including your tiny charge."

"I know but...*whew*!" She gave a shaky smile. "Maybe I'll hold off on those lessons."

He slung his arm around her shoulder, unsure if it was because he needed the stability or if he just needed to be close to another human being right now, and they headed back to the car.

"Come back to my place?" she said. "I'll get you some tea and something to eat. From the feel of her, Rocky needs some food too."

"Rocky?"

"It's what I'm naming her for now. At least until I can look for her owner. Hopefully someone will claim her."

"Rocky fits her, considering where she was found." He was grateful she hadn't offered him alcohol. Although he wasn't sure why he thought she would. "Anyway, I accept on both counts."

Jessie's knees were still knocking by the time they made it back to her place. What she'd witnessed had been both thrilling and terrifying. And it had shaken her to her core. Cabe and Gloria could have both plummeted to their death and the thought of that...

He'd looked done in too, and who could blame him. He'd done all the work. If they hadn't been there, how long would it have taken for help to get there? Sure, Doug had gotten there within about fifteen minutes, but Cabe was already almost at the top by the time he arrived.

She directed him to the sofa and urged him to sit down.

"I'm fine," he said.

Dumble evidently had to get his two cents' worth in, because he started in immediately. "Not the only one. Not the only one."

He'd been repeating that phrase almost nonstop for the last week, and she had no idea where it had come from. When he caught sight of the dog, he gave his whistle and said, "Good doggy."

When she turned to glance at Cabe he was making a face at the bird. "Sorry. I know he's annoying."

"No, he's fine."

"I'll be right back. I'm going to give Rocky something to eat and drink."

Once she set two bowls on the floor, the dog immediately drank. So far she seemed perfectly fine, settling in to eat the food.

Going back into the living room to ask Cabe what he wanted to eat, she glanced at him. "Oh! Your butterflies have come off."

It was almost a week, but evidently the sweat and exertion had decided to do the rest of the job.

Moving closer, she examined the dirt-streaked skin, surprised when he didn't try to brush her away. "It looks good. I think it'll do."

Warm fingers curled around the nape of her neck. "Thanks for sticking around."

"Where else would I be?"

"You could have left."

A sense of mirth went through her. "You took the car keys with you. I'd have had to hot-wire your car, something else I know nothing about."

His thumb took a slow, treacherous course, moving from just behind her ear all the way down her neck. "Is that the only reason why you stuck around?"

"No," she whispered, realizing it was true. Nothing could have dragged her from that dome while he was up there fighting for someone's life. It had moved her in a way she didn't understand. Didn't want to examine.

Before she had time to analyze her thoughts anymore, his lips came up and caught hers, pressing tiny kisses all along her bottom lip, before sucking it into his mouth. The sensation sent fiery signals along her nerve endings, obliterating everything in their path.

The shock of seeing that rescue unfold in living color and the reality that he could have been killed at any point during it still hung in the foggy areas of her mind. She'd been so scared. And then after the woman was lowered and whisked away, Cabe had hung out on those jagged rocks for several minutes not moving. She'd thought at first he'd been hurt too, distracting her as she looked Rocky over for injuries. The relief when he finally started moving down had held her transfixed at the base of the Dome. It held her transfixed even now, as his kisses started reawakening parts of her body that had been sleeping for a while. Until that first trip to the Dome.

And until now.

She thought she'd succeeded in putting those feelings to bed. Or maybe bed was what it was going to take to squash out those embers. If so, she was all in.

It was Sunday, and she was off for the rest of the day. That suddenly seemed like a huge luxury. And to spend it with this man...

She shifted on the couch, straddling his hips in a way that said she'd be satisfied with nothing less than full contact. The Full Monty. She wanted her hands on the butt she had glimpsed that first day at the clinic. In reality it had teased at her every time she'd seen him since then. Every time she'd spent time with him. Maybe it had been leading up to this the whole time.

And maybe this was what it would take for her to stop feeling that sense of yearning.

Vaguely she became aware of strange sounds coming from behind her, but since Cabe's lips had pushed aside the V-neck of her shirt and were now getting tantalizingly close to areas that were screaming for his attention, she tuned it out. Until he stopped.

God! He wasn't going to leave, was he?

She leaned back to look at him. "What is it?"

He nodded at something behind her. "It's him." She twisted around and heard the sound again. She realized it was Dumble. He was staring at them, his head twisting this way, then that, making the most obnoxious kissing sounds known to man.

She swallowed, then slowly turned back to Cabe. Jason had hated it when the bird taunted him. Had gotten truly angry about it at times.

But Cabe didn't look angry. He was smiling.

"I'm really not up for a threesome today." Then Rocky appeared at the base of the couch. "Make that a foursome. You wouldn't happen to have a bedroom in this place, would you?"

"As a matter of fact, it's right down that hallway. And it has a door that can be closed. Let me just barricade her in the kitchen." Jessie scooped the puppy up, a sense of euphoria taking over as she put Rocky in the kitchen while Cabe came over and tipped her small dinette table on its side and put it in front of the door.

Then he turned to her and put his arms under her butt, scooping her up so fast that she squealed, having to wrap her calves around his back to keep her balance. Well, she guessed she didn't have to ask if he'd changed his mind. He evidently hadn't. And neither had she.

"It's down the hall, first door on your right."

Every step he took was torture; the rhythmic press and release against the most sensitive part of her seemed geared toward driving her crazy.

And it was working.

Dumble and Rocky were left behind as Cabe slid into her bedroom and closed the door by leaning against it. Then he kissed her on the lips, seeming in no hurry to move from this spot. Fortunately, he had taken his climbing vest off before getting into the car, so he was left with just a long-sleeved T-shirt.

While he continued to kiss her, she bunched the shirt in her hands and tugged it upward, but her thighs were pinning it in place. She squirmed, but still couldn't pull it free.

His lips went still. "Need some help?"

"Yes."

He started walking toward her bed and then leaned over it and let go of her, bracing his arms on the mattress. The sudden lack of support made her fall onto the soft surface.

He chuckled, then went onto his elbows and kissed her nipple through her own T-shirt and bra. The sudden contact made her arch against him, eyes closing as she moaned.

And then he was gone.

Her eyes sprang back open and found him hauling his shirt up his taut stomach and pulling it over his head. It went onto the floor.

She sat up and started to do the same, only to have him stop her. "That's my job."

Warm hands slid her shirt up her torso, taking their time when he reached the curves of her breasts. And then her shirt too was gone. Whisked away and dropped on top of his. The juxtaposition of her clothes on top of his seemed to carry a weird intimacy. She pulled her glance away from it before she read more into it than she should.

Lean hips met her view, and her hands couldn't resist sliding around them until she found his jeans-covered butt. "You should have worn your other pants."

"My other…?"

She slid her fingers into his back pocket. "Hmmm… it would have made things so much easier."

He caught her meaning and laughed. "Those jeans didn't survive their ordeal."

Her calves slid around his and held him in place. "It's okay. I think we can figure something out."

Her fingertips skimmed around the bare skin of his waist, taking in the changes in topography formed by the different muscle groups. This man was certainly not soft. Her eyes settled on the area behind his zipper—definitely not soft.

She popped the button on his jeans free and then slowly slid the fastener down, hearing a hissed breath from above her when she purposely put more pressure than necessary on what was behind that zipper.

Pushing his jeans and briefs down his thighs, she reached behind him and squeezed his glutes, her eyes closing as she acted on the fantasy she'd had for the last week. God, they didn't disappoint. That soft layer of skin was stretched tight over muscles that were unbelievably hard. That rippled beneath her touch.

Just like what was right in front of her face. Hard and warm, and jerking with a need that she could definitely understand.

The hands on his ass reeled him in until she could just…

Slide over him.

The groaning sound from above her was all the affirmation she needed to know that he liked what she was doing. A lot. As did the gentle pull against her scalp that said he must have her ponytail bunched in his hand, the way she'd done with his shirt. The mental picture was almost too much, ramping her need up higher than it had ever been. But when she slid her tongue slowly along his length, that same grip on her hair was used to ease her free.

When she looked up, his eyes were clamped shut, a muscle working frantically in his jaw before slowing. Then he looked at her, and his gaze was molten silver, scorching over her before his hands settled on her shoulders. With a single push, she fell back onto the mattress, and he shed the rest of his clothes, pulling something from his wallet before he leaned down, settling his elbows on either side of her head.

"Not fair," he muttered against her mouth. "So not fair."

She smiled her response. Oh, it was plenty fair. And fun. And incredibly hot.

What he lacked in the area of communication, he made up for in things that didn't require a whole lot of talking. And she found she liked it. Liked using the reactions of his body as a guide for what he liked.

And so far, he'd liked pretty much all of it. A lot.

So had she.

He sheathed himself. But where she expected him to just hunch down over her and drive himself home, he didn't. Not that that would have been a bad thing. It wouldn't have. She was ready.

But evidently, he wasn't.

Reaching behind her, he unclasped her bra and

tugged it free of her body, tossing it behind her. Then she felt him move between her legs, before standing up completely.

"No!"

"Shh… I'm not leaving. Not a chance."

His hands covered her breasts, kneading them with a gentle motion that was unbelievably erotic before moving on to her hips and then lower.

That first touch was electric, and she arched up with a low moan as his thumb stroked over her, moving in time with the rhythm her hips set up. Soon it wasn't enough. She needed more. So much more.

Her arms reached for him, as the point of no return became visible…unavoidable. "Cabe…please." The words carried a quiet desperation that she hoped he caught.

He did.

He was there in a flash, muscles bunching in his arms as his hands lifted her hips off the mattress, so he could drive home in one stroke. Then she was full. So unbelievably full, as he moved inside her. It was an ecstasy she'd never experienced. With anyone.

There'd always been too much talking. Too many questions about what she liked, what she didn't. This was what she liked. Being able to concentrate on how he made her *feel*.

And it was…overpowering. Overwhelming. Just like seeing him on that mountain had been. This time she didn't need carabiners. Didn't need belay devices. She just needed him, ratcheting her higher and higher with each stroke of his body.

She was right. This was what she needed to do away

with that awful tension that had been building inside her ever since she met him.

Her legs pinned him against her even as he continued to move, continued to tighten the gears. As he held her up with one hand, his other returned to stroke her, making her hips jerk against him. As her need increased, so did her speed. It didn't matter what he was doing at this point, because she could only focus on that peak of the mountain that was so close. So so close. So...

Then she shot past it, sailing out into open air as her body spasmed around him. On some level she was aware of his shouted cry above her, of his hands gripping her hips, of his movements that came at lightning speed before slowing. Her own body slowed as well, as she floated down, eyes closing as she tried to hang on to those few last seconds of dreamy sensation before they were gone.

She drew in a deep breath, one arm curling around her head as she tried to regather her senses. Then he slid free, and she frowned.

"Sorry. My phone is buzzing."

Her ears picked up the sound coming from somewhere beside the bed.

Well, at least he wasn't lying to get out of there.

Although maybe he should have.

She sat up in a rush. What had just happened here? Yesterday, she'd been thinking of all the reasons she didn't want to get involved with anyone. Of how little she even knew about Cabe.

Of how hard it was going to be to trust again.

Of course you didn't need to trust someone to have sex. Right?

She might have agreed with that argument a few minutes ago, but right now she wasn't so sure. Because sex could lead to caring.

And she didn't want to care.

Not right now. Maybe not ever.

God...she was so confused. So... She felt like she was the one stuck on that mountain, dangling in space, trying to gather enough strength to get herself down in one piece.

And she couldn't do that if she let herself get emotionally involved all over again.

So while he pulled on his clothes, she pulled herself together and dragged the bedspread around her body, so that she felt at least a little less vulnerable.

Then she forced herself to look at him, even as he finished his call and shoved his feet into his shoes. "Hey, this can't change anything between us, okay? This was just good clean fun that—" she forced herself to use his words from the other day when she'd almost kissed him "—that was a whole lot of nothing."

"Of course."

The words came fast. Too fast. With a sense of relief that was unmistakable.

She should have felt a relief of her own, but instead there was just a quiet sense of unease as if her brave-sounding words were just that. Words. Words, that, like her proclamation, meant nothing.

She might be able to say that what they'd done had changed nothing, but she had a feeling it was all a lie.

That what they'd done had changed things in ways that she couldn't yet understand.

But she had a feeling it would become all too clear as time went on.

So all she could do was hold off the inevitable for as long as possible, and hope that whatever changes today had made could be undone.

Which meant, she couldn't sleep with him again. And while she wasn't going to say that to him directly, as he gave a quick goodbye salute and left her room, as he walked past Dumble who made more obnoxiously loud kissing sounds, she was going to make it very clear by *her* actions, that no further action was required on his part. Then she fell back onto the bed and tried to make herself believe it.

CHAPTER SEVEN

HE HADN'T HEARD from her in almost a week. And as he sat with the guys at the squad house and ate the chili someone had thrown together for lunch, he wondered why that surprised him. It shouldn't. But his part in her seminar series was coming up in two days. Maybe she'd decided to kick him off the schedule. Not that he could blame her.

The last thing he'd expected when he came down off that mountain was to feel what he had as he'd leaned his weight on her as they'd walked to the car. He'd felt a sense of companionship. A sense of belonging that was alien to him.

But that probably had more to do with the way Jessie made people feel than it did with actually belonging in her circle. She had a way about her that was warm and inviting and made those around her feel special.

He'd fallen for that spell. Until after they'd had sex, and *she'd* been the one to say the words that he should have said. But hadn't.

And he wasn't even sure why.

Letting himself believe in fairy tales would be a big mistake, even if she hadn't made it clear that the sex had been as meaningless as the handshakes she'd given to him at that first seminar.

But he wasn't sure it had been as meaningless to him. And that bothered him on an elemental level. He'd never had a hard time separating his personal life from his professional, but now he found that thoughts of Jessie were encroaching even in the very spaces he held sacred.

Doug's voice came across the table at him. "You sure you're okay? You've seemed on edge ever since you got called in on Sunday."

In the back of his head, he heard Jessie's bird making those lip-smacking sounds. If he wasn't careful, Dumble wouldn't be the only one making those noises at him. His squad buddies would too.

"I'm fine."

"Whatever you say, bro." Doug grinned at him in a way that said he wasn't buying whatever Cabe was shoveling. "Which reminds me. We probably need to practice for our demo in a couple of weeks. We need to get the timing down."

Since Cabe had had no idea if they were still in the lineup, all he could do was say, "Sure. Whenever you guys are ready."

They'd figured out that Brad and Doug would be helping with the demo. Cabe would be their lead climber, since they needed Soldier to alert to Brad, who would be hiding in one of the outcroppings of evergreens at one of the spots on the Dome. Brad would follow him up as the second person on the climbing team and work the brake. They wanted to be able to accomplish the mock rescue in a half hour, so the observers weren't standing around long enough to get restless or bored, which meant they needed to coordinate things almost down to the minute.

Brad spoke up. "Do you want to shoot for tomorrow?"

Perfect. So he needed to decide whether or not to call and talk to Jessie to make sure she hadn't changed her mind. Or he needed to just let things ride and hope for the best. Maybe he could show up on Saturday for the first part of his three sessions as if nothing had happened. She'd said it changed nothing, right? So maybe he should just take her at her word. They were both professionals. They could both handle working together these three times.

Then that would be that. He'd go back to his yearly vaccination schedules with Soldier, just like he'd planned back when she'd helped put his dog back together again. He fingered the spot on his cheek that she had patched. So far it had held.

Whatever had happened between them—whatever he'd had to patch back together again—would hold too. He'd make sure of it.

"Yes, let's shoot for tomorrow." Like Dumble, it seemed like all he could do was parrot his friend's words back to him. Well, he needed to shake himself out of his funk, before someone really took notice. And started to dig for the reasons behind it. He honestly didn't care if someone figured out he'd slept with someone. But Jessie might. And that mattered to him a whole lot more than it should.

So he would just keep on pushing forward and do his best to keep what had happened under wraps. Until it all blew over. Or until the butterfly bandages he'd slapped over those tricky emotional areas fell off of their own accord.

* * *

The calf wasn't budging.

The thing about being a vet in a rural town was that sometimes the calls were a whole lot different than they were in the city. Fortunately when she'd gone through vet school, she'd shot for a mixed practice degree—which encompassed both small and large animals—never expecting to use her large animal vet skills in San Francisco. But she'd hoped someday she'd be able to do both. So when Doc Humphrey's job request had come through, she'd been able to honestly say that she had expertise in both areas. And now, here she was. Under a cow. Trying to get her baby out of her.

If she could just reach one of its tiny front legs…

The owner was up by the heifer's head with a lead rope, to help keep everyone safe. When the call came through, Farmer Jonas said he'd woken up to the cow covered in sweat and straining. It was obvious she'd been working for a while. If Jessie could help it, she didn't want to hook a calf puller to it unless there was no other choice.

Which was why she was lying spread-eagled on the ground with her hand searching for those elusive legs. Without them moved into position, the baby's head wouldn't have enough room to be born.

Found one!

Just as quickly, the leg slipped from her grasp, and she had to start all over again. Feeling the head and following it down, down, down, until she felt…a leg! Using all her force she pulled it up next to the head and then reached for the second one. There!

The muscles in her arm were cramping from the effort and she could understand why Cabe had seemed so drained after rescuing that woman off the mountain.

Cabe. No thinking about him right now.

She'd pretty much chanted that to herself every time he came to mind. Sometimes her brain listened and sometimes it didn't. Like when she was asleep and couldn't fight against it any longer. Then the time in her bedroom played back through her dreams in stunning detail, causing her to wake up drenched in sweat.

Just like the heifer that she should be concentrating on. Forcing Cabe once again to move away, she hauled the baby's second leg up and lodged it beside the first.

Now she just had to hope the cow had enough left in her to push. Jasmine wasn't just a milk cow and a valuable asset to a family farm, she was also a pet, the farmer's kids finally convincing him that they should be allowed to name her. The rest was history. This baby was going to be her last, then when the baby was weaned, and her milk dried up, she would be retired to live out her days as a beloved family pet in a green pasture.

If Jessie could just get one more push out of the girl.

She slid her arm free. "Okay, Jasmine, come on, you can do it." She glanced up at the farmer, who'd sent his kids away once he realized the cow was in trouble. "I've gotten the front legs forward. Hold her while I give her a dose of oxytocin to stimulate her contractions."

Fortunately the hormone could be administered through the muscle, so she quickly pulled out the pre-prepared syringe and injected it. Jasmine was so tired, she didn't even flinch. Not a good sign

"Come on, girl. Show us what you've got."

Another minute went by. Then two. And then…

A push. A good one.

It was followed by another, and finally she saw those two tiny feet emerge, exactly as they should have when this whole process had started hours ago. She glanced at her watch. An hour had gone by since she'd arrived on-site. Hopefully for both mom and calf, she hadn't been too late.

There! The head. "Almost there, Jazzy."

"That's what my kids call her."

The farmer's voice pulled her from her trance. She smiled over at him. "She looks like a Jazzy."

The shoulders emerged as Jessie focused on the baby's open eye, which she could just see through the sac, willing it to…

Blink! It blinked! Yes! She'd hoped they'd be able to at least save the heifer, but the fact that the baby was still viable…

One more push and the tiny creature was delivered.

As if energized by the birth of her calf, Jasmine came up sternal, reaching around to start cleaning her baby.

As long as she could do the rest herself, and the baby wasn't in trouble, Jessie was okay letting her bond with the gal. "You've got yourself a new little heifer."

"Good. Now if I can just keep my kids from naming this one too." He removed the lead rope from the cow and let her stand to finish the job, while Jessie cleaned up and put away her gear. She needed to wait for the placenta to emerge and for the baby to get to her feet. But it looked like this might be one lucky mama and baby.

"I think it's safe to call the kids back out here."

"Thank God. I had no idea how I was going to explain it to them if one or both of them died."

He used his phone to call the house and within seconds, Jessie heard the shrieks of three little kids as they ran to their beloved cow's stall.

"Is she okay?" The oldest girl, who looked to be about twelve, was leaning over the rails looking anxiously at the pair.

"She's just fine. But let's give her some time with her baby before you go in there, okay?"

"Okay."

The two other kids were peering through the slats; the youngest one had a blanket clamped close to his chest.

Jessie's throat tightened. She'd always thought she would have children by now. But vet school had been long and exhausting, and Jason just hadn't seemed interested in having a family. She'd convinced herself she didn't need it either. But now...?

What would it be like to have your biggest worry be about whether or not your kids would name a farm animal?

She shook the longing away and finished her job. The placenta emerged perfect and whole, and the baby was now on her feet, nursing with loud slurps that made her smile. She was strong, seeming no worse for wear after the ordeal her mom had gone through in getting her into this world.

"I don't know how we can thank you. I really appreciate your coming right out."

"It was no problem." She'd had to reschedule three of her appointments, but her clients had understood. She imagined Doc had had to do this more than once.

Her legs had finally stopped shaking, and Jessie could now draw a deep stress-relieving breath.

She smiled at the kids, cooing and laughing over the new baby, although they'd probably seen lot of animal births on this farm. But this cow was different. And this birth was special.

Like making love to Cabe had been? Was that why she'd been so desperate to put him in his place afterward. Because it had been special, when she didn't want it to be?

Maybe.

Which was probably why she'd been avoiding calling him to confirm that he was still coming on Saturday.

Surely he would have contacted her and let her know if he'd planned on backing out.

But it wasn't professional on her part. It wasn't what she'd done when preparing for Lillian's arrival. Because Cabe was special?

Oh, God. He was not special. He couldn't be. She did not need this right now.

But no matter how uncomfortable seeing him was going to be, she was going to call him and do the right thing when she got back to the office. Confirm he was coming. And maybe soften what had felt like a harsh ending to their encounter on Sunday. He'd been called to what might have been an emergency, and all she could do was rattle out words about nothing changing and blah, blah, blah…

How would she have felt if the roles had been reversed and she'd been called to help Jasmine, while Cabe was busy throwing the same words at her?

She wouldn't have appreciated it.

So she would do what she could now that she'd had time to realize the difference between what she'd done and what she *should* have done at the time.

She would apologize. And hope to hell he accepted it.

Margo had told him she'd been called away on an emergency and that she might be a while. But she said it was okay for him to wait, if he wanted to. Since the waiting room was empty, he did. He really didn't want to just show up on Saturday and hope for the best, even though his brain argued it would be the easier path. Easy wasn't necessarily the best path.

Rocky found her way over to him and yapped at his feet. He scooped her up, smiling as she licked his chin. "Are you still here, girl?" He glanced up at Margo. "No luck finding her owner?"

"Not yet. I almost think Jessie's hoping there won't be one."

The door to the clinic opened with the breezy sound of canned wind chimes—a holdover from Doc—and Jessie swept through. He blinked at the ponytail that was half falling out, some of her blond strands curling around her face. Her black jeans were covered in some kind of grayish dirt and her light blue shirt… Well, he didn't even want to think about what that large dark spot was on her left breast.

She headed toward Margo, who held up her hand for her to stop.

"What is it? Another emergency?"

"I have no idea. Look behind you."

Jessie's head turned in his direction and her eyes widened, lips parting. "Cabe…"

He stood, his glance going to Margo's face and seeing blatant curiosity there. He set Rocky on the ground. "Can I bend your ear for a minute? Outside?"

"Oh...of course." She glanced down at her clothes, her hand going up to shove back a loose hank of hair that draped over her shoulder. Rocky pawed at her leg until she picked her up. "Can you give me about ten minutes?"

"Sure."

As she went by, Margo said, "Your next appointment isn't for a couple of hours. I wasn't sure how long you'd be over at Jonas Tate's place."

"Good call. Thanks."

She disappeared into the back, leaving him alone in the waiting room. With Margo. Who had to be dying of curiosity. Well, this was one thing he was not about to discuss with anyone except for Jessie.

So he picked up the nearest magazine, so he didn't have to carry on a conversation with her, and flipped through it, reading nothing. But the very act helped keep him from thinking about all the things Jessie could say to him.

Like, "thanks but no thanks."

He took surreptitious glances at his watch in between page turns. Seven minutes went by and the door to the inner office opened once again, and Jessie emerged. Her hair was neatly in place, although it was wet as if she'd showered. And she was dressed in fresh clothes. If he hadn't seen her a moment earlier, he wouldn't have believed the quick transformation was possible. And when she came and stood over him, he could have sworn the scent of fresh honeysuckle followed her path.

"Care to get some coffee? From the coffee shop down the road?"

That last sentence was a little louder than the first one had been, and it was probably for the benefit of the receptionist, although her gaze never strayed there.

"Sure. Where did Rocky go?"

"She's in my office in a playpen."

That made him smile as he got up and held the door open for her. They left the clinic, but when he started to head toward his car, she shook her head, a half smile on her face. "Do you mind if I drive this time? That way I won't be stranded if you get a sudden call."

A reference to the precursor of their lovemaking, when she'd waited at the bottom of the Dome for him to finish his rescue. But she'd said she would have waited even if she'd had her own car. That and her smile said her words had been a joke.

But right now, it was hard to separate things that were funny from things that weren't so funny.

He waited for her to unlock her side of the door and climbed in. Suddenly the scent of honeysuckle was no more, and it was replaced by the smell of...

"Oh, God. Sorry. Maybe we should take your car after all so mine can air out."

That made him laugh. "Your emergency call was to an organic fertilizer factory?"

"Kind of. A cow in labor. She and I got up close and personal for a little while."

Kind of like he and Jessie had. Well, without the lingering aroma, he would hope.

So they got out, while Jessie opened all the windows on her car and headed over to Cabe's. His vehicle didn't have the same smell at the moment, but he was sure there were days when he was sweaty and the aroma was pretty rank. And his mom had always called cow manure the smell of fresh country air. He'd never really minded it.

He drove the few minutes to the Café Parisienne, although he couldn't imagine anything less like his mental image of Paris than the simple coffee and sandwich shop. He parked, but before he could open the door to get out, she asked. "Do they have takeout?"

"They do. I'll go in and get them. What do you want?"

"A cappuccino, extra whipped cream."

That made him smile. From cow poop to extra whipped cream. The woman was certainly a patchwork of contrasts. He found that he liked it. She could get down and dirty with the best of them. But she could also enjoy the frillier things of life. His ex had always chafed at how "small town" Santa Medina was. And when they'd divorced she'd made a bigger change than that. She moved away. The funny thing was, while she'd pressed him to start a family, she'd never pressured him to move away from their hometown. And really, of the two, he would have been more likely to give in to the second request than the first.

He got their orders and returned to the car, handing her her paper cup. "Here you go."

Climbing back into his seat, he set his drink on the cupholder, watching as she removed her lid and blew across her beverage for a few seconds before snapping the cover back on.

"Can we go out by the meadows?" she asked.

"Tuolumne?"

"Yes, if it's okay?"

"Not a problem."

He drove the fifteen minutes to the park area and showed his pass to get in. He then found one of the parking areas where they could look out over the water of the lake.

"Well," she said. "I know you wanted to bend my ear. But I'd actually planned to call you when I got back to the clinic today. I wanted to apologize for not getting in touch with you about Saturday's seminar and to say I hope you're still willing to come and present." She paused. "I also want to say I'm sorry for the way I handled…er, things on Sunday. You got a phone call which, for all I knew, could have been an emergency, and I started blasting you with things that were of no importance."

"They were."

"What?"

He sighed. "They were of importance. You don't have to apologize. I actually came to apologize for much the same thing. Sunday was unexpected, and I can only chalk it up to the adrenaline generated by the rescue and…" he had to bite out the next words. "Emotional exhaustion. It felt good just to do something…normal."

Sunday had been anything but normal, but it was the only word he could think of to describe it without making things weirder than they already were between them.

"Normal." She laughed. "Okay, well that might have been 'normal' for you, but it was pretty extraordinary by my standards."

His brows went up, even as he fought to contain a

laugh of his own. "I was talking in generalities. But as far as specifics go? Yes…pretty extraordinary."

"Not that it can happen again," she was quick to add. "Right before I moved to Santa Medina, I broke up with a longtime boyfriend. Let's just say the end wasn't pretty. So…"

"You're not in the market."

"Not at all."

A frisson of relief mixed with something else went through him. "I can well understand. I went through a messy divorce, myself, some years ago, so be glad your relationship never got to that point."

"Believe me, I'm thankful for that every day. Especially since he was stealing meds from me."

He turned to look at her. "Seriously?"

"Yep. Worse, he was taking a portion of the narcotics that were meant for my dog who had cancer. We were living together at the time and treating her with pain meds and chemo drugs to extend her time, but…" She took a deep breath. "He offered to treat her while I was at work. And now I understand why."

"How did you find out?"

"Her meds ran out quicker than they should have right about the time he'd weaned himself off pain meds after a shoulder injury— he's a minor league pitcher. There's more, but suffice it to say, now more than ever, I don't like secrets." She shrugged. "So, like you said, I am definitely not in the market anymore."

"I understand, truly I do. I know firsthand what it's like living with an addict." It was on the tip of his tongue to say more, but something held him back.

"Margo mentioned that you were divorced. You and your ex-wife were high school sweethearts, right?"

She'd jumped to the conclusion that the addict he'd been talking about was Jackie. While he might not want to talk about his dad, he also didn't want to let her believe something that wasn't true. "Yes, we were, but Jackie wasn't the one with the problem. It was my dad. He was an alcoholic."

She sat there for a minute without saying anything. "I didn't know."

He was surprised Margo hadn't told her. They'd all gone to the same high school together. Jackie and Margo were good friends, in fact. Margo didn't speak to him for a while after the divorce was finalized. It appeared time healed all wounds, since they were on speaking terms again.

Thoughts of his dad skittered through his head. Well, maybe it didn't heal all wounds. Because the damage caused by his relationship with his dad had ultimately wrecked his ability to give Jackie what she'd needed. And if there was one thing about his marriage that he regretted the most, it was that.

"Jackie and I knew each other a long time, but once we got married she realized she didn't know as much about me as she thought she had." He cocked a shoulder in a half shrug. "So she left."

"I'm sure that was hard. I thought I knew Jason, but once we moved in together..." She winced, then smiled. "To top it all off, he couldn't stand Dumble."

Just like that, she popped the bubble of melancholy that had taken over the conversation. And he appreciated that more than she would ever know.

"Dumble? No! I can't even fathom how that would be possible."

"Are we talking about the same Dumble?" Jessie

laughed again, and he found that he really liked the sound of it. Lilting and musical, the sound kind of melted into him every time he heard it. Which always made him tense. He didn't want anything sliding past the layers of armor he wore. Which meant he had to stay on his guard, because if he wasn't careful…

Well, he could find what he'd always been looking for, while foisting on her what he wouldn't wish on his worst enemy: him with all of his worn baggage and problems. Jackie hadn't been able to deal with it, why did he think someone else could?

Jessie took a sip of her coffee and leaned back against the seat, staring through the windshield. "Who knew places like this existed in the world? It's so calm. So serene."

"It is right now. But wait a few months. Yosemite can rage with the best of them. The roads up here close once late fall arrives."

"I hope I at least get to see the snow up here before that happens."

"It's beautiful in winter. Once the roads close, people visit it using cross-country skis."

"I see I'm going to have plenty of classes to take. Mountain climbing…skiing…"

"You've never skied?"

Her nose crinkled. "I've water-skied, but nothing involving snow."

It was on the tip of his tongue to offer her pointers on that too, but he didn't think they'd be well received. Especially since they were still trying to find their way through the aftermath of Sunday.

"Well, if you get the chance. Do it. There's nothing quite like it."

She took another long drink of her coffee. "I will. Thanks. So we're good on the other issue? And you're okay with coming on Saturday?"

"Yes." He frowned for a second. "Didn't you say you wanted to see the demonstration before that happened?"

"Well, I think I got as close to a real rescue as I want to get. No preview needed. I trust you guys to do what you do best. I'll just print up a pamphlet telling people it's at the Stately Pleasure Dome, and I'm sure they'll find it."

Well, that was pretty much it. He couldn't think of anything else that needed hashing out, and if she was okay with where things stood then he was too.

Except for that little part of him that had just raised its hand and asked to be heard. Nope. Not happening. He ignored the request and gave Jessie a perfunctory smile, and they headed back to town.

CHAPTER EIGHT

CABE'S SECOND SEMINAR went as well as the first one had, and as Cabe stood at the front answering questions from the people who flocked around him, Jessie couldn't help watching him with admiration. Was there anything the man didn't do well?

He and Soldier had put on a first-class performance just like they had the previous week, and she'd learned things about Cabe that she hadn't known before.

Oh, she'd known he was in the army. But what she hadn't known was that he'd had a friend who had gotten lost in a deeply wooded area and hadn't been found until it was too late. That had sparked his desire to join a search and rescue team. And although she'd known that Solder was adopted from the shelter, she didn't know he'd been a natural and had taken to SAR training with gusto.

She'd also noticed that while he talked about his mom, he'd never mentioned his dad, which was understandable after what he'd shared with her. If she'd thought the ending with Jason had been bad, she couldn't even imagine living with an alcoholic for your whole childhood.

She waited until the crush of people became just one

or two before she headed up to the front of the room. Soldier greeted her with a wagging tail, his droopy features at odds with that single happy-looking feature. It made her smile and reminded her so much of his owner. Cabe had many of the traits that Soldier possessed.

Bending down to pet him, she murmured, "Good job, buddy."

An old man stepped up to him. "Hey, your dad would have been proud. A shame that it ended the way it did."

In a flash, Cabe's demeanor changed. Oh, the smile was still there as big as ever, but his eyes had hardened to flint. It made Jessie want to shrink back. She'd seen Cabe laughing. She'd seen him intense. She'd seen him upset. And over the last week and a half they'd seemed to come back to where they'd started. But in all of her dealings with him, she'd never seen him like this.

Exactly how bad had his childhood been?

"Yes, you're right, it was a damned shame." And that one stilted sentence ended the conversation, the man turning to leave, as the one person left smiled at Cabe and gave a quick congratulations before she too turned and headed for the door.

Jessie took her hand off Soldier's head and waited for the door to close one last time before looking at him. "Are you okay?"

"Yeah. No. Hell, no one's mentioned my dad in a very long time. At least not to my face."

"I know he was an alcoholic, but you think he wouldn't have been proud of you? In some way, shape or form?"

He fixed her with that same hard steely look. "Oh, I don't just think. I know. He wasn't proud of anyone.

Not even himself. He didn't just drink, he was a fall-ing-down-until-someone-put-him-to-bed drunk. He was literally the definition of someone committing suicide by bottle."

Her heart went still. And she could see why he'd been so short with the older man. "I am so sorry. I can't imagine what that must have been like for you." She drew him over to one of the chairs and sat down with him. The clinic was closed since it was a Saturday, so no one was around, not even Margo, who was on one of her infamous fishing trips. "And your mom?"

"She finally divorced him when I was fourteen, after years of begging and pleading with him to stop drink-ing. And after a couple of black eyes that she explained away as accidents. He died of cirrhosis at the age of forty-two."

"God. Did he hit you too?"

"No. Only my mom."

Jessie swallowed. You would never know from being around Cabe that he'd grown up in an abusive house-hold. But then again, lots of people kept dark secrets and covered them with a flashy smile. Just like Jason. Only it wasn't quite the same thing. In fact, when she'd first met Cabe she remembered thinking how much darker he was than Jason. She guessed she now knew the reason for that. Had that played into his divorce?

Not something she was going to ask him. So she said, "Is there anything I can do to help?"

He peered at her for a long moment. "I don't think so. After all this time, it is what it is. My relationship with my dad, or what little of it there was, is set in stone. There's nothing anyone can do to change it. Or him. It's too late."

"For him, maybe. But not for you. You've done well for yourself. Your dad might not have been proud of you, but you should be proud of yourself."

If anything, the tension in his face and jaw increased. "Easier said than done. As is not perpetuating any cycles that he set into motion."

Something about that made her shiver. Did he drink?

"And you're afraid you might perpetuate them how? Do you get falling-down-until-someone-puts-you-to-bed drunk?" She waited for a moment and then he shook his head. She gave an inward sigh of relief. "From what I can see you're a mature, caring individual who is in the business of rescuing people."

Something shot a bolt of lightning through her, making her sit up. "Was your friend the only reason you joined SAR?"

He gave her a hard smile. "I think you went into the wrong profession."

She was right, she sensed his dad was part of that equation. But he'd put her firmly in her place, and she knew better than to dig any deeper. But she couldn't blame him. It was really none of her business. But despite some of her earlier missteps with him, she cared about him. More than she probably should.

"I'm in exactly the right profession. Working with animals probably saves me a lot of grief."

"Oh, undoubtedly. Because, believe me, working with people is hard. Very hard." He smiled and stood up. "And now that you know the ugly, bitter truth about my childhood, can we promise we won't talk about this anymore?"

"Yes. I promise." She promised to not talk about a whole lot more than just his past. Or examine her current state of emotions, which were a jumbled mixture she wasn't sure how to sort through. Or if she even should. Part of that was probably wrapped up in how deeply he cared for Soldier.

Weren't people suckers for men with puppies?

Yep. She was starting to consider Cabe a friend—kind of, sort of—and she didn't want to do anything to mess that up. At least not any more than she already had. No more mining for information about him. She knew as much as she needed to know. As much as she wanted to know.

"Thanks," he said. "I appreciate that. And Doug, Brad and I ran through our mock rescue for next week and it went according to plan. It should take around thirty minutes at the most. Maybe less, depending on how tired I am that day."

The thought of how tired he'd been the time he'd rescued that woman came back to her. Did she, or anyone, really have a right to expect him to put on a show for the masses? "Cabe, if it's going to be too much, please don't think you have to go through with it."

"No, I want to. It's not just about the demonstration and letting people know about the SAR program. I think it's important for people to know how dangerous climbing can be. Maybe they'll take more precautions. Put in the redundancies that we talked about a couple of weeks ago."

Kind of like she'd done in trying to keep from falling into a pool of emotions where he was concerned?

Well, like he'd said, maybe she needed to realize how dangerous it was to let herself get hung up on someone without knowing if they were a good match. Look how that had worked out with Jason.

"Yes, you said redundancies are always good. I did remember that much."

He smiled and this time his face softened. "Yes, you did. As long as you keep remembering that you shouldn't get into any trouble."

Ha! That showed how much he knew about her. Well, right now she was swimming as fast as she could away from the whirlpool that was her heart and hoping beyond hope that she could make it safely to shore before she was sucked under completely.

Demonstration day—or D-day, as Brad referred to it—had arrived. Cabe was more nervous than he normally was. Not because they would have an audience, but because any training practice had the potential to go sideways. And after Soldier had been hurt a month ago, he wondered if he should be taking chances with his dog's life like this. But Soldier was well trained for this, and he had to keep up that training or there was even more potential for him to be injured. It was like a redundancy that he'd talked about with Jessie.

Doug, Cabe and Soldier stood at the bottom of the Dome with about twenty people milling around, waiting for them to get started. It was almost one thirty and he'd seen no sign of Jessie yet, which surprised him. He'd spoken to her on the phone this morning and everything seemed to be in line. Then he saw her hurrying toward them.

"Sorry," she said. "There was a problem with Jasmine's calf, and I had to go."

His head tilted. "Jasmine?"

"Never mind, I'll tell you about it later." She greeted Doug and Terry—who'd come out to watch. "Thanks for coming and helping with this. Is Brad already up there somewhere?"

"Yep, he's there," Doug responded.

She glanced at her watch. "Are we ready?"

"Whenever you are."

"Okay, let me just get everyone gathered."

Cabe watched as she motioned for those who were here to watch to come closer, and she introduced everyone. "You guys already know Cabe and Soldier from the last two weeks. But this is Doug Trapper, one of the team members on the Santa Medina Search and Rescue team. Bradley Sentenna is our mock victim…you can meet him afterward. And then…" She glanced at her notes. "Terry Jordan…can you raise your hand so people can see you? There he is. He's the head of the search and rescue team here."

She looked around. "So I'm not going to give a lot of explanations, I just want you to see this fantastic team in action. If you have questions afterward about how to get involved, I'm sure any one of them can send you in the right direction." She smiled. "Okay, Cabe, handing it over to you."

Cabe nodded to her and then caught Doug's eye, silently asking if he was ready.

"Yep. Go."

Pulling the piece of Brad's shirt out of a notebook, he called Soldier closer and let him sniff it. The dog lifted his head, probably recognizing Brad's scent right away. And then he was off, scrambling up the hill, giving a braying bark every time he found where Brad had set his feet. They hadn't wanted to make it too easy, so Brad had jumped from one rock to another, trying to throw Soldier off the scent. When his dog got to that

exact spot, he swept along a path that any grid maker
would be proud of and then picked up the scent again.
He took off with sure feet, heading up the Dome. Ten
minutes later, the dog stood stock-still and barked and
barked. Brad stood up from his hiding place and waved
a piece of ripped cloth.

"Help! I need help!"

His voice carried down with enough realism that a
few people whispered among themselves.

Cabe and Doug got to work, donning their climbing harnesses and equipment as Brad sank back into
the bushes. Soldier might have been able to make it up
that slope, but they'd chosen one that would require
him and Doug to using climbing gear.

They went through the whole process of checking
each other's gear, even though they'd both done thousands of training climbs. It didn't matter how many you
did. All it took was one mistake. One slipup to spell
disaster for everyone involved. It was about keeping
everyone safe.

"Belay?" he called over to Doug.

"Belay on."

"Climbing."

"Climb on."

Cabe started up the face of the rock and went until
he found the first anchor bolt. He quickly hooked into
it and then waited for Doug to follow him up. The procedure repeated until they reached Brad. They brought
him out of the trees so people could see them pretending to check him over and treat him. And once done,
they slowly helped their injured and lost climber head
back down the Dome.

Once down, he glanced at his watch. Twenty-eight

minutes. Not bad. Rewarding Soldier with a treat, Brad wiped the fake blood from his head to much applause.

Then, armed with the pamphlets Terry had printed up, they talked with people for the next half hour or so. There was a lot of general excitement about the program and those who couldn't or weren't able to go through a stringent training program still wanted to help. There were other options available, whether working in dispatch or even just raising awareness of the program.

He glanced up, his eyes seeking out Jessie before he realized what he was doing and then turned his attention back to the next person in line. He hadn't seen her, but surely she wouldn't have left until it was over.

Except she had. There was no real reason for her to stick around.

Maybe that calf she'd mentioned had taken another turn for the worse.

She'd talked about doing something for those involved in the mock rescue afterward as her way of saying thanks. She hadn't said what it was, though, just that it would take about an hour. They'd all said they could be there for whatever it was. Maybe it was some kind of reception at the clinic.

Then the people were gone, and Jessie reappeared as if by magic. Her smile was brilliant, and when she looked at him, there was this gleam…

There wasn't a gleam. It was his imagination.

"Hey, guys, can you follow me?"

He tilted his head. "Are we walking? Driving?"

"Walking."

Okay, that was weird. Where were they walking to?

There were no restaurants up here, other than a local store that carried necessities for hikers or campers.

He looked at the other three members of the SAR team and Brad just shrugged. But they followed Jessie as she walked down the road, around the turn and then around another, sharper turn, and then Cabe saw them.

People. A whole slew of people. There had to be a hundred of them, at least. Music started as the Santa Medina marching band began playing, and as they got closer, four members of what he thought was the color guard, moved to the front of the gathering with some kind of rolled-up paper. And when they paired off, moving away from each other in a synchronized movement, the scroll unfurled. Across the enormous dark blue field appeared the words *We're so Proud of You!* in bold white letters.

Cabe stopped walking, and when his eyes somehow met Jessie's he knew…*knew* that that message was for him. Was because of what she'd overheard in her clinic last week.

She came over and shook each of their hands and gave Soldier a treat.

He looked at her. "How did you…?"

"Actually, Margo did. I asked her to get the word out that we wanted to do something special for you… for the team and she hit it out of the ballpark. Everyone in town who was free today came out."

From out of the crowd stepped Doug's wife. Then Terry's grown children. Brad's sister and parents followed them. And he spotted Doc Humphrey, who gave him a gruff nod, out in the crowd as well. And suddenly, there was… Cabe's mom. They all came over and hugged their loved ones. As his mom wrapped her arms around his waist, bitter tears crawled up his throat looking for an exit. He held them in, hugging her tightly, and looked over her shoulder, realizing Jessie had slipped back into the crowd.

He didn't see Margo yet, but he'd bet she was out there somewhere.

But what he didn't understand was how one of the most talkative people in Santa Medina had managed to keep this a secret? Actually she hadn't. Maybe it hadn't been meant to be a secret from anyone but the team itself.

But it was one of the most special things anyone had ever done for their team. For him, personally.

And although Margo had been the mouthpiece, Jessie had initiated and orchestrated the gathering. Jessie…a kind and caring soul who would go to tend a sickly calf, just because someone called her and asked her to. One who adopted a lost and frightened dog that had been trapped on the dome. One who'd treated Soldier's wounds with gentle hands. The same hands that had patched Cabe back up.

Letting go of his mom and guiding her to stand beside him, he looked at her and said words he should have said many, many years ago. Words that out of his anger and bitterness he'd not been able to bring himself to say. "Thank you, Mom. For everything."

Her hand went to her mouth and tears shimmered in her eyes before she turned and buried her face in his chest, her shoulders trembling. When he glanced at the other members of Santa Medina's SAR, he saw similar scenes of tears and smiles and…gratefulness.

Terry had lost his wife six months ago, so this gathering had to be bittersweet for him, but he stood there in the embrace of his kids and looked like the luckiest guy on the face of the planet.

Cabe was beginning to realize just how lucky this town was to have the new veterinarian. Everyone had loved Doc and had sworn there'd never be another one like him, but he knew for a fact that there was. And it was Jessie.

He managed to catch sight of her once again and mouthed, "Thank you." He was pretty sure he was speaking for the whole town. And Jessie gave him a nod that said it all. She was happy to do it.

He leaned down to listen to something his mom said to him and when he looked up again, Jessie was nowhere to be seen.

She was probably in the crowd somewhere talking with people, because she was good at that. Such a great advocate for both animals and for the community as a whole.

Someone came over and handed him a bag. "This is for Soldier. They're made specially for dogs by a shop in Mariposa. When Jessie told us about this two weeks ago, we found a store that makes them from scratch. I hope he likes them."

"Thank you." He took a small steak-shaped treat from the bag and handed it to Soldier, who gobbled it up. He laughed. "I think he approves."

By the time things ran their course and he'd stopped by the refreshment table with his mom, the floral tablecloth blowing in the breeze, it was starting to thin out. Margo was manning the refreshments. He gave her a grin. "You're a sneaky one, Margo."

"What can I say? You guys deserve it. But it was really Jessie's idea."

"Well, thank you." He'd said the words so many times, he wondered if they'd be etched on his tombstone. He glanced around again for Jessie but didn't see her. "Speaking of Jessie, is she still here?"

"No, she left about a half hour ago. Not sure why. Maybe she had a patient."

"Yes, maybe she did."

But for some reason, he didn't think so.

He waited around and saw his mother off, promising to set up a time for lunch with her soon. It had been ages since he had, and it was long overdue. Jessie's reception had helped him see to that.

He thought she'd probably helped him with a whole lot of things without either of them realizing it.

Well, she was probably exhausted, so first thing tomorrow, he would run over to the clinic and give her a proper thank-you for everything she'd done for the community. For him.

If anyone had deserved this party, it was her. With her new ideas and new enthusiasm, she could very well breathe some new life into a town that had sat steeped in tradition for far too long.

Her reach had even extended into the station house, where Terry had agreed to take on Carrie, the shelter dog. Already she was ensconced on a leopard-print pillow fit for a queen. And he was pretty sure the rows of kibble that lined their pantry shelves was proof that she was already well loved by the men who spent so much time at the station.

Yep, Jessie had reached into hearts throughout Santa Medina. She wasn't Doc. But maybe she was exactly what this town needed—what *he* needed—at this moment in time.

CHAPTER NINE

JESSIE HADN'T BEEN able to stay yesterday. The scene between Cabe and his mom had been too raw. Too painful. Especially knowing what she did about his father. The weight of it had been etched on Cabe's face, and she'd wondered if she'd made a terrible mistake in opening the reception up to the general public. She hadn't really thought about his mom when she'd asked Margo to organize things. Hadn't even realized she still lived in town. But she was glad so many members of the community had shown up in support.

Then she saw Cabe say something to his mom. Watched as the woman turned and sobbed into the paramedic's chest. Watched as he looked up over his mother's shoulder and mouthed "thank you" at her. She'd turned away in tears.

The gathering hadn't been the wrong thing.

But something else might very well be. Because what she'd thought—hoped—might be a temporary clog of emotions concreted itself into something that could not be brushed away or hidden. And as she stood there, she was suddenly terrified that he was going to read the truth on her face. And there was no changing it. No denying it. She loved the man.

Despite the terrible truths she'd learned from her last relationship. Despite learning a deep painful truth about Cabe. Or maybe that was part of it. She'd done exactly what she was afraid of doing and had fallen head over heels for him. And it horrified her. She had no idea what to do about it, except to bury it deep and hide it. From him. From Margo. From the world.

As she sat in her empty clinic on Sunday morning, she tried to figure out what to do about it.

Maybe he felt the same way. But she didn't think so. It wasn't like she could just walk up to him and ask him. Because if he didn't…

She would be devastated. Would want to run. Because her fight-or-flight instinct had always been firmly rooted in flight. After all, she'd fled San Francisco right after learning about Jason's addiction, and although it had been the right thing to do, she'd still taken the easy route and left town.

And found Santa Medina. A place she was coming to love deeply. Almost as much as she loved Cabe. Did she really want to walk away from everything she was building here—her career, her new practice, her new friends—if it turned out that Cabe didn't care about her in that way?

Maybe now was the time to learn a new way of dealing with conflict. The question was, could she do it?

Sleep had been a long time coming last night, although she'd texted Margo this morning to thank her for everything, including cleaning up afterwards.

Her phone made a pinging sound. She glanced down at it.

You're welcome, Jess. Oh, and by the way, Cabe was looking for you after you left. I told him you probs had a patient who needed you.

She had. Only the patient had been her. She'd needed to take some time for herself to think about what she was going to do, now that she'd found herself in a situation that could become very awkward for everyone. She wrote Margo back, avoiding the elephant in the room.

Thanks for covering for me.

Her phone pinged again.

No probs.

Margo cracked her up with her abbreviations, but it was on par with her rather eccentric nature.

Just as she put her phone away and started to vacate the chair Margo normally sat in, the chimes went off over her front door. Looking up, she saw it was… Cabe.

She was horrified.

Not only by what she'd been thinking about, but her gardening clothes and her messy hair. She honestly hadn't expected anyone to stop by.

"I thought I might find you here. Or Dumble did. He was yelling 'Get back here' over and over when I rang the bell."

"Oh, God." Despite the feelings of melancholy that had overwhelmed her for the past twelve hours she could still find humor in her bird. "He hates it when I leave. I guess if I ever have a break-in though, it might come in handy."

"It might." He took a couple of steps closer. "I wanted to come by and say thank you for yesterday."

She just stopped herself from parroting Margo's response, complete with the abbreviation for *no problem*. "That wasn't just me, it was everyone. We're all grateful for the work you do."

"And I'm grateful for what you do. This town is incredibly fortunate to have you."

"The town." Her heart sank lower.

"Yes. Several people have mentioned it, even Doc Humphrey. Did you know he was there?"

"I did. He was the one person I specifically invited. He wants to meet with me tomorrow afternoon to see how things have been going." She pulled in a deep breath. "Santa Medina is a special place."

"Yes, it is."

"Being here has been...well, I'm the one who feels fortunate."

He took a few more steps. "Do you?"

Looking into his eyes and trying to see anything there that might give her hope, she nodded. "I do."

His fingers touched hers and a bolt of emotion spiraled through her. She was so confused. So very mixed up about her place here in the town. Her place with him.

But one thing she did know. If this was going to end badly, she was going to make sure it ended spectacularly. On her terms. She was going to make sure he knew exactly how she felt about him. And then it was up to him. But maybe there was more than one way to show someone what they meant to you.

Her fingers curled around his. "Like I said... I feel very, very fortunate." She drew the words out slowly, infusing them with as much seduction as she knew how.

He looked as confused as she felt...for about half a second. Then, using her grip on his hand, he tugged her toward him, so fast that it knocked the wind out of her for a second.

"Jessie, do you have any idea what you..."

The rest of his words were lost as his lips came down on hers. God! Was that an admission? A prayer? An oath?

Right now, she didn't care, because hope—which had been looking for the tiniest of crumbs to devour—evidently found the fuel it needed and went drag racing through her veins, tires spinning, gravel flying.

And then there was no stopping this. And she didn't want to, even if she could.

She kissed him as if there were no tomorrow. Because for them, there might not be.

"Your place?" He lifted his head to look at her.

"No. Here."

His brows went up. "Are you expecting anyone to walk through that door?"

"No. No one's coming."

He smiled. "In that case..." Taking her with him to the door, he engaged the dead bolt and pulled the front blinds.

Then putting his hands on her hips, he walked her back toward him, sending her pulse soaring. Her hips hit his and what he wanted was very, very evident. That was good. Because she wanted it too.

Suddenly they were in the private exam room, and they couldn't get each other's clothes off fast enough. He leaned in and bit her lip. "Remember that mechanism that you promised could hold me?"

Breathless with need, all she could do was nod.

With a quick movement, the hands on her hips lifted her onto the exam table. He planted his palms on the table on either side of her thighs and leaned in to kiss her. "Which way is down."

It took her a second before she realized what he meant. Then, her breath in her throat, she murmured, "Left pedal."

He must have found it, because the table began its slow descent. Then it stopped. "That looks just about right."

"Right for—Oh!"

He hauled her to the very edge of the table, her legs spreading to accommodate his hips, and then it was all too clear what he was thinking. Because nestled between the V of her thighs was a very eager looking body part.

And then Cabe kissed her in earnest, and she took him. Took everything he had to give and hoped she could give back even more. She wanted to lay out all of her hopes and dreams on this table and prayed those offerings were enough for him. Enough to build a future on…together.

"Where is it?"

"Excuse me?" He leaned back to look at her with horrified eyes.

"No, not that. *That*, I can find. With both hands tied behind my back. Want to try?"

"Don't." Groaning, he pressed his forehead to hers. "You drive me crazy...do you know that?"

She hoped so. Hoped she drove him crazy enough to think this thing between them might just work. Might be something real. Something to cherish.

Smiling up at him, she said, "In that case, the thing I'm looking for starts with a *c* and ends with an *m*."

"Oh...*that* that."

"Yes, *that* that."

He opened his palm, like some kind of awesome magician, and there appeared a square wrapper, its cellophane top already ripped open.

"How did you... Never mind."

She took it from him, and this time, she did the sheathing, drawing the act out for as long as she could stand, her fingers trailing over each inch of naked skin as she rolled it down him.

He felt alive in her palm, reacting to each touch, each squeeze, each change in pressure.

"Enough, Jess. God. Enough." He trembled against her, pushing her hand away. "I need time to get you ready, to—"

"No. I've been ready ever since you got here." With that, she leaned back, supporting herself on the narrow table with her elbows. "Come see."

With that, he took himself in hand and found her. Slid home with a loud groan that echoed through the tiled room.

Her eyes shut as she relished each tug and thrust that brought her nerve endings to spectacular life. That made butterflies take flight behind her closed lids. Fluttering wings that surged higher with each new movement. Taking him deeper. Harder.

The wings coalesced until she could no longer tell one from the other, a beautiful kaleidoscope of color that pulled together, getting tighter and tighter until…

They exploded apart, taking her with them as surge after surge of pleasure poured over her…through her. Cabe wrapped his arms around her hips and drove hard and fast, groaning again as he found his own release.

They stayed there for several minutes, the sound of their breathing loud in the room.

Her eyelids slowly parted to find him staring at her with a weird expression. No one said anything for a second or two, then he broke the silence. "Hell. That was…that was…"

"I—I think I love you." The words stumbled out before she could stop them. They hung there like orphans hoping to find a place where they were wanted.

Oh, God, that was not how this was supposed to go. She'd wanted to ease into it. Feel him out a little more before taking that polar plunge. But now that she was all the way in, she could feel her skin turning frigid, her muscles cramping with fear.

"What?"

The single word hit her with staccato force, paralyzing her. But not him evidently, because he slid away from her with a fluid motion that made her want to weep. How easy it was for him to just pull…free.

What hope had dined on was evidently not enough to keep it going, because its engine sputtered and then died. And all that was left was Cabe, staring at her with this inscrutable expression.

She sat up in a rush. Well, she'd done it. Exactly

what she'd said she was going to do. She gave a choked laugh. And she ended it just like she'd said she was going to. Spectacularly. With no ambiguity. No lingering questions.

"I think you should leave, Cabe."

He dragged a hand through his hair. "I can't... Hell, Jess, I can't give you what you need. What you deserve. Let me explain why—"

"No. No explanations needed. You've made it very plain. And it's made my decision easier." She pulled in a deep breath. The fact that he'd shortened her name and made an endearment out of it—all the while dropping a guillotine—just made everything that had happened here that much worse.

"Please. Leave."

See? She could throw staccato phrases right back at him.

Without another word, he gathered his clothes, but he didn't put them on in front of her. Instead, he turned and walked out of the room. Her last sight before he shut the door behind him, was his spectacular ass. The ass that was walking away from her for the very last time.

"Doc Humphrey is back..."

"She's only been here two months, but..."

"Think it might be a man? Of all things..."

"She saved our calf."

He'd come to the diner to get a quick cup of coffee, four days after leaving Jessie's clinic, and was surrounded by snatches of conversation. He'd only been half listening until that last phrase came through loud and clear: "She saved our calf."

It could only mean they were talking about Jessie. He put all of the phrases together and came up with…

Jessie was leaving town?

Why?

Dammit, did he have to ask? It was pretty obvious. It was because of how they'd left things. No. Not "they." It was because of how *he'd* left things. He'd all but fallen headfirst over his tongue in his effort to find the right words after she dropped that bombshell about love. To let her down easy.

Because, in the end, it didn't matter how he *felt*. Feelings were transient fickle things. He'd seen that firsthand. And if Cabe's life experiences had taught him anything, it was that he did not have what it took. To be a good husband. To be a good father. It didn't matter how he felt. Unless he could *do*, the feelings meant nothing.

So he'd had two choices, when Jess had told him she loved him. He could either hurt her now. Or he could hurt her later. Because there was no getting around it. He *would* hurt her.

By not knowing how to talk through his feelings.

By holding back emotionally because he was afraid of being rejected.

By pretending he *had* no emotions during the times when they were the most important thing. Just like he'd done when Jessie had told him she loved him. Just like he'd done with Jackie during their marriage.

All his father had *done* was display his emotions. Every damn emotion he'd ever had. And most of those had been bad. Had been hurtful. Every time Cabe had a negative emotional reaction to something, a little voice inside his head had whispered, "See? Just like the Daddy-o."

He could go through the laundry list of reasons he'd racked up about being wary of emotional attachments. Every year that list got a little bit longer until he was convinced he didn't need anything but Soldier and his work.

And then along came a sexy veterinarian that had him doubting himself all over again. She made him want to try. Made him want to fight.

But was his motive to add to her life? Or suck the life away from her?

And that's why he'd stood there with nothing to say. Because in truth, what could he say in the flaming aftermath of sex? Fantastic sex that had obliterated his expectations for all time. Nothing. Because he had no idea if that quavery little voice in his head was the sex talking. Or if they were from those elusive emotions that had become tangled around her from day one.

But if she's leaving.

Wasn't that her choice?

If so, she was going to make this awfully easy on him. And impossibly hard.

Maybe the best thing he could do for himself, for both of them…was to sit at home in the dark and do some heavy lifting in the emotional department and see if he could move some furniture around. Maybe, he'd find where he'd hidden his damned feelings.

Maybe then, they'd finally tell him what he needed to know: Go after her? Or just let her go?

CHAPTER TEN

DOC HUMPHREY STOOD there glaring at her. "What did you do to my damn files?"

"I digitized them. It makes it easier."

His gaze softened for a second. "I suppose I should be thanking you, rather than grumbling."

"I'm glad to have you back, Doc. Even if it's only for a day or two a week. Are you sure you don't want more?"

"No. Retirement isn't for me. Not right yet. But neither is taking over the clinic again. My tremors are better, thanks to some newfangled meds. But it's just a matter of time. And I might like puttering in that garden you set up out front."

She shook her head with a smile. "We agreed the house was yours. But the garden is mine."

Jessie was doing her best to hold true to staying the course. With some help from friends, she'd moved Dumble, Rocky and her few possessions into the small apartment over the garage and let Doc move back into the house he'd lived in most of his adult life.

So far it was working out well. At least the apartment was.

She wasn't as sure about the whole "not running"

thing. What she did know was she couldn't do her thinking in that house, where every day brought a reminder of what they'd done in that bed. It was going to be hard enough facing the memories from the clinic. Of witnessing those impossibly blue eyes shuttering themselves against her.

Maybe she'd decide that moving back to San Francisco was the right thing to do. But right now, when her wounds were too raw, too impossibly painful, she didn't trust herself to make any major changes.

The man surveyed her, then dropped into the chair next to hers, his voice suddenly soft. "How's it been going? Really? I've been around a long, long time. I saw those glances you and Cabe gave to each other at the gathering."

"Gathering?"

"What the town did for the SAR team."

"Oh." What else could she say? She could lie. But somehow it didn't seem right. And Doc was eventually going to realize she was avoiding Cabe. She'd already decided to ask him to take over Soldier's care and any exams. Although he'd already told her he'd feel better not having to do any surgeries.

"Things have changed, though, haven't they?" His hand covered hers. "Surely he wasn't that hard on you, girl." The gruffness in his voice belied the deep concern she heard just below the surface. It would have been worse if he'd come at her with accusations and disappointment.

"No. He wasn't. Everyone in the town has been wonderful." So many conversations came back to her. Delivering that calf for Farmer Jonas and his fear of his kids naming the baby. Patching up Soldier and watching the townsfolk rally around the SAR team. Hearing Cabe's heartbreaking confession about his father. Was that what some of this was about? His dad?

It didn't matter. If he was so damaged that he didn't have the capacity to love her, then she wasn't going to settle for anything less. No matter how much she enjoyed his company. No matter how much his love-making meant to her. Some people might not need the words, but she did. She'd had them her whole life from her parents...from her extended family.

And she deserved them. Just as much as Cabe deserved hearing them from whomever he was involved with.

"I love this town, Doc. It's just that..." How easy it was to think of him that way. Because of the impact the town had made on her.

"Do you love something besides this town?" He gave a sigh and patted her hand. "You won't find a man better than Cabe."

"I know. He...he just said he can't give me what I need." She avoided mentioning her ill-timed confession of love.

He puffed out his cheeks. "What is it you need, Jessica Ann Swinton?"

She stared at him for several seconds. "Jessie isn't actually short for Jessica, and Ann isn't my—"

"I know all that, but it's what I would have named you if you'd been my daughter."

She laughed to keep him from seeing how touched she was by his words, by the meaning behind them. But really, did the man actually know how impossible he was?

His wily eyes said he did, and he just didn't care.

Why couldn't she be more like him? With less care and a more "live and let live but do it my way" attitude.

She could see why people loved this man. He snuck up on them while they weren't paying attention and... *boom*! You loved him.

Wasn't that exactly what had happened with Cabe. He'd snuck up on her while she wasn't looking...and she fell in love.

"So you haven't answered my question. What is it you want?"

Looking into Doc's rheumy eyes and grizzled face, she said, "I want Cabe. But I want all of him. Not just the part he's willing to let me have."

So what was she going to do about it? The old Jessie would have run and not looked back. But the Jessie she *wanted* to be was telling her to stay...but to really examine her reasons for doing so and consider the ramifications, if it turned out that Cabe really didn't want love. And then, only then, could she be at peace with her decision.

And maybe she'd give Cabe some space to think without the pressure of her constant presence. Maybe he couldn't care less if she stayed or went. But the thought that he might, made her feel better.

She curled her fingers around Doc's and squeezed. "Would you mind if I took a few days off? If there's an emergency, I'll be right upstairs. I just need some time to think."

"Go ahead and think, girl. But give yourself permission to go after what you want. Even if what you want turns out to be not quite right for you in the long run. Like my trial run with retirement."

"Thanks, Doc."

They both stood up, and she was shocked when the man caught her in a bear hug that she thought might squeeze the life out of her. Then he released her and headed over to where his rusted file drawers used to be. "So where the hell did you put the actual files, anyway?"

On that note, she went through the door and closed it behind her. She wished she could catch the town in the same bear hug that Doc had just given her. But she couldn't. But she was going to try to love them every bit as hard as Doc had. Every bit as hard as she loved Cabe.

Then she headed up the stairs to her little apartment, which held most of her earthly possessions, including Dumble and Rocky, the pup they'd rescued from the Dome. The bird gave her a sideways look the second she opened the door. "Not the only one."

"Not the only one, what, Dumble? I have no idea what that even means."

The bird looked at her. "Not the only one." He gave a loud squawk as soon as the words were out.

Jessie laughed at his response until she could laugh no more. Until her laughter turned to silent tears that crept down her cheeks and seeped into the lonely areas of her heart.

Cabe avoided the diner for the next two days. The last thing he wanted or needed right now was to hear the latest gossip about Jessie. Because he was pretty sure he'd heard all he needed to hear. That she was thinking of leaving because of some man.

It was pretty obvious who that man was. So what did he do? Confront her and tell her not to be stupid.

That this town needed her and that she shouldn't take off because of one foolish idiot who'd failed to keep it in his pants.

The crass phrase made him cringe. Because whether he admitted it out loud or not, the sex *had* meant something. It had meant too much, actually. He hadn't guarded himself like he normally did, and she'd slid in below his radar.

Even Soldier noticed the change in him since Jessie's confession. And unlike him, his dog mirrored back his moods better than those silly fortune-teller rings they used to sell. Or maybe they still did. He was pretty sure his ring would have an easy time of it. It would show black. All the damn time.

But was he willing to let her leave town over someone like him? Maybe he could go and tell her something like, "Well, if I could feel anything for anybody, I would have picked you."

And if that wasn't some kind of morose greeting card message, he didn't know what was.

So why not go over with no plan in mind and tell her why he had done and said what he had. Which had pretty much been nothing. Oh, he'd tried, but Jessie had been too hurt to listen at the time. But maybe now that a couple days had gone by, she'd be more receptive. And maybe this time, he could actually come up with some better words.

Fortified by that, he decided to pay her a call. In person. Before it was too late. And since it was Sunday afternoon, she was pretty sure to be home, right?

So he made the short drive over, surprised when her little blue car wasn't in her parking space. Instead, there was a gray sedan that looked fairly new. Maybe she'd bought a new vehicle.

They hadn't actually said when she was leaving, but he'd assumed it wouldn't be until she'd found another vet to take her place. What if he was wrong?

At the door he hesitated. What if some stranger's face met his? What if Jessie's smile never greeted him again?

Realizing he'd forgotten to draw a breath, he sucked down a couple of gulps of air, feeling suddenly lost. Feeling suddenly afraid to see what was on the other side of that door.

But whether he was afraid or not, it would change nothing.

So he knocked. Waited. Knocked again. Louder this time.

After a few more minutes, he thought he heard shuffling from inside.

"Jessie?"

The door flew open. "Dammit it, Cabe. I was in the middle of the best dream I ever had. I was in the... well, on some island somewhere. And it was a place I could actually get some sleep!"

"Doc? What are you doing here?"

"Nice to see you too, Cabe. Thanks for the warm welcome back."

"Back, as in...?"

"Yep, I'm working at the clinic again."

The news made him reel backward as if he'd been struck by lightning. He'd thought he had more time. After all, it had taken Doc a while to find Jessie. "You're back full-time?"

"Would that be so unbelievable?" He stepped back.

"Get in here before I decide that visiting my dream island is preferable to standing here gabbing with you."

Cabe moved into the space. It looked exactly the same as when Jessie had lived here. But then again, that was because she hadn't gotten around to changing out Doc's decor. He guessed that made it nice for Doc to come back to.

"Sit, and I'll get you some coffee. The pot is still on."

"No thanks, I'm good." Doc's coffee was thick and black, and the most unappetizing brew he'd ever tasted.

"So if you don't want coffee or chitchat, what are you here for?"

Yeah, what was he here for? He had no idea. But he certainly wasn't going to tell Doc any of that.

Doc took a closer look at him, then this godawful smirk appeared on his face. "You expected to find Jessica here instead of me, didn't you?"

"Jessica?" He faltered for a minute. Was the man worse than he'd been before? "Do you mean Jessie?"

"Of course I mean her. Who else would I mean?"

He couched his next words in the vaguest terms he could think of. "Did Jessie move?"

"Yes, she moved. Didn't she tell anyone besides me?" The smirk vanished as suddenly as it'd appeared.

"I've been busy for the last day or so, so maybe she did. I...just wasn't aware she was leaving."

The man's eyes narrowed. "Oh, I think you knew *something* was going to hit the fan, didn't you?"

Okay, so he hadn't failed memory-wise in the short time he'd been away. He was as sharp as ever. Cabe glanced at the man's hands for a long moment.

"Steadier than you expected? The big city doc had

some concoction that slowed down my shakes. At least for now."

Which explained why Doc was back at the clinic. But that still left the question of where Jessie was.

"I'm really glad, Doc. Was it your idea to take the clinic back over?"

"Let's just say it was a mutual decision."

"Hell, Doc, let's stop dancing around the subject. Is Jessie gone for good or not."

"Pretty sure that's something you should be asking her yourself."

Yes, it was. And if she had already left Santa Medina?

What had he expected? That even though he didn't want to take the cake out of the baker's window and share his life with it, that it would somehow magically just stay there for his viewing pleasure? That he could go and stare longingly at it whenever he wanted to? Imagine the taste of it on his tongue? What it would be like to call it his?

That's kind of exactly what he'd thought.

Until that option was no longer there. Until the threat of never seeing that cake again loomed on the horizon. Never was a very, very long time.

That word made an area of his heart hurt in a way he hadn't felt for a very long while. The spot spread its tentacles out until they wrapped around the entire organ, squeezing it tighter and tighter.

Mourning her.

Because he loved her.

But what if love wasn't enough. It hadn't been enough for his mom who had given and given and given to a man who'd given nothing in return.

But would Cabe truly let that happen? Would he let Jessie waste her life on him? Or was he willing to stand up and fight to give her what she needed. No matter how hard it was. No matter how alien it might feel to do so.

It didn't feel alien with Soldier, did it?

No. It didn't.

He took a deep breath and looked Doc in the eye. "I take it she's gone back to San Francisco."

"Not quite."

The prevarication made him laugh.

"Come on, Doc. If you get me an address, maybe I can get you back to your nice cushy retirement spot."

"I'm kind of liking where I am, to tell you the truth." He gave a dramatic pause. "I would get you an actual address, but I can't remember it and they got rid of my file drawers. And right now Margo's—"

"Gone fishing." He finished Doc's sentence for him.

"Yep. Some things around this town never change."

Maybe. But Cabe was about to see if some things could change. For the better. Namely…himself.

"I guess I'll have to try to find her myself."

Doc laughed. "I didn't say I didn't know where she was. I just said I couldn't remember the address. She's right upstairs. In the apartment over my garage."

CHAPTER ELEVEN

JESSIE TRIED TO sit in her new place and do some thinking, like she'd promised Doc she'd do, but it was harder than she expected. She felt lonely and so out of sorts that she didn't know which end was up. For the thousandth time, she wondered if she should just go back to her parents' house in San Francisco. But she had a feeling those old sayings about never being able to go home again held an element of truth. It had been almost a week since she and Cabe had made love in that clinic, and she'd heard nothing from him. Not that she'd expected to.

And she was no closer to making a decision about him. Although Dumble had.

He recited "Not the only one" constantly now, and she was pretty sure it had something to do with Cabe. Maybe he'd made the odd comment and Dumble had picked up on some emotion behind the phrase.

She'd video chatted with her mom yesterday and, between gasped sobs and with a voice that was almost too hoarse to speak, she'd somehow gotten her story out. Oh, not about the sex parts, but about the rest. About how she'd fallen in love with Cabe, and that he was the most wonderful man, but with a terrible dad who had somehow robbed his son of the ability to be happy.

"Get this. He never told his son he was proud of him. Not one single time."

By the time she was done, her mom was crying along with her.

"I love him, Mom, but I just don't know what to do."

Dumble threw his two cents' worth in from beside her. "Not the only one!"

"Probably not, buddy. But it sure feels that way."

"What is your heart telling you to do, Jess?"

Over the last three weeks, she'd gained some important perspective. She missed Cabe so much she could barely breathe. Could she really face him again? God. She just didn't know.

"It's telling me not to give up. Even when I probably should."

Her mom dabbed at her eyes with a tissue. "Maybe that's the very time you shouldn't. When you should just hold on a little while longer."

"You always did see the best in every situation."

"Maybe because I got my happy-ever-after, and he's a pretty good one. It sounds like Cabe is as well. So make very sure, before you make any permanent decisions. We would love to have you back home, so don't take this the wrong way, but I feel like Santa Medina is where you belong. No matter what Cabe decides."

Maybe that's why she'd felt so weird whenever she thought about running back to San Fran.

"I think you're right. And, you know what? I think I can handle it."

Her mom leaned closer to the screen. "I absolutely know you can."

"I love you so much. And I'm so glad you guys are my parents."

Her mom blew her a kiss and Jessie pretended to catch it in her hand. "I'll call you if anything changes."

"I'll be right here. Cheering you on, no matter what."

With that they ended the call. Her dad had already left for work hours ago, but she already knew he would support her decision too. She went outside and sank on the little bench in her garden and tugged at a weed here and there. Doc was in the office today and had given her an update. He seemed happy to be back at work. Well…as happy as his gruff manner would allow him to be.

But he'd probably be glad to know she was going to stick around Santa Medina.

No matter what Cabe decided, it wouldn't change her decision. She loved him. Would love him for a very long time. But she would make her life in the town that she also loved.

Sliding from the bench and getting down on her knees, she began to weed the garden in earnest, so caught up in the task that she almost missed the shadow that fell over her.

Until she heard her name.

"Jess?"

She looked up, shielding her eyes against the glare of the sun. Then her breath left her body in a huge whoosh.

Realizing she was just sitting there staring at him, she lifted her chin a fraction. "Cabe? What are you doing here?"

"I could say that I'm Doc's errand boy, but would you believe that?"

"No."

"How about the fact that the whole town is mad at me, and they believe you're leaving Santa Medina because of me."

"They would be wrong about me leaving. But if I did leave, they'd be right about the reasons." To soften the words, she allowed the merest hint of a smile to cross her lips.

"Would you mind standing up, you're making me uncomfortable down there."

"There are enough weeds for two." She smiled again. "Down here."

"Weeds."

"It seems some of us have more than others."

He knelt beside her and at once she was transported back to a month ago, when she'd reveled in his touch, in the scent of his skin. She closed her eyes against the memories for a minute.

He didn't say anything, just went about the task of pulling stuff up.

She touched his hand. "Uh-uh. That's a flower."

"How can you tell the difference?"

He stared at the plants, most of which were still in their early stages. She understood his confusion.

"You eventually learn which ones should stay and which ones should go. But it takes time and experience."

He took her chin and tilted it, so she looked up at him. "Like emotions."

The fact that he caught what she was aiming for surprised her. "Yes. Exactly like that."

He sighed. "When you told me you loved me, I was shocked. The fact that you could know it with such certainty…amazed me. Scared me." He looked into her eyes. "You'll never know how much it scared me."

She pulled up another weed to avoid looking at him. "I think I do. Because I was just as scared. But I couldn't…" She tried to find the words. "I couldn't bear to go through life wondering what might have happened if I hadn't said the words. I didn't want the regret of not knowing." She gave a slight shrug. "And now that I do, well…"

"Except you don't." His jaw worked, a muscle twitching as if he fought something inside him that was probably telling him to hold it in. To not let whatever it was out. "I feel it too."

The words hung between them and hope surged. But it wasn't enough. Not at this point in her life. Not after all the heartache she'd suffered at someone else's hands.

"Feel what?" This was so important. So very important. She couldn't let him sit on the side of the pool and dip his toes in whenever he wanted to. She needed to hear the words. If he couldn't get past this…

Please, Cabe. Just say it.

If he could sacrifice in this area, he could sacrifice in others. Just like she would sacrifice for him.

"I love you." He closed his eyes and then opened them again, the blue irises seeming to be infused with a light that hadn't been there before. "I do. I have all along. I just felt it wasn't enough. The words…they mean nothing, if I can't give you what you need."

"Cabe." Tears prickled behind her eyes as she hugged him close. "You just did. You gave me exactly what I needed."

"But if I can't say *rah-rah-rah* every time you want me to, or—"

"Have I ever asked you to do that? I'm not a super *rah-rah-rah* person, if you haven't noticed."

"I don't always talk things out."

She took his chin between her thumb and forefinger and wiggled it back and forth. "You don't think I talk enough for the both of us?"

"Well…"

"Be careful with that answer, buddy."

He laughed, seeming to relax all at once.

She got serious. "I don't know what you think I want from you, but I think it's a whole lot less than you think it is. I want companionship, can you give me that?"

He nodded.

"I want to periodically hear the words. Not all the time. But sometimes."

He nodded again. "I can do that."

"I want children, can you give me that?"

"I want to, but…"

There was a long pause that made her hold her breath. Then something in his face changed. Got softer, his glance going to her midsection in a way that made her swallow.

A huge feeling of relief made her want to laugh, but she held it back. She didn't know why, but she sensed he'd kicked down some mental barrier and had come out on the other side. She forced herself to remain matter-of-fact and keep things light.

"But nothing." She looked closer. "Unless you have a problem with sperm count."

He looked shocked, and this time she did laugh. "Okay, I take it those guys are pretty good swimmers."

"As far as I know." His brows went up. "You can find out for yourself later."

He waited as if expecting her to come up with some more conditions.

She smiled. "That's it, Cabe. I'm now ready for your expectations."

"Mine?" He swallowed. "Okay. I would ask for your patience as I learn to tell—" he motioned to the garden "—flowers from weeds."

"That's easy."

"I would like honesty."

She sensed that one came from a place deep inside of him. A place of hurt and sadness. And she wanted to weep for him. But that's not what he'd asked for. So she held it inside her.

"I'll give you honesty."

"And I want to make you proud."

This time she couldn't hold back the tears. "Oh, Cabe, you've had that since the time I watched you rescue Gloria from that mountain. I love you. And I'm very, very proud of you. More than you'll ever know."

He pulled her against him and held her there for a very long time. This time he smiled. "It looks like we've come to a working agreement."

"I think we have, indeed, Mr. McBride."

He kissed her, then looked at her. "Why didn't you tell me your real name is Jessica?"

She laughed. "It's not. And that could have only come from Doc."

"Yes, it did. And he seems rather put out by his missing file cabinet." He stood and held out his hand for her. She took it, and he pulled her to her feet.

"Oh, wait! I have one more demand," she said.

The expression on his face made her laugh. "No, it's nothing terrible. I should have said it's a request, not a demand."

"What is it?"

"Is there any way you could…um, rip a pair of your jeans right along here…" she traced her fingers down his right buttock, "and periodically walk around the house in them?"

His choked laughter told her she'd hit the right button. In more ways than one.

"I think that can be arranged." He glanced toward the garage. "So you're living there right now?"

"Yes I am."

He gave her a smile that she could only describe as calculating. "Does there happen to be anyone else up there right now?"

"Just Dumble and Rocky, but they probably don't count."

"Dumble might. It depends. He tends to be a tattletale."

"Yes, he does. He also knows how to parrot certain, possibly embarrassing, sounds."

His lips pursed. "That could be a problem. How loud exactly are you planning to be?"

The hope that had died a hard death, was back on top…making its triumphal lap around the track.

"I can be as loud as you want me to be." She thought for a second. "Well, I'd rather the whole clinic not hear us."

"I can agree with that."

She led him up the stairs and into the apartment. Rocky ran over to meet both of them, doing a dance on her hind feet. He scooped her up. "Well, hello there. Still no owner?"

"I think her new owner is going to be me."

The second he set the dog down and Dumble saw him, the bird bobbed his head up and down, his comb raising high on his head. "Not the only one! Not the only one!"

The words were pitched so high, they were almost a scream.

"Weird. Ever since we moved into the apartment, he's been repeating that constantly. Do you know where he got it from?"

"I do, but that's a long story. And I think it can wait a while." He took her in his arms and kissed her as Dumble swiveled between making smooching sounds and loud screeches, and Rocky whined at their feet. "A very long while, if those two—and I—have our way."

CHAPTER TWELVE

SHE FINALLY GOT her wish to see Tuolumne in the snow. How fitting that it was on the first anniversary of their marriage. And it didn't disappoint. It was gorgeous with snow sweeping across the meadow and clinging to their Dome—as she had come to think of the Stately Pleasure Dome. It had brought her pleasure, in so many ways.

Her skis pulled to a halt so she could take it in. Her cheeks were on fire and her hat was askew, but she didn't care. The temperatures today were well below that of her disastrous polar plunge, when she'd blurted out that she was in love with him, while he was still trying to process his feelings. Still trying to process whether he was capable of being a good husband. A good father.

But process them he had. His seeking her out had proven more than anything, that he *did* have what it took to give her what she needed. Because really? Her needs weren't all that great:

She wanted to be loved. By Cabe.

She wanted to have babies. By Cabe.

She wanted to prove that he was everything he needed to be and more. Because he was Cabe McBride.

And he. Was. Enough.

His father's tragic life and death had scarred him in ways that no one could truly understand. But she trusted him to keep remodeling himself into the person *he* could trust. Because she suspected he hadn't trusted himself in a very long time. Maybe even never. But he was learning to.

His arms slid beneath hers, coming to wrap around her midsection. "Are you sure the doctor said this was okay?"

"Hey, I pulled a calf yesterday, I think a little skiing isn't going to do either of us any harm."

By "us" she didn't mean her and Cabe. She meant her and Cabe and the little one she was carrying inside her. It was just a little peanut, too small for others to notice just yet, and she wanted to keep it that way for a little while longer. To be the secret that only she and Cabe knew about. Because each second he was with her, was another second he could prove to himself that he truly *was* the man she saw when she looked at him. They both had some growing and changing to do. But they were helping each other do exactly that.

"Did I tell you that Mom and Dad are actually thinking about moving to Santa Medina?"

He nuzzled her ear. "Why is that surprising? We have the best vet in the whole country."

"I think you might be a little biased."

"Speaking of biased. Did I tell you I saw Farmer Jonas yesterday in town?"

"No. How is he?"

Cabe chuckled. "He said to tell you, and I quote: 'They named that damn little heifer.' He didn't seem too happy about it, but said you'd know what he meant."

She spun around in his arms and said the words she'd repeated to him time and time again. "See? We *are* magic. When we're together, good things happen."

"So, naming 'that damn little heifer' is a good thing?"

"Yes. It's a very good thing. Because it means she's going to grow up and retire out in that pasture with her mother and live a long and happy life."

"Ah, yes, I can see how that is a very good thing." He kissed her lips, slowly deepening the contact until she was breathless with need. Then he pulled back. "I think you're the one who's magic. So when I retire, will you let me share your pasture with you?"

"I have a feeling we'll both have to be very old and very gray before that happens."

He straightened her hat. "I can feel myself graying as we speak. Which reminds me, we'd better head back before someone sends SAR out to find us."

"Yes, because we all know how that will go. They'll find us long before we want to be found. Especially with Soldier on the trail."

Cabe had made his peace with Dumble and could be found padding through the kitchen before dinner with the bird perched on his shoulder. Dumble had unfortunately picked up a few more choice sayings which Jessie was going to have to talk to him about. Not Dumble, but Cabe who thought it was hilarious to teach her bird urban slang that wasn't fit for work. And Soldier and Rocky got along famously. It was as if they were made to be a family.

As they turned to go, Jessie threw one last look at her surroundings. "I am the luckiest girl on Tuolumne Meadows."

"Sweetheart, you're probably the *only* girl silly enough to be out on Tuolumne right now."

She gave him a secretive smile. "That doesn't make me any less lucky, does it?"

"No, it doesn't. So, then, am I the luckiest man out here?"

She gave him a hard peck on the lips. "Yes, you are. And I'll show you just how lucky when I get you home."

Without any urging whatsoever, Cabe began retracing their path across the snow, that fine ass of his moving faster than she'd ever seen it go. Well, maybe not faster...

Suddenly her skis picked up speed as well. And yes. She was the absolute luckiest girl in all of Tuolumne.

* * * * *

MIRACLE TWINS FOR THE MIDWIFE

LOUISA HEATON

MILLS & BOON

For Nick, my constant support and cheerleader.
Thanks for everything. x

CHAPTER ONE

New York, New Year's Eve

DR HENRY LOCKE would have preferred to stay at home. He liked it there. Home was his refuge. His quiet place. His books were there. His piano. His bed. The apartment was high enough that he wasn't too bothered by traffic noise, but if he was at home whilst rush hour was going on he simply put on some classical music to help drown out the frantic sounds of horns and sirens down on the streets below.

But it was New Year's Eve, and his brother Hugh was over visiting from England, and he'd turned up at Henry's door, insisting that they help to bring in the New Year.

'We're going out! Put on your glad rags, brother dear, we're about to paint the town red, white and blue.'

He'd tried to protest, but Hugh had been having none of it.

'You think I can go out drinking on my own, knowing you're sat at home with your head between the pages of a book? Come on! You're not at the hospital tonight, you've got a rare evening off, so we're going to enjoy it.'

They'd started the evening at an Irish pub called Shamrocks where, to Henry's surprise, Hugh seemed to actually know some of the regulars. It turned out they'd been at university together and so, whilst his brother had knocked back pint after pint, Henry had nursed a glass of wine and smiled and chatted, all the time wishing he was back home in bed, catching up on some much-needed sleep.

Work had been heavy of late. A lot of difficult deliveries, a lot of emergencies. Every time he thought he could finally get some rest in an on-call room his phone would chime and he would get called back to the ward. It didn't help that they were down on staff numbers. Covid had caused a few of the staff to quit. Others had simply migrated to other hospitals.

Ideally, they needed at least one more OBGYN attending, one more registrar, and a couple of certified nurse-midwives. They had agency staff, but that was never the same. All those changing faces, and having to teach new people almost every day, it seemed. HR had just informed them, though, that they'd employed a couple of new people, so that would be good. They needed regulars. They needed people to stay. Then maybe the rest of them could relax a bit more.

That was one of the reasons he hadn't wanted to go out tonight. It was his one night off, his first in God only knew how long, and he didn't want to waste it by spending it doing something he disliked.

And now he was being dragged towards a club that had bass music thumping out so loud he could almost feel his teeth vibrating. It was the sort of thing he hated.

Why, oh, why couldn't Hugh have just suggested a movie instead?

He eyed the exterior of Liquid Nights. A burly door-man stood by the door, checking IDs and occasionally letting people in by unhooking a red rope between two metal poles.

'This looks great!' Hugh said, dragging Henry over to the queue. 'I bet there are lots of lovely ladies inside, just desperate to be blown away by our charming English ways.'

Henry doubted it. Though his own English accent was popular with his patients and his friends, he doubted that Hugh, who was almost struggling to stand upright after his alcohol consumption, would find a lady who might succumb to his drunken charms. But who knew? It was New Year's Eve and maybe his brother might manage to persuade some lovely local to let him kiss her as the New Year rang in?

Henry checked his phone. Eleven thirty-two p.m. He'd make this his last port of call, then once the New Year was here, convince his brother that it was time for him to go home. He didn't want to be a party-pooper but, as Hugh said, this was his only night off and he'd planned on sleeping.

They slowly made it to the front of the queue and entered the club. Instantly Henry was plunged into a dark, humid and extremely loud room. Hugh turned to him, grinning madly, trying to say something, but Henry didn't catch a word of it. He tried shouting into Hugh's ear that he needed him to repeat it, but it was almost impossible to be heard. Clearly all you could do in this place was drink and dance, as most of the clientele seemed to be doing.

Everyone was up close, bodies writhing and bopping to the music, hands in the air. He smelt sweat and alcohol and the choking smoke of dry ice. As Hugh went in one direction, towards a trio of ladies who appeared to be celebrating a bachelorette evening, Henry headed towards the bar to get himself a drink.

It took some time. There were huge crowds surrounding the bar and his *excuse me* and *sorry* were lost in the noise of the music vibrating from overly large speakers.

Eventually he made it to the bar and waved a note at the barman to catch his attention, successfully managing to order a white wine by pointing at the bottle after the barman had trouble hearing his order.

How did anybody enjoy this?

Looking out over the thick undulating crowds on the dance floor, he thought he spotted Hugh, propping up a wall and trying to charm an amused brunette who was wearing a tiara with pink chicken feathers on it and a pink sash saying *Bride-to-Be.*

Seriously, Hugh? You aren't going to get anywhere chatting up the bride!

He turned back to accept his glass, and was just about to move away and head for a corner as far away from the speakers as he could get when he felt someone stumble over his feet and splash his chest and trousers with a drink from a cocktail glass.

His first reaction was to steady her by catching her arm with his, and then he looked down at his shirt to check the damage.

I should have known better than to wear a white shirt.

A red stain was soaking through across his chest.

Her mouth moved. She said something he couldn't quite catch.

He saw a mass of blonde curls as the woman dipped into her handbag to grab at a handkerchief, and then she began dabbing at his shirt, pressing the material against him here, then there, then lower. Then she paused, bit her lip and looked up at him, and he was suddenly hit by a bolt of *something* as she looked uncertainly into his eyes.

Her lips moved again, forming words he still couldn't hear because of the damned music, and then she nodded downwards. Towards his trousers.

Still shocked by his startling reaction to this woman, he quickly gathered himself and looked down as well. And, yes, there was a small twist of lemon peel stuck to his crotch. He picked it off, and then didn't know what to do with it. Just throw it away?

It was as if his brain wasn't quite working properly, because the woman standing before him was *stunning*. Which couldn't be, because he'd had strong words with himself about reacting to beautiful women just lately, and he'd sworn to himself that getting involved was *strictly* off the menu! There was to be no falling for anyone, no getting romantically attached, no acting on lust, no noticing women, period! The only women he interacted with were his patients, and his relationship with them was strictly professional anyway.

Henry and romantic entanglements never worked. They always ended badly. He wasn't very good at romance and he struggled with dealing with other people's emotions. So this sort of thing was not meant to happen!

He stood there, kind of dumbstruck, one hand holding his glass of white wine, the other holding the lemon twist. He opened his mouth to speak, to ask if she was all right, but she just shook her head and pointed at her ear. She couldn't hear him either, damn it!

Henry put down his glass, and the lemon twist, on the bar. He wanted to be able to apologise. Wanted to buy her a new drink in case it was his fault that hers had spilt. But this music was far too loud.

He pointed to a door marked *Exit* and she nodded.

He hadn't realised how hot and stifling it had been inside until the welcome cool breeze of outdoors washed over him as they stepped outside. The door-man moved aside to let them pass and they took a few steps to one side of the door.

'I'm sorry about that,' he said. 'You must let me buy you another drink. Or at least pay.'

He began to rummage in his pockets for his wallet, but she reached out and placed a hand on his arm, stopping him.

'No, thanks. I didn't want to be here anyway, so you've helped me escape.'

He smiled. 'You too? I thought I was the only one who didn't want to be here.'

'Clubs not your thing?' she asked, smiling up at him.

She wasn't that much smaller than him. He was just over six feet tall. She seemed to be about five ten. Maybe a little less if you took away the huge amount of blonde curls.

'No, I'm afraid not.'

'Nor mine.'

He nodded in acknowledgement. Glad to be able to talk, rather than shout to be heard. She intrigued him, this woman. He'd never seen her before—but then why would he? His whole life seemed to revolve around the hospital lately, and if you weren't a patient, or a member of staff, then it was sometimes easy to forget that there was a whole wide world out there, full of people and places yet to be met or explored.

'You're… English?' she asked, her head cocked to one side.

'Yes. Oxford born and bred. Henry— Henry Locke.'

He held out his hand and she reached for it. As he clasped his hand around hers he felt a surge of something undefinable rush through him, so when she let go he placed both hands back inside his trouser pockets, so that he didn't do it again. She made him nervous. She made him consider breaking his promise to himself. He could still feel the imprint of her hand, even though he wasn't touching her any more.

He rocked back and forth on his feet. Kept glancing away, almost as if he were looking for his escape route. And yet…he knew he didn't want to go. Something about her made him want to stay. For just a few moments longer.

'I'm Natalie.'

He smiled. It suited her. 'Pleased to meet you, Natalie.'

'You too. I hope I haven't ruined your shirt.'

'Oh, this old thing? Don't worry about it.'

'You must let me pay for the dry cleaning.'

'Nonsense.'

Behind them there was a blast of noise as the club door opened and out came Hugh with his arm draped around the neck of a hen. He waved at Henry and staggered over.

'Hey, this is Brandy! She and I are going to have a party of our own. You okay to get home, brother dear?'

Henry nodded. 'Fine.'

Hugh blearily peered at Natalie. 'Who's this? Have you pulled?'

Henry looked at Natalie, mortified. 'Please let me apologise for my crass brother. Alcohol appears to have shut down the politeness centre of his brain.'

She laughed—a beautiful sound. 'That's okay. If you can't drink tonight, when can you?'

Hugh and his new lady-friend headed off down the street. Henry felt his cheeks flaming with embarrassment. His little brother always had been the most exuberant member of the family.

'Sorry about that.'

'It's okay.'

They both watched his brother and his temporary companion disappear around a corner.

Natalie shivered.

'Are you cold? Here, let me…' He shrugged off his suit jacket and draped it around her shoulders.

'Thanks.' She snuggled into it.

He felt that he should leave. It didn't matter about the jacket; she could keep it. His brain was screaming at him. *Walk away whilst you can! Save yourself!*

But he found himself staring at her instead. Entranced by her soft blonde curls, and the way shadows contoured her face. The small uptilt to her nose…the soft-looking plumpness to her lips. She wore a dress with thin straps, the colour of midnight and sparkling with sequins, and her feet were in strappy heels. Painted toenails. An ankle bracelet. A small, dainty tattoo on the side of her left foot that he couldn't quite make out.

And then he realised that maybe all the staring was going to creep her out.

'Are you...um...going to make any New Year resolutions?' It was the only question his befuddled brain could conjure up, inoperative as it was in its current confused state.

She nodded. 'Yes. I'm going to start afresh. Not let the past hold me back. I'm going to put everything into my new job and make new friends. Be a good neighbour. Stay away from guys. You?'

'Ah...um...yes. Same. Stay single. Not let my past hold me back, but learn from it...you know, that kind of thing...'

He kept staring into her face. She had the most exquisite eyes and wondered what colour they were. Blue? Green? It was hard to tell at night. But they were bright, and intelligent, and yet also somehow haunted. It was that shadow, that darkness, that intrigued him. It was as if she was trying to mask something—but then perhaps that was the past she'd talked about? Henry knew all about painful pasts. And the yearning to escape them.

'Ten! Nine! Eight!'

They both heard the countdown begin inside the club.

Henry looked nervously at Natalie. Clearly they were about to ring in the New Year together. Two complete strangers.

'Seven! Six! Five!'

His mind raced. What was the etiquette here? They'd just met, and the standard practice as the New Year was rung in was to cheer and celebrate with those close to you with a hug and a kiss. But they'd both admitted that neither of them wanted to get into anything, so...

If he were to kiss Natalie, how should he do it? On the cheek? On the lips?

He stared at her mouth, torn with indecision.

'Four! Three! Two!'

He looked at her eyes, as if seeking direction. Or maybe just permission. He really wanted to kiss her, despite his rules—because, hey, it was just one kiss, right? It wasn't going to lead to anything. He'd kiss her, wish her a Happy New Year and then leave. He'd be enigmatic. She'd go on with her life and tell her friends about the mysterious stranger she'd once kissed at midnight and he kind of liked that image. Kind of liked being a character in her story, even if it was for the briefest association she'd ever had in her life. It didn't matter that he'd never see her again. Did it?

'One! Happy New Year!'

The roar of voices from inside the club, the cheering and the whistles being blown, caused them both to laugh at how silly it all was. She looked up at him shyly, almost coquettishly, and he knew she wouldn't mind if he gave her a brief kiss.

He smiled and took a tentative step forward, bent his head low and moved in to give her a peck on the cheek. It seemed gentlemanly. Not too forward. Not too brash. Not assuming that she wanted more.

But the skin on her cheek was baby-soft, her hair smelled like flowers, and after he'd pressed his lips to her cheekbone, still with his hands in his pockets, he suddenly lingered, his senses going crazy at her scent, her softness.

She turned to look at him with questions in her eyes. Her face so close to his. She looked down at his mouth, then back up to his eyes again. Uncertain? Hopeful? Wanting?

'I…'

His throat had stopped working. The words couldn't be formed. His breath was gone from his lungs. His senses were all in complete disarray as she reached up to cradle his face and brought his lips back to hers.

He closed his eyes and kissed her.

The sun, already high in the sky, was streaming through his bedroom window when Henry awoke the next morning. He blinked rapidly, trying to clear the sleep from his eyes, his body deliciously content.

And then he remembered.

Turning his head, he saw a mass of blonde curls on the pillow next to him. Natalie was lying on her front, facing away from him, her delicious hair splayed all over his white pillowcase, her bare arms cradling the pillow. The smooth sweep of her back, bare down to the crease of her bottom, where a bedsheet covered her modesty, was marked by a small array of silver scars.

He swallowed hard. As mind-blowing as it had been last night, this was *not* the way he'd hoped to ring in the New Year—by breaking the only vow he'd made for himself!

Not a great start, was it?

Sighing, and rubbing his hand over his face, he turned the other way and picked up his phone to check the time. He couldn't remember setting the alarm. He and Natalie had stumbled into his apartment, frantically removing his shirt and her dress, and they'd practically fallen into bed, unable to tear their hands away from each other long enough to be able to set an alarm.

Nine thirty-four a.m.

He immediately sat up straight, his mind roaring into action. He had a scheduled C-section at midday.

Once he'd showered and cycled to work that would leave him cutting it fine, that was for sure.

Henry glanced down at the still-sleeping Natalie. Should he wake her? What would he say? He really didn't want to have that awkward conversation over breakfast, promising to call her when he knew that he wouldn't. If he was going to start this year afresh, he had to forget about this little setback and start anew *today.*

He pushed aside the sheet, grabbed jersey boxer shorts, trousers and a shirt, and headed into the bathroom. He'd wash, shower, brush his teeth... And then apologise for leaving her, explain that he was running late for work, and hopefully avoid the conversation that he just knew she'd want to have.

Would she see him again? Would he call her? They should do this again sometime.

No.

No. No. *No.*

He couldn't afford to do any of that. No matter how amazing last night had been.

Flashes of it coalesced in his brain. Their frantic kisses...her hot breath against his neck. The feel of her as he plunged deep inside and the way she'd arched her back as she gasped...

His body stirred in response, so he turned the shower setting to *Cold* and stepped into the chilly spray, gasping himself and holding his breath as the icy water ran down his body.

What am I doing?

He quickly washed his hair and then stood for a few moments with his head under the spray, trying to gather his thoughts and empty his brain of last night.

Okay, so he'd messed up at the first hurdle, but he was a man who believed in second chances, so he had to give himself that opportunity.

Turning off the water, he rubbed his hair with a towel, then dried off his body before getting dressed.

Would she be awake when he went out? Would he have to turn away so she could get dressed? Would he have to have that awful conversation with her whilst his back was turned?

It didn't seem right, but he had to do it. He was a gentleman above all things and she deserved the truth. This couldn't be anything more. They'd had one great night and that was all. It ended here. Memories would have to be enough.

Resting his hand on the door, he took a few moments to breathe deeply, then grasped the handle and stepped out. 'Are you awake? We need to—'

The bed was empty, save for crumpled sheets and askew pillows. He noticed that her midnight-blue sequined dress was gone from the floor and—he padded into the hallway—yes, her high heels were gone, too.

'Natalie?'

There were no signs of her.

She had left. Just like that.

'Maybe she didn't want to have that conversation either,' he mused aloud, not sure whether to be elated or disappointed by her disappearance.

As the elevator took her down to the ground floor Natalie struggled to slip her feet back into her vertiginous heels. The bell pinged, the doors slid open, and an elderly couple came in just as she was pulling the hem of her short dress down to cover more of her thighs.

'Good morning,' she said awkwardly.

The woman raised an eyebrow and said, 'Happy New Year.'

Natalie smiled at them both, aware that the gentleman—the woman's husband?—was looking at her with a smile on his face.

His wife swiped at his arm with her rolled-up newspaper. '*George!* Eyes front!'

He snapped to it and Natalie stood up straighter, diving into her handbag to grab her phone and check the time.

Nine forty-seven a.m.! Thirteen minutes to get to her first day at work in her new job! What would they say? And she still had to go home to get changed first. She couldn't barrel up to the hospital dressed in this!

She closed her eyes, cringing at her own impulsive and ridiculous behaviour.

Why had she kissed him like that outside the club?

Why? Why did I go home with him? He could have been anyone! An axe murderer!

Though he hadn't looked like one. He'd seemed quite respectable.

But wasn't that what the neighbours always said when they were interviewed on the local news the morning after a newly discovered bloodbath?

He seemed so nice! Kept himself to himself. No trouble at all...

There were messages on her phone. Her mom and dad wishing her well at her new job. One from her best friend Gayle, who still lived back home in Montana.

New Year, new start! I have no doubt you'll be a great success!

How to tell her she'd stumbled at the first hurdle? That she'd headed out for one drink to ring in the New Year and had ended up falling into the arms of a man and *going home with him!*

That wasn't like her at all. Natalie didn't take risks like that. She had sworn off men after Wade's betrayal.

She blamed loneliness. It was a dangerous thing.

She'd moved away from all her family and friends. Leaving them behind in Montana to go and live and work in New York, after securing a post at Heartlands Hospital in Manhattan. Arriving barely a week ago in the Big Apple, she'd moved her few possessions into a tiny stamp-sized apartment and for the first couple of days had been afraid to go out into the streets.

She wasn't used to a bustling big city. She had lived on a farm for most of her life, her surroundings mountains and plains. Back home she could sit with her thoughts in relative peace and quiet. Sit by a stream to think and listen to the birds. There were vast open swathes of ground filled with horses or cattle. Not this metropolis filled with soaring skyscrapers, bumper-to-bumper vehicles, horns blaring, and thousands of people all busy with someplace to go, who thought nothing of bumping into you and passing on by without even an apology.

So she'd stayed in her apartment, eating what little supplies she had brought with her, talking to no one except her family over the phone. She'd missed them terribly. Felt homesickness for the first time after leaving them all the day after Christmas.

But as New Year's Eve had crept closer she'd felt a determination creep into her soul, telling her that hiding away in her apartment was not how she'd imagined her life in the big city. She'd come here determined to go out and claim what she wanted. So, set on ringing in the New Year, her new life and her new job, she'd headed for the first club she could find. Liquid Nights. And she'd made it in, struggled past all those happy people to get to the bar. Ordered her first ever Cosmopolitan, because she'd read about them once. And then, before she'd even taken a sip, she had managed to trip and spill it all over a guy's shirt. A very nice man's shirt.

She'd been *mortified.* Tried to apologise. But their voices couldn't be heard.

As she'd seen his face in the flashes of the light in the club she'd thought, *He has a kind face.* The kindest face she'd seen since moving there. Dark short hair, slightly wavy. Dark-framed glasses. Strong, defined jaw. And he was tall. Over six feet, for sure.

He'd caught her arm as she tripped, steadied her, but he hadn't gripped her hard. His touch had been gentle, steadying, and the second she'd got her footing he'd let go and smiled, despite the Cosmopolitan staining his perfectly white shirt.

He'd made her heart pound. That was for sure! He'd just seemed so…considerate. Gentlemanly. And then he'd tried to say something to her, but the music had been so loud it had been impossible to hear him. He'd been the first person to be kind to her here, and so when he'd indicated they head outside she'd agreed. Even though he was a stranger, she figured she'd be safe if they stayed by the doorman outside. She wouldn't stray from there, she'd told herself. She wasn't stupid.

Outside in the cool air, she'd heard his voice. His accent. British! And had found her first impressions had been correct. He was a gentleman. And he was kind and thoughtful. And he'd listened to her talk. And then the countdown had begun, and he'd kissed her on the cheek, and she'd been so taken by him, so determined to accept who she was now, she'd taken his face in her hands and pressed her lips to his. Just to see. Just to see if kissing him would be as wonderful as she'd imagined it to be!

And it had been. The excitement and the joy and promise of the New Year being rung in had worked a little magic.

It was hard to describe, but if she had to, she would say it had been like two lonely souls finding each other. Finding hope. Delighting in the other. Needing more. Craving more. Neither of them willing to go home to spend the night alone.

Somehow they'd made it back to his place, and even before they'd walked through the door they'd been removing each other's clothes.

Her need for him had been like a raging hunger. As if she'd been starved for too long and somehow believed that she could eat as much as she wanted at this buffet and the calories wouldn't count. Because it was New Year's. It was special. It was a night like no other. And somehow Henry—beautiful, handsome, body-like-a-Greek-god Henry—had understood her needs and her damaged body as no one had ever done before.

She'd believed sex had been great with Wade. Whenever they'd got together their lovemaking had been frantic and wild, and she'd believed it was exciting because they'd taken each other in small snatches of time, in places they ought not to have. A restaurant bathroom. Wade's car. Once they'd even done it out-side in the park!

Wade had been her mystery man, from out of town. He'd seemed knowledgeable and worldly and he had made her head spin. She'd not been able to get enough of him, and had wondered if everyone else's relation-ship was like hers. Full of excitement and raw impulse and spontaneity.

Only now she could see all that for what it was. Wade had never taken her home to his place *because he couldn't.* Their lovemaking had been illicit and thrill-ing because Wade had been hiding a massive secret. One she hadn't known about.

She'd thought that his obvious desire for her meant that he loved her. That she was special because she aroused so much passion in him! She'd believed whole-heartedly that Wade would ask her to marry him.

Only he couldn't do that either.

But Henry... Henry had taken her back to his place and he had shown her how a man should be with a woman. Their passion for each other had exploded, yes, but he'd also been able to tease her and slow everything down. He'd taken the time to make sure she was satis-fied over and over again before taking his own plea-sure, and every time she'd thought she was exhausted, and would no longer be able to reach those dizzying heights one more time, Henry had proved her wrong and taken her there, delighting in her every gasp and sigh. They'd laughed together. Giggled. Rested. Then begun all over again. And all her fears that he would see her scars and stop had faded away like magic.

She'd fallen asleep in his arms, sated and happy

and strangely feeling completely safe, considering they barely knew one another.

She'd woken with a start to the sound of a door closing, blinking her eyes open and reminding her that she was somewhere strange and not in her own apartment. The events of last night had flooded back and she'd sat up, pulling the white sheets up to cover her naked chest.

Heart pounding, she'd leapt from the bed to look for her clothes. Her dress had been on the bedroom floor. *Where was her underwear?* Grasping the sheet to her, she'd frantically elevated pillows and checked bookshelves, and eventually spotted the black lace undies hanging off the corner of a large medical textbook. The title hadn't registered. Her main thought had been getting dressed and getting out of there before the lovely Henry came out of the bathroom and asked to see her again.

Maybe.

Maybe he wouldn't want to, but either way she hadn't wanted to stay and have that conversation. This was not how she was supposed to have started her new life in the big city. And she'd had no idea of the time! The sun had been up, and she'd been able to hear the traffic down below. She had to start her new job today!

Why didn't Henry have a clock anywhere? And where was her phone?

She'd grabbed her tiny clutch, found her heels in the hallway, where she'd kicked them off, and wrenched the door open. She'd paused briefly in her flight, wondering if she ought to leave a note.

But what would have been the point? Nothing can come of this. I'm staying single, like I promised myself,

so I will just have to be a notch on this man's bedpost.
A pleasant interlude for two lonely people.

When the elevator doors pinged open on the lobby floor, she raced past the elderly couple and headed outside to get her bearings. She looked left, then right, raised her hand for a taxi and jumped into the back seat of the first one that came along.

'Inwood, please.'

CHAPTER TWO

THE TRAFFIC GODS were kind and the taxi driver got her home in less than five minutes.

'Please stay, I'll be one minute!' she said, then ran inside, unzipping her dress and struggling out of it before her front door had even closed.

She grabbed a pair of jeans, a white tee and a cream-coloured cardigan, and raced back outside to the taxi.

'Heartlands Hospital, please, as quick as you can!'

'Someone dying?' the taxi driver asked with a smirk, looking at her in his rear-view mirror.

'Me, if I don't get there before ten a.m. I'm late for my first day at work.'

'You a nurse or something?' he asked, pulling back out into the road.

'Yes. A nurse-midwife.'

'Guess you'll be seeing a lot of babies in September, then? After last night?'

She nodded, not really listening, as she pulled out her compact mirror to check her hair. Sometimes her curls could go wild and frizzy. Sometimes she'd get awful bedhead. But actually, despite her acrobatics last night, her hair looked decently presentable. She wished she could have had a shower, but she had wet wipes in her purse, so she used those to freshen up her face and remove last night's make-up.

She tried not to think of how Henry might have looked in the shower. She'd heard the water running as she'd crept out. Tried not to let her imagination go wild with images of soaping him down and getting a daytime look at that excruciatingly gorgeous scar-free body of his that had been hidden beneath the plain white shirt and dark pants.

Those muscles...that tight little butt...

By the time the taxi pulled up outside the hospital she felt fresh and ready to go, despite only having had maybe three hours of sleep.

Luckily, her first report this morning would be to HR, not to the ward. She wasn't due to go to the ward until midday. They'd allocated her two hours to get all her paperwork done. Get her ID made. Her picture taken. Sign all the documents she needed to.

God, I'm starving!

She paid the taxi driver and got out, looking up at the impressive building set in the heart of Manhattan. The façade was all glass and steel, the hospital's name set in dark block lettering just above the entranceway. She was about to go in when the aroma of freshly baked hot doughnuts hit her, and she turned to see a street cart off to one side. She bought a doughnut and began eating it quickly as she headed into the main building, her eyes scanning the list of departments in the lobby. Human Resources was on the third floor.

The doughnut was delicious. Warm, sugary-sweet dough, with powdered sugar and a hint of warm strawberry jelly in the middle. She felt as if she could have eaten three or four of them! But one would have to do as she got into an empty elevator and pressed the button for the third floor.

She brushed her fingers against her jeans to rid them of excess sugar and licked her lips, trying to take in a deep breath and steady her nerves. She'd made it! After all that! The frantic drive home, the frantic race to the hospital... She hadn't screwed up her first day, the way she'd screwed up the start of her New Year, no matter how amazing it had actually been.

She smiled to herself, reliving moments from last night. Almost laughing at how wild and crazy it had been to do something so completely out of character! But it had been worth it. To feel like that. To be carefree and confident in herself again.

She wondered who he was? What he did for a living? Whether he'd been relieved or not to find his apartment empty when he'd emerged from the shower? Was he missing her? Would he have liked to see her again?

Doesn't matter. The answer would have been no. No matter how tempting he was.

She thought about that for a moment and felt sad. She couldn't help it. Despite her vow to stay away from men and not get involved, because she couldn't trust them, she was still an old romantic at heart. And there was a tiny part of her that still hoped that maybe Henry had been the magical prince? The knight to save a damsel in distress?

She shook her head. No. Women saved themselves these days.

But still...he had been amazing.

Ping!

The elevator slowed to a halt to let on some people

from the next floor. The second the doors slid open she looked up—and froze, her breath catching in her throat.

There stood Henry. Dressed in a smart shirt and pants, with a body-fitting waistcoat, a *stethoscope* draped around his neck, and a hospital ID clipped to his belt.

For a moment their eyes met, but neither of them could say or do anything! Then, as the elevator doors started to close, Henry stepped forward to grab a door with his hand and stop it, so he could step inside with her. A woman hurried into the lift also, and hit the button for the fourth floor.

Her face flamed with heat. *He was here! He was a medic of some kind...*

Suddenly the image of her panties caught on the corner of a medical textbook flashed into her mind. An obstetrics textbook written by Dr Robert Yang, one of America's leading obstetricians...who worked here at Heartlands...who was one of the reasons she had applied for a job here. With the best. To learn as much as she could.

How had she not realised?

She couldn't look him in the face. She had never imagined she would run into him again. And now she had to stand side by side with him, not able to say a thing, not to explain running out on him this morning.

Ping.

Third floor.

Without looking at him, she hurried out and let out a huge breath as behind her the elevator doors closed and it moved away. She'd escaped! Her explanation could come another time. Or maybe never. All she'd have to do was avoid him. It was a huge hospital.

But, oh, that obstetrics book… What kind of doctor was he?

Please don't let him be on my ward. Please don't let him—

'Natalie?'

She turned, cheeks flaming once again. He stood before her. Must have got off at the same floor as her.

'Henry.'

He gave a small, embarrassed laugh, and then smiled—and *boy, howdy!* Did she love his smile! Warm and genuine. Her attraction to him skyrocketed in that moment, because she knew what lay beneath that clean-cut Clark Kent exterior. Henry might be a gentleman, and kind and considerate, but in the bedroom he was a master. With a body that was… *mmm, edible!*

But she couldn't stand there appreciating that, because—*damn it*—things had all just got incredibly complicated.

She'd thought him a one-night stand. Her first ever and only one-night stand. Someone she'd never have to see again. Someone she wouldn't have to explain her scars to. And it had been better than it had ever ought to be for a first time.

But this was her new start. Her new job. Her first day, for crying out loud! And… She. Had. Sworn. Off. Men. They didn't choose *her*. They didn't put her first. They used her. Thought she was only good enough for a bit of cheap fun, if Wade's actions were anything to go by.

He'd broken her heart. She had been too gullible, too keen to look past the red flags she'd noticed. She had believed him to be the most wonderful person she'd ever met. And now she was doing the same thing with Henry.

Because of one hot night? Because of a charming smile and a scorching body? His ability to give her multiple orgasms?

No. She refused to get lured in again! She'd made a serious mistake with Wade. She would not repeat her past errors.

'What are you doing here?' he asked.

Her mind whizzed with possible lies, but she knew she wasn't a liar—and besides, she knew what it felt like to be lied to. Honesty was the best policy in this situation.

'It's my first day here.'

He nodded. 'That new job you mentioned… Here? Which department?'

He suddenly looked uncomfortable, and she realised that maybe he didn't want her here.

'OBGYN. I'm a certified nurse-midwife.'

'Ah, I see.'

And there it was. He *didn't* want her here! She saw his eyes darken. Saw the way he looked everywhere but at her, as if he were embarrassed or appalled at this news. And, even though she'd expected it, it *still hurt*.

'Look, I know this isn't ideal. For either of us. But it is what it is and we're both grown-ups; we can deal with it in what I hope will be an adult way.'

She babbled fast, checking all the time to make sure that no one passing by might be listening in.

'We were together one night, had some fun, but that's all it needs to be. We can sweep it to one side and forget about it. We can both get on with our jobs and forget the fact that we've…seen each other naked and done things to each other that maybe, in the light of day, feel a little embarrassing, but…um…the thing is…the thing *is* that we are mature people and we can forget about it and move on. Right?'

As she spoke, she could see he was peering at her. Oddly, at first, and then smiling, as if amused by her words. She wasn't sure what to make of the sudden change, and then he suddenly tapped at his chin.

'Um…you have a little something…' he said.

She frowned. 'What?' She touched her own chin with her fingers and felt, then, the blob of red jelly that she must have missed when eating the doughnut. Her cheeks flamed once again. 'Oh. Thanks.'

She licked her finger clean and wished her heart would slow down a little. Shame was overwhelming her. She did not know how to deal with this. She'd never done it before. Never had to have this excruciating—

'You're right.'

She looked up at him. 'I am?'

'Yes. We need to work together, and to do that we must put last night behind us. As wonderful as it was…' he added quietly, almost sounding wistful.

So he'd thought it was wonderful too? That was good. That made her feel better. 'Okay. Well, I need to get to HR. They're expecting me. And you, no doubt, have a lot to do, too.'

'Prepping for a C-section at midday. Maybe you can join me in the OR, if you have the time?'

She would love to be in his OR! But she didn't want to seem too keen. Or make him think that she was keen on *him*.

'I might still be in orientation.'

'Okay. Well, I'll see you around, Natalie.' He smiled and turned away, heading for the stairs.

She couldn't help but look at his neat little butt as he did so, knowing not only how it looked in the flesh, but also what it was like to touch. And what it was like to bite…

'See you around, Henry,' she muttered, almost in disbelief that this was happening to her.

She'd become a different person with him last night. Bold. Sexual. Revelling in the joy of her body for the first time since the accident. Telling him what she wanted him to do to her. Urging him on and returning the favour in kind, time and time again. Finding the confidence from knowing it was a one-time thing and she'd never have to see him again.

And now they had to be professional and work together.

As if it had never happened.

So, this wasn't ideal. Natalie. A nurse-midwife in his own department. Of all the hospitals, in all the world, she had to be working in his.

It was a complication he didn't need. But they'd both been clear with each other from the very beginning. Neither of them wanted a relationship.

And yet…it was going to be difficult, with his memories from last night still fresh, replaying in full technicolor and high definition in his mind's eye. He could still smell her scent. Her hair. Her body. Could remember what she tasted like…

And those scars…what has she been through?

He took his time scrubbing for the C-section, turning his thoughts away from the delectable Natalie and reminding himself of his patient and her history.

First time mother with gestational diabetes. Thirty-six weeks. The baby was already estimated at being over ten pounds, so they'd opted for a C-section, as Mum was quite a small lady, only five foot five, and a normal vaginal delivery would be a risk for both of them.

As he headed into the theatre, he quickly scanned the faces, looking for Natalie. She had blue eyes. Would struggle to contain her mop of curls beneath a scrub cap. He knew that now, but he didn't see her there.

He went over to his patient, who already had her spinal block placed. 'How are you doing, Helen?'

'I'm nervous!'

He saw her teeth were chattering, which could sometimes be a side effect of the nerve block.

'That's to be expected, but you're in good hands, and when your husband is ready he'll be here to sit by your side. We won't start without him.'

He smiled at her, knowing how scared she must be. A Caesarean was quite routine for him. He performed many of them each week. But for the patient it was often their first time. Surgery was a big deal, and this operation was considered major abdominal surgery. So many people thought it was something easy, but it could still take its toll on the body and needed a proper recovery time.

He knew, though, that Helen had a good support network at home. Her husband Cole was keen to get stuck in, and both their parents lived close by. Plus, Helen had three older sisters with children of their own, who were all excitedly waiting for her to bring the new baby home and ready to help out.

The door to Theatre opened and in walked the husband, who sat down on the small stool positioned by his wife's head and took hold of one of her hands.

'Ready?'

She nodded, teeth still chattering.

Cole looked up at Henry in question.

'That's normal. So, are we ready to meet your son?'

'Yes.'

'Good.' He took hold of some pincers and pinched at Helen's abdomen, high and low. 'Feel that?'

'N-no. N-nothing.'

'Just as we like it. Okay.' He eyed the people in his team. 'Let's make a start. Scalpel?'

Tess, his scrub nurse, passed him the blade and he made the first horizontal incision. It didn't take him long to get through the various layers. Skin, fat, rectus sheath, the rectus, the parietal peritoneum and then the loose peritoneum, exposing the distended uterus. He opened up the uterus and Tess began suctioning amniotic fluids as he reached in to grab the baby and pull him out. His head was down low.

'You might feel some pressure, Helen.'

'That's okay. I'm doing all right.'

'So am I.'

The head was out. Tess handed him the bulb for suctioning the baby's nose and mouth without having to be asked for it. They were a well-versed team in Theatre, Thankfully, there were no signs of meconium, so the baby wasn't in distress.

When that was done he delivered the baby's shoulders, and then pulled out the rest of him. A very large, chunky baby, wet and slippery, who immediately began to cry. He clamped the cord, cut it, and then held the baby over the blue cloth sheet to show Helen and Cole their son.

'Here he is. Handsome fella.'

'Oh, my God!'

He heard Helen begin to cry and passed the baby to another nurse, who draped him and took him over to the warmer to be fully suctioned, dried, and have some initial tests undertaken, like blood sugar, weight and measurements.

Whilst the others took care of the baby, he delivered the placenta and then began the suturing process, which was probably the longest part of the procedure. Best of all the baby was crying, so were Mum and Dad, and there'd been no haemorrhage. It had been straightforward—just as Henry liked them to be. He would never get bored with C-sections.

When he was done, he spoke to his patient. 'We'll keep you monitored in post-op for an hour or so—just to keep an eye on your vitals and any bleeding, okay?'

She nodded, smiling with happiness.

He went over to the warmer, where Dad was already busy taking pictures with his cell phone. The nurses there were not concerned. All had gone well, and he felt that rush of adrenaline at yet another excellent outcome.

He never allowed himself to get nervous before surgery. His patients deserved him to be on top form. His nerves always came later—afterwards. When the last stitch was in and he could do no more. That was when the enormity of the situation would fall upon him and he would know that he had evaded disaster yet again.

It made him feel good to keep on bringing new life into this world. It was a snub to the darkness that had taken so much from him. A two-fingered salute to what he had faced, losing his own daughter before she had even been allowed the chance to take her first breath.

I've beaten you again.

He scrubbed clean and headed down to his office to write up the notes. He met his mentor Dr Robert Yang on the way, who was dressed in flowing blue scrubs as he himself headed into Theatre.

'All good, Henry?'

'Absolutely. Straight in, straight out. One healthy boy—once we get his blood sugars sorted.'

'Marvellous. That's what I like to hear.'

'You got something good?'

'Patient with uterine didelphys being transferred in from Brooklyn.'

Two uteruses? That was amazing! 'I'd like to see that.'

'I need you to cover the floor as Serena's not in yet.' Serena was another attending. 'But join me when she gets here.'

Robert walked on by and Henry gave a low whistle. Two uteruses! Was the patient pregnant in both? Dr Yang hadn't said. But it would be a historic case to see and be involved in. The kind of thing that made careers. That got your name noticed. And Henry had ambitions. To be the best. To become as well-known and as well respected as his mentor.

In his own office, he sat down and logged into his computer. He began typing, and was lost in his own little world when a voice began to make its way into his senses. He stopped and looked up.

Natalie.

She was being shown around the floor by Roxy, one of the other midwives. 'This is the dirty laundry room. This is Dr Yang's office. And this…'

Roxy smiled in his doorway. 'This is Dr Locke, one of our attendings.'

Natalie smiled at him and came in, hand outstretched as if she'd never met him before. 'Nice to meet you, Dr Locke. I'm Natalie, the new nurse-midwife.'

He smiled at her impressive improvisation skills and stood to take her hand, happy to play along with the pretence of them being strangers. 'Pleased to meet you, Natalie,' he said, trying not to pay too much attention to how it felt to be touching her again.

It was as if there were sparks in the air between them. Electricity tingled through every nerve-ending in his hand, sending bolts of excitement up his arm and straight down to his groin. Clearly his body remembered!

He sat down before it became obvious how excited he was to see her again. He was just in scrubs, after all.

'How did your C-section go, Dr Locke?' asked Roxy.

'Very well. Mother and son doing fine,' he answered, looking directly at Natalie, unable to tear his gaze away.

She'd been a stunner at night-time, but in the daytime she looked amazing! Those unruly curls, her large blue eyes, her face devoid of make-up…she could easily be a model. But she was more than her looks—he knew that. She was kind, and she had listened to him talk, and her laughter when he'd whispered naughty things into her ear had been hypnotic and delightful.

It had made him feel as if he always wanted to make her laugh and smile.

Only he couldn't. He *wouldn't*.

Natalie had been his for one night only, and he was not going to allow himself to be drawn into another relationship. He'd rushed into a relationship before and it had ended terribly, crushing his heart and his spirit. He'd taken some time off work to think about what he wanted to do with his life afterwards, and he'd re-alised his work was what was important to him if he was going to feel any balance at all.

'You're busy,' said Roxy. 'We'll leave you to it. Come on, Nat. Let me show you where the staff room is. There might be some chocolates lying around.'

He watched them go and let out a pent-up breath.

Things had to get easier, surely?

'Dr Locke's delicious, right?' whispered Roxy con-spiratorially.

'I guess…' Natalie didn't know how else to respond. Say yes and admit she found him attractive? Or say no and have Roxy think she was weird for not notic-ing how dishy the attending was? So she'd opted for a safe middle ground.

'He's got that sexy specs thing going on, and you'd think he was this geek, right? But you can tell from his clothes, and when he's in scrubs, that he's got a de-licious bod!' Roxy leaned in even more. 'Once, Saf-fron saw him taking off his scrub top in the changing room and she said he was all muscle with a washboard stomach. I mean…can you imagine?' Roxy feigned swooning.

Natalie laughed and swallowed hard. Saffron was

right. He was exactly like that. And more. But he wasn't just a hot body to be admired. There was more to Henry than that. He'd been kind, funny, polite. A good listener. An attentive lover. Considerate. Neat. And she had no doubt there was a whole lot more to learn about him. Even if she would never get that chance.

I don't want to know more about him. It was one night. That's all.

And, though her experience with her ex, Wade, made her yearn to want to know more, she knew it would be dangerous to do so. What if she thought he was perfect?

Then I'd most definitely be wrong.

'Tell me about Dr Yang,' she said, trying to redirect the conversation.

Roxy chattered on about their fearless leader and head of OBGYN, whilst she made them both a drink in the staff room. Natalie was pretty much ready to start work now. She'd had her orientation, signed all her paperwork, got her ID. All that was left was to start taking care of patients. It would be the best way for her to settle into a new job.

Back home, when she'd first qualified, she'd had to shadow another midwife for a couple of weeks before she could look after her own patients, and it had been only after that point that she'd felt like she had truly started. She assumed the same would be true here. She was keen to get stuck in. She'd come all the way from Montana to New York to start afresh and she just wanted to get started.

This was her new slate. Her new life. Free of all the trauma that Wade had wrought upon her heart and soul. She wanted to be successful here, to prove to herself, and to him, that she was better than all that sordid business he had dragged her into. Ruining her name and her character.

Just thinking about it now made her angry. She'd been the innocent party! She'd believed he'd loved her! How was she to have known his secret? That he had a wife and children in the next town over? She'd thought he loved her. The heat between them had been *undeniable*. A heat that she had mistakenly believed to be love…

But she'd been a naïve fool, and hated herself for not having seen the signs that now, with hindsight, had been all too clear. His only calling her from a cell phone number. Never going to his place. Saying he worked most weekends. No public displays of affection. No shopping and eating in the next town over, and never at any popular places. She'd felt special, and he'd made her feel that way after having lived most of her life back home being ignored or expected not to make a fuss.

That was what happened when you were the youngest of six kids. By the time Natalie had come along, she'd simply had to fit in with the others. No special treatment for being the baby of the family. She'd just been another mouth to feed. She'd vowed to herself that when she grew up and had a family of her own she'd only have a couple of kids. Maybe three, at the most. So that she could give each of them the attention and love that they deserved.

And be the best mother ever.

Wade had taken that from her, too. She'd thought they would settle down and start a family. She'd often dreamed of carrying his child, even though he'd told her that they needed to wait a little longer. That they'd do it one day soon. And worst of all? She'd *believed* him. Fooling herself that they were both heading in the same direction. That they both wanted the same things. To discover the truth had devastated her.

She consoled herself with a chocolate from the tin, and then accepted the mug of coffee that Roxy served her.

'So, what made you come to Heartlands?'

'Well, I live in a very small town back in Montana. We have a medical centre there that I worked at, but it's a very small department and any patient that was complicated or considered high risk was sent to a bigger hospital, as we didn't have the facilities. That was good for the patients, of course, but it often left me feeling like I wished I could experience more. I enjoy learning new things, and so I started looking to see who else was hiring. I'd never been to New York, so I applied and got the job.'

'That's fantastic. But you'd never been to New York? Ever?'

Natalie shook her head. 'Nor have I ever left the country.'

'You're serious?' Roxy looked shocked.

Natalie laughed and nodded.

'Wow. I mean, I can't imagine not having travelled to other places. Are you, like, a homebody?'

She shrugged. 'I do like being at home.'

She thought of her bedroom back home. The pale pink wallpaper that had been there since her teens. The framed certificates on the walls. The family dog, Scoobs. The horses. Mucking out. Mom yelling at Dad for bringing bits of farm equipment into the kitchen and leaving grease stains everywhere. Dad's heavy sighs and winks at Natalie when her mother wasn't looking. Her sisters borrowing her things. Her brothers hogging the family bathroom every time they went on a date and emerging from it in a cloud of body spray.

It was noisy and raucous at home, but she missed them all anyway.

She'd never, ever thought to leave. Not until Wade had stained her name and her reputation.

'Excuse me…?'

Natalie started at the sound of Henry's voice from the doorway and turned to look at him, her cheeks flushing. Exactly which part of her conversation with Roxy had he overheard?

'I've just been notified of a case of foetal hydrothorax coming up from the first floor. It needs a thoraco-amniotic shunt. Would you like to scrub in, Nurse Webber?'

Natalie looked over at Roxy. 'Would that be all right?'

'Absolutely! Go for it. Learn from the best.'

Nat turned back to Henry. Smiling. 'Yes, please.'

'All right. See you in the OR.'

When he disappeared, it was as if he'd taken all the air from the room. Natalie suddenly felt herself deflate, aware of the way she'd shot to attention when she'd heard his voice. 'Wow. I've never seen that procedure.'

'Nor have you seen his magic hands at work. I tell you, one glance at him over that surgical mask and you'll fall in love. It's the eyes. And his hands. It's like watching a master at work. We've *all* fallen for Dr Locke. You'll have your turn now.'

Natalie laughed nervously. 'I don't think so.'

'Think you're immune? Think again. Just remember you're safe, though. He doesn't really date. Keeps himself to himself. We reckon there's some big tragedy in his past that he doesn't speak about. Makes him more enigmatic, if you ask me.' Roxy sniffed and glanced at her nails before abruptly changing the subject. 'Want me to show you where the scrub room is, or can you remember?'

'I remember.'

But Roxy's warnings sounded ominous, and now she was beginning to doubt her acceptance to join Henry in the OR.

'Then go get 'em, girl!'

He'd not meant to listen in. But after the call from Dr Fox on the first floor, about a twenty-eight-weeker with persistent fluid build-up in its chest, impacting lung development, he'd called to prep a theatre for the procedure and had heard her voice as he'd neared the staff room.

He'd intended to walk straight past, assemble his team and check to see if Serena was in yet, but he'd heard Natalie talking about wanting to see more complicated cases and before he'd known what he was doing, he'd asked her to join him.

It's fine. I do know what I'm doing. It's just one colleague asking another colleague if they'd like to see an interesting case, that's all.

He was scrubbing his hands when the door to the scrub room opened and she came in, tucking her curls beneath a scrub cap.

She looked up at him hesitantly. 'Hi.'

'Hello.' He reached for the nail pick. Decided to

make this businesslike from the offset. 'Patient is a thirty-six-year-old woman, twenty-eight weeks and two days pregnant. Fluid was noticed at the twenty-one-week scan, but it was only a small amount so they decided to monitor and refer to a maternal-foetal medicine doctor, who performed an echocardiogram on the baby. Thankfully there was no mediastinal shift on the heart, but the fluid has built up significantly in the space between the lungs and the chest wall.'

'Okay.' She began to scrub.

'Dr Fox performed a foetal thoracentesis to drain the fluid, but it just returned, so we need to do this procedure now, before there's damage to the lungs and heart.'

'Did Dr Fox take a sample of amniotic fluid to see what might have caused this?'

He was impressed that she knew about that. Especially if she wasn't used to seeing complicated cases. 'He did, but won't get the results back until later today.'

'And what exactly will we be doing?'

'Placing a pigtail catheter into the baby's chest. This will allow the fluid to drain into the amniotic cavity. It gives the best chance of stopping the lungs from under-developing.'

'Okay. How many of these have you done before?'

'About ten.'

'And are they always successful?'

'They have been so far.'

He smiled and then, fully scrubbed and sterile, headed into the theatre to take a look at the scan images that Dr Fox had sent up. It was as if he could breathe again. His heart had been thudding. He could see quite clearly the build-up of fluid in the baby's chest.

Tess helped him gown and glove up, he checked that

the mother had received sedation, and then he used the scanner to check the baby's position in the womb, just as Natalie came in, too.

'Come and stand near Tess. Then you'll be able to see everything. Everybody… This is Certified Nurse-Midwife Natalie Webber, joining us on a permanent basis.'

Everybody said hello. There were smiles and nods.

'Okay, let's make a start.'

He made a small incision in the mum's abdomen through which to pass the needle that contained the catheter. Using ultrasound, he guided it into the womb and into the baby's chest, stopping in the pleural gap where the fluid build-up was. The mother's sedation passed through the placenta to the baby, so the little one was also sedated, and thankfully didn't move during such a delicate procedure.

He looked up briefly at Natalie and saw that she was utterly engrossed in what he was doing. It made him smile. He was all about education. He wasn't grand-standing. But he really wanted this procedure to go well. After all, it was the first time she was seeing him at work, and for some strange reason, he wanted to impress her.

'Deploying the catheter now.'

He pulled back allowing the first part of the catheter to unfurl in the pleural gap, then withdrew a bit more until he was outside the chest wall and in the amniotic space. He deployed the rest of the catheter. It sprang into a recognisable pigtail curl that would help to hold it in place until the baby was born.

'That's amazing,' Natalie said. 'And that will help drain the extra fluid into the amniotic sac?'

He nodded, removing the rest of the needle and stitching up the small incision he'd made in the mother's abdomen. 'We'll keep her under obs for twenty-four hours, then she can go home. In about a week, she'll get a scan to measure how much fluid has been removed.'

He stepped away from the patient, removing gown and gloves. Natalie did the same, depositing hers in the same bin as him before they went back to the scrub room.

'Such a simple thing, yet it works! And the mom didn't even need major surgery for it to happen.'

'Yep. It's done on an outpatient basis.'

'That's remarkable!' Natalie shook her head, as if she couldn't quite believe it.

'Medicine is capable of many remarkable things.'

'It is. But it needs remarkable people to carry it out.'

Her cheeks flushed. He liked that. Was thankful for her compliment. He smiled a thank-you, knowing he had to get out of there before he said something stupid back, like, *Hey, do you want to get a drink later?*

'Well, I must be off. Dr Yang has a unique case that I want to catch up on.'

She nodded. 'Okay. Thanks again.'

'You're very welcome.'

He stared at her a moment more, realising that the more time he spent in her company, the more he liked her, and that it hadn't been an error of judgement when he'd taken her back to his place. There *had* been something special about her. He'd not imagined it.

Natalie was a good person. And potentially a real threat to his vow to remain steadfastly single and not get into any complicated relationships. What had he heard her say? That she came from Montana? A small town? Was here to start a new life in the big city? He didn't want to ruin that for her. She deserved her new start.

'Okay. I'll see you around.'

'You will.'

And he left, heading to his office to write his notes and then track down Dr Yang and the double uterus, determined to think about his work and not the curly-haired blonde who seemed to be at the forefront of his mind.

Natalie had been given the care of a forty-weeker called Felicity. She had been contracting regularly for the last six hours and was here alone, without a birth partner. The baby's trace looked good. It was handling the contractions well. No decelerations or anything to give any concern, and at the last check mom had been eight centimetres dilated.

Felicity puffed on the nitrous oxide as another contraction died down.

'How are you doing, Felicity?'

'Oh, my God, these are killing me!' she said, her head dropping back against her pillow.

Natalie wiped her brow with a cold, damp facecloth. 'Want anything stronger?'

Felicity shook her head. 'No. I can do this.'

'Okay.'

Natalie was just readjusting one of the transducers when Felicity's water broke in a gush.

'You nearly got me!' she said, and smiled. 'But that's a good sign. Things are moving on and some of the pressure should feel better now.'

Felicity began to puff on the nitrous oxide again, as Natalie checked the patient's notes one more time. She liked to be careful. Didn't want to miss anything. Especially on her first patient in her brand-new job!

It was always a worry...that something would go wrong. And working on patients who were placing their lives and those of their children in her hands was always stressful.

People could be litigious in today's society. They complained over the smallest thing. But Natalie had always taken anything like that as a learning opportunity. At her last hospital, back in Montana, a new mother had made a complaint about one of Natalie's colleagues, saying she'd been mean to her during labour. Ordering her about and therefore ruining that mother's birthing experience.

Since that day, Natalie had worked hard to make sure that all her comments and all her behaviour towards her patients were kind and considerate. Because it was a special experience. It was their child's birthday. No matter what, it would be a day that would be long remembered by those parents, and Natalie would have a starring role. She wanted everyone to remember her fondly.

She noted that there didn't seem to be much mention of the father of the baby in Felicity's notes, and clearly he wasn't here, either. Was he just squeamish and waiting at home to celebrate with a cigar? Or was he not in the picture at all?

'I feel like I want to push...' Felicity breathed after the contraction had died down.

Natalie noticed that she was trembling, which could

be a sign of transition. She would need to examine her to check that her cervix was fully dilated.

'Okay, let me check you first, though. We don't want you pushing too early, because if there's any cervix left over and you push too soon it could swell up.'

Natalie admired Felicity's strength. Here she was, birthing her baby without a partner. Trying to do it without an epidural or pethidine. Just the nitrous oxide She had spirit and determination.

'You're doing brilliantly, you know.'

'I'm not, though.' Felicity began to tear up. 'Look at me! Here alone! No family. No boyfriend. What kind of mother am I that I'm bringing this child into the world without support? He'll be all alone. No father to teach him things.'

'Hey, now. There are a lot of kick-ass mothers out there bringing up their children single-handedly, without families or partners, and they're doing a brilliant job.'

'I wanted so much more, though. I thought everything was perfect! That I'd get the dream, you know?'

Natalie laid her hand on Felicity's. 'You can make the dream by yourself. Be the best mother ever. If he has you, then this little boy has all that he needs.'

Felicity began breathing in the nitrous oxide again as Natalie checked her.

'You're ten centimetres. You can begin pushing with your next contractions and I'll alert your doctor. It's Serena Chatwin, isn't it?'

Felicity nodded, still breathing in and out on the mouthpiece. 'I didn't have a father growing up,' she wailed. 'I really wanted my son to have one.'

'Can I ask what happened to your partner?' Natalie asked gently.

'He made me feel like a queen. Then I found out he had two other girlfriends, both of whom had also had his kids.'

Felicity looked down and away, as if she was too ashamed to make eye contact. Natalie stared at her. She knew exactly how that felt. That sense of betrayal. That feeling that you'd been such a fool.

'What kind of role model did I choose for a father, huh? It's laughable.'

'He made you feel special. And you believed him. There's nothing wrong in trying to believe in love.'

'But I should have known!'

'How? People who deceive can often be so charming. And we often take others at face value. We want to believe the best of them. No one goes out there deliberately assuming everyone is a liar. Don't beat yourself up about it. You did nothing wrong.'

Natalie picked up the room's phone and notified the desk that Dr Chatwin's patient was about to start pushing.

'She's in a C-section. We'll send in Dr Locke. He's free.'

Natalie's heart pounded against her chest at the news. 'Okay. Thanks Roxy.'

She put down the receiver and watched the CTG tracing as Felicity's next contraction built, tracing the shape of a very jagged, very high mountain on the paper.

'You need to start pushing with the next one.'

'I'm scared.'

'Don't be. I'm here with you, and Dr Locke will soon be here to help, too.'

The contraction ebbed away. 'What about Dr Chatwin?'

'She's in surgery. But Dr Locke is very good, I promise you. He's very kind.'

'Okay...'

'So, when the next contraction comes along I need you to take in a deep breath and push down into your bottom. And you're going to try and do that three times with each contraction, okay? I'll help you.'

Felicity nodded.

The next contraction began to build.

'Okay. Deep breath in and...push!'

Felicity bore down and Natalie began to count to ten, watching and checking at the same time to see how well her patient was pushing. Sometimes first-time mothers didn't always push in exactly the right place, but Felicity seemed to be doing very well. The baby's head was already there and she could feel hair.

Behind her, there was a knock at the door.

'Come in!' she called.

The door opened and there was a small swish of the curtain as Henry came into the delivery room. 'Hello, Felicity. I'm Dr Locke. Keep doing what you're doing and I'll get ready.'

Natalie felt her body become aware of his presence behind her and she wanted to turn and watch him, to soak him in, as if just looking at him would somehow allow her to feel full and sated. But she couldn't. Her patient came first. So she concentrated instead on coaching Felicity and counting to ten and soon it actually became quite therapeutic.

'How is she doing?' asked Henry.

'Pushing well. Baby's head is right there.'

Natalie stepped back, so that Henry could sit on his stool at the end of the bed, and moved to the side to hold one of Felicity's legs.

'You're doing brilliantly, Felicity. Baby is right here—want to feel?'

Natalie watched as Felicity reached down to feel her baby's head. 'That's him?' Her face lit up with wonder and awe.

'That's him. He's so close now,' whispered Natalie. 'Here comes another contraction. Breathe in. And now push! One…two…three…'

Natalie couldn't help but remember the countdown that she and Henry had listened to outside Liquid Nights on New Year's Eve. She'd felt so nervous, hearing the numbers drop, knowing that most people would find someone to kiss as the New Year arrived and the only person she could do that with was the man upon whom she'd spilled a drink. A man she didn't know at all. A man who had introduced her to the pleasures of the flesh in a way that Wade never had. Because those pleasures with Henry, as far as she could tell, had been honest.

But he was a man she now had to find a way to work with, without letting what had happened between them complicate matters. And she knew, watching him work now, that that was going to be very difficult indeed.

She helped mop Felicity's brow as Henry took over coaching her through her contractions. She noted the laser-like intensity in Henry's eyes as he focused on his work. Trying to ensure that Felicity didn't tear as she began to crown.

'That's it. Little bit more. Little bit more. Tiny push…and pant!' He nodded, the skin at the corners of his eyes creasing as he smiled. 'Head's out. One or two more pushes and your son will be here.'

Felicity nodded, her determination now on show, knowing that the finishing line to all this pain, all this discomfort, was nearly in sight, and that the grand prize—her very own baby—was within reach.

'You're amazing,' encouraged Natalie, dabbing at Felicity's face and offering her a sip of water through a straw. 'You're about to be a mom,' she whispered, smiling and, as she always did since the accident, feeling a pang of envy.

'Another one's coming!' Felicity said.

'Okay… First shoulder's out…can you push again for me?'

She bore down with a groan, and suddenly out came her baby boy, along with a whole lot of hind-waters that splashed all over Henry.

Natalie looked up at the wall clock. 'Three thirty-two p.m.'

Like the gentleman he was, Henry didn't even mention it, or react. He clamped the cord, cut it, and then draped the baby on Felicity's chest. Where her son began to cry, loudly, in protest.

'Oh, my God, he's so tiny! And so beautiful!'

Natalie draped a small towel around the baby quickly, so that he didn't lose too much body heat, smiling as she did so, and rubbing the baby boy's back to help his lungs. She then used a bulb to suction fluids from his mouth and nose, but it was clear the baby wasn't having any problem with his breathing. He was letting everyone know that he wasn't happy about being evicted from his cosy womb.

'Well, his lungs are fine,' Natalie said, still drying him off.

Felicity looked up at her. 'Thank you so much for helping me.'

'Hey, you did all the work.'

'But you got him here safe. You and Dr Locke. Thank you. Thank you so much!'

Henry smiled. 'Has he got a name yet?'

She nodded. 'Wyatt. Wyatt Edward, after my grandfather.'

'That's perfect. It suits him,' Natalie said, smiling. 'Do you want a shot of Syntocinon to help get the placenta out?'

Felicity nodded, and Henry quickly injected it into her thigh. But she hardly seemed to notice, so wrapped up was she in admiring her baby boy. Just as it should be.

'You've got a very minimal tear here, but it should heal on its own. You did great.'

Wyatt was just beginning to settle down, his initial protest now calmed as he lay against his mother's chest and heard her reassuring heartbeat.

'I need to weigh and measure him,' said Natalie. 'I'll just take him for a moment and then you can have him right back, okay?'

Felicity nodded again.

By the time Henry had examined the placenta and checked Felicity's bleeding there was nothing more to do, so he gently covered her with her blankets and offered her another sip of water.

'I bet you're dying for something more,' he said.

'Coffee would be great.'

'I'll see if I can get one rustled up. How about some toast, or a sandwich?'

Felicity smiled gratefully. 'Yes, please—whatever's easiest.'

'I'll go and sort that out for you.'

Natalie watched Henry go, surprised that he was doing that. Usually providing the after-birth nourishment was something that fell to the midwives. At her old hospital the doctors would come in, perform the important part of delivering the baby, and then disappear again. It was the midwives who did all the duties of tending to their patients afterwards. She liked that about him. It was nice and considerate.

Baby Wyatt was doing well. He had an APGAR of nine, his reflexes were all there and he was a healthy weight. Wrapping him up in a new blanket, she carried him back over to Felicity.

'Here he is. All seven pounds and two ounces of him.'

'Wow. It's hard to think that moments ago he was inside of me.'

'Crazy, isn't it?'

Henry came back with a small tray. There was coffee, a plate with two biscuits on it, and a pre-packaged sandwich. 'Egg salad was all that was left, I'm afraid.'

'It's fine. Thank you.'

'How's your pain level?'

'I'm sore, but I'm fine.'

'Well, if you need anything, use the call button and

one of these fine ladies can organise some painkill-ers for you.'

Natalie smiled at him and then he left.

'Is there anything else I can get for you?' she asked Felicity.

'No. I have everything I need.' Felicity stared down at her son, as if unable to tear her eyes away.

'Okay. I'll give you some time together, and then someone will come round to take you to the postna-tal ward.'

'Thanks.'

Natalie gathered her notes and quietly left the room. The birth had gone brilliantly and mother and baby were well, which was the most important thing. She sat at the desk and began to fill in the delivery notes and update the board.

'Hey, how'd it go?' asked Roxy as she passed, car-rying an armful of linen.

'Healthy baby boy.'

'Great! Find everything okay? Need any help?'

'I'm good.'

'Fantastic. When you've updated the computer, why don't you go take a break? About twenty minutes?'

'Perfect. Though you might have to point me in the direction of the hospital cafeteria.'

'So, tell me about the blonde,' said Hugh, who had called on Henry's mobile as he sat in the cafeteria.

He decided to play innocent. 'What blonde?'

'The one I saw you with last night! Curly-haired, doe-eyed… Tell me you got yourself a piece of that.'

Henry rolled his eyes. His brother could be so crass sometimes. 'I wished her a Happy New Year.'

'Yeah, with what body part?' Hugh laughed. 'Seriously, mate, it was good to see you looking that way.'

'What way?'

'Interested in another woman. After what happened with Jenny you deserve some happiness, bro.'

'Thank you.'

'I mean it. What happened was awful. No denying it. Losing the baby...everything. But it's been killing me to see you alone all the time when you've got so much to give. I was happy for you.'

Henry smiled sadly. 'At times I thought I'd never get through it.'

'But you did—and look at you now. In New York. In your dream job. Seeing in the New Year with a hot blonde. So, tell me, was she good?'

'A gentleman never tells.'

Hugh laughed. 'Aha! So she was! You dog!'

Henry grinned at his brother's enthusiasm. 'How was your...erm...date?'

'Awesome. I'm in her bathroom as we speak.'

At that moment one of the radiologists stopped by his table. A young woman. Very attractive, clearly wanting to speak to him. 'I've got to go.'

'We'll speak later, yeah?'

'Yes.' Henry clicked off his phone and looked up.

There was a radiologist, judging by her uniform, talking to Henry. Natalie had sought him out in the cafeteria and was now waiting for the young woman to finish flirting with him—which was clearly what she was doing. The young lady was smiling a lot. Laughing. She played with her hair at one point, and kept tucking it behind her ear. And then she even reached out and touched Henry, trailing a single finger down his forearm.

Unbelievable.

She watched Henry curiously, trying to gauge his response. Wondering whether he would respond to this obvious flirtation in kind? Whether he would draw a slip of paper from his pocket and scribble down his number to pass to this woman? Something...

But with Roxy's words echoing in her brain—*he doesn't date*—she saw Henry shake his head, looking back at the woman with apology.

Natalie watched with bated breath to see what the woman would do next. She shrugged, smiled, then walked away—and Natalie let out a huge breath that she hadn't realised she was holding.

After waiting a moment or two, she carried her tray towards him and stood beside him. 'May I join you?'

He looked up, smiled, and indicated that she could sit.

'Thank you.'

'You're welcome. How's your first day going?' he asked, sounding as if he was really interested.

'Well, I had an awkward encounter earlier on, but I think I survived it—despite the blob of jelly on my chin the whole time.' She smiled and sipped at her drink. 'And then I got to see a fabulous surgery, so that was good too, and then I helped deliver a baby. So...excellent.'

He smiled at her, and there was genuine warmth in his eyes.

'How's *your* day going? Do you always get hit on when you're on your break?'

'Oh. You saw that?'

'Everyone did.' She smiled back.

Was he blushing? It was the darnedest thing! Cute, too.

'That was Amelia. We worked on a case together a few days ago. She's nice, but…not my type.'

'And what is your type?'

He looked up at her and raised an eyebrow.

'Curly-haired blondes who spill drinks on you?' she asked.

She couldn't believe she was flirting with him herself, but it was as if she couldn't stop herself. There was something about Henry that just brought it out of her—and hadn't he already seen who she was? Every excruciating inch of her…scars and all?

Henry laughed and pointed at her coffee. 'Just don't spill that on me. That's all I ask.'

'I'll try not to.'

He was looking at her tentatively. As if he had something to ask but wasn't sure about whether he could. But right now she was feeling brave, so…

'Go on. Say what it is you want to say.'

'I noticed your scars.'

Ah. Here we go.

'Yes.'

'What happened?'

'A car accident. I ended up having a lot of surgery.'

'And are you okay now?'

She smiled. 'I'm getting there.'

CHAPTER THREE

'So, TELL ME how it's going. Is everybody nice?'

Natalie lay back on her couch, holding the phone against her ear as she chatted to her mom. 'It's going great. And yeah, Mom, everybody's nice.'

She couldn't help but think of Henry. The shock of discovering he worked there. The embarrassment of standing in front of him with jelly on her chin on that first day. The tactful way he'd told her about it. The way he'd invited her into the OR. Watching him deliver a baby, unable to tear her gaze away. Flirting with him in her breaks. Seeing him in the corridors each day.

It was getting harder and harder to pretend that nothing had happened between them.

'And you've made friends? I've always heard that people aren't that friendly in big cities.'

'I've made friends. There's a great midwife called Roxy. She's funny and kind.'

'And?'

'And what?'

'What about the doctors? Anyone…interesting?'

'Mom.'

'What? I'm just asking if the doctors are nice!' she protested innocently.

'No, you're asking me if there are any nice men here. And, if you don't mind me saying, you're being very stereotypical. A lot of doctors are women.'

'I know, I know!'

There was a brief silence, as there always was when Natalie and her mother tiptoed around each other, so as not to cause offence. It was even more important now, what with them being miles away from each other.

'You know what I'm asking. This is hard for me. Do you know how it feels to have you all those miles away so I can't see if you're doing okay? If you're looking after yourself?'

'You never worried about that when I lived at home.'

'Because I could see you every day with my own eyes. I didn't have to worry.'

'And now you do?'

Her mother sighed, impatiently. 'You're alone in a big city. Of course I worry.'

Natalie didn't know what to say. She'd never felt noticed by her mom. Had never heard her mother say that she worried about her. But what if she just hadn't seen it from her mother's point of view?

'I'm doing fine, okay? Don't worry about me.'

'Well, I'm going to, anyway. What are your neighbours like?'

'My neighbours are quiet. There's a Russian lady who lives next door—Mrs Petrovsky. She brought me over a welcome bowl of borscht.'

'What's that?'

'Some kind of beetroot soup.'

'Oh. And work's fine?' she repeated.

'Great. Busy. Complicated.'

'You wanted "complicated" from what I remember.'

'I certainly got it,' she said wryly, thinking about Henry, but knowing she couldn't tell her mother about him.

'You went through a lot, honey. What that man did…he changed your entire life. Your whole future! I'm allowed to ask if there's any chance you're going to be happy there.'

'I know.'

She appreciated her mother's concern. Back home, when she'd been recovering from the accident, not too much had been said about what her injuries meant for her future. Her parents had brought her home from the hospital and everyone had nursed her, yes, but no one had actually spoken about what it all meant, only said, *It'll all work out. You'll see.*

She'd wanted to rage at them sometimes. How did they know? They couldn't! Their words were empty and nonsense.

Now… It just made her uncomfortable.

'I'm not looking for a relationship, Mom. You know that. I'm just here to work.'

'Well, just try and make good friends, okay? You've got used to pushing people away since the accident, and you don't want to be all alone in the big city.'

Was her mom right? Did she push people away? Maybe she was a little prickly, but wouldn't anyone be? Her whole world had come crashing down. Her whole future had changed because of a man's lie. A man she'd trusted with her whole heart. And he'd ruined it. Ruined everything. And had there ever been an apology from him? No.

'Mom, please don't. I don't want to argue with you.'

She'd woken with a headache this morning and,

despite a good seven hours' sleep, she still felt tired.
There was a deep ache in her body that didn't seem to
disappear, despite all the body stretches and yoga she
attempted. So her irritation was at surface level. Her
mom didn't need to do much more digging.

'I don't want to argue with you either. It's just…'

'Just what?'

'Let us be here for you, honey. Even if we are miles
away, we're still at the end of the telephone. All you've
got to do is call.'

Her mother sounded so sincere, so caring and loving in that moment, Natalie could almost have cried.
In fact, she could feel the tears building up behind her
eyes, the backs of them stinging and watering as she
fought to keep them contained. There was a painful
lump in her throat.

'Thanks, Mom.'

There was a silence at the other end. Maybe her
mother was fighting the same reaction? That made her
smile a little. Perhaps she had misread her mother all
along? Maybe she hadn't ever ignored her—she'd just
been busy? She'd had six kids. Had a house to run, a
job of her own. Perhaps her childhood hadn't been as
bleak as she'd imagined? She had had a roof over her
head and food on the table every day. So what if affection and love hadn't been shown all that much? Perhaps
her parents had showed her that they loved her in other
ways? Like her mother was right now?

'I've got to get ready. I'm due in for my a shift.'

'Okay. Well, take care, and promise you'll call me
at the weekend?'

'I will. And…thanks. For everything.'

'My pleasure, honey. Love you. Bye.' And then her mom was gone.

Natalie put down her phone and stared at it for a moment. Had she been so wrapped up in her own suffering this year that she'd forgotten what her accident had meant to her parents? They'd nearly lost her, after all.

How had they felt, receiving that call from the police and being told that she'd been involved in a terrible accident? They must have felt awful. Terrified. But had they shown it? No. Natalie had woken up in the ICU, covered in wires and tubes, and her mom and dad had been sitting by her bed, smiling, holding her hands and telling her that she was going to be okay. That they were going to get her through this. And they had visited every day. Steadfast. Stoic. Accepting all the news that had been delivered to them.

My God. Why didn't I notice that before?

Because she'd been hurting, that was why. So wrapped up in losing the man she'd loved and then hearing from the doctors that her abdomen and pelvis had been so damaged in the accident that it was extremely unlikely that she would ever fall pregnant.

The physical scars on her body showed some of her pain, but she knew the scars on her heart were just as bad.

She was a romantic. She'd always dreamed of love. Of finding her prince and settling down and having babies with him one day. It might seem old-fashioned to some, but she was an old-fashioned gal.

She'd wanted it all. The white picket fence. The two point four children. A dog. Maybe some backyard chickens. A house with cherry trees in the garden. A husband who loved her, adored her, and would make the most wonderful father, cradling her belly as her pregnancy grew, just as excited as her to see who they had made together.

All of that gone. Taken from her. By Wade. The most deceitful bastard she'd ever had the misfortune to meet.

Her cell beeped, reminding her she had ten minutes to get to work.

She stood in front of her bathroom mirror, running her hands through her curls, and then stared at her pale face before splashing it with cold water to try and freshen up. Her eyes had gone a little red, but hopefully that would have passed by the time she got to work.

Henry was locking up his bike when he noticed Natalie heading into the hospital. His first instinct was to call out her name and catch up with her, but he managed to stop himself just in time. Instead, he watched her go in alone, and then waited a few minutes to ensure that he didn't have to share a lift with her.

Because the last three weeks had been really difficult!

Difficult in that he'd begun to realise that Natalie was more than just one hot night. She was fun. And popular. Everyone at work spoke about her kindness to her patients—something he'd witnessed himself—as well as how nice she was as a colleague. She'd really fitted into their little obstetrics family so well. She was generous and friendly. Her laughter made everyone smile, and she was a hard worker, too, putting one hundred percent effort into everything she did.

He'd met her in one of the corridors yesterday, coming towards him. He'd seen her before she'd seen him, and just as he'd decided to turn around and go another way she'd looked up through her curls and smiled at him and—*bam!* It had been like being socked in the gut.

All he'd been able to do was smile and say, 'Hi, how are you doing?'

'Good, thanks. Busy, you know?'

'Yes, yes. Me too.'

It had felt so awkward. When he'd wanted it to be anything but. He'd opened his mouth to say something else. *Anything else!* But he hadn't been able to think of what to say, because he'd been so busy fighting his brain, which had wanted him to yell, *I'd love to see you again.*

But there was no way in hell he was going to say that. His mind and his body would just have to get used to that fact—because he didn't date colleagues. He didn't date full-stop. Despite all the flirting in their breaks. Despite the secret smiles they often shared.

'I…er…must get on.'

He'd waved a manila folder at her, as if it were the most important document on the planet, and passed on by, cursing himself for being an idiot and knowing she must think him one, too.

So he didn't need to run into her again, after yesterday's little debacle.

He counted to ten. Slowly put his cycling helmet into his backpack. And then he strode into the hospital, his eyes scanning the lobby area for her and noting to his relief, that she wasn't there. He pressed the button for the lift and waited.

'Hello, Henry.'

He jumped and turned to see Natalie standing beside him, holding a takeaway cup and straw. She must have gone to the hospital coffee shop before heading up to their floor.

'Hey. Hi. How are you?' He could feel heat filling his face.

'Ready for another shift!'

The lift pinged its arrival and they both stepped inside, along with four other people.

The silence was incredibly uncomfortable for him. His body was so aware of her proximity, his senses going into overdrive at the aroma of her body scent. Something floral. Spring meadowy. That kind of thing. And on her…

Dear God…

He needed to think of something else. *Quick.* So he began listing the bones in the human body. Alphabetically, to make it harder.

Er…calcaneus, capitate bones, carpals…

On the second floor two people got off, giving the rest of them more room, so he sidled over to the back corner of the lift, hoping she wouldn't notice, giving himself some respite from her delicious scent.

An image danced in his head of rushing over to her and kissing her, pressing her up against the back of the lift…

Cervical vertebrae, clavicle…

She moved to take a sip of her drink, gently enveloping her straw with her full, soft lips. He couldn't help but look. Saw thick pink fluid move up the straw. Strawberry milkshake? He looked up at the roof of the lift, trying not to think of her lips and what they had felt like on his body all those weeks ago.

Coccyx, cuboid bone…

Another ping and they were at their floor. He held back, trying to think about how he could avoid having to walk with her into the department.

She turned to look at him. 'You not getting off here?'

He swallowed hard at the easy double meaning. 'Er…no. I've got to go and check on a patient who came in through the ER yesterday.'

'Oh, okay.'

The lift doors slid shut on the sight of her sucking at the straw again and he sagged back, as if all his breath had left him in one go.

What was it about her that kept alerting him? Kept turning his body on? They'd had one night.

It wasn't the first time he'd had a one-night stand. Occasionally he indulged in them—once he'd made it absolutely clear to the woman that it would go no further than that one night. He had fun, he got the urge out of his system, and he moved on. But *Natalie*?

Was it because they worked together and he kept seeing her? She'd just started here, so it wasn't as if she was going to leave, and neither was he—he'd come here to work under his mentor, Dr Yang.

So I need to accept that I'm going to see her every day.

But how? When she kept smiling at him the way she did? When he could barely control his body's craving to have more of her? Even though that went against every rule he had? What did other guys do when they had to keep on seeing a woman they'd slept with in a professional setting?

Henry got off at the next floor, even though he didn't need to be there, and went over to the large glass frontage of the hospital and looked out. Relaxing his shoulders, he let out a long sigh, then gave himself a stern talking-to. Was he really going to try and avoid her every time he saw her? It was hardly the adult thing to do. No. He just had to get on with it—and that meant no more hiding but treating her the way he treated everyone else. As friends.

So he turned around and headed for the stairs, trotting down the flight of steps that would bring him to his own floor. Sucking in a deep breath to reinforce his new attitude, he stepped into the OBGYN wing with renewed vigour.

He had nothing to fear. Natalie didn't want anything from him. It had been just a bit of flirty fun. Their night together was *over*. She was settling into her new job and doing well. He needed to get on with his own.

He consulted with Dr Yang on the patient with a double uterus. He'd been able to perform the ultrasound scan and discovered that she was pregnant in one, but had a smallish fibroid in the other, which shouldn't cause any problems.

Then he sat in an outpatients clinic for most of the afternoon, seeing his list of patients who were considered high risk. Multiples. Gestational Diabetes. A baby with spina bifida.

When he was done and it was almost time to go home, he went to the staff room to make himself a hot drink as he'd not had one all day.

The door to the staff room was open and he noticed Roxy whizz by. 'Hey, what's the rush?' he asked.

She stopped briefly in the doorway. 'We're swamped! I don't think any of us have managed a break all day. I was just going to relieve Penny and hand over to the night shift.' She eyed him by the kettle. 'Don't suppose you'd be willing to make everyone a drink and take it to them in the delivery rooms, would you? I know it's a big ask.'

'It's fine. I don't mind doing that at all. You go and let me take care of it. How many midwives are on?'

'Nine.'

He nodded. 'Do they all drink coffee?'

'Is the Pope Catholic?' She laughed and glanced at her fob watch attached to the front of her uniform. 'Got to go. Can I leave that with you?'

'Absolutely.' He smiled as she whizzed away again.

Sometimes it could get ultra-hectic on OBGYN. Every room would be filled with a labouring mother, and somehow they'd all go into late labour at the same time, so it was imperative that the midwives stayed with their patients.

He didn't mind making them all a drink. In fact, he knew they'd be appreciative of it, and he liked to support his colleagues, whether they were consultants or porters. The position they held in the hospital didn't matter to him. People were people, and he believed in treating everyone the same.

He managed to find nine clean mugs and made nine hot drinks, placing them on a tray with a jug of milk and a small bowl of sugar, as he wasn't sure who had what.

He began his round, knocking on doors and delivering drinks to thankful midwives. Danielle said she could kiss him. Carlita gave him an appreciative hug. Janine called him a godsend. At the fourth room he knocked on the door, and when he heard a voice call, *'Enter!'* knew he had located Natalie.

'Just me,' he said popping his head around the curtain. 'I offered to do refreshments for everyone.'

'Oh, wow! That's amazing. I haven't had a sip of anything since midday, and my stomach thinks my throat has been cut. Thank you so much!'

He laid the tray down next to her. 'I didn't know how you took it, so help yourself to milk and sugar.'

Natalie took a pink mug, emblazoned with a slogan that said *World's Best Midwife* and added a small splash of milk.

He thought she looked a little tired, but if she'd been on the go all afternoon, with no chance of a break, then it wasn't surprising. But even so she still looked beautiful.

She stirred her drink and took a grateful sip, then grimaced. 'Urgh!' She frowned at the mug. 'Is that milk off?' She sniffed at the coffee and turned her face away in disgust.

'Er...no. It was a new carton I opened. Totally in date.'

'Not being funny, but it tastes rank.'

'Oh...' He felt a little embarrassed that his coffee-making skills had not impressed her. 'Want me to get you something else? You need to stay hydrated.'

'Maybe a glass of water?' She placed the mug back on the tray. 'Sorry. I know you were trying to be nice.'

'It's fine. I'll take everyone else their drinks, then come back with water for you.'

'Thank you, Henry.'

She smiled at him and it did things to his insides. So much so that he simply smiled back, grabbed his tray and left the room.

He took a quick sniff of the milk. It was fine. Maybe

it was the coffee itself that wasn't to her liking? Maybe too strong, or something?

He delivered the rest of the drinks, then returned to Natalie with a beaker of water, half filled with ice, which brought a huge smile to her face.

'Perfect. Thank you. This is very kind of you.'

'Well, Roxy said you'd all been rushed off your feet, so…' Henry looked over at the patient. 'Anything interesting?'

'Running like clockwork. She's just taking a nap after having an epidural placed. I'm waiting for someone to take over, then I'll be off home.'

'I think the night shift have arrived, so someone should be along soon.'

'Great.'

She smiled at him again, and he suddenly realised he'd have to think of something else to say to her or make his excuses and leave. And, as he couldn't think of anything to say… 'Well, I'd best be off.'

'Doing anything nice tonight?' she asked.

'Er…no. Well, I'm staying in. Catching up on some reading, maybe.'

'What do you like to read?'

Did she genuinely want to know, or was she just being polite? 'Crime. Thrillers. That kind of thing.'

'Oh, I love those too!'

'I can always recommend a couple of books if you'd like?'

'I would like.'

He smiled back at her—and then she was called over to her patient as she woke from a brief nap.

The woman looked at Henry askance.

'I'm a doctor, but don't mind me. I just came in to see Nurse Webber. I'm leaving.'

'Thank you, Dr Locke. For the drink.'

Her smile went straight to his heart.

He nodded and left the room, telling himself he'd done a half-decent job in not being tongue-tied and genuinely acting like a normal guy who worked with a normal woman.

Surely he'd given no sign that being in her presence still affected him?

Now all I have to do is repeat that each time we meet and it'll be just fine...

By the time she left work that evening Natalie was absolutely shattered. It had been a long eight-hour shift, without a single break. She'd had nothing but the water Henry had so kindly brought to her room, and no toilet break either. Her legs ached, her whole body ached, and she was so hungry she felt sick.

She knew she needed to get something into her system—*quick*. So on the way home she grabbed a pretzel from a street stall and quickly began to gobble it down. Every mouthful of malty dough seemed like heaven at first, but by the fourth bite she began to feel a little strange, and had to stop in the middle of the street and peer at it, to see if it was off, or had gone stale, or something.

The taste it had left in her mouth was odd and, disgusted, she threw it into a trash can and hurried home. Back in her apartment, she rifled through her food cupboard, trying to find something that would appeal. She fancied something sharp-tasting, so crunched her way through a pickle or two, and then decided to make herself a vegetable curry. She had all the ingredients, and even a spare packet of garlic and coriander naan bread, too.

She turned on the radio and sang along to some music as she cooked. The recipe called for one teaspoon of medium curry powder, but she wanted something with a kick, so added two and a half—almost three. She chopped up a red chilli pepper too, and dropped that into the mix, along with extra cumin.

It smelled delicious, and her empty stomach rumbled in anticipation as she served herself a huge bowl of the stuff, with some soft, fluffy jasmine rice, and settled down to watch some trash television.

The food hit the spot perfectly, taking away her earlier nausea, which she put down to simply not getting a break at work. She'd been on her feet all afternoon, so it was only to be expected; it had probably been a drop in blood sugar.

She didn't recall falling asleep in front of the television until the noise of a siren racing past her window awoke her to the news that she'd got a stiff neck. She scrambled to her bed and settled down instantly, soon waking to her alarm that went off at six. She had an early shift today, and needed to be at the hospital by seven a.m.

Propping herself up on an elbow, she turned off her alarm and swung her legs out of bed—and suddenly got hit by a wave of nausea.

'Whoa…'

She took some deep breaths and steadied herself as she got to her feet and headed to the kitchen to make herself a coffee. She figured it had to be dehydration. 'd hardly drunk anything yesterday, and when she'd come home she'd eaten and then fallen asleep straight away. So she grabbed a glass of water and necked it whilst she waited for her coffee to brew.

Such a crazy day yesterday! She'd gone from one patient in advanced labour to another. Barely sitting down. On her feet all shift. If she hadn't been tending to her patients she'd been answering phone calls, and had even gone down to the ER at one point, to help assess a seventeen-year-old girl who'd come in with a suspected ectopic pregnancy. Thankfully, it hadn't been. She'd not even been pregnant. It had turned out to be an appendicitis.

Then Natalie had gone back to OBGYN and straight into seeing yet another young labouring woman. The one she'd been with when Henry had brought her that drink.

Bless Henry! What a kind thing to do. Not many attendings would have done that for the midwives, and apparently he'd taken every one of them a drink—which was so considerate. He was a good man and she liked him very much.

She poured herself a coffee and went to take a sip. But when the scent of it hit her nose, she recoiled.

'Urgh! What *is* that?'

She swirled the drink around in the cup, staring at it, trying to work out why her coffee smelt so awful. The same thing had happened at work yesterday, when Henry had brought that coffee. But the coffee at home and the coffee at work were from two separate sources, so the only common factor here was her.

Maybe my tastebuds are changing?

She made some toast with strawberry jelly on it, and thankfully that tasted normal and good, so she ate it in full. She filled a reusable cup with iced water and headed off to work—but not before she picked up a couple of the books she'd read recently, intending to show them to Henry to see if he'd like them.

It was great that their working relationship was going so well after they'd spent the night together. It showed that they were being mature. That they were adults. She was proud of them both.

But it wasn't easy by any means. It was hard to look at Henry and not think about what he'd done to her that night. How his lips had felt against her skin. The caress of his hands. The weight of him on top of her. The feel of him inside her...

She almost purred just thinking about it...

When she got to work she sat down and listened to the handover of patients from the night shift. There were a lot of ladies in Postnatal now, and only a few labouring. Two in early labour, who were going to go back home and wait for more regular contractions, and two who were staying. Natalie was assigned Shruti Kaur, a first-time mother, thirty-nine weeks pregnant and six centimetres dilated.

She knocked on the door and went in to introduce herself. 'Hello, Shruti. My name's Natalie and I'm going to be looking after you for most of today. How are you doing?'

Shruti smiled. 'I'm doing all right. This is my husband, Kamal.'

She smiled at the man seated beside her bed, who looked at Natalie and raised a hand to say hi.

'Pleased to meet you both. I'm going to take a quick look at your notes and acquaint myself with your case, but if you need anything just ask, okay?'

'Thank you.'

Natalie sat down at the small desk in the room and opened up Shruti's folder to begin reading. The pregnancy had been conceived naturally, right before the couple had been due to begin IVF.

'You got pregnant all by yourselves?' she asked, smiling. They must have been so pleased!

'Yes. We were told I couldn't get pregnant without help as I've got scarred fallopian tubes from pelvic inflammatory disease.'

'Wow. How was that diagnosed? Through a laparoscopy?'

'Yes. They tried to remove the adhesions, but said there was substantial scarring as they were close to the ovaries.'

Removal of adhesions was usually more successful if they were closer to the uterus, rather than the ovaries.

'It says here you tried to get pregnant for four years before you decided on IVF?'

'That's right. We'd had our initial visit at the clinic, and we were all ready to start injections. They always do a pregnancy test, just in case, before they start that, and ours was positive.' Shruti reached out for her husband's hand and smiled.

'Well, that's amazing. I'm so happy for you.'

And she was. Truly.

It could be a real shock to hear that you might not be able to have children. After her own accident, she'd come around in the ICU to be told she'd suffered tremendous damage to her pelvic area. Her pelvis had broken in three places, her uterus had been torn and her fallopian tubes damaged. Surgery had also removed one ovary. The attending had sat on her bed and gently explained that the likelihood of her getting pregnant without help was extremely low.

'It would be a miracle,' he'd explained softly, as tears had run down her cheeks.

'But miracles can happen,' she'd argued.

He'd nodded, yes, but in his eyes she'd seen that he thought she was deluding herself. In that moment, she'd hated him. Hated all her doctors. Hated Wade!

Miracles can happen.

It was something she'd clung to, desperately at times, because more than anything she wanted to be a mother...

A sudden hot sweat bloomed all over her body, and she realised that she needed to eat something quickly or she was probably going to be sick.

'Would you just excuse me for a moment?' she said, forcing a smile before rushing from the room and hurrying into the staff room.

She needed her locker key, but she was all fingers and thumbs and dropped it on the floor before she could get it into the lock. Then the key got stuck, typically, and she had to slam at the locker door with her open palm before it would turn.

There was a cereal bar in there, with dried strawberry, cranberry, and white chocolate chips. Probably not the most healthy of snacks, but it would do.

Bam! The lock opened and she rifled through her bag to find it. She ripped it open and took a large bite, sighing as she chewed, feeling her stomach settle and wondering just what the hell was going on.

The coffee tasting odd...the pretzel...the tiredness... the nausea this morning... It was almost as if—

No. It's not. It can't be.

Pregnant. That was the word that had bloomed in her mind. But that was impossible. Because the doctors had said it would be a miracle. But...

Miracles can happen. That's what I said.

No. It couldn't be that. She thought back to her night with Henry. They'd used protection. There'd definitely been condoms.

And condoms are...what? Ninety-eight percent effective?

Ninety-eight! Which meant that out of hundred women who had sex, two would get pregnant using a condom. But surely that meant two people who were ultra-fertile, right? Not people like her, with damaged insides and only one ovary.

No, this had to be exhaustion, or stress, or...

Her mind went blank, only focusing on one thing. Well, there was an easy way to test her theory, wasn't there? But she didn't want to do it. Because she knew that if she did pee on a stick she would begin to hope that a miracle *had* happened, and when it turned negative—which it most definitely would—then she would only experience that crushing disappointment and loss all over again. And she didn't want to go through that.

No. I'm not going to do it. Whatever I'm feeling will pass. I'm sure it's exhaustion and dehydration and low blood sugar. That's all it can be. It will pass. I will not get my hopes up.

Besides, getting pregnant by Henry was not the way she wanted to start a family. He was a man who had only been after a one-night stand. He wouldn't be interested in her in any other way. He'd told her. And she'd told him the same. Her dream was to be married and in love before starting a family, and as she didn't feel able to trust any man right now, getting pregnant from a one-night stand was not how she was going to do things.

No. This isn't happening. I won't allow it to happen. I'm just tired.

'Oh, hey, Natalie! Glad I caught you. I've brought in a couple of books—'

She turned to look at Henry, tears in her eyes. He was always around. It was as if she couldn't go anywhere in this place without running into him. And she didn't want him to see her this way. Confused. Frightened. Feeling ill. Emotional.

And now she was having these stupid ideas about being pregnant just because she'd slept with him. It was ridiculous! She was overreacting. She had to remember she'd been through a lot lately. Not just with everything that had happened with Wade, but with moving away from her home and her family.

New jobs were stressful enough as it was. Learning new systems, having to remember everyone's names, learning new protocols, understanding the hierarchy and politics of a place. She didn't also need to have to avoid the hot attending she'd slept with! Who was being, oh, so mature and kind and considerate, bringing her drinks and books, making her wish for a second night, maybe a third. But she knew that she couldn't, and...

'Are you okay?'

The concern in his eyes was genuine.

She sniffed. Smiled. 'I'm fine! Honestly. Ignore me.'

There was a pause. A hesitation. A look of doubt in his eyes, and then, 'I could never do that.'

He stepped towards her, took her hand in his. A

simple gesture? An overture of friendliness? Or was it something more?

She looked at him. What did he mean? Her hand felt electrified by his touch and she didn't want to remove it.

'No?'

Her parents had used to ignore her quite easily. And Wade had taken her for granted. Dropping her the instant his secret was revealed and ignoring her calls from the hospital as she lay in bed, hooked up to drips and machines.

'No. Sit down with me. You look like you need a moment.'

He took her arm, gently guided her towards a couch, then sat down next to her. The concern in his eyes was so intense she almost didn't know how to deal with it.

In his other hand were a couple of books, which he set down on the low coffee table.

'For me?' she asked.

He smiled. 'I thought you might like them.'

She eyed the small pile, noting the authors and titles. They were definitely the kind of books she'd like. And he'd thought about her...brought them in for her. That was so thoughtful.

'You're a very kind man, aren't you, Henry Locke?'

'I try to be.'

'Of course you are. I mean, you save babies. How could a man who saves babies be anything but kind and lovely?'

He frowned, as if he wasn't sure how to answer her question.

'Sorry. As I said, ignore me. I'm feeling emotional.

You don't have to stay with me if you're busy. I'll be fine on my own.'

She looked at his profile. Studied his features intently, wondering what it might be like to have made a baby with this man. Silly idea, though. She was letting her mind run away with her. Her brain was stubbornly refusing to accept the truth of her situation. She would probably never get pregnant without help, so why was she allowing herself to imagine and hope?

'Do you want to talk about it?' he asked. 'About what's bothering you? I'm a good listener. I may not be able to help, but I'm a good listener.'

She smiled. 'You're sweet…but I have a patient waiting for me, and if I ever got started on all my issues we'd be here all year,' she tried to joke as she got to her feet. 'Thank you for the books. I look forward to reading them.'

She laid her hand on his shoulder as a gesture of thanks and then she walked away, heart thudding, telling herself that walking away was the best thing to do.

All too easily she allowed herself to fall for men who were nice to her. It was pathetic, really! Was she so starved of affection that she'd done this to herself? Wishing and hoping that maybe Henry was different from Wade?

In the doorway, she turned and looked back at him.

He was watching her still, concern etched deeply across his features.

He really does care. Doesn't he?

'Let's meet up later,' he said. 'When you've got a break.'

'Why?'

He smiled. 'No reason. We'll go for a walk. Shoot the breeze, as you Americans say.'

She nodded. Spending time with him always made her feel better. His simple gaze accelerated her pulse. His touch could make her feel so alive. The rest of the time she wondered if she simply walked around like a zombie.

But for now she had a patient waiting. 'I'll page you when I'm free.'

CHAPTER FOUR

HENRY SAT IN the staff room, looking down at the two paperbacks he'd brought in and wondering what Natalie's tears had been about.

Seeing her so upset had pained him, and he'd realised with a sudden shock that he couldn't bear it and wanted to make her feel better.

Henry walked over to her locker and placed the books down in front of it. He scribbled on a piece of paper:

I don't need these back.

He signed it with an H. For a moment, he briefly contemplated whether to add a kiss, but decided against it. Because other staff members might see it and start the gossip going, however innocently. And he didn't like to be talked about at work. Not like that, anyway. Not about his private life. That was why he'd never told anyone about Jenny.

Jenny had struggled with her emotions. He'd often found her crying. But whenever he'd tried to help she'd lashed out at him, or yelled, or told him to go away, leaving him feeling helpless. And hopeless. Feeling that everything was going wrong and there was nothing he could do to stop it.

Seeing Natalie cry had reopened that memory box, but instead of brushing him off she had welcomed his touch. Had been grateful for his offer of a listening ear. It had made him feel bold. That he could be there for her even if he couldn't have been there for his wife.

He couldn't bear to witness another woman falling apart. So he vowed, there and then, to help her as much as he could. Even if it was just to listen.

Maybe it would heal them both?

'Okay, Shruti, you need to push, okay?'

'I can't! I'm too tired!' Shruti cried.

Her husband, Kamal, pressed his forehead to his wife's and said something low in Hindi.

'You can. I believe in you,' said Natalie. 'Now's the time to dig deep and get this baby born.'

There were some late decels in the baby's heart rate with every contraction. Each time Shruti bore down the baby's heartrate dropped dramatically. If she wasn't able to push him out soon, then they'd have to go to the OR.

The attending, Dr Serena Chatwin, sat positioned between Shruti's legs, which were up in stirrups. She'd already got forceps placed and was helping Shruti with her pushing.

'One last big push and we can get the head out. We're going to do this together, you and I.'

Shruti nodded, face contorted in pain.

Natalie felt for her. She and Kamal had had such a long journey to getting the baby they had wanted for so long, and she knew that her patient must feel as if she was failing at the final hurdle. But Natalie knew her patient had the strength in her. Every woman did. She just had to believe that she could find it.

'Shruti? Remember all those dreams you had of having your own baby? All that trying? All the upset you went through. That's behind you now. Because right at this minute your precious, much-loved and much-wanted baby is right there, waiting to be born. It's up to you now. One big push and you'll be able to hold your baby in your arms and shower him or her with all the love you've been waiting to share. One big push is all you need. So when that next contraction comes, I want you to take the biggest breath you've taken all day and give it your all. Can you do that?'

Shruti listened and nodded, a look of grim determination settling upon her face. 'It's coming now.'

'Okay.' Natalie looked down at Serena and nodded.

Her patient sucked in a deep breath and pushed hard, and the baby's head finally got around that difficult corner and began to crown.

'Okay, little pushes…little pushes and pant!' ordered Serena.

Shruti breathed heavily in and out as Serena unlooped the umbilical cord from around the baby's neck. It was no wonder those decels had occurred. Every time the mom had pushed, the cord had tightened. But now the baby was free, and he slithered out almost on his own.

'It's a boy!' cried Kamal, cradling his wife's face as Serena laid the newborn baby boy on Shruti's stomach, before clamping the cord and cutting it.

'You did it! Well done!' cried Natalie, beaming with pride and staring down at the new life.

It was a life that this couple had been told would never be possible without help, and look at what they'd achieved. Medicine didn't always know the answers and there *were* miracles. And now this lovely couple had finally achieved their dream of becoming a family.

A dream that Natalie knew would never come true for her, because she didn't see how she'd be able to trust someone enough. Yes, still she wanted that romantic ideal of marriage and a family. But Wade had set her back with his lies and deceit. She'd believed him to be head over heels in love with her. How could she trust anyone else?

She helped dry off the baby, then positioned Shruti's precious son to begin breastfeeding after she'd run all the checks and measurements on him. Then she left the family to settle, before she moved them to a post-delivery room.

She met Henry in the hospital grounds, over by the memorial garden. It was a small, green area, laid with pathways, interspersed with bushes and flowers, and even a small goldfish pond protected by fencing.

'I…er…wanted to apologise. About earlier.'

'You have nothing to apologise for,' he said.

'I know… I just…' She blushed as she looked up into his face, staring into his eyes as he stared back at her, feeling so many feelings right now she wasn't sure how to react.

Henry might genuinely be the first man ever to see her for who she was. She had been intimate with him and he had seen her body, had not been appalled by its myriad of scars—had, in fact, been delighted by her body. Had brought her to the heights of ecstasies she had only dreamed of.

But he'd been more than that. Had done more for her than that.

He hadn't ignored her. Or taken her for granted.

'I'm not used to being *seen*...' she began, not sure how to explain her complex life and history to this man in one short moment, but knowing that she wanted to at least try. Her emotions were all over the place just lately. 'And I just feel that...that you *do* see me. And not because you want to use me, or take advantage of me, the way men have done to me in the past. You seem genuine, and kind, and I wanted to say that...' She looked once again into the beautiful blue of his eyes. 'That I see you, too. And so far... I like what I see. So, thank you. Again.'

She laughed nervously, wondering just what the hell she was doing, spilling out her feelings like this. Randomly, in the hospital garden. This was different from the flirting they'd been doing. This was serious stuff.

'I don't normally get emotional,' she went on. 'I was just feeling a bit weird and you caught me at a vulnerable moment. I didn't want you to think I was crazy!' Another laugh. Embarrassed. Nervous.

He was smiling at her. 'You're not crazy by any means.'

They came across a bench and Henry indicated that they should sit down. She felt nervous suddenly. She had no idea what was going on in her body and, yes, of course she could just be imagining the whole thing. But what if she *was* pregnant? And this man was the father? He'd been a fabulous one-night stand, and a great flirty friend, and an amazing colleague—but did that make him good father material? Or would he abandon her as Wade had done?

'Well, I appreciate you saying that.'

'Easy to say when it's true. I know our relationship didn't start off in the most conventional way, and that we've both…felt things…but I am here for you. If you're homesick, or whatever it is that's bothering you.'

He thought she was homesick. Okay. She could run with that for now. 'It has been bothering me. Being away from home, not having anyone to lean on.'

'You can lean on me,' he said.

And she could tell that he meant it.

'You're sweet,' she replied, and impulsively she leaned over and pressed a soft kiss to his cheek, before getting up and hurrying away, feeling his eyes upon her the whole time.

She headed to the cafeteria to grab some lunch. She felt as if she was fizzing after her chat with Henry… full of nervous energy. She breezed past most of the sandwiches, craving something with a bit of a kick, and selected some chilli and rice.

As she sat at the table the aroma made her mouth water, and the chilli itself, when she tasted it, was awesome! Not mild at all, but with quite a kick to it. She wolfed it down, sad when it was gone too soon, and wondering if the café assistants would think her a pig if she went back for a second helping?

She sat staring the food counters, tapping her foot rapidly against the floor…deciding. Deciding it didn't matter what the assistants thought. She got up to rejoin the queue, but as soon as she'd stood and begun to take a few steps realised that she'd begun to feel decidedly queasy.

Maybe I've eaten too fast?

She began to hiccup, with each lurch of her stomach making her feel worse, and knew she had to get to a bathroom. There was one just outside the cafeteria doors, and she raced into it and opened the nearest stall and threw up her lunch.

Afterwards, she felt marginally better.

Was the chilli off? Or was it too spicy? Or could this possibly be what I'm terrified of it being?

Pregnant. That was what she was scared of the most. And yet at the same time it was what she wanted most in the entire world, and that was why she was scared to admit it. To take a test and see.

Because if she was, then it wasn't the right time. This wasn't how she wanted to have a child. A child should be conceived in love, not from a one-night stand. Although, doing the job she did, she saw plenty of babies who'd originated that way.

Because if she was, then her whole world would turn upside down.

Because if she *wasn't*, then she would have allowed her hopes back in and that was a difficult box to close again.

At the sinks, she rinsed her mouth out with water and stared at her reflection. She looked tired. Exhausted, even. A bit green about the gills. She shook her head, telling herself she was being stupid even to consider that she might be pregnant with Henry's baby. But she knew she had to take a test to find out.

She felt bad about taking one of the tests from work. She felt she ought to buy her own from a pharmacy on the way home. But she knew she couldn't wait until then. She needed to know *now*. Needed to see that it was actually negative so she could forget all this mental turmoil about whether she was or not. And when she *wasn't* she'd know she had a bug, or something. She'd stay at home. Let it pass. Then return to work feeling better and brighter and move on with her life.

She and Henry were in a good place right now. As long as he didn't think she was a nutjob because one minute she'd been crying and the next smiling and kissing him on the cheek.

She sneaked into a bathroom on the delivery floor with her test and, taking a deep breath, peed on the stick. She placed it on the toilet cistern and turned her back on it.

I can't believe I'm feeling so scared!

She knew it would say negative. But a tiny part of her—the part that had been devastated when that doctor had sat on her bed and told her it was unlikely she'd ever have children naturally—wanted it to be positive. Because... Well, she didn't know why. To show the doctors that they were wrong? To have the child she'd always craved?

Because having a child with Henry would be...

She wanted to think it would be good.

But she was terrified, too. If it *was* positive, then her whole life would be on a new trajectory—and not in the most ideal circumstances. Her parents were very traditional in their views and believed in marriage before kids. Would they be angry with her? And what about Henry? He'd made it clear he wasn't interested in a relationship, even if he *had* said he would be there for her. That she could lean on him.

But he'd meant as a friend, right?

She checked her fob watch. A minute had gone by. Too early to look…

But she couldn't resist. So she leaned forward to grab it and closed her eyes, stood up straight and steadied her breathing. Until she felt ready to look.

And then she opened her eyes.

Two lines. Two very strong pink lines.

Pregnant!

Natalie gasped and sank to her knees, her back sliding down the stall door as she stared in shock at the test before her. She was pregnant with Henry's baby! Pregnant! With a baby naturally conceived, despite her injuries, despite using protection! How was that even possible?

Life finds a way.

Her mother had said that when she'd heard the news that Natalie probably wouldn't have a child of her own. She'd clutched the cross at her neck and told her that if it was meant to be then life would find a way.

At the time, she'd thought it was just her mother, clinging desperately to her religion and her belief in God, believing that somehow the Lord would one day provide her daughter with the family she so desperately wanted. That she was saying it just in reassurance, because she wasn't sure she believed it. But wanted to offer her hope.

And somehow her prayers had come true.

'I'm pregnant…' she whispered to herself out loud, needing to hear the words. To make it seem more real.

The temptation to do another test, just to make sure she hadn't had a false positive, was strong. But she knew she didn't dare take another test from the hospital stores. She would buy one on the way home.

But what was she supposed to do now?

All her symptoms added up, but was she supposed to just come out of the stall and return to work as normal, without saying a word to anyone? Her whole life had just changed in an instant! A major event had blown the wind from her sails and yet she was expected to behave normally.

What else am I meant to do?

Her 'glass half empty' nature told her she was still very much in the early, dangerous days of the first trimester, and with her internal injuries she had no idea if the pregnancy would remain viable anyway. She could miscarry. She could lose it. What was the point in telling people and going through all the upset and turmoil if that was going to happen anyway?

So…no. She'd keep it to herself. Especially from Henry. Henry seemed the kind of guy who would do the right thing. But how did she really know? And what would be the point in telling him if she was just going to lose it?

For now, she decided, she'd keep it to herself.

Three separate pregnancy tests had sat on the kitchen counter earlier that morning and all of them were positive. There was no mistaking it.

Natalie had simply stared at them for a while before heading into work, mind blown, utterly unable to comprehend the news, still feeling numb when she bumped into Henry as he arrived on his bike.

'Morning. You okay? You look like you've seen a ghost,' he joked.

She was going to be a mother. In a few months.

Unless the world did what it usually did and went all to hell.

'I didn't get much sleep last night, that's all.'

I'll need to get some folic acid.

The pregnancy probably wouldn't last anyway. First pregnancies often ended in miscarriage, but for the time she was pregnant she needed to do her absolute best in keeping healthy. Just in case.

Just in case I go full term.

'Did you see the news?'

She blinked. 'What news?'

'The lady on TV? Giving birth to her own grand-children? Fifty-seven years of age and being a surro-gate for her daughter. Now that's one hell of a surprise, huh?'

I've had my own surprise.

'Surprise pregnancies? Yeah.' She smiled weakly, waiting for him to finish locking up his bike.

For so long she'd been the midwife. And now, pos-sibly, she would be the patient. The aspiring mother-to-be on the bed. If she made it to full term, who would be her birth partner? Her mom? Henry? Who knew? The first would be extremely disapproving of her hav-ing a child out of wedlock, and the other... Well, she didn't know enough about the other, truth be told. But she felt he would offer to be there. He seemed gentle-manly. He seemed as if he would want to do the right thing. But...

I've been so wrong about men before and look what happened to me!

And if the pregnancy did last? Where would she live? The apartment she rented was a shoebox, the cheapest she could find. She couldn't raise a baby in that place.

'I couldn't imagine my mother carrying my baby, could you?'

'Your mother? No.'

But could you imagine me?

They were all gathered together for the morning handover from night shift. Henry stood at the back of the room and became acutely aware of Natalie's presence the second she entered, with only minutes to spare. He watched her edge her way through to a spare seat. Saw the way she tucked a stray curl back behind her ear. The way she smiled at someone who moved their legs to one side, so she could pass and sit down.

He thought of the kiss she'd given him yesterday. How her lips had felt against his cheek. How it had made him feel. How he had felt running into her this morning, hoping no one noticed how he looked at her. Hoping no one registered his growing feelings for Natalie upon his face. He was concerned, though. She looked pale. Tired. He glanced back, concerned for her, worrying, hoping that she wasn't ill, and let himself gaze at her in what he hoped was an unobtrusive way.

The handover began and he started scribbling notes on his notepad, as he always did when he received the updates for his patients. He didn't like to miss anything. He wanted to know if there'd been any changes overnight. Any test results that might have come in.

Dr Yang was speaking. '…and I've got a macrosomia case that's been transferred over from Queen's. Baby is already weighing in at about ten pounds. Could be a complicated delivery. So, I'll need a midwife. Any volunteers?'

Natalie raised her hand.

'Thank you, Nurse Webber. And I'd like you, Dr Locke, to assist me with that case.'

Henry nodded, glancing at Natalie, who'd turned to look at him. Now, what *was* that expression in her eyes? Concern? Was she worrying about how he'd be with her after yesterday's kiss? Even if it had been only on his cheek?

The case was interesting. Foetal macrosomia meant a baby that was considered much larger than average. It could be caused by gestational diabetes in the mother, or simply excessive weight gain, but the delivery could be complicated by uterine atony—where the womb didn't contract after birth, so there would be heavy postnatal bleeding.

At that moment Dr Yang's phone sounded and he glanced at it. 'Our case is here. Natalie? Henry? Shall we?'

Henry excused himself as he sidled past his colleagues, and then waited politely for Natalie to leave the room first, so he could follow.

Ahead of them, Dr Yang strode down the corridor, his step brisk, stopping only to check at the desk on which room his patient had been put in.

'Room Seventeen, people! Now, let's remember, Mom is scared. She's away from her home base and has no one to support her. Nurse Webber? I'd like you to try and make her feel as comfortable as you can—understood?'

Natalie nodded. 'Yes.'

'Okay. Let's go.'

Dr Yang opened the door to the room and strode in as if he owned the place. He was clearly the king of this department, and all the staff and patients were his subjects, whom he was honouring with his presence.

'Hello, Lakeisha, my name is Dr Yang, and these are my colleagues, Dr Locke and Nurse Webber. Now, we're all here to take care of you and get you through the next hour or so.' He smiled and turned to Henry. 'Can you present the case, please?' He passed over the notes.

Henry flipped open the file. 'Lakeisha Waring, twenty-four years of age, thirty-nine weeks and three days pregnant with her first child. Strep B negative. Normal first pregnancy otherwise, fundus measurements always measuring high, no excessive amniotic fluid reported, current weight estimate of just over ten pounds.'

He smiled at Lakeisha when he finished.

She gave a small clap. 'Marvellous, Doctor. You've done your bit—now let me do mine.' She stuck mouthpiece delivering the nitrous oxide to her lips and began to suck on it as her contraction built.

She was already attached to a CTG machine and Natalie stepped forward to check it. 'No visible decels. Baby is coping well, it seems.'

Dr Yang smiled like a proud father as he turned to talk to Henry. 'I'd like you and Natalie to stay with Lakeisha and monitor her until she gets to ten centimetres. Then call me immediately—understood?'

'Yes, sir.'

Yang waited until Lakeisha had finished her contraction. 'I'm going to leave you in my trusted colleagues' capable hands, but I'll be back for the big

finish, so you just relax and let us take care of everything, okay?'

And then he swept from the room.

Lakeisha looked at Henry and Natalie with surprise.
'Did that dude just tell me to *relax*? With a ten-pound
baby about to burst from my vajayjay?'

Natalie nodded, smiling. 'He did.'

'I'll give him *relax*.' Then she began to huff and
puff again, as another contraction began.

Natalie looked at Henry, hesitantly, holding out her
hand for the notes.

He passed them over. 'I ought to examine her,' he
said.

'Okay.'

'Could you do a basic set of obs? Get her BP and
temperature for me?'

'Sure.'

There was definitely something happening between
them, although he was completely unsure what. He
liked being in Natalie's company, and often found himself seeking her out. Looking for her.

He waited for Lakeisha's contraction to be over. 'I
need to examine you, if that's okay?'

'As long as you're gentler than the last lot. I felt like
a side of meat.'

'I'll try. But if things get uncomfortable you just let
me know and I'll stop, okay?'

'*Relax? Uncomfortable?* You guys sure don't know
how this feels.' Lakeisha turned to Natalie. 'Do you
think we'd tell guys to 'relax' if they had ten-pound
babies coming out of their wazoo?'

Natalie laughed as she wrapped a blood pressure
cuff around their patient's right arm. 'I hope so!'

'I don't think so. I think if guys had the babies they'd have found a different way, believe you me.' She grimaced as Henry began his examination.

'Sorry. Just a moment longer... Yep, you're about nine centimetres.' He removed his glove, discarding it in the clinical wastebin, then washed his hands. 'How are you feeling?'

'How do you expect?'

He smiled. 'You're in the best place. Anyone coming to hold your hand, or...?'

'No. The father made a run for it the second I got pregnant again.'

'What about your family, Lakeisha?' Natalie asked.

'They're at home. Covid.'

'Oh, I'm sorry. Well, I guess Henry and I will have to do.'

'Never thought I'd give birth with only strangers here.'

Natalie smiled. 'Well, we'll introduce ourselves a bit more, so we're friends, not strangers.' She turned to look at Henry, and he saw there was some colour back in her cheeks, mischief on her face. 'You go first. Tell Lakeisha all about yourself.'

Ah... He could see what she was doing. This wasn't about letting Lakeisha feel she wasn't with strangers— this was about Natalie trying to find out more about him. He smiled at her, but he never gave out too much personal detail at work. He always kept the details he did give trivial.

He turned to smile at Lakeisha. 'I'm Henry. Originally from Oxford, England. I have a brother called Hugh, who was over here recently, but he's gone back to the UK now. My father was in the marines and my mother was a nurse—which is where I get my love of medicine. I guess you could say I'm an introvert. I like music and books. Dog person, rather than cats, though I like both. I prefer dark chocolate to milk, strawberry milkshakes over vanilla, and my favourite ice cream is mint choc chip.'

He glanced at Natalie with a special smile, to show her that he'd cleverly evaded her probing.

Natalie narrowed her eyes at him, pursing her lips with amusement. 'I'm Natalie. I just came to New York after living my entire life in a small town in Montana.'

'Whereabouts?' asked Lakeisha. 'I've always wanted to go the country.'

'Near Scobey? Heard of it?'

Their patient shook her head and then began to suck again on the nitrous oxide.

'I don't like crowds or busy places,' Natalie went on. 'I miss the hills and the animals we had on our farm. I miss my family and my best friend, Gayle. I miss my dog. I like to dance when no one is watching. I sing in the shower because that's the only place my voice sounds great.' She laughed, placing a hand on her belly as if she was hungry. 'And my favourite ice cream is rocky road.'

'Okay, my turn.' Now that the contraction was over, Lakeisha seemed better able to talk. 'I'm Lakeisha. I'm about to have an amazing son. I fall for all the wrong guys and make terrible decisions. I love to eat dip and salsa and salted popcorn, which explains my waistline even when I'm not pregnant. I don't like sweet things at all and…' she breathed in '…and I think you're gonna need to pass me a bowl or something. Because I'm gonna puke!'

Natalie hurriedly passed a long blue bag that looked like a sock to Lakeisha, who groaned and held it close to her mouth, but didn't vomit.

'Why do I feel this way?'

'Could be transition,' suggested Henry.

'Oh. Delightful.' Lakeisha lay her head back against the pillow, still clutching the blue bag. 'I'll keep this, if you don't mind?'

'Be our guest.' Henry smiled and went to stand with Natalie. 'You have a dog?' he said.

She smiled at him. 'Back home, yes.'

'What breed is he?'

'He's just a mongrel. Nothing special.'

'All dogs are special.'

'You ever think of getting one yourself?'

'One day, maybe. But not now. It'd be wrong to work this many hours and leave it home alone, or in doggy daycare.'

'Perhaps one day when you settle down and have kids?' Natalie asked.

She was probing again. He could hear it in the tone of her voice. She was asking if he saw that in his future one day. He had to admit that for some reason he liked her asking these questions. He was enjoying the fact that she wanted to know more about him. It proved that they'd been more than just one crazy night.

'Maybe. One day.'

He'd never rule that option out. But he didn't see it happening for a long while.

His eyes fell upon the trace. It was still looking good, though there were early signs of the baby's heartbeat dipping with each contraction. Nothing too significant, but enough to make him think that maybe the baby was tiring of labour.

'How long have you been contracting?' he asked Lakeisha.

'Half a day.'

'Everything okay?' Natalie asked in a whisper beside him.

It was difficult having her this close. Close enough to touch. But he couldn't let it unsettle him. Despite the fact that just being near to her gave him the urge to reach out and touch her. It would be enough to just touch her arm. Her hand. Her cheek…

'Baby's tiring,' he said.

Lakeisha was beginning to tremble, her whole body shaking. 'What's happening?'

Henry stepped away from Natalie's proximity. 'Trembling like this is normal…don't worry. It's your body in transition.'

'F-f-fun,' she said, teeth chattering.

Natalie took her hand. 'You're going to be fine.'

'Tell that to my vajayjay.'

Henry smiled. 'I'm just going to have Dr Yang paged. I'll be back in a moment.'

Outside in the corridor, he felt as if he could breathe again. That moment, standing so close to Natalie and breathing in her scent, had been like torture. A terrible yet delicious and tempting torture. His senses had gone into overload, his body reacting to her and needing her desperately, like an addict craving a hit. Stepping away and trying to pretend that everything was normal had been agony.

'Page Dr Yang to Lakeisha Waring's room, please,' he asked Roxy, who was on the desk.

'Sure thing. Hey, you're in with Nat, right?'

He nodded. 'Yes?'

'Is she okay?'

'I think so. Why?'

'I don't know… I thought she looked a little tired today.'

'I think you're describing every hospital employee on this planet.'

Roxy laughed. 'Ain't that the truth?' she said as she picked up the phone to page Dr Yang.

Henry headed back to the room.

'She's feeling the urge to push.'

That was what Natalie greeted him with, the second he walked through the door.

'Great, I'll get ready.'

Henry checked his trolley, to make sure he had all the sterile packs and equipment he'd need, and got gowned up as Natalie began guiding Lakeisha through how to push. This was her first try at delivering vaginally.

Behind him, Dr Yang knocked and then entered the room. 'All systems go, I hear?'

'Yes, sir.'

Dr Yang stood for a moment and watched Lakeisha pushing to judge the quality of it. 'You're doing excellently, Ms Waring.'

Lakeisha gasped for air. 'I'm so glad you approve!'

Dr Yang examined the trace and then moved to stand next to Henry. 'Baby is getting tired,' he said in a low voice.

'I know.'

'I say we give her half an hour to try and do this

herself and after that we intervene—unless that trace
tells us otherwise.'

'Agreed.'

Dr Yang turned back to Lakeisha. 'Okay, with these
next contractions I really need you to push as hard as
you can.'

'What do you *think* I'm doing?' Lakeisha yelled.

'I think you're doing great, but I know you can do
better. This is a big boy, so it's going to take you some
enormous effort to push him out,' answered Dr Yang
in his normal, no-nonsense, let's-just-get-on-with-this
voice.

'Is he okay?'

'He's doing fine, but he's getting tired. It's showing on the trace.'

Lakeisha nodded silently and frowned, and Natalie
proffered her a small sip of water.

Dr Yang began to glove and gown up, standing behind Henry, who had seated himself between the stirrups and was checking baby's station and position.

'Okay, good… He's face down, just as we want him.
He's doing his part—now we need you to do yours.'

Lakeisha sucked in a breath and began to bear down,
grimacing with the effort of pushing hard. Clearly she
no longer had time to make jokes with them and meant
business.

Dr Yang looked on.

This was a large baby, but Henry really thought she
could do it. It was possible. The largest baby Henry
had ever seen born vaginally had been nearly eleven
pounds, and though there'd been a bad second-degree
tear, there'd been no awful complications.

But still he was alert, as he always was, ready to

leap into action if needed. And he knew they could act fast, if it was required.

They could see the top of the baby's head now, and it was thick with dark hair.

'You're doing well, Lakeisha! Baby's right there. Keep pushing hard.'

'I'm *trying*!'

Dr Yang went over to Natalie. 'I'll take over coaching. Can you get the NICU staff paged—stat? Just to be on the safe side?'

She nodded.

Dr Yang dampened a cloth and wiped Lakeisha's face. 'Okay, another breath and then bear right down into your bottom. One...two...three...'

Henry looked up from his place between the stirrups and with a look asked Dr Yang to check the trace.

He watched as he checked the peaks and troughs and saw that the baby was not coping with the delivery at all well now.

Dr Yang turned back to Henry and gave him another practised look that said, *We need to get this baby out—stat*.

'Okay, Ms Waring, your baby is getting tired and I think you need some help. I can use a ventouse, which is a suction cup placed on the baby's head that I can use to help pull him out as you push.'

'Do it!'

Henry placed the cup, but after a few tries it was clear it wasn't working.

'Okay, change of plan to forceps,' said Dr Yang. 'And I may need to make a small cut to help facilitate his birth.'

'I don't care—just get him out!'

Natalie returned to the room with the NICU team, who checked the prepped warmer and the oxygen and then stood behind Henry, ready to take the baby when he arrived.

Henry made the cut after injecting a dose of local anaesthetic, and then positioned the forceps around the baby's head. 'Next big push we need to get the head out, okay?'

'Okay.'

Lakeisha's face filled with a determination that was very familiar to Henry and to most OBGYNs. It was the look of a woman who had reached a wall and had decided that even if the wall might try to stop her she was going to power on through it anyway. Because her baby was at stake and Mother Bears would do anything to help their babies. She was tired, and she was hurting, and she was vulnerable and alone, but still she would find the strength somewhere—even if it took her own last breath to do so.

She sucked in a huge lungful of air, scrunched her face up tight and began to push, a growl straining from her throat and her teeth clenched, her face a mask of pain and exhaustion, yet also filled with determination and good old-fashioned gumption.

And it was working! Baby's head had come out.

Henry quickly discarded the forceps and used his hands to help manoeuvre the shoulders, and then baby was out. Big and floppy, and totally done in by the shock of the birth.

Henry swiftly handed the baby boy over to the NICU team, who surrounded him in an instant and got to work.

'Is he okay?' cried Lakeisha.

'They're working on him now,' Natalie said, taking her hand in hers and rubbing it.

But Henry could see her bleeding wouldn't stop. 'Dr Yang?'

Dr Yang tried to feel for the top of Lakeisha's fundus, to help massage the womb down, but it was as they'd feared. Her uterus was atonic and wouldn't shrink back after such a big baby, and neither was the placenta making an appearance. She'd already lost so much blood...

Henry looked up at Lakeisha. 'You've done a brilliant job in getting your son here, but your womb isn't contracting, so we need to get you to the OR.

'I'm not going until I know my son is okay.'

Natalie bent forward. 'I'll stay with him. I'll sit with him. He won't be alone. You have my word.'

'But...' Lakeisha looked from Natalie to Henry to the team of NICU staff, still gathered around her baby like bees around a flower. 'I need to know he's okay!'

Henry bit his lip. This was one of the hardest parts of his job. He needed to save this mother from bleeding out, but that wasn't her priority at this moment. She needed to know her baby was all right.

'Lakeisha? I understand you want to put your baby first—I get that. But if we don't get this bleeding stopped then you might be too sick to look after him. If you want to look after him, then you've also got to take care of yourself.'

Lakeisha looked at him, paling.

But luckily, at that moment, her baby let out a small cry.

Lakeisha sobbed, her hand suddenly covering her mouth. 'He's okay?'

'He was struggling to breathe, but we've got him,' said someone from the NICU team.

'All right, Doctor. Do what you have to do. You promise you'll stay with him?' Lakeisha asked Natalie.

'Every second until you're back from the OR,' she promised.

'Okay...'

'Okay, let's go!'

Henry and Dr Yang began to roll the bed from the room and rushed their patient straight through to the OR, leaving Natalie and the baby behind.

CHAPTER FIVE

LAKEISHA'S BABY HAD been stunned and exhausted by the birth process. It happened. And, although it happened frequently, it wasn't a situation that the staff took calmly. Their absolute focus was on those babies. Warming them. Drying them. Giving them oxygen. Trying to stimulate them into taking a breath.

Baby Waring did breathe on his own, but that minute in which he hadn't shown any response at all had been terrifying for all involved.

But now he'd begun to make respiratory effort and everyone breathed a sigh of relief. He lay wrapped in blankets, in Natalie's arms, awaiting the first cuddle with his mother.

Natalie stared down at the baby boy. He'd weighed ten pounds and three ounces, so he was more than a decent size for a newborn! And he was adorable. Thick black curls beneath his blue knitted hat. Chubby cheeks. A cute button nose. And dark, curious eyes.

She held him in her arms and she wondered…

Wondered about whether she would get through this pregnancy and hold her own child. Wondered about whether this pregnancy was going to be as problematic as all her other relationships. Wondered about Henry and what secrets he might be hiding. But, most of all, what would *her* baby look like?

She'd never allowed herself to think about it at all. Why put herself through such torture? Why waste hours dreaming about something she'd never thought she'd have. And yet now... Now there was a chance. And she could dream and she could hope and she could be scared. Because having her own baby was something she'd hoped for *so much*!

She was pregnant. She had all the symptoms. Even now the nausea was present, but was being kept in check by the bliss of sitting here, holding a baby in her arms.

What would it feel like to watch her belly grow?

What would it feel like to experience new life kicking and stretching inside her?

'You have a mom who loves you very much,' she whispered. 'And I'm going to be a mommy, too, but don't tell anyone because it's a secret.'

Natalie smiled, because she knew her secret was safe with him—but also because it was the first time she'd actually said it out loud somewhere other than in the safety of her own apartment.

She suddenly felt so happy. Despite everything. Despite the fact that this wasn't a perfect situation and she wasn't having a child the way she'd hoped to and there would be so much to sort out. Moving. Affording the baby. Taking time off work when it was born. How would she deal with childcare? There was a nursery here at the hospital, for staff members, but was there a waiting list? Did she have to enquire about it now? There was so much she didn't know.

And she couldn't help but think about Henry saying that one day he would get a dog. One day he would settle down and have a family. He did dream of it. At least he'd said so, anyway. But she was firmly still in the friend zone.

'Problems for another day,' she told the baby. 'But not today. Let's just get you reunited with your momma, huh?'

Natalie heard footsteps and looked up, seeing Henry dressed in scrubs coming towards her. It appeared that Henry was one of those lucky people who looked good in anything. Clothes. Scrubs. Naked…

She felt her cheeks bloom at the thought, and then a sudden bolt of lust hit her low in the gut. She began to tingle, feeling her body respond at the thought of him.

He pulled off his scrub cap and gave her a quick smile. 'How's the baby doing?'

'He's doing brilliantly after his slow start. How's Lakeisha?'

He grimaced. 'We couldn't stop the bleeding. We had to do an emergency hysterectomy.'

'Oh no! Poor Lakeisha.' She knew he'd be feeling really sad about that. No doctor liked to make that choice in surgery, but if they had no other option, then that was what they had to do.

But to hear that kind of news…she knew what it had felt like to be told she might not be able to have children and that had hurt like hell, but to know for sure? To know that your womb had been removed…

'I'd like you in there with me when we tell her. I feel we have a bond with her, and it will do her good to have familiar faces there.'

'Okay.' She stood up to put the baby back in his crib. 'Is she in Recovery?'

'Yes, she's awake, but a little groggy still.'

Natalie tucked baby Waring under his blankets and began to wheel him to Recovery with Henry by her side. She felt a little awkward. Knowing she was keeping this secret from him, fighting her physical craving for him. It was as if all her wiring inside had been mixed up by an amateur and parts of her were firing on all cylinders, when clearly it was inappropriate right now to be wanting to tear Henry's clothes off and take him like an animal in the linen cupboard, whispering her secret into his ear.

She risked a side-glance at him. 'I didn't know that your mother was a nurse.'

Henry nodded. 'Yes, she was.'

'What kind?' she persisted, knowing she could never walk in silence with him. She needed to talk to him. Needed to know what she could about him. To try and work out who he was. To discover his secrets.

'She was a scrub nurse.'

'Oh. I guess she had some tales to tell?'

A faint smile touched his lips. 'A few.'

Natalie stopped, shaking her head and smiling. 'You're really not going to give me anything, are you?'

Henry turned to look at her, clearly enjoying this game between them.

'I want to know about you,' she told him. 'Who you are. What makes you tick.'

'Why?'

He seemed amused, as if he was wanting her to say *Because I'm interested in you.*

'Because I want to know.' She stared at him then, lowering her voice. 'We were intimate. We shared one incredible night and…' She shrugged. 'I just feel like

I want to know you better. To understand you. Understand who I got involved with.'

He smiled at her. Did he seem glad that she felt that way? Even though they'd told themselves *not* to get involved? Not to pursue anything with each other.

Maybe he wanted to know more about her, too?

They stopped outside the recovery room's doors.

Henry stared at her so intently she almost wilted beneath his strong gaze. It was as if he was assessing her, deciding internally whether to say any more. She hoped he would give her something. *Anything!* Some iota of information that would help her understand him a little better and decide what kind of man he was.

'Would you like to meet me for a drink?' he asked. 'There's a favourite place I like to go to and I haven't shared it with you yet. Away from here. Just a coffee. Maybe a bite to eat?'

This was it. She knew it. The moment in which she could either decide to plough on alone or accept his invitation and allow herself to get in deeper with this man. The father of her baby.

I don't want to be alone.

'I'd like that.' She blushed as she said it, heat flooding her face as her stomach rolled with nerves.

He nodded. 'After work?'

'Sure.'

Henry pushed open the recovery bay doors and indicated where Lakeisha was. She looked tired and pale, but most of all relieved that it all seemed to be over.

She perked up at the sight of the crib and a broad smile crept across her face. 'Is that him?'

Natalie beamed. 'It is! All ten pounds and three ounces of him. Do you want to hold him?'

'You bet.'

'Let me prop you up a bit,' Henry suggested, pushing a button on the bed that elevated the back-rest, so that Lakeisha was in a sitting position.

Natalie scooped the baby into her arms, smiling all the time, because this was the best part of her job. Handing a healthy baby over to a healthy mama for the first time.

'Oh, my Lord! He's so precious! He looks like me!' Lakeisha gazed down adoringly at her son.

'Does he have a name?' Natalie asked.

'Kofi. It suits him, don't you think?' asked Lakeisha, examining her son's little fingers.

'It's perfect,' agreed Natalie.

But as she stood there she could feel her nausea coming back in a big way. She needed to get something to eat. One of the ginger cookies she'd brought with her in her bag. Maybe a drink of something tangy, like fresh orange juice.

Perhaps it wasn't the pregnancy sickness. Maybe it was nerves because of the big news they had to tell Lakeisha, about her emergency hysterectomy. That this baby would be the last she'd ever have.

'Lakeisha, you lost a lot of blood after delivery and, as you know, we had to take you into the OR,' Henry said gently.

Lakeisha nodded.

'We did all we could to stop the bleeding, but we were unsuccessful. So, to save you, we had to perform an emergency hysterectomy.'

Natalie watched their patient carefully. She herself knew what it was like to receive such massive news.

'Oh. I see.'

'I can talk you through the surgery, if you'd like? Answer any questions you may have.'

'I can't have any more children?' She looked down at Kofi.

'You won't be able to carry any more babies, no.'

Natalie couldn't bear it. Panicking, she glanced at Henry. 'Could you...er...excuse me a moment?'

And she quickly left Henry and Lakeisha behind as she hurried to the staff room and her locker, hating herself for leaving Henry so suddenly, in the lurch.

Hurriedly she wolfed down a ginger cookie or two, sighing with relief as they instantly settled her stomach. But her heart was with Lakeisha and what she'd just discovered, and she wanted to tell the world that sometimes miracles happened.

Her hand went to her belly.

Natalie had left so suddenly. One minute she'd been smiling at Lakeisha, gazing adoringly at baby Kofi, and then it was as if a shadow had crossed over her and she'd suddenly made her excuses and left.

It was most definitely odd, and when he found her moments later in the staff room he was really beginning to get concerned. 'You okay?'

'Fine.' She stared back. 'Just tired, you know?'

He felt it must be more than that. She'd seemed terribly upset at hearing they'd performed an emergency hysterectomy on Lakeisha. Almost like it was *personal* news. He thought back to their night together. To her scars. She'd had hip surgery, that was clear. But there'd been other marks. Laparoscopy scars. And a jagged silver line across her pelvis.

A car accident, she'd said. But what if it was more

than that? Could Natalie not have children? Was that what this was all about?

'If you don't want to go for that coffee later, we can postpone to another time.'

She looked up at him. 'No. I still want to go.' She managed a smile.

'You're sure? I don't want to push you into anything.'

'No. It'll be good to talk. Away from the hospital.'

He nodded. 'Okay. I'll pick you up later.'

The Central Park Café was situated on the northeast side of Central Park. It was small, intimate, yet busy, with servers busy attending tables, delivering trays of drinks and pastries, as well as a long queue at the counter that led out through the door, of people popping in to get takeout orders.

'We certainly got here at the right time,' Natalie said, as Henry pulled out a chair for her by the window so that she could sit down.

He smiled. 'It helps to book a table. I rang ahead, because I knew it would be busy. It always is.'

Natalie looked a lot better this evening. There was a bit more colour in her cheeks and her eyes were bright. It was incredibly strange, seeing her in casual clothes and not her CNM uniform. She wore an off-the-shoulder white top, that was slightly cropped, and black jeans with some boat shoes. A messenger bag was strapped across her chest.

She lifted it off and hung it from the back of her seat. 'Do you come here often?' she asked, before shaking her head and laughing. 'I can't believe I just asked that.'

He liked it. 'Actually, I do. I pass this place most

mornings when I cycle in, and if it's not too busy pop in for one of their breakfast sandwiches.'

A server welcomed them and handed them a menu. 'I'll come take your drink order in just a moment.' And then she disappeared to clear a table.

Natalie perused the menu with enthusiasm. 'I hope they've got something good. I'm starving!'

'Good. Pick anything. My treat.'

She smiled at him over the top of the menu. 'Well, aren't you kind? I'll have a decaf latte and their spiced scampi and peppered potato wedges.'

'Sounds great. I'll join you.'

They put their menus down, gave the server their order and then turned their attention to each other.

'So, how are you?' he asked.

'I'm good.'

'I'm glad to hear it. Lakeisha's case was difficult.'

Natalie glanced out of the window at a mother pushing her child along in a stroller. 'Some cases just get to me, that's all. I like Lakeisha. She's great. It's just that I know what a battle she's got ahead of her.'

'Her recovery, you mean?'

'More the mental and emotional side of things. That was big news you gave her today. I think sometimes we medics give patients news like that and then we walk away to deal with other things. And they're left there, reeling, with no one around to support them.'

'Is that something you've experienced yourself?' he asked softly, leaning in to reach for her hand upon the table. 'You know you can talk to me about *anything*, don't you?'

She smiled, blushing. 'Of course.'

She looked down at their hands and he wondered if he'd imposed on her.

'Were you…?' He paused briefly as the server arrived with their drinks, then when she was gone again looked Natalie in the eyes. 'Were you ever given big news like that?'

Natalie withdrew her hand and looked down and away, out of the window at Central Park. It looked so green and vibrant out there. People were sitting on the grassy areas. Others were on benches, reading books.

'Once upon a time I was, yes.'

'You don't have to talk about it if you don't want to. I just thought I'd let you know that…well, I'm here, if you ever want to.'

She looked at him then with such intensity, such a need to share, that he thought she just might unburden herself. She was considering him, weighing her options, he could tell, and so he sat there, trying to look as open and receptive as he could. He wanted her to share. He wanted to help. He wanted to listen.

He wanted to show her that he could be her friend.

And maybe more?

He'd never felt this way about a woman before, and that was strange. Jenny had outright refused to talk to him about anything, and he'd wondered if he just wasn't cut out for romantic entanglements. That maybe he was faulty in some way. But now Natalie had come along and she had made him wonder. Had made him want to know her deeply.

'There's something about you, Natalie.' He smiled, watching with wonder as the twinkle returned to her eyes at his compliment. 'I don't know what it is, but you make me want to…'

'Want to what?' she asked, taking a sip from her tall latte.

'Makes me want to be with you. All the time. I look for you in the hospital. I can't stop thinking about you. And when I'm with you...' He laughed, because he couldn't quite believe he was sharing these thoughts with her, but was completely unable to do anything to stop himself. 'You make me smile. You terrify me. You make me want to show you that I'm a good guy.'

'Wow,' she said. 'That's nice to hear. So you're a good guy?'

He nodded. 'I'd like to think that maybe I'm one of the best. I save babies' lives, remember?'

'That's right. You do.' She looked back at him, head tilted, a broad smile across her face. And then their food arrived, hot and steaming. 'You inspire me, too.'

'I do?'

That pleased him. He could feel his body's senses coming alive. He wanted to touch her again. Wanted not to have a table between them. To explore her the way he had on New Year's Eve. Though technically it had been New Year's Day. Very early in the morning!

'Of course. But...'

Ah, the dreaded 'but'.

'But we need to be careful. I think we both have a lot of baggage, and we need to pick through that carefully before we do anything rash.'

'What do you consider "rash"?' he asked, leaning across the table and speaking in a conspiratorial whisper.

He saw her gaze drop to his lips. Saw her take in a breath.

'Something we might both regret.'

* * *

They took a walk through Central Park. This time of the evening it was beautiful. Busy still, but it was nice to walk along its pathways and admire the trees as they passed the zoo, and stroll under the bridges, where a trombonist was playing a version of 'Greensleeves'.

They decided to sit down on one of the benches that lined most of the paths in the park, and sat opposite an elderly couple who were feeding some biscuit crumbs to a load of birds.

'My feet are killing me.' Natalie lifted up her right foot and rolled her ankle, before doing the same with the left one.

Henry sat down beside her, his arm draped across the back of the bench, behind her shoulders. He wasn't touching her, but she kind of liked the proprietorial nature of it.

'I guess we walk miles in our job,' she said.

'Here. Give me your feet.' Henry reached down and swung her legs around, so that he was a little further away. He now had her right foot in his hands and was removing her shoe.

'Oh, no, don't do that! My feet are probably all horrible and sweaty.' She tried to pull free.

'Your feet are lovely. Like the rest of you.'

She watched hesitantly, hardly daring to breathe, as his masterful hands expertly massaged her ankles and metacarpal bones…her toes, her lower calf muscles. She couldn't look at his face. Could only concentrate on his hands touching her, caressing her, easing out the aches and pains in her feet.

She fought the urge to groan with satisfaction as, slowly, she began to relax more and tried to enjoy it.

Henry seemed to know exactly what she wanted. Exactly what her feet needed. A perk of being looked after by a medic, who knew where all the knotty little problems might be.

A smile settled upon her face and finally she looked up at him, wondering whether to tell him about the baby. He seemed so wonderful. So kind. So caring.

But I thought the same about Wade and I was wrong. Why tell him if I might lose this baby anyway?

She was still in the first trimester. Still early on. Anything could happen. Why tell him and ruin his life if it all went to hell?

'Other foot.' He lifted her left foot, dropped her shoe and began his massage again.

'You're very brave. Massaging feet that you barely know.'

He grinned. 'I'm familiar with the rest of your body. Although I think I neglected these feet the first time around.'

It was a reference to their night together. She coloured as she remembered it too, and how it had felt to have his fingers and hands exploring other places on her body.

Had it suddenly become hotter? She wanted to fan herself...

'Do you ever imagine your future?' she asked suddenly. She needed to know exactly *what* he imagined, as if it would somehow give her a clue.

'Sometimes.'

'What's in it? Marriage? Family?'

He stopped to look at her. 'What do *you* imagine?'

She looked away at the old couple, now sitting holding hands. Content with being in each other's company. Not needing to speak.

'Finding true love. Someone I can trust. Someone I could have a family with. Nice house. A dog...' She smiled, remembering their previous conversation about pets. 'What about you?'

'That all sounds perfect to me.' He smiled at her and let go of her feet, after he'd slipped her shoes back on.

She'd kind of liked having her bare feet exposed to the air, and now the shoes felt alien. Compacting. Harsh.

'And are you looking for that special someone?' she asked. 'Because back when we met you were off the market. Has that changed?'

He raised an eyebrow, smiling at her. 'What are you offering?'

What *was* she offering? She'd love to tell him that technically, his family had begun. That she was already carrying his child. But she was scared. Doing so would launch them both into the unknown. Right now he was smiling at her, and she was happy being in his company, getting to know him better. Telling him would change all that. He'd back off. He'd want time to think. And during that time she'd be left in the lurch. Again. She was done with waiting for men to make up their minds about where they wanted to be. This new life was supposed to be about her taking charge.

'I'm thinking of lots of things I could offer right now. But I'd hate to scare you.'

'I'm not that easily scared.' He smiled.

CHAPTER SIX

NATALIE WAS FEELING terrified about her twelve-week scan. What would it show? Would she hear a heartbeat? Would everything be normal?

She'd already seen her primary care physician, who'd confirmed the pregnancy, and she'd had an early scan at eight weeks, due to her medical history. Everything had been fine then. The baby was a small, curled bean. With a beating heart. But that was all. And a lot could happen in four weeks.

She was slightly reassured by her continuing symptoms. She'd always told other prospective mothers that nausea was a good sign that the pregnancy was progressing normally, although she'd never truly understood just how *bad* that nausea could be.

But the most terrifying thing about the scan was that today would be the day that she would actually see her baby. No longer a grey bean, but a foetus that would be baby-shaped. Legs. Arms. Moving. A real person. She knew realistically that it was there, growing in her womb like a plant, but today would make it official that she was out of that first terrifying trimester. Once she *saw* that baby—its human shape, how it moved—and heard its heartbeat it would become real. And if she were to lose it after that... The heartbreak would be so much worse than she dared imagine.

She wanted this baby so much!

It was a miracle that it had survived this far. Somehow navigating its way past all her scar tissue and implanting anyway. And growing! Her body was definitely more curvaceous, and there was a tiny bump that she was managing to conceal by deliberately picking scrubs one size too large.

It had been difficult concealing the news of her pregnancy. There'd been so many times she'd wanted to tell people. Henry, obviously. And Roxy, who'd become a close friend to her since she'd started working there. Soon she would have to start telling people, and then the questions would begin from everyone.

Henry.

Her heart ached at the thought of him. How would he react? Part of her wanted him to smile and scoop her up in his arms, kiss her and tell her that everything would be fine. That he would look after her...that they would work this out. That he would be there for her and the baby and that, somehow, they would get to know each other better.

They'd been spending a lot of time together lately, out of the hospital, and each time he'd walked her home to her door and pressed a gentle kiss to her cheek, even though she craved so much more.

She had this dream that soon he would tell her everything, because he'd recognised that they were family now. That she would discover he truly was a good guy and didn't have any skeletons or ex-wives in his closet. Or current wives!

But she knew it wouldn't happen like that. Life never

turned out the way she hoped. She could hardly expect him to whoop for joy at the news that his one-night stand was pregnant, no matter how much he seemed to like her.

Imagine the gossip in the hospital. Everyone would know! And he was a man who liked to keep his private life private. She didn't imagine he'd be all that impressed.

I can't worry about all that right now. I just need to get through this scan and find out if my baby is okay.

It wasn't particularly cold out, but Natalie didn't want to be recognised going into the antenatal clinic. So she put her crazy curls under a hat and wore a face mask. She figured she'd sit in a corner and keep her head down by reading a book, or something. She'd be incognito.

It felt odd, not going straight to OBGYN But she managed to get inside the hospital without anyone recognising her, and she stood in the doorway of the antenatal clinic and scanned the room first, making sure there was no one there that she knew.

Convinced she was safe, she went over to the reception desk. 'Hi, I've got a scan at one o' clock?'

'Name?' asked a receptionist she'd never met before.

'Natalie Webber,' she said in a low voice, checking around her once more.

The receptionist smiled. 'Take a seat, Ms Webber, and you'll be called through soon.'

'Thanks.'

The clinic was busy. But she knew she was one of the first on the afternoon list, and she hadn't turned up until the last possible moment, so it wasn't as if she had to sit there and wait for all these other women to be seen first.

There was a corner seat free and she went and sat down in it, over by a small playpen filled with plastic balls for younger children. Pulling one of the books that Henry had lent her from her bag, she began to read.

She was the patient now, and that felt strange, bringing back dark thoughts of her previous time in hospital. The last time time she'd been a patient she'd had bad news delivered to her, and she hoped she wouldn't have any more now.

There were three scanning rooms. The door of the first one opened and a woman stood in the doorway, dressed in scrubs. 'Mrs Oliver?'

A woman who looked to be about five months along got up and entered the room.

Natalie looked back down at her book, but none of the words were going in.

'Miss Cortez?'

Natalie looked up again, her nerves increasing. And this time she noticed Henry, who'd come striding into Antenatal, carrying a thick folder which he passed to the lady at Reception.

Lifting her book, she held her breath. What was he doing here? He shouldn't be here! Not today of all days! She could have gone anywhere for her scan, but there'd been no appointments except at this clinic that fitted in with her shift times. She'd thought she'd be safe. Henry hardly ever came down to this department unless he was specifically called.

He was smiling and chatting easily to the lady behind the reception desk, and Natalie could see the way the young receptionist was looking up at him.

All smiles and head to one side with a tinkly laugh. Clearly flirting with him!

'Ms Webber?' called a voice.

Oh, no.

She saw Henry frown and turn to look at the roomful of women to see who would stand up. He'd clearly recognised the name.

What to do? Pretend I'm not here? No. I can't do that! I need to know my baby is all right. I have to go in there!

With trembling legs, Natalie got to her feet and tried to hurry through to the room without looking directly at Henry.

And she almost made it, too.

'Natalie?'

She stopped, heart in her mouth, stomach in knots, before turning to look at him and meeting his gaze over her mask. She pulled it beneath her chin. Gave a rueful smile.

'What are you...?'

And then realisation dawned in his eyes as guilt flooded her face, and he stood there, hands on his hips, looking down at the ground, before walking over to her and pulling her to one side.

'Are you pregnant?' he whispered urgently.

'Maybe...'

He stared at her, his face a blizzard of emotions. Anger. Shock. Surprise. Upset. Fear. Disbelief. She saw them all hit his eyes, and much, much more.

'I need to go in, Henry. They're waiting.'

'Then I'm coming in with you!'

'What? No!'

'Is this not my baby?'

She stared at him hard and swallowed, her mouth having gone incredibly dry with nerves, as she debated all the possible lies she could tell. But she knew she wouldn't say any of them, because she'd hated it when someone had told lies to her. It had ruined her world and her life.

She knew Henry had to be wondering. Wondering why she'd never mentioned her pregnancy to him in the last few weeks. Or even last night, when they'd gone to see that movie and she'd fallen asleep halfway through. He'd nudged her awake at the end and she'd made excuses about not having slept very well the night before.

'It is.'

It was as if she'd hit him with a fist the size of a house. At one point she thought he might need to sit down, he went so pale.

'Then I'm coming in. And you and I are going to talk.'

He pushed past her to enter the room where the sonographer waited.

Natalie smiled a quick greeting to the woman, who said hello, before removing her now useless mask and hat, freeing her curls, and lying down on the bed.

Henry sat on the chair beside her.

'Dr Locke! Are you Dad?' asked the sonographer with a big smile, unaware that he'd only just learned this news himself.

'I am,' he said, somewhat shakily.

Natalie glanced at him, then turned back to answer the sonographer's questions. She would deal with Henry's anger and shock later. What mattered right now was the baby.

Marissa, the sonographer, ran Natalie through a few

questions. How far along was she? What was the date of her last period? What symptoms had she been experiencing? Was there any pertinent medical history she ought to know about?

'Erm…yes. I was involved in a car accident some time ago.'

'What injuries did you sustain?'

Natalie glanced at Henry, knowing that he would be hearing this for the first time. 'I broke my pelvis. My uterus was ruptured and I lost an ovary. I was told I'd probably never have children.'

'Ah, yes, I see that now. You had an earlier scan four weeks ago?'

Natalie guiltily glanced at Henry, feeling her cheeks fill with heat. 'Yes.'

'And was this a natural conception?'

'Yes.'

'Okay. Well, we'll take a look and see what we can see. The last scan was normal, and your baby was measuring at eight weeks exactly. You've been referred to Dr Yang, our specialist OBGYN, to monitor the pregnancy, considering your previous injuries?'

'Yes…' Natalie didn't want to look and see what Henry felt about these revelations. She figured he'd still be in shock about the pregnancy, never mind anything else.

'So, if you can just loosen your trousers, I'll put on some gel and get going. It can feel rather cold, okay?'

'That's fine.'

'Have you drunk plenty? Do you have a full bladder?'

'Yes.'

Self-consciously, Natalie unbuttoned her trousers,

pulled down the zipper and exposed her lower abdomen to the room.

Marissa tucked some paper towel into the top of Natalie's panties to protect her clothes from the gel.

'You've already got a little bump. Look at that!'

And then she pressed the transducer against Natalie's belly.

CHAPTER SEVEN

HENRY DIDN'T KNOW what to feel—apart from completely blindsided. He'd never suspected this. Not *this*.

Pregnant

Natalie was pregnant with his baby. And she'd known about it for some time!

A rush of emotions was threatening to overwhelm him.

When he'd found out Jenny was pregnant it had been entirely different. She'd been in her small studio, painting. He'd used to love it in there. The smell of the paints, the multi-coloured paint splatters everywhere, covering every surface... Pots and jars of brushes, canvases on the walls and stacked on the floor... Her most recent commissions wrapped and ready to be shipped to their new homes.

Jenny's style could only be described as vibrant. She loved colour and used splashes of it to emphasise a figure. Nature and animals were her forte. So, for example, if she was painting an elephant the animal itself would be grey, and painted in detail, yet behind the elephant would be an expressive multitude of colours. Pinks, reds, greens, oranges, blues, yellows...

Her work had become more popular after one small

piece had been bought by a minor celebrity, who had shared the work online, and suddenly Jenny's website and email inbox had become much busier with requests.

Usually whenever he'd gone in to see her working she'd been frantically at it, brush clamped between her teeth as she concentrated on some tiny detail like an eye. So that day, when he'd gone into her studio and seen her just standing there, staring at a canvas, without her usual frantic movements, he'd smiled and asked her if everything was all right.

'Uh-huh,' she'd said, still staring at the canvas he couldn't see.

'Are you stuck?'

He'd gone to stand by her, turned to look at the canvas. His eyes had opened in surprise. Because she'd not painted a rhino, or a raccoon, or a giraffe, but instead a baby, curled up tight inside a womb.

Puzzled, he'd asked her, 'Is that a new commission?'

'No,' she'd said, turning to face him. 'It's ours.'

Henry had frowned. Theirs? It wasn't typical of her usual work, and he'd had no idea where they would put it, but...

'It's nice. It's different...'

'No, Henry!' Jenny had reached for his hand then, placed it against her belly and said again, 'It's *ours*.'

It had taken a second or two for him to realise what she was actually telling him. But when it had sunk in he'd been so happy! Whirling her around the room, whooping and yelling with happiness, not caring one iota that he was probably getting paint all over his suit.

'We're having a baby!'

He'd been so happy. *They'd* been so happy. Unaware

of the tragedy that was awaiting them. And now it could happen all over again. He could lose everything.

It was as if he could barely breathe. He was afraid to inhale too deeply, in case he somehow unbalanced what was happening and caused everything to crash. These next moments were fragile. What he was about to see could ruin him all over again, and he wasn't sure he was strong enough to survive another disaster of the heart.

He'd done a double-take out in Reception. He'd brought down a file that they'd received from a primary care physician, ready for a patient they were hoping to scan later that day, and though his brain had registered the name 'Ms Webber' being called, he hadn't for one moment thought it would be Natalie.

He'd seen movement, glanced up just to check that it wasn't by some crazy coincidence *her*, and he'd seen the curls, tucked inside a hat. He had recognised her in an instant, even though she'd been trying to hide behind a face mask, and in that moment, when her eyes had locked with his, his brain had simply been unable to compute why she was there.

Because it had to be a mistake, right?

Some cosmic joke?

He'd know if she was pregnant. They'd spent so much time together lately. He'd even seen her last night! She would have said something, surely? Though, to be fair, she had been asleep for most of it...

Oh. Now it all makes sense!

The weird symptoms that she'd passed off as exhaustion from work. Looking pale. Sneaking snacks. The tears that seemingly flowed so easily every time she helped a mother give birth. Before, she'd smile and look happy for them, but…

But, no. It was real. And she'd stood there in front of him, like a remorseful child in front of a headmaster, and told him that, yes, she was pregnant—with his baby.

And now he sat in an ultrasound room as a father. *Again.*

He still couldn't wrap his head around that word. Because the last time he'd hoped to be a father it had all gone terribly wrong. Who was to say that it would go right this time? Especially since Natalie had just revealed the exact nature of the injuries from her accident…

He decided to concentrate on the face of Marissa, the sonographer. She had the screen turned away from them, as was the usual practice, until she could turn it to show the happy parents that everything was all right. He stared intently at her face. Waiting for the inevitable frown. Waiting for the solemn information that this pregnancy wasn't viable.

'Any history of multiples in either family?' Marissa asked suddenly.

Multiples?

'No. Not in mine,' said Henry, shocked.

'My cousin has twins,' said Natalie.

Marissa smiled. 'Well, they didn't pick up on it in the first scan, but…so do you.'

She turned the screen and there, exactly as she'd just told them, were two babies. One behind the other.

'Separate sacs, so non-identical. That's carried down from the mom, so you probably released two eggs from that remaining ovary.'

Two babies.

Two eggs.

Non-identical twins.

Twins.

Henry wasn't sure if he was even breathing. He stared at the screen in absolute shock, then turned to look at Natalie and saw that she looked just as shocked as he!

'That's why I've got a bump already? That's why I've been so sick?'

Of course! Henry recalled now the multitude of times over the last few weeks when Natalie had hurriedly excused herself from a room. He'd thought on occasion that maybe she was running away from him. He'd been beginning to get a complex about it! Especially when at other times they'd seemed to be getting on so well.

It had been morning sickness?

How did I not realise? I'm a bloody OBGYN, for crying out loud!

With hindsight, it was obvious.

But...twins. Twins!

'Are they...all right?' Henry managed to ask, even though he could see quite clearly from his spot by the bed that they looked good to him.

'Looking good!' said Marissa perkily. 'I'll just get some measurements, and then we can listen to the heartbeats, if you'd like?'

Henry looked down at Natalie. Saw her lying there, vulnerable...afraid. He realised all she had been through these last few weeks. Why hadn't she told him? Why had she kept this news to herself? Because of the accident she'd mentioned? Maybe she'd thought she'd never make it to today? Maybe she was just as stunned as he to see that this pregnancy was viable?

He watched as Marissa checked the Nuchal folds, femur lengths and amniotic sacs. 'They're measuring a good size. Twelve weeks and two days for Baby A and twelve weeks and three days for Baby B.'

Baby A. Baby B.

Henry had used those terms many times before with his patients, but he'd never understood before the sheer impact of those words. He wasn't just going to be a father to one child, but to *two*.

Suddenly the small room was filled with the sound of first one heartbeat then another. Fast. Like runaway trains. It choked him up a little. He could feel a lump in his throat and was glad that at this moment he wasn't expected to speak. Because right now he doubted he'd be able to say anything.

He stared at the babies on the screen.

They were his.

He was going to be a father.

Natalie was glad to be lying down. *Twins!*

'I never suspected... Even for a moment... I've barely been able to hold on to the thought of one baby, never mind two.'

And Henry had discovered it with her.

'How was this missed before?' she asked.

'I can't say,' said Marissa. 'Maybe one of the babies was much smaller at the time. Baby B is still positioned right behind Baby A.'

This was a pivotal moment. She had nothing to hide from him anymore. It had become difficult these last few weeks, coping with the morning sickness that seemed to last all day, lying to her friends and telling them that she was all right, even though she knew they'd noted how many times she'd come into work looking off-colour. Blaming it all on tiredness.

Now she could tell them all. Because Henry knew.

It was a huge stress off her shoulders.

Having to keep a secret was the worst thing in the world!

No, this wasn't how she'd expected Henry to find out, but he had, and it was done, and quite frankly she could already feel some of the weight being lifted.

All she had to do now was get these two babies safely through six more months.

No. Five more months. Twins come early.

Less than half a year to get her life sorted. To find a new apartment. To buy all that they'd need. How was she going to do that? One baby was expensive enough...

Marissa gave them a few copies of the ultrasound pictures and Natalie sat up and wiped the gel from her belly with blue paper towel.

'I'm going to check you've got a follow-up appointment soon with Dr Yang,' Marissa told her.

Natalie nodded. 'Well, we work with him. I'm sure we can chat to him about it.'

'Of course. He's a specialist in multiples and, considering your history, I think you've picked a most excellent doctor to see you through this.'

They both thanked her and left the room, going back out into the bright lights of the antenatal clinic's reception area.

Natalie carried her coat and her mask in her hands

as they went out into the main hospital corridor. She turned to face Henry and smiled nervously. 'Surprise...'

Henry still looked in shock, but he gave a brief laugh. 'It certainly is. How are you feeling?'

'Nauseated, and... I don't know. I wasn't expecting twins. I wasn't expecting to see anything really, with my history.'

'About that... Can you tell me what happened?'

Natalie glanced at her watch. She had thirty minutes before the start of her shift. 'Aren't you working?'

'I have time for this.'

She nodded and took him over to a couple of chairs in the corridor, where they sat down.

'I knew this guy. Wade was his name. And... I thought we were in love. Well, I was in love with him. Utterly. We seemed such a great match. He was handsome and charming. He made me laugh. Most weekends we'd go out for a drive somewhere...see the sights. This one time we were driving, and somehow Wade lost control of the car. The sun got in his eyes, or something, and the next thing I knew we were careering into the next lane. We hit a truck and the car flipped. Witnesses say we rolled three times and came to land on the roof. I was knocked out, thankfully, so I didn't experience any pain until afterwards. I was rushed to hospital with three fractures of my pelvis...damage to my fallopian tubes and my womb. They removed an ovary, but managed to save my uterus. I was told the likelihood of my getting pregnant without assistance would be a miracle. Guess they were wrong about that!' She gave a bitter laugh.

'And Wade? What happened to him?' asked Henry.

Natalie shook her head and grimaced. 'His *wife* arrived.'

She watched as Henry took this in.

He looked down at the ground. 'I'm sorry.'

'I couldn't believe it. I kept waiting for him to come to my bedside. To apologise. To say that they were splitting up, or something. I kept texting him. Asking him to come and see me. Only he didn't. But *she* did. Her name was Bea. She stood at the end of my bed and told me she was sorry I'd been hurt, but she'd been hurt more, and that Wade was a serial adulterer. She said that if I still wanted him I could have him, as she was walking away.'

Natalie shook her head.

'I'd just been told I wouldn't ever get pregnant without a lot of medical help. I felt I'd lost my ability to have children. I hoped that I wouldn't lose him too, at first. It all seemed too much. But then I got angry as more and more time passed. Obviously I didn't take her up on her offer. He had kids. Two boys. Six and nine years of age. How didn't I know? How didn't I see?'

'The same way I didn't know that you were pregnant. Why didn't you tell me? You must have known for weeks!'

Natalie looked down at the ground. 'I'm sorry. I just...' She ran out of words and shrugged.

'You and I have got a lot to sort out.'

'I guess we do.'

'I'll speak to Dr Yang. Go over your medical files—if you'll allow me to?'

'Okay.'

'And we'll take the rest of this one day at a time?'

She nodded. 'I guess.'

They stood looking at one another awkwardly.

'Henry?'

'Yes?'

'I need you to be honest with me. I can't be lied to again. It's too much. So, tell me this, at least. I know I've been to your apartment, and it didn't look like you had someone living with you, but... Are you married? Do you have a wife or a girlfriend I need to worry about?'

He stared intently into her eyes. 'No. I used to be married, at home in England, but we got divorced. That's all over now.'

She stared back at him, seeing the truth in his eyes. Believing him. 'Okay. All right. Then one day at a time it is.'

'One day at a time.'

He took her hand in his and gave it a reassuring squeeze.

Finding an empty delivery room, Henry closed the door behind him and walked over to the window, rubbing his hands through his hair, unable to actually believe what just happened.

The day had begun so innocently. So *normally*.

Now this. A father. To twins.

What if the same thing that had happened to Jenny happened to Natalie? After hearing her story about Wade—how she was lied to, deceived—he knew Natalie deserved to know the truth about his and Jenny's baby. But how could he have told her in that moment, when all she'd needed from him was reassurance that he wasn't about to bolt and leave her behind.

He couldn't have told her then. It had not been the time to stress her out unnecessarily. But he would have to find the time to do so soon.

She has to know.

But what would be the best way to let her know?

I could invite her round for dinner. We need to talk more anyway. Get to know each other properly if we're going to be parents.

If.

It could all go wrong. His track record in these matters didn't bode well. Nothing had worked out for him so far—why should he expect this pregnancy to be any different? Even though they'd found no specific reason for the stillbirth of his last child, they were up against so many unknowns with Natalie's internal injuries.

Oh, God, I'm going to lose them, too!

The thought of Natalie going through what Jenny had…

Henry sagged as he stood by the window, feeling all his fight go out of him at that moment. He'd put on a front just now. Pretended to be strong for Natalie. But he was terrified.

Turning, he left the room, going to look for her, finding her about to go into a patient's room.

'Natalie?'

He saw her turn, see him, smile. 'Hey.'

'Look, I've been thinking… We've both got a lot to unpack over the next few months and…um… I think it would be a good idea for us to sit down over dinner. At my place. Discuss a few things.'

'Oh…um…sure. That sounds good, I guess…'

He smiled. 'Great. Can you do tonight? Tomorrow? The weekend?'

She laughed. 'Tonight's fine. Say, eight o'clock?'

'Perfect. What kind of things do you like to eat at the moment?'

'Anything tangy.'

'Sweet and sour chicken?'

She nodded. 'Sounds good,' she said again.

'Okay. I'll see you this evening, then.'

'You will.'

She smiled at him, making her eyes gleam, before she entered the patient's room.

Henry stood there for a moment, quite unable to believe that he was actually inviting a woman to his place for a meal. It had been a long, long time since he'd invited someone to dinner. The last woman he'd brought back to his New York apartment—in fact the only woman—had been Natalie.

And now he was inviting her again.

Because they were going to become a family.

If everything worked out right, that dream he'd always had could be about to come true.

How was he supposed to feel about that?

He had vowed to stay single, and now here he was, going to be a father to twins, inviting the mother of his children for a meal.

Boy, how the tables could turn!

Natalie peered up at the building in front of her. She'd been here once before. On New Year's Eve. Or rather, New Year's Day. In the early hours. Stumbling into the elevator. Unable to take her hands off Henry, her lips pressed to his as they struggled with clothes, desperate to get inside his place and consummate their lust for each other.

If they'd known ahead of time the results of that night, would they still have done it?

She stepped through the revolving doors and across the lobby. She didn't recognise it. But why should she? That night she'd only had eyes for Henry, and if there'd been a trio of dancing pink elephants in the lobby she probably wouldn't have noticed.

It was very stylish. Black marbled floor with hints of white and gold. A welcome desk behind which stood a suited building manager, who smiled at her approach.

'May I help you, madam?'

'I've come to see Dr Locke on Floor Ten.'

'You have his apartment number?'

'I do.' She smiled, feeling her stomach bubble with nerves as she headed towards the elevator and pressed the button.

She was still reeling from the news today. The severity of her nausea was now explained, by the news that she was carrying more than one baby! And what had once seemed like a simple new life in the big city had changed in an instant into something wholly more complicated and involved.

She'd vowed to remain single as she began this New Year, and yet here she was, into March now, pregnant with twins and about to have dinner with the father of her children.

How crazy was that?

She'd called her family. Told them. Of course they'd been full of questions! Her mom had wanted to see her. Asked if she could visit. But she'd got no room to put her mother up, so she'd promised to fly home for a weekend visit soon.

The elevator doors pinged open and she stepped

aside as a woman pushing a stroller with a screaming toddler in it whooshed past.

Natalie watched her go…watched her struggle to answer her cell phone as her child protested and tried to climb out of the stroller, face all red with tears, and wondered if that was her future.

Nervous about what awaited them both, she stepped into the elevator and pressed the button for the tenth floor. She felt her stomach drop as the elevator raced upwards, and before she knew it she was on the tenth floor and walking towards Henry's apartment. There was the ghost of a memory here. Her laughing, feeling Henry's lips against her neck as he vainly searched his pocket for his keys. She'd tried to help him, hands wandering, finding an entirely more interesting bulge in his pants and focusing her attention on that instead.

Natalie felt her cheeks blush with heat, unable to believe that she'd been so brazen with him. But hadn't she been throwing caution to the wind, truly believing that it was just for one night only? That if she *acted* confident she'd *be* confident?

She raised her hand and knocked on his door. Clearing her throat and trying to look normal. She'd spent an age deciding what to wear. They'd been out together so many times already, but this seemed more official.

She heard him slide off the keychain and then the door opened and there he stood, dressed casually in dark jeans and a black tee, revealing the muscles in his arms and his narrow, flat waist. Natalie tried hard not to think too much about what lay beneath those clothes.

'Hi.' She smiled.

'Hey, come on in.'

He stepped forward to kiss her on the cheek. She

closed her eyes. Paused. Revelled in the sensation of
his lips once again on her skin. It was sending her pulse
rate rocketing, and her temperature had soared by what
felt like five degrees. Would she ever get used to it?

Natalie stepped past him and into the apartment,
her eyes widening slightly as a rush of memories returned. Searching for her panties. Her bra. Finding the
heels that she'd kicked off haphazardly in this very
hall. Grabbing her bag and trying to be as quiet as she
could as she unlocked his door and snuck away whilst
he was in the shower.

Now she could focus on the things that had only
been in the periphery of her attention that night. The
framed paintings on the walls. A tiger set against a
splash of bright colours…a hissing snake about to at-
tack, framed by explosions of green and orange.

'Interesting art.'

Henry smiled and nodded. 'I…er…know the artist.'

'Oh?' Natalie peered closer at the painting of the
snake, tried to decipher the author's signature. It looked
like *J Locke*…

'My wife painted them.'

She turned to stare at him, wondering what kind of
man kept his ex-wife's paintings on the wall? A man
who still had a thing for her? Who hoped to re-estab-
lish their relationship?

Henry must have seen the questions in her eyes.
The doubt. The fear.

'Don't worry. It's totally over. I just happen to really like these two. I had about twenty, and sold most
of them, but these I bought from her before we even
got married, so…'

She shook her head. 'You don't have to explain yourself to me.'

'I do, though. We're going to be parents. Hopefully.'

He smiled and led the way to his living room. A large open space that was very masculine. Lots of dark furniture. Black couches. Black cushions. White walls. Lots of green plants, either on the walls or trailing from pots up on high. There was a huge television in the centre of the room. A piano beside it. And a gaming system.

'You like to play?'

'On occasion. Can I get you a drink?'

'Do you have orange juice?'

He nodded. 'Fresh, with pulp.'

'Sounds perfect, thank you.'

He nodded and indicated a couch. 'Take a seat. I'll be back in a moment.'

Natalie slowly lowered herself onto the couch and made a soft sound at finding how wonderfully comfortable it was. She settled back, adjusting a cushion behind her, just as Henry came back with a tall glass of fresh orange juice that he sat on a coaster on the black glass coffee table in front of her. He sat opposite with his own glass.

'Hope you're hungry?' he said.

'I'm always hungry. Anything to stave off the nausea.'

'I'm sorry you've been suffering.'

'It's certainly been difficult hiding it.'

Henry looked awkward for a moment. Then curious. 'Can I ask why you didn't tell me?'

She looked up at him as she took a sip of her juice. Right to the meat of the conversation already?

'Good question.' She sighed. 'I was scared. Plain and simple. Shocked to even be pregnant in the first place. And then, because of my situation, my history, I just assumed I wouldn't make it through the first trimester. I didn't see any point in disrupting your life until I had something definite to tell you.'

'Like today?'

She nodded. 'Like today. I needed to see that scan. I thought if they told me that everything was going okay, then I would find a way to tell you. I promise.'

'You would have told me?'

'Yes. Even though I know it's not something you wanted or planned after a one-night stand. I figured you were a guy who'd want to start his family from within marriage. Out of love.'

'We don't always get what we want. Often we get what we need…'

'If I hurt you, that wasn't my intention. I was trying, in my own faulty way, to protect you from pain.'

He pondered her words solemnly, then nodded.

'I've had some time to get used to this idea and I do want them. I want them very much. These babies.' She laughed. 'Still seems strange to say that. *Babies*. Plural.'

Henry agreed. 'You're right. It sounds crazy. Unreal. If you'd have told me I don't think I would have believed it, so I'm glad I was at the scan.'

'You must have done a double-take when you realised they were calling for me.'

'I'll say.'

Natalie laughed. 'I'm sorry, Henry. That you discovered it in that way. I would have wanted to tell you in a nicer way. Maybe sat you down for a coffee in the hospital cafeteria…broken the news…surreptitiously slipped the scan pictures across the table to you…'

He smiled. 'Life likes to play with people, that's for sure.'

She thought back to the crash. To seeing Wade's wife walk into her room. 'It does.'

They were both silent for a minute, and then Henry got to his feet. 'I'd better start cooking. You must be starving, and it's been a big day for both of us.'

'Can I help you?' she asked.

'If you'd like.'

She followed him into the kitchen. Saw that it was an extension of the living area. All sleek black surfaces. The only colour in the kitchen came from the large bowl of fruit on the centre island.

'Here. You measure out and rinse the rice and I'll chop up the chicken.'

It was nice cooking with Henry. He was at ease in the kitchen and clearly cooked a lot for himself. He whizzed from cupboard to drawer, selecting implements and pots and pans. His skill with a knife was undeniable, and he had the chicken cut up within seconds, before sliding the meat into the hot wok he was using to cook with.

The meat hissed and began to sizzle as Natalie chopped peppers and onions. The onions were strong and began to make her eyes water.

Henry noticed and grabbed a piece of paper towel. He stood in front of her, dabbing at her eyes. 'Okay?'

She nodded. 'Thanks.'

He did little things like that, she'd noticed. Like in the park, when she'd mentioned her feet hurt and he'd massaged them. Like when he'd brought all the mid-

wives drinks because they hadn't got away for a break
or a drink all day. Other things, too. Little things. Smiling at her over his mask in the OR. Raising an eyebrow as if to ask if she was okay. Sharing a joke with
her that he thought she'd like. Bringing her books he
thought she might enjoy.

She'd got so used to not being noticed that to finally
be *seen* was just…nice. Odd. But strangely comforting.

She studied Henry's face carefully as he concentrated hard on gently mopping away her onion tears.
He was an extremely handsome man. Brilliant blue
eyes, dark hair, a square, dashing jaw peppered by
stubble at this time of the evening. And he was being
so gentle with her!

For a brief moment their eyes met. And being that
close…staring into each other's eyes…became incredibly intimate. And uncomfortable.

Natalie had to laugh and turn away, desperate for
more but afraid to let it happen. They'd already had so
much news today —did they really want to add a new
frisson to their relationship?

Soon the rice was gently simmering away, and the
kitchen was filled with enough delicious smells to
make her stomach begin to rumble. She watched Henry
as he stirred the chicken and vegetables together in the
sauce, reduced the heat. She saw the muscles flex in
his arm, felt her gaze drop to his beautiful backside
in those dark jeans, and felt another stirring far below
her midriff.

'Tell me about your wife. What kind of woman was
she?'

Natalie needed to know. Needed to know what kind
of woman had snagged this man into marriage. What

kind of woman had made this man think, *Yes, she is the one I want to be married to for the rest of my life.*

Henry thought for a moment. 'Her name is Jenny. She's English—like me. She was an art student when we met, madly into painting—as you've already seen. And she was the complete opposite of me.'

'Opposites attract?' Natalie smiled.

'I guess… I like neatness and order. Jenny likes anarchy. Disorder. Disarray. I was the one who put away clothes. Jenny didn't care if they hung off the backs of chairs, or stayed on the floor because she'd missed when she'd thrown them into the laundry basket.'

She could hear the admiration that Henry still had for his ex-wife in his voice. Did he love her still?

The thought made her anxious, even though she knew she had no claim on this man romantically. They might have made two babies, but that did not mean they would have a relationship going forward. They hadn't established what they were. Or what type of claim they had on each other.

'We had a whirlwind relationship,' he went on. 'Too fast, probably. But Jenny was manic—she actually got diagnosed with bipolar just after we got married—and rushing into a relationship seemed to make sense to her. It was how she was. It was how she did things. In a rush. Chaotic. Just reacting.'

'Was it bad? Did she have to take medication?'

Henry drained the rice and began to serve it onto two plates. 'Yes, she did. Sometimes she'd forget to take it, but mostly she remembered.'

Natalie wondered what had broken them up? Had it been the bipolar? 'What happened between you two?'

Henry passed her a plate after adding some of the

sweet and sour chicken, and indicated that they should go through to the living area, where there was a table and chairs for them so they could sit down and eat. He didn't speak until they were seated, but she could see he looked extremely uncomfortable.

'I find it hard to talk about the next phase of my life. I've not spoken about it with anybody from work. No one knows.'

He was asking for her discretion. She got that. And if she wanted to know about this man she had to give it. She made a zipping motion across her lips and smiled.

'Jenny fell pregnant.'

Natalie stared. This was what she had dreaded. She knew he'd been married, knew there was an ex-wife out there—but children, too? Her simple, ordinary life was becoming more and more complicated by the minute, and now she'd learned that her own children, if they made it through the pregnancy, would have a half-sibling. She would become part of a blended family, with all the baggage that entailed.

'Oh.' She pushed the food around on her plate. Despite her hunger, she found she didn't really want to eat, but the nausea kept insisting.

Eat, or I'll make you regret it!

'We'd not planned it, and when she found out she stopped taking her bipolar medication, because there'd been a report about some risks during the first trimester.'

Natalie said nothing, just continued to listen.

'Her bipolar symptoms returned, but she refused to go back on the tablets and instead turned to her painting. Mostly she was manic. On a high. Working furiously in her studio, creating painting after painting.

Never stopping. Never resting. Working all through the night. There were occasional lows, during which she'd sleep for almost an entire day. And because of the highs and lows we didn't pay as much attention to her pregnancy as we could have, and didn't notice when towards the end of the pregnancy the baby's movements were slowing.'

Natalie locked eyes with Henry, suddenly dreading what was to come.

'The baby...a girl...died in utero.'

Henry took a moment to gather himself as he moved to the window of his tenth-floor apartment and looked out across the city.

Natalie's heart broke for him. What he and Jenny must have gone through! That was awful... She'd helped mothers give birth to stillborn babies and knew it was one of the most heart-wrenching things any midwife had to do. They had to remain stoic and detached as much as they could, to protect themselves, but also show that they were human and grieving along with the family, maybe shedding a tear or two in private. It was a hard enough situation for the midwife. God only knew how awful it must feel to be the parents who went through that terrible trauma.

'Jenny...she...er...went downhill afterwards. We thought it was postnatal depression, but the bipolar complicated matters. We couldn't get her stable on her meds and she began to suffer hallucinations. And then she tried to kill herself.' Henry looked at Natalie. 'I got her into a private treatment facility for her own safety. To help her deal with her grief and bipolar issues. She refused to see me.'

'Why?'

'She blamed me. Said her life had been fine until she met me and that everything had gone wrong as soon as we got married. So you see…that's why I haven't let myself get close to anyone since then.'

'What happened wasn't your fault.'

'But she was right. Her life *was* fine until she met me. I'm a doctor. I should have been on top of things. Found her meds that would keep her stable. Supported her better after the stillbirth delivery. But I was grieving myself. I tried my best. I really did. But I failed.'

Natalie felt fear assail her. What had been the cause of their baby being stillborn? What if it was somehow genetic and the damage had been passed onto their twins? She already had a difficult enough path in front of her, because of her injuries from the car accident. What if another danger had been added, now, too?

'I can see it in your eyes,' said Henry. 'You're wondering if our babies will be affected, too. But I have no idea if they're at risk. There were no significant findings that explained the stillbirth.'

'I think I'm allowed to be scared, Henry, after you telling me this.'

'I know. And this is why I don't get close to anyone.'

She tried not to show how much it hurt that he'd retreated from her as he stepped away from the window and began to pace the room.

'Don't get me wrong, Natalie. I'm going to be there for you and the babies. I'll support you through everything, and somehow we'll work this out. I just don't know how yet.'

Work this out? He made it sound as if she was some sort of business problem that he was managing. Were they just words? Was Henry trying to keep an emotional distance from her?

'Okay… Well, we'll just have to take it one day at a time. Like we said before. And I'll be vigilant. But I can't feel them moving yet. It's still too early.'

'You'll feel it earlier with twins—you know that.'

'I do. And I'll keep you informed.'

If he was going to sound businesslike, then so would she—even if inside she felt incredibly disappointed that she didn't seem to be getting any closer to him. She was carrying his babies! She was going to be the mother of his children!

I'll give him as much reassurance as he needs.

Henry escorted her home. It was dark, and he didn't like the idea of her travelling home alone in the big city. Especially not now.

He walked her right up to her door, waited for her to find her keys, and when she turned to say goodbye, with a smile, he leant in to kiss her on the cheek—as he always had before.

He wasn't sure if he should, because now their relationship had changed. In fact, he hesitated…looked into her eyes to see if his peck on the cheek would be welcome. But she smiled, shyly so he kissed her, inhaling the soft scent of her skin, feeling his senses overwhelmed with need and want, before he stepped back and watched her go inside.

She gave him a small smile before she closed the door, and afterwards he turned to go home.

He felt relief that he'd finally told her about Jenny, and what had happened to their daughter, and he was grateful to finally feel some of that burden lifted by sharing it with someone. But Natalie was probably the worst person he could ever have shared that with, simply because of the situation they found themselves in.

Had he terrified her with his past? Would she honour her words about keeping him informed about the babies? Or would she run for the hills, back to the safety and security of her family? She had no one in this city apart from her work colleagues and him—and what was he to her, really? A one-night stand that had evolved into a complicated friendship.

Today had been dazzling in its confusion. To find out he was going to become a father. To twins. Then to learn of Natalie's internal injuries, which could threaten the pregnancy. Telling her of his own difficult past.

He wanted to be able to celebrate the fact that he was going to be a father—wanted to love these babies. But he refused to let himself.

He could not allow himself to have hope.

Or to want. Or wish.

He had to remain at a distance until these babies were safely delivered, but it would be, oh, so difficult because of his growing feelings for Natalie.

They'd been complicated before, but now... Knowing that she was growing his children within her... He wanted to wrap his arms around her, hold her close and keep her safe. He wanted to kiss her and never let her go. Let her know that she was his and that he would be there to protect her for as long as she needed.

But was he being crazy? He'd failed Jenny—ruined his wife's life. Could he really take the chance on not ruining another?

Natalie had accepted his kiss goodbye, but did she

think that was all it was? Was he being a total idiot for assuming that she would somehow read something more into it? As if he was some sort of prize catch for any woman?

Because he didn't feel that way. Not at all. He felt as if he might ruin Natalie's life if he wasn't careful. What he needed to do—what would be safest for him to do—was take a step back until these babies were born and in that immediate postnatal period. Then, and only then, would he allow himself to truly love them. Then, and only then, would he allow himself to care about Natalie.

But who am I kidding? I already care for her. I can feel it! I'm fighting it every day! But I'll just have to hide it.

Natalie had been assigned the patient with uterine di-delphys—two uteruses—as apparently she had gone into early labour.

Dr Yang had prescribed tocolytics to try and prevent or slow the contractions overnight, but nothing seemed to be working, and Claudia Bateman was now in fully established labour.

'Monitor her closely, Nurse Webber,' Dr Yang had instructed, asking her to contact him the second she got to ten centimetres or the baby showed any signs of distress.

In the meantime, Henry kept popping into the room to check on this special patient, too.

'Hi, how's everything going, Claudia? Nervous?'

'Yes. It's too early! She's only thirty weeks.'

'We're keeping a very close eye on you and the baby. Natalie here is one of our best midwives.'

He smiled at Natalie and she smiled back, thankful for his faith in her abilities and his compliment. She'd had a difficult night last night, after Henry had dropped her off at home. Her mind had been whirring with thoughts, her emotions and fears pulling her this way and that. She'd not known what to think!

On the one hand she wanted to be cautious about this pregnancy, but after seeing the two babies on the scan yesterday…hearing their heartbeats… It was hard not to be optimistic and start daydreaming about the kind of life she was going to have. The kind of mother she was going to be.

She'd hated Henry walking away, leaving her at her door, knowing he was going home to his place whilst she stayed at hers. She'd started wondering about what kind of family they'd be. Was it just going to be her and the twins? Would she be a single mother, with Henry taking them at weekends? There was definitely something between them. Physically they were attracted to one another, and emotionally she wanted to be close to him—to feel that maybe they could become a family. He had escorted her home and kissed her on the cheek, as usual. But there'd been something in his eyes last night…an expression she couldn't define.

Henry had promised to be there for them. To support them. But what did that mean?

Financially? Physically? Emotionally?

Natalie wanted to dream of having it all! The cute babies and the hot guy who adored her and loved her. The white picket fence around a beautiful home in the suburbs. The two of them raising their babies with love and affection and laughter.

Who wouldn't want that?

But she sensed Henry's uncertainty. He'd told her outright—*'We'll work this out. I just don't know how yet.'* And she'd felt it in the distance he'd kept from her as he'd walked her home. Always at least two feet away, hands in pockets, when she'd yearned for him to walk with his arm around her shoulders. She'd felt it in that kiss goodbye. On her cheek. A kiss that *friends* might give one another.

She'd gone to his place last night hoping to cement their new relationship, but it was just as uncertain as it had always been.

She understood his uncertainty. Of course she did! She had it herself. But…couldn't he make a leap of faith? Couldn't he show her that she meant something to him? That she was worth something? More than just the physical carrier of his children?

Natalie was in a situation in which she needed certainty. Not vague promises. And Henry wasn't giving her pie-in-the-sky promises—he was telling her the truth. Outright. That he didn't know how they were going to do this.

Was it enough? Enough for a woman who'd just found out she was carrying twins?

Natalie dragged her attention back to Claudia, who was trying to breathe through her contractions. When her latest one was over, Natalie began asking her questions.

'Did you always know of your unique situation?'

Claudia shook her head. 'No. I only found out when I went for my first pregnancy scan.'

'It must have been a shock?' said Natalie, understanding how such a revelation could rock your world.

'That's an understatement! To find out you're some kind of medical anomaly... It makes you very popular all of a sudden.' Claudia smiled ruefully.

'One for the textbooks?' asked Henry.

'For sure!' She crunched through an ice chip. 'It's like the doctors forget...no offence intended—' she glanced at Henry '—that beneath the anomaly you're also a human being. With feelings. With worries. All they see is how different you are. How they can write a paper on you and get it published.'

'Like you're being used?' Natalie mused.

'Exactly! Yes, I'm different—but I'm also just the same as every other woman in this place. I'm going to have a baby for the first time and I'm terrified. That's what should be important. Dr Yang was the first doctor who saw me for who I am. Not *what* I am.'

Natalie wondered what Henry saw her as. As a woman terrified to have not just one, but two babies? As a first-time mother, who was petrified because of her past injuries? As a woman who had the same fears as every other mother? Getting through the pregnancy, giving birth to healthy babies and becoming a mother to them... Or did he just see her as a problem to overcome? Something to work out? He was a very private individual. What would happen when everyone heard that they were going to have twins together? The gossip was going to be unstoppable in a place such as this.

'Well, thankfully you have someone who loves and supports you. That must mean everything when you feel the world is against you. Where *is* Alex?'

Alex was Claudia's husband.

'He left the camera in the car. He's just gone to fetch it.'

Henry was keeping an eye on the trace, tracking back through the last few contractions.

'Everything looking good there, Doc?' Claudia asked.

'Absolutely.' Henry smiled. 'Natalie, can you get me a set of obs, please?'

'Sure.'

She busied herself checking Claudia over. Everything was looking good. Her pressure was stable, her temperature was perfect...

Natalie bent over to pick up the pen she'd just dropped, and when she stood she felt the room reel a little as a wave of nausea overcame her.

She must have made a noise. Perhaps groaned a little. Because suddenly Henry was at her side.

'What is it? Are you all right?' he whispered, low and urgent.

'Yeah, I'm just feeling a little...' She rubbed at her stomach, knowing she needed to get something to eat.

'Go. Take a break,' he insisted.

'I'm fine.'

'No. You're not. You need to look after yourself.'

'Is everything okay?' Claudia asked. 'You're whispering. It's not nice when you're labouring and people whisper.'

Natalie was about to protest that everything was fine, but Henry got there first.

'Nurse Webber's fine. Just pregnant. I'm telling her she needs to eat.'

Natalie felt her cheeks flame with heat. *He was telling a patient!*

'Oh, congratulations!' Claudia said, reaching for another ice chip. 'How far along are you?'

'Just three months,' she muttered, not sure if it was tempting fate to talk about the twins so openly to anyone.

'You'll feel better soon, then, but that morning sickness is a killer, isn't it?'

Henry turned to Natalie. 'Go on. I'll come and check on you in a minute.'

'I'll be back shortly,' she said to her patient, glaring at Henry before leaving the room and heading for her locker, where a bevy of biscuits awaited.

In the staff room, armed with ginger biscuits and a banana, she sat on one of the couches, her feet up on the table. That had been a close one! Those waves of nausea could just hit her out of nowhere. But she would never complain about it. It was a good sign and it meant that the babies were still doing well.

A few moments later Roxy came into the staff room, saw Natalie with her feet up and laughed. 'Like that already, is it?'

Natalie smiled. 'You know how it is…'

'You're telling me. Mind you, you do look a little peaky. Everything okay?'

At that moment Henry came in. He sat beside Natalie and looked her over. 'Do you want to tell her?'

Natalie glared at Henry again. Did he want to tell the whole world?

'Ooh! Tell me what?' asked Roxy, settling down beside them both.

'I'm…er…pregnant,' Natalie said, feeling terribly awkward and embarrassed. She wasn't ready to tell people yet. The more people she told, the more real it made the babies and the more she grew attached. And if something went wrong…

'You are?' Roxy's eyes widened and she gasped out loud. 'Oh, my God! Congratulations!' She threw her arms around Natalie and gave her a squeeze. 'I guess I should have known. You have looked quite green for a while, always rushing off to the bathroom, but you know how it is…you don't like to suggest something like this, because if it isn't true… How far along are you?'

'Three months.'

'Really? Oh, you should be feeling better soon, then. Unless it's twins!' Roxy laughed again, then stopped when she saw Natalie and Henry passing looks between them. 'It's *twins*?'

Natalie nodded, then smiled, unable to stop herself being caught up in Roxy's awe and wonderment as she squealed her delight.

'Who's the father? You've never mentioned a boyfriend.'

Natalie glanced at Henry again, not wanting to tell his secret unless he was the one wishing it to be known.

'I am.' Henry turned to face Roxy and smiled.

'You're kidding me?' Roxy looked from one to the other. 'Really? How? When?'

'We met at New Year's…' Natalie admitted.

'You did? Oh, my God, I can't believe it!' Roxy shook her head. 'And so you two—you're an item?'

Natalie didn't know how to answer that.

'We're working it out,' Henry said diplomatically.

'Who's in with Claudia?' Natalie asked, suddenly changing the subject, not wanting the conversation to carry on in a direction in which she didn't want to hear the answers.

'Dr Yang and her husband, Alex.'

She nodded. 'Rox, could you give us a minute?'

'Sure! Absolutely! Must give the lovebirds their moment alone!' She grinned wildly, grabbed a chocolate or two from a tin on the table and sauntered out through the door.

Natalie looked at Henry. 'So we're suddenly telling people now?'

'You're beginning to show.'

She straightened her uniform over her hump. It was more noticeable in this than in scrubs. 'You do realise that everyone will know by the end of the day now?'

He nodded. 'I don't care.'

'You don't?'

'No. You're what's important.'

'I am?'

'Of course you are,' he insisted.

How important am I to you, Henry? she wanted to ask him.

But she was too scared of hearing the answer in case it was the wrong one. *Because you're carrying my children.*

When all she wanted to hear from him…from anyone…was, *Because you mean the world to me. And I would lay my life down on the ground before you if it would keep you safe.*

But no one had ever said that to her. Or treated her in that way.

And she doubted Henry would say it, either.

She wanted him to take her face in his hands and bring her lips to his. She wanted him to settle beside her on the couch and wrap himself around her and hold her close, whispering sweet nothings into her ear and making her laugh and smile.

What the hell is going on with me?

'How are you feeling now? Stomach better?' he asked.

She nodded, slightly mollified by the soft, caring tone in his voice. 'I ought to get back to Claudia.'

'Take your time. I don't need you passing out during her delivery.'

Henry stood up and turned to go.

'Henry?'

He stopped. Looked at her. 'Yes?'

'I...' She couldn't think what to say! She needed some reassurance, that was all. Needed some sign from him that this was all going to turn out well. But those words and questions got stuck in her throat, so she copped out with another question. 'Have you spoken to Dr Yang yet about me?'

'No. Not yet. I was going to sit down with him later on today.'

'All right,' she answered quietly, and watched him disappear through the door.

Frustrated, she threw her banana skin onto the low table, angry with herself. Why couldn't she just ask him outright for what she wanted? Why didn't she demand to be treated better? With more consideration? With more...what?

Emotion? Feelings? Commitment?

How can I demand that of him? Knowing what he has already gone through?

Her stomach had settled now. She picked up the banana skin and dumped it in the bin. Took a drink of water and then headed back to Claudia.

CHAPTER EIGHT

CLAUDIA'S BABY WAS born three hours later, emerging into the world with an attempt at a roar, before she was rushed off to the NICU for monitoring and help with her breathing.

Natalie was clearing up the room, clandestinely watching Claudia being cared for and comforted by her husband, Alex. He was being the perfect partner. Holding her hand tightly. Telling his wife how much he loved her. How proud he was of her. How their daughter was beautiful and just like her momma. Asking her if there was anything she needed.

She wished a man would look at her in that way. Wished Henry would. Sometimes she thought that he did, but then convinced herself she was just imagining things.

It was strange. Confusing. Hoping for something that just a few months ago she'd been trying to stay away from.

How quickly our lives change.

'I need to see my daughter,' Claudia cried, dabbing at her eyes with a tissue. 'I haven't even held her! She needs to know her mom loves her.'

'I can take you,' Natalie offered.

Claudia sniffed, looking over at her with hope. 'You can?'

'Sure. I can grab a wheelchair and take you up now. Give me a moment to call NICU to let them know, and then I'll grab you a chair.'

Claudia beamed. 'Thank you!'

'No problem.' Natalie smiled back, glad she could help.

Once the room was cleared, she headed off to the desk to dial the NICU and tell them they'd be receiving a visitor. Then she grabbed a wheelchair and whisked Claudia and her husband off to the elevator, as the NICU was on the next floor up.

As they headed out onto the NICU floor Natalie saw Henry and Dr Yang talking to one of the neonatal specialists. She saw Henry glance up, do a double-take, and then he was striding over to her, taking her arm and pulling her politely off to one side.

'What are you doing?' he demanded.

'Claudia wants to visit her daughter.'

'Please tell me Alex pushed the wheelchair?'

Natalie frowned. 'No. I did.'

'Are you crazy?'

'I beg your pardon?' she asked incredulously.

'Natalie…you shouldn't be pushing patients around in wheelchairs. Not in your fragile condition.'

'Who are you calling fragile?'

He sighed. 'You're not. Obviously you're not. But the babies could be. They've already got enough difficulties without you hauling patients around.'

'I see. This is your cack-handed way of trying to keep me safe. Is that right?'

Henry tilted his head this way, then that, as he considered her question. Then he smiled, sighed, and said, 'Possibly. I'm sorry.'

'No, it's good. It's just… I have to be able to do my job, Henry.'

'I know. Just…don't take any unnecessary risks, okay?'

'Okay. So, do you want to push Claudia over to see her daughter, then?'

He nodded. 'Fine.'

They both went back to Claudia.

'Your daughter is over here in this bay,' Henry told her. 'She's doing well. Please don't be concerned by all the wires and cables. They're there to monitor her heart rate, temperature, blood pressure…and that one there on her face is giving her supplemental oxygen.'

Henry parked Claudia up and put the brake on the wheelchair. Claudia stood up to peer inside her daughter's warmer. Her husband, Alex, went to the other side to peer down at her.

'She's beautiful!'

Natalie stared at them, wondering if she would have this moment in a few months' time. But she would have two cribs to visit. Would her babies make it to nine months? Or would the scarring on her womb prevent it from expanding to its full size? Would her scars rupture? Would she have to deliver her twins as an emergency? She'd seen enough parents sitting by their babies' empty cribs to know that she did not want to have that in her future.

Her heart ached in that moment.

'I've spoken to Dr Yang,' Henry said in a low voice as he came to stand beside her.

'What did he say?'

'That he wants to do a detailed ultrasound himself.'

'Did he sound worried? Did he say I was high risk?'

'No. He said it's a complication, but that if we monitor the babies regularly, then we should be okay.'

'What does he mean by "regularly"?'

'Every two weeks.'

Natalie nodded. It would give them all peace of mind to do that, so if any problems began to present themselves they could be right on it. 'Did you tell him about what happened with Jenny, too?'

Henry nodded, looking glum. 'I think I surprised him.'

'I'm sure you did. Listen, do you fancy grabbing something to eat together at lunch? About one? In the main cafeteria?'

'We should—with the gossip mill firing on all cylinders.'

'Okay. I'd better get back. Can you get a porter to bring Claudia down?'

'I will.'

Natalie smiled at him and walked away, but the second her face could not be seen by him she frowned. Was Henry's main focus the babies? It was hers, too, but she really would like a sign that he felt something for *her* as well. She herself was finding it difficult to work out how she felt, but she did at least acknowledge she had feelings for Henry.

Of course she did! How could she not? He was hot. Her hormones were raging and she was carrying his children! They were going to be a family and she wanted to spend more time with him. Hence the suggestion of lunch. They still had a lot to sort out, but she wasn't trying to drag him into a relationship he didn't want.

Even if I want one.

They'd been getting along so well together. The time she'd spent with him had told her that he really was a good guy. Maybe one of the best. And she truly trusted that he had no further secrets lurking in his past.

She knew about his past now. Knew his secrets. There was no current wife or girlfriend hiding in the wings. Henry wasn't using her. He was free and single, so she felt she could trust him in that regard. But... did he feel anything for *her* at all? Beyond friendship?

She needed to know. Because if she knew he didn't think of her in that way then she could stop hoping. She could get on with her life and put these babies to the forefront. Be the best mother she could be.

But if he *did* feel something for her...

Well, that would be a different story, wouldn't it?

If he had feelings for her they could build on that— and maybe, just maybe, she could get her happily-ever-after?

Henry spotted Natalie sitting over by a window. She already had food and drink in front of her, so he gave her a quick wave and indicated that he'd grab himself some lunch, then join her.

He'd been a bit reluctant when she'd suggested it. Even though they'd only told Roxy about their unconventional set-up, he understood that they would become the focus of gossip. Which he didn't like.

Plus, every time he was in Natalie's company he found himself fighting his needs. Soaking her in. Admiring the colour of her eyes. That little side-smile she sometimes did when something amused her. The wondrous way in which she laughed.

He loved working with her. She was very dedicated to her patients and he had no doubt that she would be a great mother. But...he couldn't let his feelings for her run away with him. He needed to keep up that wall. Because he'd been through a major loss before. He'd lost a child and a wife and he knew how devastating that could be. And what would be the point in getting attached to these babies and to Natalie if it happened again?

It was the only way he could keep his heart safe. Because he wasn't sure he could go through the trauma of losing those he loved again. Jenny, back in England, was still trying to rebuild her life, even after all this time. So best to try and not love at all.

But he felt that maybe he was already fighting a losing battle, because ever since she'd spilt that drink all over him in Liquid Nights on New Year's Eve, and looked up into his eyes with shock and apology, he'd been a little lost. She'd affected him from day one, and when he'd realised he was going to have to work with her he'd struggled.

Now she was carrying his twins. Precious, precious cargo! He couldn't believe he was being given another chance to become a father. All he wanted to do was wrap himself around her and keep her safe—because if he could do that, then maybe it would go some way towards atoning for what had happened to Jenny. Maybe it would show the world that he was worthy of having happiness. Having the family that he'd been craving for quite some time now.

He took his tray over to her table. Tea. A baked

salmon fillet and a jacket potato. A small orange jelly with fruit pieces for dessert.

Henry sat opposite her, noted that she'd gone for the curry option, with some rice, and that she'd almost finished. 'Hey.'

'Hey, yourself.' She smiled.

'How are you feeling?' he asked.

'A bit better, I think. Nausea has eased up.'

'Maybe it's on its way out?'

'I hope so. It's been awful.'

He glanced over at a line of nurses standing in the queue, who all seemed to be stealing glances their way and whispering. 'Grapevine is in full swing. That didn't take long,' he said.

'Never does in a place like this. Is it bothering you?'

'Somewhat. I'm a very private person. Knowing that everyone here is aware of my private life is going to be a little difficult to deal with.'

'But you're not embarrassed?' she asked.

'About you? This? No.'

'Good.' She smiled. 'Because we need to be united for these babies. We have to be strong.'

He nodded.

'Speaking of which... I'm going to start looking for someplace else to live. I thought I'd better let you know. My place is a shoebox. Definitely not big enough for me and twins. And, yes, I know it's still early to be making plans, but it can take a long time to find a good place in the city.'

'I'll keep an eye out for you. Although...' He trailed off.

'Although what?'

He laughed. 'My apartment is big enough for us all.'

He shook his head, not quite believing what he might be offering.

Am I offering?

She stared at him. 'Are you suggesting I should move in? With you?'

He shrugged. He really didn't know. He'd thought about it, but not really come to any conclusions. He'd originally assumed the babies would live with Natalie and he would take them at weekends. But if her place was that tiny...

If he was going to get this miracle chance of being a father, he wanted to be there every minute of the day for them. He didn't want to be a part-time father!

'I want to be there for them as much as I can.'

'Which means what...for us?' She blushed.

'I don't know.'

'Are we going to be more involved than friends?' she asked quietly, clearly nervous, clearly ready to run if he said the wrong thing and embarrassed her.

She was talking about having a relationship with him. About them being a couple! And though he longed for it, he was scared of it, too. What if it all went wrong? Losing the babies would be bad enough... but losing Natalie, too?

Relationships could be precarious.

Every day you walked a very thin line.

'I don't know. I really don't,' he repeated.

'Do you not think of me in that way?'

He laughed. Was she being serious? He thought about her in 'that way' all the time. That was the problem!

'I think of you in every way,' he answered, his voice quiet.

'That's good, isn't it?'

It was terrifying…that was what it was.

Because he hadn't directly answered her, she persisted with another question.

'What conclusion did you come to?'

He looked around them, checking that no one was close enough to overhear. 'Are you asking me to be in a relationship with you? A romantic relationship?'

Her cheeks flushed red and he realised he'd put her on the spot. But he needed to hear what she wanted. If he knew what she wanted, then maybe he could work out how *he* wanted to be involved in all of this.

'I don't know. Possibly. I only have one night to go off, but we seemed to get along very well. And I, for one, find myself thinking…sometimes…that we could…er…give it a go.'

'For the sake of the babies?' he said.

She looked at him strangely. 'What else?'

She'd certainly given him a lot to think about. She wanted a relationship with him! That had terrific appeal. He'd wondered about it, too. She was always in his mind, even when he was at home alone, ever since they'd met, and now she was telling him she wanted them to try to be together.

Was he brave enough?

Thankfully, he was saved by his mobile phone. An alert asking him to go back to OBGYN. He was being paged by Dr Yang.

'I've got to go.'

'Of course. But think about it, Henry. I don't want to screw this up.'

Nor did he. And perhaps that was the reason why

he ought to stay away until the babies were safely here and he knew everything was all right?

It was clear to Natalie that Henry was only thinking of the babies. She'd asked him about the possibility of a relationship and that was what he'd replied. *For the sake of the babies?*

She felt upset, but acknowledged to herself that she had to be realistic. They had only spent one night together—they couldn't base an entire relationship on one night, a few lunch dates and an unexpected miracle pregnancy.

So she decided to focus on her work and entered the room of Jo and Richard Malbeck, who had come in to have their twins. Jo had naturally gone into labour at thirty-seven weeks and three days and was contracting regularly. Both babies were head-down, so that was good, too.

'These are your first babies?' she asked.

'Yes.'

'How exciting! I'm expecting twins, too,' she said, cradling her small rounded bump.

She was proud and yet also somehow shy about admitting it out loud to people. But she wanted to celebrate it. The pregnancy was going well right now, so why shouldn't she? She'd had enough bad stuff happen. It meant something for her to take the time to be happy when she could.

'Congratulations!' Jo said. 'It's scary, though, isn't it?'

Natalie laughed. 'Just a bit! Now, it says here in your birth plan that you want to stay as mobile as possible and try to have a water birth—is that right?'

'If I can.'

'I don't see why not. Everything's going smoothly right now. We'll monitor you closely, especially after the first baby is out, to make sure Baby B is in the right position for a head delivery. When the second twin suddenly gets that extra room after Baby A is out, it sometimes flips.'

'Dr Yang said that, too.'

'Feel free to move around. Take a walk…bounce on a ball. It all helps. You're five centimetres now, so I'll start filling the pool, and I'll let you know when you can get in, okay?'

'Thanks, Natalie.'

Jo got up from the bed now that she was off the monitoring trace and began to pace back and forth in the room.

Natalie wrote down in Jo's notes what she'd advised and her plan of action. She hoped that Jo would get to have the birth she'd dreamed of the same way Natalie had dreamed of her own future and her babies. But for Natalie her hopes went beyond the twins in her womb. She'd had aspirations for her and Henry, too, but could feel that hope dwindling. And it was tainting her dreams of having that perfect future she aspired to.

'I'll be back in a moment. The call bell is there, if you need me.'

Natalie headed back to the desk in the main corridor. She needed to order another warmer for the second baby and notify the NICU doctors that she had twins on the way—even though, for their gestation, they should be okay. It paid to be safe anyway.

She caught a glimpse of Henry at the end of the corridor. As usual, he looked absolutely gorgeous, completely unaware of the effect he had on her. She tried not to stare, to get on with her work, but found she couldn't tear her eyes away. And then he looked over too, and caught her eye.

For a moment they just looked at one another, and then Henry gave her a nod and headed into a patient's room.

She wished so badly that he would take a risk on them. But she understood his need to try and protect himself after his own past trauma.

I miss you.

'Hey, bro, what's up?'

Henry was all aflutter at Natalie's suggestion of having a relationship and he needed to talk to someone—so he'd called his brother.

'I need to ask your advice.'

'Sounds serious.'

'It is.'

'So, what's up?'

'You know that girl we were talking about? Who I met on New Year's Eve?'

'Yeah?'

'Well...' He sucked in a breath. 'She's pregnant. With my babies.'

'Babies? More than one?'

'Yep.'

'Wow.'

'I know. Tell me about it. I really, really like her, Hugh, and I think I've offered to let her come and stay with me when the babies arrive, because I don't want to miss being around them, but...'

'But you're scared?'

'Wouldn't you be?'

Even if Natalie wasn't pregnant, he'd be seriously doubting his rule not to get involved.

'There's definitely something between us. Something stronger than mere attraction. I consciously seek her out. I think about her *all the time*. She's never out of my mind. I feel better in her company. I feel lost when she's not there.'

'So, what's the problem, bro? That sounds great. Like you've got feelings…real feelings for her.'

'I have.'

'Then go for it. What'll happen if you don't? You could miss the chance to be really happy at last. I want that for you. After all you've been through.'

Henry nodded. Listened. It was just so hard to know what to do for the best and keep his heart safe.

Natalie alerted the front desk when Jo began to push. She was in the pool and doing well when Henry came in to assist with the delivery of her twins.

He glanced at Natalie and gave her a nod of acknowledgement. A quick smile.

She smiled back. 'She's been pushing for a couple of minutes.'

'Okay, let's see how you're doing, Jo.' He put on the longer gloves they used for pool deliveries, and dressed in a gown to cover his everyday clothes. 'Ah! I can already see a head of dark hair.'

'Definitely mine, then,' joked Richard, Jo's husband, who had a full head of dark hair himself.

'Not the time, honey…' breathed Jo.

Richard stroked her arm. 'You sure? I thought you always had time for my sparkling wit?'

Jo glared at him, then sucked in another breath before pushing again.

Natalie coached Jo through her breathing, counting from one to ten again and again, managing to get three counts per contraction so Jo could give her all. Beside her, Henry watched carefully, helping to facilitate the birth with careful manipulation of Jo's perineum and vulva to prevent tears.

'You're doing great, Jo. We might get the head out on the next one, so I'll need you to listen to me carefully, okay?'

Jo nodded, sucking in another breath and bearing down like a champ.

'Nearly there!' Richard encouraged, peering down between his wife's legs, his face a mask of hope and excitement.

Jo growled with the effort, her face red, straining really hard.

"Little push for me…and another…okay, pant!' Henry instructed.

Natalie looked down. The head had crowned and was out, naturally turning towards Jo's right inner thigh, the little face was scrunched-up, the babyblissfully unaware of what awaited it in the world. As always, Natalie was in awe of the miracle of birth, and today it seemed even more miraculous, knowing that she might very well be doing this herself in just a few months!

Would Dr Yang deliver her babies? Would Roxy assist? Would Henry be mopping her brow and calling her *honey* and stroking her arm? Or would she be in a delivery room all alone?

The thought made her blood run cold and she looked

at Henry, saw his face was a mask of concentration and determination. His strong arms were waiting, ready to catch this first baby.

He would be a good parent, she knew. And he wanted it as badly as she did. He must do, or she couldn't bear it.

'One more push, Jo!'

Jo bore down hard.

Henry smiled with delight as the first baby, a little girl, slid out into his waiting hands. He adjusted his grip and then lifted Jo and Richard's daughter up onto Jo's belly as Natalie draped the baby with a towel.

'Congratulations!'

Natalie caught Henry's eye then. He looked at her as if to say, *This could be us.*

At least that was how she interpreted it, anyway.

She smiled and nodded as Henry clamped the cord and Richard cut it. The baby burst into loud protest at her arrival, now that she was no longer in the lovely warmth of her mother's womb.

'I can't believe it! She's gorgeous!' Jo gasped.

'I'm so proud of you, honey.' Richard pressed his face to his wife's and kissed her on the cheek, before stooping to kiss his daughter.

Both Natalie and Henry smiled, enjoying this moment they got to share. Henry even winked at her!

Her stomach did a little flip. What did that wink mean?

It meant something, right? It meant something to her, anyway.

She knew Henry's reluctance to get into a relationship. Maybe this was his way of sending a silent message? *This could be us.* Something he couldn't say out loud in the room, because right now the moment was about Richard and Jo and *their* babies.

Whatever it was, she liked being included by him. Loved his secret smile, the twinkle in his eyes, the warm way he looked at her. It did incredible things to her insides!

'Honey, take the baby. Another contraction's starting.' Jo passed her newborn daughter over to her husband, who took the baby reverently, as if she was the most precious thing he'd ever had the privilege to hold.

Natalie wrapped another towel around the baby, saying, 'Keep her warm.' Then she returned to kneel by the pool again, as Jo began to breathe through her contraction.

'I need to check the position of the second baby, Jo—okay?' asked Henry.

'Okay...'

Henry performed the internal examination quickly, then withdrew. 'Good news. Baby's head down, so you can push with the next one.'

'I've already done this once. Do I really have to do it again?'

Henry smiled. 'I'm afraid so. There are no short-cuts with twins.'

He glanced at Natalie again.

He was right. There were no shortcuts. No cheat codes. No magic button. Having twins was double the work, but double the reward.

Natalie tried to imagine herself holding one of their babies and Henry the other. The thought made her glow. Made her feel as if she wanted to pull Henry close and hold him tight.

Jo began to push again.

'You can do this!' urged Richard.

Natalie needed this birth to go well. She felt somehow that if it did then it would be a good sign for her own pregnancy. That their twins would get through this pregnancy safely, without any mishaps or dangers or emergency procedures.

'Just a couple of pushes to go,' she said, joining in with the encouragement.

It took four more pushes. Four hard, strenuous pushes. And then out popped a little baby boy. One of each!

Jo began to cry, as did her husband, and because of her hormones Natalie found she was fighting the strong urge to cry herself. She had to keep wiping at her eyes, and her face stretched wide into a smile as both babies were checked and found to be extremely healthy. No need to go to the NICU, APGARs were excellent, and the new little family were left alone to get used to each other.

Natalie headed to the linen room to get new sheets for the bed and Henry followed her in.

'That was amazing, wasn't it?' She turned to face him, her smile brighter than the sun.

'It was. It made me think of us.'

'Me too,' she answered, glad that he'd felt the magic of that moment as well.

For a moment they just stood there, looking at one another. Natalie felt a yearning inside her that was so strong she wasn't sure she'd be able to contain it. The need to touch him. Just once. To feel him in her arms again. Her hunger for him burned like a flare, white-hot, and she could see in his eyes that he wanted her, too.

But then an alarm bell sounded and they were ripped violently from the moment, knowing they had to push aside whatever it was that they themselves wanted and answer the call.

Henry led the charge, bursting from the linen room, his eyes scanning the corridor to see the red alarm light strobing wildly outside Room Eleven.

They both ran as fast as they could, bursting into the room to see a woman on the bed, writhing in pain, her baby's head already out, and Roxy looking up at them in a panic.

'This is Clare. A late walk-in. Baby's head was out when she got here and now it's a shoulder dystocia.'

Natalie rushed to Clare's side as Henry donned gloves and immediately began to assess the situation.

'Page Dr Yang,' he ordered, as other staff ran into the room. 'How long has she been pushing?' he asked Roxy.

'She can't remember.'

Natalie could feel her heart in her throat. A shoulder dystocia was one of the most terrifying things to happen in a birthing suite. A true emergency. Staff would have only minutes to get the baby out safely.

Clare writhed on the bed. 'Help me!'

Natalie's heart ached.

'Don't push yet,' Henry said. 'We need to release baby's shoulder from behind your pubic bone first.'

A nurse rushed back into the room. 'Dr Yang is in the OR, Dr Locke.'

Henry nodded, and Natalie knew he would be feeling the pressure of being the only doctor there at the moment, having to make decisions and deliver this baby to its mother, keeping them both safe.

In that instant she admired his fortitude and bravery. He did not shirk from his duty, he did not dither, and he knew what he had to do.

'Let's get her into the McRoberts Manoeuvre.'

McRoberts involved getting the patient to lie on her back with her legs pushed outwards and upwards, towards her chest.

'I'm going to press firmly here—okay?' Henry told Clare, positioning his hand on her abdomen, just above her pubic bone, trying to manipulate the baby from above.

But Natalie could see that, although it had helped somewhat, there still wasn't enough room for the baby. 'What about an episiotomy?' she suggested.

'I agree. Clare, I'm going to have to make a cut to help ease the baby out—okay?'

'Do whatever you need to! Just get it out!'

It was over in a matter of seconds. As soon as Henry made the cut, then applied abdominal pressure again, the shoulder was released and the baby slithered out, its face screwing up into an almighty roar on arrival.

A palpable relief filled the room. Natalie looked across to Roxy, who grinned, and then she looked at Henry, who gave her a quick smile before returning to his work.

'Is it okay?' asked Clare, who couldn't see her baby as it was surrounded by staff over at the warmer.

'Baby's doing great,' said one of the paediatricians. 'We'll have him over to you in just a moment.'

Clare sank back against the pillows. 'Thank God! And thank you, guys. Thank you so much!'

'Hey, you did all the work,' Henry said, busy stitching.

'But you saved us.'

'All in a day's work.'

The baby was brought over to Clare moments later, with the paediatrician explaining that sometimes babies born after a shoulder dystocia suffered from something called a brachial plexus injury—a stretching of the brachial nerve. But any numbness or discomfort should pass after a few days.

Clare herself had suffered some tears, as well as the episiotomy, but her bleeding was well controlled and she'd only need a few extra days of rest.

They all left Mom and baby to bond, and Natalie got ready to head for home. It had been a long day.

'Setting off?'

Henry stood in the doorway to the staff room, leaning against the doorjamb, arms folded, stethoscope still draped around his neck. He looked so yummy in that moment that Natalie had to turn away and take her time getting her stuff from her locker.

'Yes. I'm ready for a hot bath.'

'Not too hot, I hope?'

She smiled, closing her locker. 'No, don't worry.'

She walked over to stand before him, her coat draped over one arm.

'What you did in that room was amazing.'

'It's what I'm trained for.'

'But you saved that baby's life.'

'We all did.'

She smiled. 'Don't be so modest. You're an amazing man, Henry Locke, and I know, in my heart, that you're going to make an amazing father, too.'

He looked at her then, in such a way that caused

everything else in the world to just fall away. Sounds muted...details blurred. All she could see was his eyes and the need in them. The yearning. The want. Her whole body was responding in kind, and before she knew what was happening Henry had moved towards her in a rush, taking her face in his hands and bringing her lips to his in a sweet, gentle kiss, as if fearing that if he waited he would change his mind.

Natalie dropped her coat as she brought her hands up to hold him tightly against her, moaning slightly as his kiss deepened and her every nerve-ending sprang into action, awaiting a caress, a touch...

Being kissed by Henry was even more magical now than it had been on New Year's Eve! Maybe it was the fact that she'd had to wait so long to enjoy it again, or maybe it was because this time they knew each other, so it was different and held more meaning.

No longer were they strangers who'd met on a night out—two lonely souls, each with a heartbreak they'd been trying to hide. Now they knew each other's pain. Now they were stepping forward into something new. She was carrying his children. Her hormones were raging. And the intensity of Henry's kiss was mind-blowing. Earth-shattering.

She needed more. Wanted more. But suddenly he took hold of her upper arms and pushed himself away from her, letting go and taking a step back.

'I'm sorry. I...' He met her gaze then, and she saw in his eyes a deep grief, before he turned and walked away.

'Henry!' she called after him, her heart breaking. *What had just happened?*

The kiss had been amazing. How could he regret that?

'Henry Locke! Don't make me run after you!' she called.

Henry stopped. Turned. Came back to her. 'We can't do this. *I* can't do this.'

'Can't do what?'

'Allow myself to have feelings for you. It's too much. It's too difficult.'

He wasn't looking her in the eye.

'I'm sorry for kissing you just now. I should have stopped it before it even began. But I will be there for the babies, Natalie. Anything they need. *You* need. Moral support—whatever. But I can't do this…with you…right now. I'm sorry.'

And he walked away.

Tears were already trickling down her cheeks as he rounded the corner and disappeared from sight. It was as if he'd taken all her hopes and her dreams with her. Taken them from her. Given her hope, then stolen it away.

Just like Wade had.

He had made her think that everything was going to be okay. Let her dream. Let her make wishes for her future. And then he'd torn it all down, shown her that he wasn't available and that she was actually very much on her own.

How could Henry do this to her?

If they couldn't be together then…what was the point?

Would they be working together for evermore and sharing their children? Would she be seeing him every day? Torturing herself with what might have been?

She'd never felt more alone than she had in that moment as he walked away.

At least Wade hadn't left her pregnant…

Suddenly Natalie didn't want to be there any more. Not in Heartlands. Not in New York. The yearning to run back home, back into the bosom of her family, was incredibly strong. She knew her parents missed her. Knew that they would rally round and be there for her as she raised these babies. And Montana was a lovely place to have kids. All that nature… Those wide-open spaces, the animals on the farm…

What did she have here? Her tiny apartment and traffic. No one to help her out.

I've made a terrible mistake. Again.

CHAPTER NINE

HENRY STOOD IN an empty patient's room, pacing back and forth, frustrated. Angry! Furious with himself! Why on earth had he *kissed* her? All it had done was prove to him how perfect they were for each other, how beautifully they fitted, how much he wanted more.

But the second—the very second—he'd realised he'd wanted every part of her, to be with her every day, to wake up with her, go to sleep with her, his brain had begun to scream at him.

This could all go wrong. You could lose these babies and her and then where will you be?

And he'd panicked. Plain and simple. He'd not thought it through. He'd allowed his desires to overrun his brain. Had given in to his need for her and tasted her lips one last time. Fireworks had gone off inside his brain. His entire body had lit up with energy. His desire had been soaring into the atmosphere as he'd tried to soak up every last drop of her. And it had been that need, that yearning, that had warned him…

What if you lose this…? Think of what it will do to you…

He'd had to stop. Before he got in too deep. Before he fell in love. Or perhaps it was already too late for that? But something terrible might happen, and to have his heart ripped out from his chest once again wasn't to be borne.

The pregnancy might not last—and even if it did, what if the same thing happened afterwards? What if Natalie got postnatal depression? What if she suffered psychosis, the same way Jenny had? What if? What if? *What if?*

There was too much that was unknown. Too much he had no control over whatsoever. And he couldn't deal with that. That was the whole point about not getting involved with someone! You never knew how they were going to be. Okay, so Jenny had bipolar. She'd shown signs that her mental health wasn't great even before the pregnancy—and, yes, she'd stopped taking the tablets that kept her stable whilst she was pregnant.

But that had had nothing to do with their baby being stillborn. And lightning could strike twice.

The dread he'd felt ever since finding out about the twins had to count for something, didn't it? If you didn't listen to your own logic, then what was the point? He *could* be with Natalie—just not yet. He had to wait until he knew for sure that they were all safe. And then, and only then, could he possibly allow himself to venture down the road of allowing himself to become involved.

Just not now. Not whilst they were all still in danger. To do anything otherwise would be crazy, and risky—not only to his heart, but to his sanity.

I've made the right decision.

Only why did he feel so awful about it?

* * *

It was just a short break. That was all she would tell herself. A short break back home. Some time away to think. To get her head straight. Talk to her mom and dad. See what they thought. And if they all agreed she should stay in Montana, then that was what she would do. She'd send in her resignation, effective immediately, to Heartlands Hospital, and leave New York and Henry Locke behind her.

This was such a difficult time in her life. Being let go by Henry. Cast adrift in a sea of abandonment. That was what it felt like. Maybe she was too sensitive after what Wade had done to her, but it was how she felt. The desire to be surrounded by family, by people she *knew* loved her, was strong.

But if she left then she'd be walking away from the medical care that Dr Yang, a specialist in problem multiple pregnancies, could provide—and surely, her babies' wellbeing, not hers, should come first?

Look at me...casting aspersions on Henry for doing that when I know I need to do so myself.

Wasn't Henry just being sensible? Hers was a high-risk pregnancy. Twins. Prior uterine surgery. Internal scarring. Previous broken pelvis. And then there was the fact that Jenny's baby had been stillborn. They'd had no idea why. Was it something that had just happened? Or was there a reason for it in Henry's DNA?

She felt like a ticking human time bomb.

Was Henry so wrong to insist on there being some sort of distance between them? He was just protecting himself—and why wouldn't he, after all that he'd been through? Hadn't both of them been trying to protect themselves by vowing to remain single when they'd first met?

But deep down Natalie had hoped that Henry would care for her so much that he wouldn't be able to bear being apart from her. And the fact that he clearly didn't…that he'd so easily pushed her away…

That hurt.

Natalie stared down at her suitcase. She'd packed it earlier, crying all the while, shoving things in without properly folding them, grabbing stuff without really thinking about what to take.

Am I being hasty?

The buzzer on her door sounded. 'Taxi,' said a man's voice.

Natalie bit her lip and grabbed her suitcase off the bed.

The next day, Henry made it into the hospital feeling awful. He hadn't slept a wink. He hadn't been able to do anything but think of how it had felt to kiss Natalie yesterday. How it had felt to have her in his arms once again and how awful he had made himself feel by ending the kiss and pushing himself away from her.

The look in her eyes when he had done so…

Betrayal. Upset. Shock.

Disbelief.

She wanted more for them—he knew that. And so did he. But if he allowed himself to fully admit what he felt for her, the way he knew he should, then he would be putting himself at risk. And if something awful were to happen to these babies, or to Natalie, then she would need someone who could be strong for her. And how strong could he be if he was crumbling inside? He wasn't good enough for her right now. Not strong enough.

He was doing them both a favour, really.

He saw Roxy first, when he walked onto the floor. She was at the desk, just hanging up the phone, a pen shoved through the rough bun of her brunette hair.

'What did you do?' she asked curtly, one eyebrow raised.

He frowned. 'I'm sorry?'

'Natalie. She's taken some leave. But she called me last night, almost in tears, saying she needed some time to think, and when a girlfriend says that kind of thing to me, in that way, I know a boy's involved. So come on—what did you do?'

The look of hurt in Natalie's eyes flashed into his mind once again. 'How long has she taken leave for?'

Roxy shrugged. 'Don't know. But she was talking about going back home.'

'To her apartment?'

'To Montana, you fool! I mean...um...' she blushed '... Dr Locke.'

Henry stared at her in shock. Natalie was on leave? Might already have left New York? The idea that she might be gone... Out of reach! He didn't even know exactly where her home was. He might never see her again! Might never see his babies. And if she had to go through this all alone...he'd never forgive himself.

He'd never intended that to happen. He'd sworn to Natalie that he would be there for her in some way. But if she'd gone into some sort of hiding, what could he do?

'When did she say she was leaving?'

'I don't know.'

He rushed past Roxy.

'Where are you going?' she yelled. 'There's no one to cover the floor if an emergency comes in!'

Henry skidded to a stop. He needed to get to Natalie! But he couldn't put anyone else at risk.

'Where's Dr Yang?'

'Not here yet.'

'What about Dr Chatwin?'

'In the OR.'

He sighed. 'Okay. I'll wait until she's back on the floor—then I'm going.'

'To do what?'

'Beg Natalie to stay.'

Henry burst from the lift, looking left and right at the apartment numbers, then sprinted down to Natalie's door at the far end of the corridor. His fist hammered the door.

'Natalie! *Natalie!*'

He waited briefly, but impatience overrode him.

'Natalie? Please answer the door. I don't know if you can hear me, or if you're even in there, but if you are, please let me in!'

'Who are you?'

A door behind him opened and a stout woman with flushed cheeks looked out at him curiously.

'Is Natalie in, do you know?'

The woman shrugged. 'I don't know. But could you be a little more quiet, please?'

He nodded. 'Sorry.'

The woman stared at him a moment more, then closed her door.

Henry rested his head against Natalie's front door.

'You're probably gone already. I bet that I'm too late. But...' He sighed. 'I just wanted to say I'm sorry. Sorry for pushing you away. I got...scared. You mean so much to me and... I just kept thinking that things could all still go so wrong, and I wouldn't be strong enough to help you. I thought that if I kept my distance then somehow it would be easier. But then I heard from Roxy that you were taking time off to go home, and the idea that I'd never see you again just made me realise that...'

He closed his eyes in pain, trying not to accept that this might have already happened.

But then there was a click from the other side of the door, and he took a startled step back as Natalie opened it, red-eyed from crying.

'You're still here?'

She nodded, crossing her arms. 'I am.'

'You heard everything I just said?'

'I did.'

'I meant every word. The idea that you might be gone for ever was...just awful. It made me realise that even if something bad did happen to you, or to the babies, then I'd still want to be there for you. That I couldn't bear the thought that you'd be alone. Or that I would.'

'What are you saying?'

'I'm saying that I want to be with you and that... I think I love you.'

Natalie flushed and gave a small smile. 'You only think?'

He shook his head. 'I know that I do. And I know that I need you in my life every single day. With me.'

'So tell me properly.'

He smiled.

'Natalie Webber. You and I have already been through so much. The last few months have been crazy for both of us, and I want to continue experiencing the crazy with you. I want to be there with you through hard times and good times, and I want to be able to touch you and hold you in my arms and keep you safe. You're my first thought every day. I think of you constantly. I miss you when you're not with me. I rush to be with you. Seek you out. And not in a weird, stalker way.'

He smiled again.

'I want to stare into your eyes for ever and never let go.' He reached for her fingertips and locked them in his own. 'I love you.'

She smiled. 'I love you, too.'

'So this means…?'

'That we're both in a bit of a pickle!'

'But we're in it together?' he asked.

Natalie nodded and stepped closer still. 'I was going to leave. But then I thought of all the medical help the twins might need and I knew I had to put them first. And that's when I realised that that was what you'd been doing, too. Only I blamed you for acting that way, when really it was exactly what you should have been doing. I wanted you to love me, but I didn't think that you would. That you *could*.'

'Loving you is easy enough. Admitting it was slightly harder.'

'We might have some tough times ahead of us, Henry.'

'We might.' He tucked a stray curl behind her ear. 'But I think we can get through anything if we're together.'

'I think so, too.'

And then he kissed her.

And this time the kiss was even more euphoric than the last. Because this time they knew that they were destined to be together and that neither of them was hiding from the other at all. They'd both admitted their love, both admitted their fears and their flaws, and it was still all okay.

Love was what mattered in the end.

EPILOGUE

HENRY UNLOCKED THE DOOR, pushing it open wide, allowing Natalie to walk through first. His apartment had changed in the last few months. Gone was all the dark furniture, glass and chrome, and the place had had new life breathed into it by her own home decorating. There was a cream couch with scatter cushions. A fluffy rug. A low coffee table strewn with books, and a glass bowl filled with fresh cut flowers. The walls had bookcase after bookcase, and now there were photos of the two of them all around the room.

They walked into the living space and put down the two car seats, side by side, then stepped back to look down at their twin baby girls: Sophie and Esme.

'So what do we do now?' Natalie asked, and she slid her arm around his waist as she stared down at the babies.

'I don't know. I've never got this far.'

'There's not a handbook?'

He laughed. 'I'm afraid not.'

They both just stared at the two girls, falling in love with them even more. They looked so perfect.

Sophie had been born first, emerging into the world at just over thirty-three weeks with a strong cry, and weighing five pounds exactly. Esme—smaller, quieter, and more content at just four pounds twelve—had come into the world with a little snuffle, content to just be held.

Even though they weren't identical, they looked as if they could be. But in the last few weeks in the hospital they had begun to notice the tiny differences between the two girls. Esme had more hair and Sophie had her father's eyes.

'Why don't you sit down?' said Henry. 'I'll make us both a cup of tea. The girls will be awake soon and want feeding.'

Natalie nodded, sinking into the soft couch, glad to be back at home, surrounded by her own furnishings. She kicked off her boots and just sat there, staring at her two daughters. They were so perfect! So beautiful!

Eventually Henry came back through from the kitchen with a tray. There was a white teapot and two cups in saucers, a small plate of biscuits, and a dark blue velvet box.

Natalie frowned and looked up at him. 'What's that?'

Henry sank to the couch beside her and took the box, smiling. He opened it, then turned it around for Natalie to see.

Inside was a beautiful platinum ring, set with a large square cut diamond.

'I love you with all my heart and you have made me the happiest man in the world. Not just because you've given me two beautiful darling daughters, who I hope grow up to be exactly like their mother, but also because you've given me your heart and your soul, and I

can't imagine my life without you in it. So, Natalie...
Will you do me the honour of becoming my wife?'

Henry slipped off the couch and sank to one knee.

Natalie gasped, her hands clasped over her mouth
in shock. 'Yes! I will!'

She threw her arms around him and pulled him
tight, kissing his face, his cheeks, his mouth, feeling
tears of happiness well up in her eyes as she held out
her hand for him to slip the ring on.

She stared at it as it caught the light. A perfect fit.

Henry kissed her again, more passionately this time,
but Sophie and Esme chose that moment to begin to
snuffle awake.

Natalie held Henry's face in her hands, staring
deeply into his eyes. 'I love you so much.'

'I love you more.'

The twins began to protest, wriggling in their re-
spective car seats, wanting to get out.

Natalie laughed, wiping away her tears. 'Take one
each?' she asked.

Henry nodded. 'Let's do this!'

* * * * *

COMING SOON!

We really hope you enjoyed reading this book.
If you're looking for more romance, be sure to
head to the shops when new books are
available on

Thursday 19th January

To see which titles are coming soon, please visit
millsandboon.co.uk/nextmonth

MILLS & BOON®

Coming next month

SINGLE DAD FOR THE HEART DOCTOR
Karin Baine

'Is this really necessary?' Lily batted away the heart-shaped helium balloons lining her path but managed to walk straight into the red and pink streamers hanging from the ceiling.

'I think they're keen to reiterate the purpose of this scheme. That it's for heart patients only and shouldn't be abused by those hoping for a lift to hospital appointments or who want us to pop round with a takeaway. Plus it's Valentine's Day so, you know...' Finn's soft voice in her ear caused the hairs on the back of her neck to stand to attention when he was so close she could feel his breath on her skin.

'Oh, I know. Let's bring in all the clichés we can to hammer the point home.' She rolled her eyes. Being deceived by the idea of love and romance wasn't an affliction she suffered from. She left it to naïve young couples who had forever to fool themselves into thinking it could solve everything. Life, and death, had taught her it only complicated things and made life so much harder. All the people she had ever loved had died and, as for romance, it had brought nothing but heartache when she couldn't give her partners what they needed—children and time.

'Something tells me you didn't get any cards in the post.'

'And I suppose you did?'

'Two, actually.'

More eye-rolling. Not only was he handsome but he knew it. One of the worst traits a man could have.

'Let me guess, one came from a grateful young woman who found herself locked out of her house in nothing but a towel and you came to the rescue? And the other...some impressionable schoolgirl whose class had a tour of the fire station?' Boasting about how many cards he'd received was juvenile, and clearly mentioned to get a rise out of her. He had, of course, succeeded.

Finn laughed so hard she actually felt the vibration through to her very bones. 'Actually, they were from my daughters, but it's good to know what you really think about me. You'll have to take my word for it that I'm not a ladies' man who would take advantage of vulnerable females.'

Continue reading
SINGLE DAD FOR THE HEART DOCTOR
Karin Baine

Available next month
www.millsandboon.co.uk

MILLS & BOON

THE HEART OF ROMANCE

A ROMANCE FOR EVERY READER

MODERN
Prepare to be swept off your feet by sophisticated, sexy and seductive heroes, in some of the world's most glamourous and romantic locations, where power and passion collide.

HISTORICAL
Escape with historical heroes from time gone by. Whether your passion is for wicked Regency Rakes, muscled Vikings or rugged Highlanders, await the romance of the past.

MEDICAL
Set your pulse racing with dedicated, delectable doctors in the high-pressure world of medicine, where emotions run high and passion, comfort and love are the best medicine.

True Love
Celebrate true love with tender stories of heartfelt romance, from the rush of falling in love to the joy a new baby can bring, and a focus on the emotional heart of a relationship.

Desire
Indulge in secrets and scandal, intense drama and plenty of sizzling hot action with powerful and passionate heroes who have it all: wealth, status, good looks…everything but the right woman.

HEROES
Experience all the excitement of a gripping thriller, with an intense romance at its heart. Resourceful, true-to-life women and strong, fearless men face danger and desire - a killer combination!

To see which titles are coming soon, please visit

millsandboon.co.uk/nextmonth

JOIN US ON SOCIAL MEDIA!

Stay up to date with our latest releases, author news and gossip, special offers and discounts, and all the behind-the-scenes action from Mills & Boon...

 @millsandboon

 @millsandboonuk

 facebook.com/millsandboon

@millsandboonuk

It might just be true love...